VIKING TOMORROW

Also by Jeremy Robinson

Standalone Novels
The Didymus Contingency
Raising The Past
Beneath
Antarktos Rising
Kronos
Xom-B
Flood Rising
MirrorWorld
Apocalypse Machine
Unity
The Distance

Nemesis Saga Novels
Island 731
Project Nemesis
Project Maigo
Project 731
Project Hyperion
Project Legion

The Antarktos Saga
The Last Hunter – Descent
The Last Hunter – Pursuit
The Last Hunter – Ascent
The Last Hunter – Lament
The Last Hunter – Onslaught
The Last Hunter – Collected Edition
The Last Valkyrie

The Jack Sigler/Chess Team Thrillers
Prime
Pulse
Instinct
Threshold
Ragnarok
Omega
Savage
Cannibal
Empire

Cerberus Group Novels
Herculean
Helios

Jack Sigler Continuum Novels
Guardian
Patriot
Centurion

Chesspocalypse Novellas
Callsign: King
Callsign: Queen
Callsign: Rook
Callsign: King 2 – Underworld
Callsign: Bishop
Callsign: Knight
Callsign: Deep Blue
Callsign: King 3 – Blackout

Chesspocalypse Collections
Callsign: King – The Brainstorm Trilogy
Callsign – Tripleshot
Callsign – Doubleshot

SecondWorld Novels
SecondWorld
Nazi Hunter: Atlantis

Horror Novels
(written as Jeremy Bishop)
Torment
The Sentinel
The Raven
Refuge

Post-Apocalyptic Sci-Fi
(written as Jeremiah Knight)
Hunger
Feast

Also by Kane Gilmour

Collaborations with Jeremy Robinson

Callsign: Deep Blue
Ragnarok
Omega
Refuge Book 5 – Bonfires Burning Bright
Endgame
"Show of Force"
Viking Tomorrow

Nostalgic Horror Novellas

The Crypt of Dracula

The Jason Quinn Thrillers

Resurrect
Ice Sheet (coming soon)

Edited Anthology

Warbirds of Mars: Stories of the Fight!

Comic Books/Graphic Novels

Island 731
Warbirds of Mars

VIKING
TOMORROW

JEREMY ROBINSON & KANE GILMOUR

Visit Jeremy Robinson on the World Wide Web at:
www.bewareofmonsters.com.

Visit Kane Gilmour on the World Wide Web at:
www.kanegilmour.com.

Kane dedicates *Viking Tomorrow* to:
Michelle, the bravest, strongest woman I know,
whose love has seen me through the wars,
and whose side I will be at until we reach Valhalla, and after.

PROLOGUE

Prologue

The girl saw her pale face reflected in the creature's slick eyes. She smiled at the sight, and then giggled. The harbor seal, a foot longer than the girl was tall, grunted and huffed with appreciation, then it nuzzled closer to her, as it had done all week when they met by the hole in the ice.

The young girl's mother, a broad, powerful woman, sat nearby on a log. She was repairing a shirt with a needle and thread, as the girl played with the seals. At only six years old, the girl could swim nearly as well as the creatures that emerged from the hole each afternoon to laze in the scant Arctic sun. Her mother wasn't worried about her.

There were usually three or four seals, and the girl loved to play with them. She had begged her mother to create a fur hood she could wear, so she would better resemble the sleek-skinned animals. It had taken some time, but eventually her mother had presented her with a smooth, brown, full-body garment. She rarely took it off now. It was skin tight, and kept the girl's long blonde hair out of her face, but it wasn't the warmest article of clothing she owned. Still, she would happily shiver if it meant playing with her friends.

Unlike many other creatures the girl had seen, these seals were unaffected by sickness or deformities. Her parents explained that most of the animals had been changed by the wars and disasters of the old times. The girl didn't know much about those times, but as long as the seals had only one head each and no scary fangs or claws, she was fine with them.

The most daring seal—the girl had named him *Jostein*—hooted with pleasure that his new human friend was once again on the ice. While the others would come close and scamper around her, Jostein was the only seal that would touch her or allow himself to be touched.

"Mama," the girl said, "can I swim with Jostein?"

"Wait," her mother said, the woman's voice unusually terse and devoid of humor.

The girl turned to see her mother's face was drawn. She was squinting back at the shore.

The girl whipped her head around toward their home, a small two-bedroom wooden hut on the shore of the frozen bay. Her father was chopping timber with a wood-handled ax, as two men arrived on vehicles the girl had never seen before. The machines were longer than a man, with skis on the front end and treads at the rear. The sound of the vehicles buzzed out across the iced-over sea, reaching her ears only after the men had arrived at her family's log pile.

"Wait," her mother hissed in a whisper.

A sudden dread filled the girl. She did not know what the problem was—most of the visitors they had, though infrequent, were welcomed heartily. She determined to stay still and alert, until her mother told her otherwise. At her side, Jostein lifted his head and peered toward the house. The girl knew his limited surface eyesight was not up to the task, but his keen hearing and sense of smell had detected the vehicles' arrival before she had.

The two strangers dismounted their mechanical steeds and pulled long swords from their belts. The men moved with purpose toward her father, who was now brandishing his woodcutting ax like a weapon.

"Into the water," her mother urged her. "Get in and go under with your friends. Stay under as long as you can, and then stay under longer." The woman started running toward the shore, her mending dropped on the snow-crusted ice.

The girl turned her head toward the two-foot-wide hole cut into the surface, its black water already disturbed by the harbor seals, who had detected trouble and slid into the hole, nose first, with hardly a ripple. The only sound was their bellies scraping across the ice. Jostein waited for her, looking back and barking softly.

She turned toward the home just once more. The two men swung their blades at her father. An arc of brilliant crimson shot up and over their heads.

Her heart seized as a sword struck her father again. Her mother was still running for the shore, screaming.

The girl turned back to the hole and, like the seals, slid in head first.

The shock of the cold water was like being slammed in the chest with a log. There was hardly enough light to see, but she spotted the dark shadows of seals swimming around her. The cold permeated her thin seal-skin hood. Her muscles felt tight and unfamiliar as she tried to swim while blocking the vision of her father's blood from her mind's eye.

She turned upward toward the deep hole. The ice was over a foot thick. As she looked up at the circle of blue sky beyond it, Jostein slipped into the hole from above, blocking out the light with his bulk. He plunged into the water, and immediately glided to the girl, winding his body around her like a snake. She knew he was smart enough to understand the danger. He was being protective.

The blackness around her did not scare the girl at all, but the terror of seeing the men attacking her father, and the fear of what they might do to her mother, filled her small mind. She had no fears for herself. She did not think the men would come out to the ice for her, and she was wearing her seal costume anyway. If they had even looked out across the ice and seen her mother, they most likely would have thought the girl was one of the seals.

She treaded in place under the water, her head just feet beneath the hole in the ice. If the men came and looked into the water, they would see black and the reflection of the porcelain blue sky above them. Nothing more. But she would be able to see them.

If they came soon.

Her mother had told her to stay under as long as she could, but she was running out of air now. It had been over three minutes. She could usually hold her breath for three to four minutes, but the last part always hurt her chest. When her circular view of the sky started to dim at the edges, she would have to emerge. For now, she waited, her arms tired and flapping slowly to keep her from sinking.

Jostein swam around her still, nuzzling her gently. She could tell he was worried. The other seals had already fled. He stopped in front of her, looking her in the eyes. *He looks sad,* she thought. Then he turned and swam away.

Her lungs burned.

She was alone.

The brutal cold constricted her muscles, and she knew she didn't have long before a vicious cramp would set in.

She had to have air.

The girl moved up slowly, and tilted her head backward, so her lips and nose would be the first—and only—things that surfaced. As soon as she felt the frigid air on her mouth, she exhaled the last air in her chest and gulped in several fresh lungfuls. Her face was still a foot lower than the surface of the ice, hidden from the view of anyone on shore.

But her curiosity and fear got the better of her. She reached up, grabbed the smooth edge of the ice, and pulled herself up.

She wished she hadn't. Her young eyes took in the sight instantly, and she dropped back down into the icy water.

The men were leaving on their strange vehicles. The house was on fire. Her father's body was strewn on the ice in a spreading lake of blood. And her mother was tied over the back of one of the vehicles, like a sack of grain. Her long blonde hair was dirty and covered in blood, as it dragged on the ground.

The girl was young. She did not understand what the men wanted her mother for, but she understood that the woman would be dead soon, if she wasn't already.

The girl was alone now.

She waited in the water, her head out and breathing the brittle air in sharp short bursts, her nose smelling the smoke from her burning home. She counted in her head, focusing on the numbers' rhythm, trying to block out the fear and the terror, the images of blood and fire.

When she had been in the water an extra four minutes, she finally grabbed the lip of the ice and hauled herself out. The water was cold, but the frigid air chilled her worse. She flopped up out of the hole onto the ice, and lay on her back, her eyes tightly squinched shut against the cold air on her face. Her whole body shivered, and her teeth chattered. Her seal hood had come loose from her head, and her sopping wet blonde hair now framed her face. She knew she needed to get up soon, or it would freeze to the ice.

I am only six, she thought. *How can I survive? What can I do?*

She knew she needed warmth. Her head lolled to the left and she saw the flames where her house had been were already dying down, the spot instead choked with a thick, billowing, black smoke column that climbed into the sky and spread over the sea.

Where can I find warmth?

She also knew she would need food. And shelter. With the house gone, all three of those things were gone.

I will die here.

She closed her eyes again. Then she heard a noise that made all of the terror of the afternoon pale in comparison to the sensation that flooded through her now.

It was a loud, deep grunt. And it was close.

Summoning a reserve of energy she didn't know she had, the girl sat up, flipped and rolled into a crouch, one hand steadying herself on the ice, while the other spread out for balance.

A polar bear. And close.

Very close.

No doubt drawn by the scent of smoke.

The creature was no more than a few feet away, its head lowered toward the ice, its eyes locked onto hers. Its white fur had matted, yellow patches. In a few places, the fur was missing entirely, revealing black crusted skin.

The beast was huge, probably longer than her house had been wide—nine or ten feet. It had an extra hind leg, dangling out of its left flank, as if the limb contained no bones. Indeed, as she looked closer, she saw that the meaty appendage did not reach all the way to the ice, but hung limp and floppy. The other two hind legs were normal sized and powerful, although the leg supporting the unwanted twin had a knee that looked like it bent sideways. The front legs rested on the ice, the creature's thick, black claws longer than the girl's hands plus half the length of her forearms. The dark claws glistened as they lay on the ice. She noted that the creature's rear claws had sunken into the ice, which would give it traction when it lunged for her.

She stayed perfectly still, watching the creature as it watched her. The beast's odor was heavy and thick, and there was something under it, like the scent of spoiled food. She knew the bear saw her as a seal of some kind, because of her outfit, but she wasn't acting like a seal. That was probably the only reason the bear had not attacked and eaten her yet.

As she watched, the beast pulled one front paw backward slightly, the tips of the claws driving into the ice for additional purchase.

It was going to strike out.

She stood there shivering, and eyed the bear's thick fur. She looked at the beast's bulk, all sinew and muscles, and at the sheer size of the thing. As big as a house.

Warmth.

Food.

Shelter.

She slid her free hand back to the bone-handled knife on her hip.

The bear roared and lunged forward, but to its surprise, the girl also roared, and pulled out her own claw, running just as fast for the beast and leaping.

1

Ulrik stood in the wooden longboat's bow, staring at the decomposing metal remains of the once-tall, proud buildings in the distance. The structures had housed dozens of people, but now they were little more than canted skeletal reminders of an age gone by, populated by birds and creeping vines, and no longer by man. As his men paddled the ship into the crowded harbor, he lowered his eyes and saw several boats similar to his, and many groups of men armed with axes and shields, wearing leather and furs.

All had heard the same call from the ruined city of Stavanger that Ulrik had heard: there was an imminent threat to all the peoples of the North, and the greatest fighters were needed for an urgent task. Ulrik was well known throughout the region surrounding the river town of Drammen. The people there had selected him to take the perilous journey around the coast to Stavanger, to find out what needed to be done.

The letter had said to arrive by the solstice, or it would be too late.

Ulrik and his men had nearly not arrived at all, thanks to a pitched battle with a vicious band of marauders near the rocky islets of Kristiansand. He'd lost two men on the journey, and now he was ready for some answers. Whatever this threat was, he was eager to sink his ax into its skull.

Looking around the bustling harbor as the boat glided toward a rickety wooden pier, Ulrik recognized several fighters of repute. One was a man named Trond, who was roughly the size of an elk. His flowing golden beard was braided and stained with dyes. He carried a double-sided broad ax. Ulrik had heard stories of Trond cleaving men in two with a single sweep of that gigantic blade.

He also saw men whose names he couldn't recall, but with whom he knew he'd shared a battlefield in the past. There were many he did not know—neither from experience nor from tales told around tall glasses of frothy beer. He realized they must have come from much farther than he had, and he wondered how far out the message had been sent. Was the Jarl of Stavanger recruiting Swedes? Finns? The crazed, mutated warriors of Rus?

As he stepped off the boat and strode down the pier, he overheard conversations around him, and all were asking the same unanswered questions about what this great peril might be. Ulrik knew better than to ask. No one here had the answers. Only the Jarl would know, and he wasn't out on the docks to greet the arriving fighters. There would be a feast first, and then, when most of the men around him were falling-down drunk, the Jarl would explain. Ulrik knew better than to get excited about it now, on the docks. But unlike the others, he wasn't about to wait until after sunset for his answers.

He strode down the wooden walkway until he was on the beach, and his boots kicked water-washed pebbles. Those who knew him or had heard of him stepped out of his way. While everyone else was milling around, he looked like a man with a purpose. A few did not know him—not even by reputation—and two of them made the mistake of staying in his way. The first was a skinny man in tight brown leather. Ulrik walked straight into the man, bowling him over, and sending the stranger onto his ass in the wet sand. Ulrik kept walking, despite the complaints and curses hurled at his back. The second man, further up the beach, stayed in Ulrik's path intentionally, a hand out to slow or stop him.

Ulrik met the man's gaze and saw no threat in it. "Move or be moved," he called to the man.

"Ulrik the Fearless, well met. I do not plan to try to stop you," the man said. He had short, greasy blond hair, slicked back on his head, and an unkempt beard that covered a weak chin. Still, Ulrik noted the man's corded, muscular arms and his broad chest. At his side he wore a long, straight sword. His arms and legs were covered in a scarred, brown leather armor, and across his chest was a dented metal plate decorated with a painted red hammer—the claw-ended kind of hammer used to pound in nails. "I merely want to join you in seeking answers. My name is Morten."

"Morten the Hammer?" Ulrik asked, recognizing the symbol and the name. He'd heard tales of the man from Hammerfest, a nearly empty city of frozen ruins up in Lapland. Tales Ulrik didn't like. Stories of the men Morten had brutalized and the women he'd had his way with. Most of the stories involved the Laplander outwitting his foes, instead of overpowering them. Often through trickery or betrayal. Many of them were undoubtedly bluster and legend, but there was probably some truth.

"You are heading to see the Jarl now?" Morten asked.

"I lost men on this voyage," was all Ulrik said, and he took a step further toward the Jarl's longhall.

Morten again thrust his hand out, this time toward Ulrik's chest. It was enough, after a lengthy voyage, losing two friends and missing even more meals.

Ulrik, a few inches taller than Morten, and broader, with fists like frozen slabs of reindeer, stepped closer to the Laplander, whose hand made contact with Ulrik's chestplate. Another step forced the man's loosely extended arm back and bent it at the elbow. Then Ulrik slammed his forehead into the bridge of Morten's nose. Blood splattered both men in the face, splashing into their eyes.

Morten staggered backward from the blow, but his hand was already moving to a black-handled knife on his belt.

Ulrik spun and cocked his arm. He came around in a full circle, his pointed elbow mashing into Morten's ear, and knocking the man sideways to the ground.

Someone screamed out a blood-curdling battle cry from behind him, and Ulrik heard the tell-tale scuffle of leather boots on the pebbled ground.

He ducked low, just as a man soared over him. The man had tried to tackle Ulrik, and as his form sprawled to the ground several feet behind Morten's body, Ulrik recognized him as the first man he had hit. *Another damned Laplander. These two have no honor.*

Morten stirred on the ground, and since he was down there anyway, Ulrik hammered a fist into the man's face. The blow knocked Morten down and out of the fight, and made a worse mess of the man's already bloodied nose.

Before Ulrik could scramble forward to go after the man who had attempted to attack him from behind, he was bumped from the side by yet another man, this one a huge moving wall of flesh and furs—only his legs and arms were bare. Ulrik lost his balance and toppled over onto the ground. The wall of flesh was mighty Trond, who now picked up the Laplander who had attacked from behind like a coward. Trond hefted the smaller man's body and threw him up the beach as Ulrik watched, stunned at the ox's strength. Arms and legs flailed until the small man smashed to earth right where the sand and pebbles met long patches of scrub grass.

Ulrik staggered to his feet and turned his eyes back to Morten. The greasy man was awake and clambering to his feet, spitting a thick phlegmy wad of blood to the ground, while pulling his longsword from its brown scabbard.

Ulrik pulled the long handled ax from its leather loop on his belt, and yanked his cracked wooden shield off his back, gripping the curled, well-worn, leather arm straps with his left hand.

Morten's blue eyes faltered for a second, glancing back at the bustling harbor.

It was in that split second that Ulrik processed the sounds around him. Men were yelling and screaming. Some were shouting oaths, and others were promising death.

Knowing it was foolish to take his eyes off his opponent for even a second, Ulrik still did it. He let his eyes dart back to the harbor.

In the span of a few seconds, the marshy beach had erupted into a full scale battle. Turning back to Morten as the man stalked forward, Ulrik slammed the head of his ax against the metal dome on the center of his battered shield. It made a deep, satisfying clang.

"Come find death, Laplander," Ulrik said, smiling and exposing blood-stained teeth.

2

Ax versus sword. Metal versus wood and bone. All washed in sprays of blood and spittle. If not for all the screaming, Ulrik would have thought the assembled Northmen were enjoying themselves. Battle rang all around him, but he kept his focus on the Laplander.

Morten lunged with the sword point first, keeping his distance. Ulrik easily parried the strike with the head of his ax. Despite not liking the stories he had heard about the Laplander, he knew better than to trust in only stories when it came to the character of a man, and it seemed Morten's heart wasn't really in the attack. Ulrik had no desire to actually hurt the man, but if the fight went on for long, he would have no problems with further embarrassing him.

Morten's eyes darted to the other battles around the beach, while Ulrik had seen all he needed to. He would keep his gaze fixed on his opponent, now that the weapons had been drawn.

Morten thrust out half-heartedly again, and Ulrik was about to parry, when the Laplander's eyes darted again, and he yelled, "Look out!"

Not sure whether it was a ploy on the part of the man who was renowned to be a backstabber, Ulrik dove left instead of down, keeping his eyes on Morten and bringing his ax up at the same time, in case the man pressed the attack. Instead, Morten directed his attention at a new opponent. His sword flashed up just in time to stop a thin man swinging two axes down where Ulrik had been, just seconds before.

Ulrik rolled in the sand and came up in a stance at the side of Morten, just as another man came rushing in, shield first, like a human battering ram. With short dark hair and pure murder in his ice chip eyes, Ulrik categorized this man as the larger threat. Plus, the man's shield was coming straight for Ulrik's midsection. He steeled himself for the hit, but it still lifted him off the ground. The man kept running, and Ulrik lifted his ax handle high, then struck the maniacal runner on the top of his head.

The man dropped like a stone, and Ulrik landed on his feet, several yards further up the beach. He was about to rush back into the fray when he spotted Morten and the slim man Trond had thrown fighting side by side now, against three other men. At first the two Laplanders seemed outnumbered, but as Ulrik watched, he realized the two knew each other, and they fought side by side or back to back, as if they were born to it. The smaller man fought with twin hand axes, while Morten had pulled out a knife to go with his sword.

They are talented, Ulrik observed.

Closer to the harbor, Trond was barreling through men like an unstoppable storm, but as Ulrik watched, he noticed the giant man was only attacking the most aggressive and bloodthirsty of the combatants. Often with non-lethal head-butts or punches. At first look, Trond appeared out of control, but on closer inspection Ulrik saw he was picking his targets.

Then something unfortunate happened that changed the tide of the battle.

A man with a short sword took a serious swing at Trond's head, missing the larger man's neck, but cleaving off his beard with the deadly swing.

Oh, you stupid stack of testicles, Ulrik thought.

And then Trond, a man of strength unbridled and with a composure to be appreciated, went berserk.

He rushed the smaller man, swatting his sword aside before grabbing the man's skull between two massive hands and simply crushing it into a pulpy mess. Then Trond ran for the next nearest man and crushed him with a blood-drenched, meaty fist, before kicking at another and biting at a third.

As Trond lost touch with reality, all around him men detected that the brawl had become a serious killing field, and they either upped their efforts or backed off and away to the fringes of the fight—or like Trond, they lost their minds, falling into snarling, thrashing berserker rages.

Ulrik, too, could fall into a desperate, swinging rage, pummeling his enemies into oblivion. But he was nowhere near that angry today, and he saw no reason to fight these men at all. They had all come together for a common cause. He needed some way to calm the melee, but he saw no way to do it without risking his life.

To his side, Morten and his ally had knocked out their foes, the three men on the ground—two of them bleeding from several small and inconsequential stab wounds. The two victors were watching the out-of-control fight that was threatening to leave many dead or injured.

"Odin's beard," Morten's friend said. "Look at that." He pointed past the fracas to the pier, where a woman had just shoved a man off the wooden walkway and into the water. "Do you know who that is, Morten?"

Morten made no reply as the two fell silent, watching the woman.

She had long blonde hair and wore goggles with red lenses on her face. Under the thick goggles was a spread of makeup resembling a Raven's outstretched wings, only the ink was red—or else it was blood. Either was possible. She wore black leather with additional studded armored pads on one leg and the opposing shoulder. A long-handled ax hung by her side, and she marched confidently off the pier, and right into the thickest part of the fighting.

The woman jabbed upward with her left elbow as a man approached her. She had to leap slightly off her feet for the elbow to connect with the man's jaw, but the strike was so lightning fast, that the much smaller woman managed to snap the man's head backward. Before he even started to fall, she had landed back on the soles of her black boots and spun. Her high kick connected with another man's ear, sending him off to the side and into three other brawlers, knocking them all off balance, as they crumpled into the wet sand.

The woman took two more steps before a man with an ax and a beard that flowed to his waist rushed her. She sidestepped his lunge, turning and delivering the bottom of her fist to the back of the man's neck with such force and speed that Ulrik could see the man's neck bend downward as his head snapped back toward his own shoulder blades.

Broken, he thought.

The woman continued forward. When the fighting wasn't close enough to reach her, she did not pursue it. Ulrik realized she wasn't entering the fray—she was merely passing through it. And if anyone got in her way, she was putting them down. Brutally.

Morten gave voice to Ulrik's thoughts. "She is a very calm fighter."

Then a man with a beard in long braids with silver metal cones at the tips punched the woman in the side of the head, his fist slipping past her defenses. She staggered slightly to the side, and quicker than Ulrik could see, she drew a knife and slashed upward as she fell away from the man. As her arm swooped away from the man's head, a thin line of blood from the man's slit throat trailed the dark metal in her hand. And the woman, recovering her stance, launched herself into the fight, her own berserker rage consuming her as she began to drop larger fighters all around her.

Ulrik watched in awe, thinking the woman would take down every man foolish enough to confront her whirling, striking form, until Trond, still lost in his own bloodlust, headed straight for her.

3

It is a wonder we have made it this far, Halvard thought.

He stood with Jarl Gregers on the second story of one of the few skeletal buildings in town to remain roughly vertical. Most of the others had toppled, crumbled or at least fallen over to a forty-five degree angle, decades before he had been born. And at fifty-two, he was an old man by humanity's current standards. Old enough to be glad he wasn't down below in the melee.

From his perch, a hundred yards farther inland than where the bulk of the fighting was taking place, he thanked the gods he was too old to fight, and beseeched them to let his plan succeed. Despite his earlier dark thought, he knew the human race had redeeming qualities and was worth saving.

Halvard turned to the Jarl, a man of sixty, with a paunch belly earned from far too many years of drinking, after his own fighting years were done. The man had clawed and scrabbled his way to the top of the region's toughest men—often over their cracked skulls.

The Jarl leered at the fight, clearly missing the old days. A few inches shorter than Halvard, the man knew little of science or the history of the world, as Halvard did, but he appreciated a good fight.

"Now this is more like it," the Jarl said.

Halvard rolled his eyes skyward and thought, *Odin, I may have been too hasty with that 'redeeming qualities' thought.*

"Look at them, Halvard. Bloody good fighters, all of them."

As the Jarl leaned against the rusted railing to get a better look at the scrambling fight below them, Halvard saw a large man from Oslo called Trond throw a smaller man to the beach. A closer look revealed the thrown man to be a Laplander named Oskar.

That would mean... Halvard scanned the fight, and there at the edge of it he saw Morten the Hammer. Another Laplander. They were cousins. Where the one went, the other was always close by. Morten's opponent darted left as a man attacked from behind.

Halvard recognized Ulrik the Fearless, and he was glad the man had made the journey. Travel by sea was always perilous.

"Who is that?" the Jarl asked.

Halvard followed the man's pointed finger to the dock, and saw the other fighter he had hoped for the most.

"That is Val, Jarl Gregers. The woman fighter from Åland, I told you about."

As they watched, Val dispatched all threats with liquid efficiency.

"Freya's tits, the woman is good. I would have her for my own."

Jarl Gregers had been a renowned womanizer in his youth, but both men knew he rarely made headway with the ladies these days. Besides, his wife Agatha would neuter him if she thought he was cheating on her.

"Perhaps, Jarl, it would be best to keep her on the mission, and consider wooing her should they return?" Halvard suggested. The Jarl was a dullard, but an easily swayed dullard.

"Yes, you are correct, good Halvard. What would we do without your science and good counsel?"

Probably starve, Halvard thought. He was the only man in a hundred miles who had been trained by his father in the ways of the old sciences—languages, reading, maths, agriculture, engineering, biology and genetics. The sciences handed down from father to son, generation after generation, after most of the world's knowledge had been lost. A few still knew the old ways, and Halvard had done his part to train replacements for himself. Still, most of the Northmen were not interested in the lost arts and ways. Learning how to forge better blades or grow stronger crops? Yes, these were things they were happy to learn. But anything to do with the history of the world or the sciences that were mostly confined to books outside of Halvard's laboratory? They would rather drink themselves into a stupor and beat each other bloody.

As Halvard watched the fight, he realized that the fighters—all of them men except for Val—were starting to take the battle seriously. If they didn't put a stop to the brawl soon, Halvard would have very few left from which to choose for the mission.

"Jarl," he said, "perhaps now would be the time to end the fight? Before the best fighters are wounded, or before Val loses her...charms?"

The Jarl nodded and fumbled the large ivory horn from his belt. But before the horn could be sounded, Halvard's heart shot into his throat. Deep in the twists, lunges and evasions of her fight with three men, Val was oblivious to the massive Oslo man, Trond, rushing at her from one side.

Halvard looked up and saw why, just before Val did herself. The blonde woman pivoted, just in time to see an absolute mountain of a man—a full head taller than Trond—rushing at her. If she hadn't turned, he would have smashed into her from behind, and she never would have known what killed her. Now at least she would see it, but there was no time for Val to dodge the man. She did the only thing she could, and dropped down into a crouch, her arms above her head to protect her skull from the impact.

But it never came.

Instead, Trond leapt through the air, clearing her head, and just before the mountainous man would have run over the slim blonde woman like a force of nature, Trond dipped his head and the top of his flying skull rammed into the bigger man's stomach like a tree trunk. Both of the big men went tumbling to the sand behind Val, as she quickly stood, her legs apart and ready for another attack.

The Jarl's horn sounded into multiple bursts in the air, and most of the combatants stopped instantly. A few still traded blows, but they quickly quieted down. Trond stood, said something to the larger brute on the ground, and started to walk back toward Val. For her part, the woman sheathed her ax and resumed her initial course, walking toward the longhall and the neighboring ten-story building where Halvard watched.

The large man—Halvard thought his name was Vebjørn—stood and angrily chased after Val. The Jarl, seeing that the mountainous man had not lost the fight in him, huffed hard on his horn three more times. But Vebjørn still rushed for the small woman. Trond, who was walking beside her, turned his head, and saw that the man was rushing in like a frantic polar bear.

Turning fully, Trond pulled a longsword off his belt, lowering the tip to spear the oncoming maniac. Val turned as well, seeing Vebjørn's frantic rush.

The Jarl let loose a stronger, longer blast from the ox horn. At two feet long and set with silver filigree, the horn was a beauty, and when the old man filled up his portly lungs, he could let loose an epic blast of sound from the thing.

This time, the last combatant stopped. Just feet from the tip of Trond's longsword.

Halvard could see the men exchange angry words, and then Trond turned and began walking toward the tower, looking over his shoulder periodically at Vebjørn. But the larger man had lost interest and was calmly walking toward the Jarl's tower with all the others. As he got closer, Halvard saw that it was indeed Vebjørn, a man known as the 'Bear of the North.' The name fit. For the last few decades they had been seeing the occasional white or brown bear that topped fifteen feet, and Vebjørn was at least eight. Halvard didn't know why the man was so upset, but he was glad Trond and the Jarl's horn had stopped him.

He could probably kill everyone here, Halvard thought.

In a few moments most of the newly arrived warriors had clustered below the second story balcony where Halvard and the Jarl stood waiting.

Halvard was not surprised Morten the Hammer was the first to demand an explanation.

"We are here now, and we are hungry and thirsty. Jarl Gregers, why have you brought us here to Stavanger?"

Halvard could tell that the Jarl bristled at the ostentatious stranger. Either that or the man disliked Laplanders—or he had personal knowledge of this one.

"We are facing a grave time, but I will let good Halvard explain to you all. Many of you know of him, from when he traveled to your villages to teach your people new things." A low rumble of agreement filled the crowded courtyard below. Halvard had traveled most of the country about twenty years previously, assessing the population of what had been called Norway before he had been born. Along the way he had made many friends. "I expect that you will lend him your attention, as you would lend it to me. Halvard speaks of important matters."

The Jarl turned to look at him, and nodded. Then he walked away, back toward the ladder that would take him down to the ground level and the feast awaiting them all in the longhall. The Jarl might believe in Halvard, and he had used his authority to bring all these men of war to the town, but he clearly had no desire to listen to the grave news once again. Remembering the Jarl's wife, Halvard understood why.

"Gentlemen—and lady—we are facing a threat unlike anything we have known in many, many years," Halvard began, his voice already growing hoarse from using the utmost volume he could manage, to address the crowd.

"What kind of threat, Halvard?" Morten asked.

"Human extinction."

4

Val reached for a large mug of beer from the long oak table in the stone meeting room. There was nothing other than beer to drink, and although she knew better than to drink enough of it to become drunk, for now it would slake her thirst.

Eleven men from different regions of the country, including Trond, who had rushed to her rescue in the battle, stood with her. She had thanked him with a nod, and it had been all that was necessary. She knew his type: quiet and courteous...when not crushing an enemy's skull. There were far too few men like him. Most were like Vebjørn, the mountainous thug that had tried to attack her from behind. He stood in a corner, drinking by himself, already alienated from the others by his inability to rein it in when the Jarl had blown his horn.

In an opposite corner of the room stood a man she knew of but had never met, Ulrik the Fearless. At almost a head taller than her and twice as wide, he radiated calm. But under his surface, she could sense menace. She noted that while the others all grabbed beers from the table before Halvard had started to speak, Ulrik had refrained. She also noticed that he hadn't bothered eyeing her up or even looking at the others in the room, after he had briefly greeted Halvard. Instead, he had taken up his position, in the opposite corner from the Bear of the North, and his eyes never left the larger man. He wasn't staring. Val thought most of those gathered in the room wouldn't even realize what Ulrik was doing, but she understood it. He had assessed the occupants of the room and deemed Vebjørn to be the biggest threat. Ulrik leaned against the wall, as if he were disinterested and relaxed, but Val saw that his fingers were never far from the handle of his ax.

Among the others in the room was a quiet man with long, braided blond hair and a bow and quiver. His clothes were patterned like the leaves of trees, dyed many different colors, so he might blend with the forest pines. He said little, but his eyes were alert. She had not heard his name. There were a few others she didn't know, and then there was Morten the Hammer and his friend Oskar. The former had introduced himself to her, while his friend had simply looked at her chest brazenly.

"Let us begin," Halvard said, clearing his throat. "I am old, and I get tired quickly, so I will tell the twelve of you, and ask that you pass this information on to the others."

No one spoke, but many heads nodded assent.

"Do any of you know much of the *Utslettelse*—the Great Annihilation?"

Again, no one spoke.

"Very well. Over one hundred years ago, nearly sixty years before I was born, this world was a very different place. You see the remains all around you. Stavanger was once a city of perhaps one hundred and thirty thousand people. Now there are but three hundred—and it is one of the biggest towns in the North, as you are all well aware. It was an amazing world. Men traveled the skies in flying metal birds. They spoke to each other across great distances through machines small enough to fit in your hand, and weapons could be sent around the world—Midgard—to kill entire nations of people." Halvard sighed at the loss of the world's technologies.

"How do you know these things?" Val asked him.

He turned to her, a man weary with the knowledge of things others did not know. "I was taught many things by my father. He was a scholar before me, and he learned these things from his father. And from many books. I too, learned many things from the books I could find in my travels."

"You can read the old languages?" Morten asked.

Halvard simply nodded. "I can. The world was a very different place, but wars and sickness, and earthquakes and all manner of death attacked the world for many years."

"Ragnarok," Oskar the Laplander whispered.

"Not quite Ragnarok, but I am sure it must have seemed so to those who lived through it. You know that at least some of the humans of the time lived through the great cataclysms, because all of us are here." Halvard sat at a long wooden bench and drank from his mug of beer. "There were people of many kinds in those days, but our people, the people of the North, managed to withstand the sicknesses the best. That is why we all have the same colored blond hair and blue eyes. People with different colored hair had weaker constitutions and perished."

He looked around the room, as the gathered men all looked at each other and at Val's long blonde hair, swept back over her black leather jacket. She still wore her red-lensed goggles—she kept them on at all times—but none of the men were interested in looking at her eyes. They either looked at her body, as Vebjørn did, or they avoided her gaze as Morten the Hammer did. She didn't care for his hubris, but she appreciated the intelligence behind his eyes.

"There was a time when men had different colored hair?" Morten asked.

"Oh, yes," Halvard said. "Different facial features, eye color, and even the tone of their skin could go as dark as tree bark."

Some of the gathered men grunted at this. They had heard such things around campfires as children. Whether they believed the tales, Val could not tell.

"So why are we all the same now?" Ulrik's voice startled the gathered warriors, as if they had all forgotten he was in his corner.

Halvard turned to him, rubbing his fingers on the bridge of his nose. "It has to do with a science called genetics. Simply put, it is like the way your farmers create the strongest wheat by mixing different seeds. People have different things in them called genes. When mixed in certain ways, you get different results. The babies of two people with blonde hair and blue eyes will probably look the same. After many generations of not introducing any different looking people, most will look alike. But if you met a woman with hair the color of mud, and the two of you had a baby, the child might have yellow hair like you, or brown like the woman's."

"That sounds like magic," Morten said. "Or some strange curse."

"Believe me," Halvard said, "I have read the old books. It was a very normal thing once. But for many decades, the only people in the North have looked like us."

Val spoke up. "So why have you brought us? What is this emergency? What is this human extinction you spoke of?"

"Right," the old man said. "There is a problem with the genes we all have. At first they were strong. They let our ancestors survive the Uttslettelse and prosper. But too many years of the same genes, without the introduction of anything new, have led to stagnation. Much the same way a strain of weak wheat will remain weak if not crossbred with hardier strains."

Morten's face darkened. "You are talking about the barren women."

Halvard nodded slowly. "Yes. You have all noticed a lack of successful births in the last many years. It is a problem with the genes. They are, for lack of a better word, dying. I have checked with many people around the North, and I have sent messages by carrier birds to other men of science around the world. The problem is everywhere. All humans have been unable to bring new children into the world, as of the last fifteen years or so. If we cannot find new genetic material—new seeds, if you will—then the human race will die. But if we find the correct genes, even if they are as small as a grain of sand, I know other men of science who can make the necessary changes to the genes in a laboratory. We can save the entire human race. Man and woman can continue into the future. But without the help of science, there will be no more children. We will all die, and there will be no more generations to follow us."

"Please tell me," Vebjørn said before belching loudly, "it is the Ålands woman."

Val snapped her head up to look at Halvard, a scowl crossing her face.

"Of course not, no. I need you to travel far from the North, to a place where a man of science I write letters to has discovered something."

"What has he found?" Ulrik asked.

"Genetic material that might just be the last hope for humanity. But the journey is far, and as you all know, travel by sea to the south is too perilous. Too many pirates prowl the waters. You will need to travel by land. And you will need stealth as much as strength. I think nine would be a proper number."

Many of the gathered men nodded. Nine was a lucky number.

Val stepped forward. "Where is this 'genetic material' that we need?"

Halvard stood up and looked at her. "I have maps to show the way, and special equipment that will see you through. But first you'll need to choose your leader and your group for this journey."

"It will be easier if I choose men from this very room," Val said.

Morten stood from the bench. "What makes you think you will be leading this mission? You are a woman. Clearly you can fight. We've all heard stories about you, but you have nothing to recommend you as a leader."

Val walked around the table and stood in front of Morten. The red lenses of her goggles were an inch from his bandaged nose when she stopped, her hand on the handle of her ax. "I will lead, and you will follow. Once you agree to follow, the others will as well."

"Sorry, but no. You will need to fight for the position of leader." His hand slid down toward the handle of his longsword. The other men in the room remained motionless, tense.

Val tilted her head slightly, but never took her eyes from Morten. "I will not fight you, Morten the Hammer. I will need to put your craftiness to work on this trip. I do not wish to damage you, before you are of use to me."

Morten smiled and was about to say something. She spoke first. "I will not fight you, because you will be valuable to me." Val raised her arm, and without looking, she pointed at the corner of the room. "But I will fight him."

Everyone turned to face Vebjørn, the Bear of the North, a man who stood two heads taller than Val and outweighed her by a hundred pounds of lean muscle. A man who was grinning at her outstretched finger, which was pointed directly at him.

5

It was the next day, and the sky was leaden with heavy gray clouds, the humidity pressing down on the harbor and trapping the pungent smell of fish and the nearby latrines for the camped fighters.

Most were still hungover, despite the sun being high behind the sky's thick clouds. The courtyard outside the Jarl's longhall was filled with men, all eager, despite still feeling the effects of the previous night's alcohol, to catch sight of the fight that would determine leader-ship of the mission. The small but deadly woman from the islands on the far side of the Swedish lakes versus the biggest human being most of them had ever seen.

Ulrik liked the woman, but he doubted she would be able to take on Vebjørn by herself. He doubted five men, twice her size, could do it.

The woman wore her dark pants from the previous day, but she had shed her armored leather jacket, wearing only a form-fitting black tank-top. She still wore the goggles, and her face was still painted with the red downward-pointing raven's wing design, spreading down to her mouth. She strode to the center of the courtyard, which had become an arena with spectators encircling it, the Jarl and the science-man, Halvard, back on their balcony to watch.

Val stopped walking near the center of the courtyard, standing on the buckled and cracked concrete. At her side, still sheathed, was her long ax, and on her other hip was a knife and a hand ax.

Ulrik watched the crowd of men on the far side of the area part for Vebjørn. The man sauntered into the center like a Jarl or a King. *After he kills her and leads the mission, if he returns alive, he probably will be a Jarl...or a King*, Ulrik thought. The man was the size of a building, and his bare chest rippled with power. He wore just shorts and boots, and he held a long double-headed ax, like Trond's. It was so big, Ulrik doubted the woman would have even been able to lift it.

This is going to be unpleasant.

He wondered if the Jarl would have some words for the crowd, but no one seemed in the mood—least of all the Bear of the North. The man had stopped a dozen feet from the thin blonde woman, but now he simply rushed her, bringing his massive ax behind him for an overhead vertical sweep that would plunge down straight in front of him, cleaving the woman in half.

To Val's credit, she did not flee in terror. She stood still. Her hand did not even move for her long ax.

The crowd held their collective breath.

Vebjørn approached, and his ax started to come down. When he was within striking distance, Val suddenly moved—with explosive speed. She leapt to the left, twisting like a corkscrew. The long double ax missed her and the blade bit into a long soil-filled crack in the concrete.

The woman slid the wickedly shaped hand ax from her belt while spinning in the air, and she pinwheeled her legs, flipping her body around. Before her feet hit the ground, she swung hard and sank the pointed bottom edge of the ax head into the Bear's shoulder meat. The blade chewed into the muscle and bone beneath it, then came to an abrupt jolting stop.

Val, still holding tightly to the handle of the small weapon, was left suspended, her boots dangling two feet off the ground. She didn't stay motionless, though. With her other hand she pulled the black handle of the short knife on her belt, reversed it in her grip and then stabbed it into Vebjørn's other shoulder. This time the giant howled in pain.

Val scrambled up the man's back, frantic, grunting and tugging her blades out and sinking them back in, like a woman climbing a ladder. Vebjørn dropped the handle of his oversized weapon and reached with both arms over his shoulders, trying to grab the scrabbling woman who was repeatedly stabbing him. But his own massive biceps prevented his reach from being long enough.

Instead, he thrust his body backward, falling over and mashing the small woman into the ground. He drove the air out of her with the heft of his upper body's weight.

The move drove her knife so deeply into his back that only an inch of the handle showed of a seven inch-long weapon. But as the Bear rolled to his side to get up, Ulrik could see the smaller hand ax had been knocked free.

Val rolled on the cracked ground, chest heaving as her lungs tried to pull in some air. Vebjørn reached down and grabbed her by her hair, tugging her across rough concrete. She reached up, trying to dislodge him from her hair with her fingers, but he was too strong. He dragged her behind him, as he walked toward his fallen ax.

Val's hand slid down to her own long ax and quickly pulled it free from the metal loop on which it hung. She used both hands on the handle and swung it up at herself, the head of the ax clearing her head and sinking vertically into the middle of the Bear's wrist, even as the dark handle wrapped in leather cord smashed into her own face.

It was almost comical: twin arcs of blood erupted from Vebjørn's wrist and Val's face at the same time.

The Bear howled and staggered away from the woman, clutching his wrist to his chest. Freed from the massive man's hand tugging her hair, the woman was back on her feet and leaping once again. She appeared to be lunging away from the Bear, but once again, at the last second she rolled her body, stretching her arm to its full extent. She let her ax handle slide through her hand, until the very knob at the end caught in her grip.

The swing had length, which meant it had leverage, and Ulrik knew it would have the same power as a shorter swing from a stronger fighter. The edge of the ax head sank sideways into the back of Vebjørn's neck, and lodged there, trapped deep in a vertebra.

Val continued her roll through the air, and landed on her feet, her legs bending into a crouch to absorb the kinetic force. Vebjørn staggered forward, his body on a slow tumble to the broken concrete and tufts of wild grass below him. But Val was making sure. She lunged to the ground, snagging the discarded hand ax, and rolling in front of the falling mass. Ulrik thought she would be crushed under the weight of the man, like a falling tree pressing grass into soil.

But the woman struck upward with the devious pointed end of her hand-held ax, embedding the blade in the Bear's eye socket, before she performed a backward-somersault, just out of the reach of where the giant man's body would hit. Out of weapons, the woman came to a halt in a crouch just inches beyond where Vebjørn's face cracked into the concrete, three gouts of blood spurting out to either side of his ruined head and above it.

The Bear of the North did not move. Neither did Val. She stayed on her haunches, peering at the fallen man, blood gushing from her nose, and one lens of her goggles smeared, but not cracked. Her long hair cascaded down around her face.

The hungover men in the arena were quiet, but Ulrik looked around at some of the stunned faces. Not all of them would follow her into battle, but many of them looked at her with a newfound respect. *Because they know they could not have defeated the Bear.*

Eventually the woman stood. She pulled her ax from Vebjørn's neck and then used it to hack at the meat of his shoulder, sprays of blood and chipped bone arcing away from the wound, until she could pull her knife from its deep puncture hole. She gave it a shake and a spray of Vebjørn's blood sliced through the air, landing several feet away on the white, sun-washed concrete. She dropped her long ax into its metal loop on her belt, but kept the gore-drenched knife in hand. Finally she nudged the man's head enough with her booted foot until she could pry the hand ax free with a slurp.

A weapon in each hand, she looked at the men arrayed around her, many ogling her with awe, and she spotted Morten the Hammer. Standing beside him, his companion Oskar looked pale-faced and ill.

Val approached Morten until her bloody face was an inch from his.

"Do you have anything more to say, Morten the Hammer?"

He looked back at her, his face impassive. "We will follow your lead."

From across the arena, Ulrik smiled. It was going to be an interesting trip. Glancing up at Halvard and the Jarl on the balcony, he saw that the older science-man looked pleased. The Jarl looked like he was about to be sick.

6

"How far is it, this place by the sea?" Val asked Halvard. They were standing in a rectangular room with a large table at the center. It was covered in old maps, curling and with chipped edges, water stains, and in one case, a blood stain that obscured a portion of the map's land masses. The cloying scent of the many candles arrayed around them filled her nostrils, making her broken nose ache.

"It is far," Halvard said, looking grim. "I would accompany you, but I am in no shape to make it the distance. If you could go in a straight line on land, which you cannot, and if you could cover eight miles a day, which is doubtful, it would still take you most of a year, just to get there."

"And then we need to get back," Morten said. He was far more helpful since Val had revealed the depth of her skills, but he still had a defeatist attitude. Arrayed around the room were the rest of her chosen men from the original group to whom Halvard had explained the plan. Trond with his newly shortened beard and bandaged side, Ulrik the Fearless, Morten's friend Oskar, and the hunter Anders with his bow. Perched on the man's shoulder was a huge bird of prey, its head hooded with a leather sleeve. The bird's talons looked like they would pierce the leather coat. Also present was a short, broad, grumpy man named Stig. Ulrik had assured Val he was a fighter from the south of great repute. Besides the old science-man, one more man stood quietly in the corner. Halvard had introduced him to the group as his student, a man well versed in the history of the old world, from before the Utslettelse. His name was Nils, and while Val believed Halvard trusted the man's knowledge, she was skeptical of his ability to make the journey. The man was wiry and pale. She suspected she weighed more than he did. Killing him would take no effort, for Val or any other man in the room, including the aged Halvard. The other Northmen who had heard Halvard's explanations on the first day had turned their noses up at the idea of journeying so far. Even with the fate of the human race at stake, many had taken their warriors and returned home. Once those that remained had learned that the mission required stealth, they too had sent their men home. Only Val and the hunter Anders had arrived on their own, so they hadn't needed to bid farewell to disappointed kinsmen.

Val turned to Halvard, concern creasing her forehead above the red lenses of her goggles. "And how will we travel this distance? You say we cannot voyage by sea, because of the pirates. Are we to walk for a year?"

Halvard nodded, as if he had anticipated the question. "I have something else in mind. Follow me, everyone."

One by one, the assembled fighters and their historian filed out of the room after the old man. He led them outside the building and through the narrow, winding, cobbled alleys that carved up the small town. Remnants of the Old World were everywhere, but for Val, the village looked like most of the others she had seen. Rock and brick, chimneys and fireplaces. Wooden buildings and repurposed Old World things for which no one knew the names.

Val walked in the lead of their small group, following on the heels of the old man. She knew the town had been set up as an intentionally confusing maze of twists and turns to foil invaders from across the country or pirates landing from the sea. Marauders were everywhere.

She attempted to mentally catalogue their path, but soon gave up on memorizing the convoluted route. At last the old man stopped by a pair of metal doors, set at a low angle that led down into the ground. "Here we are," he said, as if that explained everything.

He bent and pulled open one of the doors. Val leaned in to help him lift the second. The doors, which looked rusted and disused, opened on well-oiled hinges. Below them was a set of stairs fashioned from laid flat river stones. The old man quickly descended and Val followed. The others came after her, and as she squeezed down the narrow stone passage, she wondered if mighty Trond would fit through.

The stairs came out into a huge subterranean room—far larger than the Jarl's longhall, and the walls were made of cracked concrete. In one place where the wall had crumbled away, it had been repaired with river stone and some kind of mortar that looked out of place. Candles lined the walls, and at the far end of the huge space were nine things the size of tables. They each had four black wheels protected by green molded armor. Each was topped by a black seat. They also had black handles that stuck up in the front and twin silver containers on the back that looked like kegs of beer.

"What...what are they?" Val asked.

Halvard turned to the assembled fighters and smiled wide with crooked teeth. "These will get you there and back. Mechanical horses. They were called ATVs in the Old World. For All Terrain Vehicles. Because they have four wheels, they were also sometimes called 'Quad-bikes' or 'Quads.'"

Ulrik approached the ATVs and ran his finger lightly over one. "These are machines? How do you make them move?"

Halvard approached him and pointed. "These were fitted with tanks for propane gas," he indicated the twin tanks on the back. "You will need to find more gas to keep them running. It will only take you a few hours to learn to ride and steer. With them you will be able to cover many miles in a day, on the roads that still cover the world. They may be old, but these vehicles are hardy. They are able to roll over most smaller obstacles like stones or tree roots."

A man approached from a small doorway at the far end of the room, which was next to an immense rusted metal door. The man was smaller than Ulrik, but covered in hard muscles, and coated in dirt and grease.

"This is Erlend. He has restored the ATVs, and he will teach you how to drive them. We have nine quads, and with Erlend, you have a group of nine for the journey. He will come with you to repair the vehicles, if they should break down."

"Hello," Erlend said, swinging a leg over the side of one of the quads.

"How do you bring these...ATVs...to life, Erlend?" Val asked, stepping forward to join Ulrik in appraising the vehicles.

Erlend turned a key on his mount, then flicked an engine switch and stood up on the kickstarter. The motor growled to life, a noise louder than anything most of the assembled fighters had ever heard—except for Val, who had once heard the roar of a polar bear up close.

Halvard startled the group by raising the massive metal door at the far end of the room, using a chain pull. Daylight flooded into the yawning space, as the vibrations from the vehicle's engine rumbled the floor. Val had just begun to step closer to the machines, when Erlend released his hand from a spring-loaded silver lever on the handle of the quad, and it shot forward, racing out the open door and onto a wide open field of grass beyond it.

Val watched, fascinated, as the man alternately sat on the ATV or stood up on it, leaning his body left and right, steering the vehicle around the field, until it was aimed at a hard-packed pile of dirt half as high as a man.

He sped up as he approached the mound and then raced up the pile, and the vehicle lunged through the air. Val's mouth fell open as he leaned backward at the last second of the quad's arc through the sky, and the rear wheels dropped into the grass and caught again, before he raced off across the field.

When Val turned to look at Halvard, who looked smug and proud, she saw that the men around him all wore expressions of astonishment or sheer terror on their faces.

"Which one is mine?" Val asked.

7

Halvard stood alone with Val at the top of one of the tallest, still-mostly vertical structures in town. It had once been a ten-story-tall apartment tower, but now it was mostly a rusted collection of bare I-beams and corroded metal stairs. The steps were coated in detritus from thousands of birds and the vegetation of several different invasive species of vine, as well as a few random trees that had mysteriously chosen to grow on the upper reaches of the building.

Halvard used the building for his birds.

At the top he had created a huge pen for the creatures. They were beautiful to behold. He knew from having read old volumes that their ancestors had been called carrier pigeons. But these birds were huge, with a wingspan of over eight feet. His great grandfather had domesticated them and had used them to converse with descendants of fellow scientists who had weathered the great annihilation. They had kept in touch through the decades, even as the world fell apart around them. One station in Venice, Italy. Another in what had been Tokyo, Japan, and another in Seattle. They shared their experiments and their failures, using the birds to converse, as their ancestors had hundreds of years before the 21st century. Only now their messenger birds were large enough to eat humans, if they were so inclined. *Luckily*, Halvard thought, *they would rather eat us out of grains.*

"You will send a message ahead?" Val asked him. It was their first time to speak alone, and Halvard had much to tell her.

"Yes. To a man named Troben, in Italy. His grandfather was from Stavanger, and he journeyed across the continent to see what remained of the world, after the Utslettelse. But he stayed in Italy, and kept in contact with us using the birds. Then his son, until Troben and I." Val was nodding, indicating she was following the story, while she appraised the huge bird Halvard called *Sulten*, which meant hungry in Norwegian.

"So this man Troben will have the genetic material for us?" she asked him.

"Yes, but there is more. Much more." Halvard was afraid she would react badly when he told her the next part. The team was about to depart in the next half hour. Even now the others were down on the ground, packing up their ATVs in preparation for departure.

"I suspected there was," Val said, turning to look up at him. "Tell me."

"After you have reached Italy and secured the genetic material, you need to get something else on the return voyage. Something crucial."

Ulrik watched Val return from the tall tower with Halvard. He had seen the bird with the mighty wingspan streak away from the roof, and he'd kept track of how much time had elapsed afterward. He knew Halvard and Val had been discussing something for some time—and even if he hadn't been paying attention, the pale cast of Val's face under her raven's wing makeup and goggles told him she'd received some grave news.

Ulrik and the others had all packed up their ATVs, the strange bikes stacked with tanks of fuel, packs of food, and Erlend's tool kit. Ulrik had suggested they divvy these things up across the nine vehicles, so if something happened to one of the ATVs—and by extension, one of the riders—they wouldn't lose all of one kind of supply.

They had spent three days becoming familiar with riding the quads. Learning to turn the vehicles without rolling them was the hardest part. You had to stand on the footplates and lean in the direction away from your turn slightly, lifting the wheel on the inside of the turn. It had taken Ulrik a while, and he had been the last to master the technique from their group, but they were all now competent riders.

Val had taken to her ATV like a seal takes to eating fish, and she had used the extra days to converse with Halvard, learning all she could about the strange parts of the world they would see, how they should go about finding more propane for the vehicles, and what kinds of food they could eat on the road.

Meanwhile, Erlend had spent time teaching Stig, the man with a perpetual storm cloud hovering over his features, how to repair the ATVs, so Erlend wouldn't be the only mechanic in their group. Anders had likewise begun to teach Trond some techniques for hunting with his bow, and how to hold the giant bird, whose name was Skjold. Morten had become the pupil of Nils, learning what he could about the world's history. That had left Morten's constant companion Oskar to help Ulrik with inventory and most days to sit on the sidelines watching the bigger man try to master the ATV.

Now, Val approached her steed, slipping her black clad leg over the saddle. Her ATV was parked next to Ulrik's. He looked at her and considered asking what was bothering her, but she didn't look open to a conversation, so he simply said, "Are we ready to depart?"

"Wait," she said. She took a deep breath of the air, then slowly let it out.

"Should I be breathing, too?" he asked.

She turned to him with a frown. "Only if you will miss the smell of this air. We might not be back for a few years."

He nodded, then took a deep lungful of the fresh seaside air. A cool breeze was blowing in from the water, and the flowers of summer were in full bloom.

Halvard stood nearby as Val kickstarted her quad, and the other eight followed her lead. The roar of the nine vehicles was like a storm of hornets. He had grave misgivings about the plan, but it was the best one they had been able to come up with. When he had revealed the additional task to Val, she had been irritated.

She turned back to look at him. He nodded at her, and prayed for Odin to keep her safe. She and her men were the last hope for the human race. Troben's message from Italy was that there were not enough brave men there who were still sane enough to undertake such a mission. He couldn't get the genetic material where it needed to go, so the burden fell to Halvard to send warriors to retrieve it. He had no idea if they could even make it to Italy from Norway. The road was fraught with peril, hostile mutated fauna and the last dregs of humanity, wrapped in their own crazed little worlds. And then, if she made it that far, she had to get back to him and with the things he had tasked her with bringing.

Val released her brakes and cruised off across the grassy field without a look back. The others filed behind her, their wheels kicking up small clumps of dirt as each launched off its starting point.

They were not traveling by sea, but Halvard realized he was witnessing history in motion. The nine warriors with the young woman as their leader were embarking on the maiden voyage of the last several decades. They were the first to travel to mainland Europe since before the annihilation.

He was witnessing the beginning of the Third Viking Age.

8

Val drove in the lead, following the road to Kristiansand, around the southern coast. The interior of the country was too mountainous—even with the ability of the ATVs to handle variegated terrain. Also, as most of the people still living in the place once known on Halvard's maps as Norway had gravitated to villages on the shore, they had kept the road mostly clear of vegetation since the Old World days. Travel along the coast would be easier.

They moved slowly and carefully the first few days, covering only a few miles each day and making good use of the small villages for meals and drink. The ATVs were a constant source of fascination for the locals, and in one case had led to an armed confrontation between Ulrik and an onlooker with no sense of personal space. After that they had sent one man into a village they planned to camp in—usually the non-threatening Anders with his hunting bird—to secure a room and the rental of barn space on the edge of town. They would then sequester the vehicles in the barn and leave one member of their party on guard, while the rest went into town for meals.

But they were halfway to Oslo now, and Val knew from experience that once they crossed over into what used to be called Sweden and was now simply regarded as 'the wild,' that the area was full of hungry creatures and few villages. They would still follow the coast in Sweden, angling down to the strait between the tip of the peninsula and the northward jutting mass of Denmark. And she hoped they would find a bridge there. If not, they would need to build a boat stout enough to take the quads, and that could take them well into winter and the following spring.

The light was fading fast, and they had already found that, even with the headlamps on the quads, traveling the rutted roads at night was too difficult. Besides, Val was eager to enjoy these last nights in Norway before they entered the unknown. Despite the lack of a proper village, she called a halt to their progress for the day.

The men grumbled, but they turned their ATVs off the road and followed her on a smaller path that was cracked and neglected, with tufts of grass and in some cases full trees growing out of it. The road wound a few hundred feet to a small island full of fractured concrete and lush trees, but the tiny bridge to the island was out, so they stopped at the end of the road instead. A tiny trail to their left led down a slope to a long abandoned concrete dock. Val drove her ATV down the slope, followed by the others. There was enough tree cover to keep them from sight for the night.

She parked her quad in some leafy trees and then began pulling her blankets from her pack. Tonight they would sleep under the stars.

"Even Skjold will not find any game here," Anders pointed out.

"This is true, but we will find plenty of fish. Perhaps you and Trond could try your luck at the broken bridge?" Val said, with good nature. She knew that no one was happy sleeping out, but there would be far more nights of this than the pampered evenings they had spent so far at the coastal villages.

They will need to get used to it. This is a good place to begin.

"Set up the camp," she told Morten. "I am going for a swim."

The rest began unpacking their needed items for the night, but Ulrik looked at her, before turning back to his task. He was the one she thought best suited for the journey. Level-headed. Calm. But if crossed, he was competent and efficient as a fighter. The hunter, the historian, the mechanic, and Trond all seemed happy to follow her lead, or in lieu of her order—Ulrik's gentle suggestions. Morten and Oskar were the two she trusted least. Morten always had the look of a man who was up to something and hoping he wouldn't be found out. Oskar was his lackey, and by association also seemed shifty. And despite Stig spending time with Erlend to learn about the ATVs whenever they stopped, lately the rotund man had been spending more time seated near Morten and Oskar at night.

If I will have problems, it will come from the three of them.

Her bath in the brisk harbor was uneventful, and she was able to sit on the small rocky beach in the last light of day, drying in the light and the breeze before dressing again in her black leather and weapons. She pulled her goggles back on again, too. She would take them off when it got darker and then stay in the shadows. She had learned long ago that the discoloration in her eyes made people uncomfortable, so she kept the goggles on around them. These moments of solitude were the only time she took them off.

As she approached the camp, moving through the trees, the sun set behind the rocky ridges of the coast, and the shadows deepened. She could hear a discussion going on as she got closer to the men.

"You saw what she did to Vebjørn," Stig said.

"I did, and it was an impressive feat, but I am still not convinced she will be a good fighter in a full melee. This journey will take us through who-knows-what kind of lands. Perhaps we will need to fight many men."

Morten, she thought. *Of course.*

"You also saw her fight many men," Ulrik said softly. "And she was very effective."

"Yes, but she was lost in a berserker rage," Morten persisted.

"Was she?" Ulrik asked.

"What do you mean?" Stig asked.

"Morten and I saw her fighting at the harbor. It looked out of control—a berserker rage, as you say. We all know what that means. We have felt it in the heat of battle," Ulrik said.

"I have not fought in any battles, but I have heard the tales," Nils interjected. "I know of what you speak."

"She fought savagely," Ulrik continued. "But with effortless grace. Each strike she dealt resulted in maximum damage to her opponent, and then she went on to the next. A minimum of movements, nothing wasted and everything gained. I have never seen a fighter like her. She did the same thing in the battle with the Bear of the North. Even when he had her down, her strikes were calculated. She never thrashed or flailed. So I ask you again, Morten the Hammer. Was it truly a rage? Or was she in complete control the whole time?"

Morten did not answer.

Instead, Stig did. "I see what you mean. I saw her at the harbor. At first what I saw was a crazy woman, but you are right. She rarely hit a single man more than once."

"Precisely," Ulrik said, again speaking in his calm, relaxed way, as if he had no real stake in the argument but was just thinking about it. But Val knew what he was doing. He was consolidating her power base in the group. "I don't know about you, but I would rather follow a leader who can keep her head, even in a crazy fight like that one at the harbor—even a woman—than a man who would go completely insane and thrash his way through a battle, possibly losing limbs or life in the process, because his mind was too far gone."

"Yes," Stig said, having come around to Ulrik's side of things. "She has made good decisions on the journey so far. Hiding the ATVs in the barns, stopping where we have. I think she will make a good leader for us. Even today, I thought we stopped too soon. I would have preferred to continue to a village. But once we unpacked, I realized just how tired I had become. Driving all day on those ATVs can suck the energy out of you. And the vibrations have made my legs numb. I think she made the right decision to stop here tonight."

Val smiled in the dark.

Stig's allegiance to Morten had been broken. Just like that. She noticed that Morten and Oskar had nothing further to say on the matter.

Six down, two to go, she thought.

Then she stepped out of the trees and into the camp, as if she had heard nothing. Anders and Trond returned a few minutes later with an immense six-foot long mackerel. It was the only fish they had caught, but they would all eat well that night.

9

When the snow began to fall, some of the men grumbled. They were stopped in a forest of thick conifer trees, to relieve themselves and shake the bone-rattling numbness of the all-terrain vehicles from their bones.

"It is summer," Oskar said, wiping away flakes from his eyes with his skinny arm. "We should not see snow for many weeks yet."

Nils spoke up. "You know that the weather can bring anything at any time. It was not always this way, though. Before the Utslettelse, the seasons were very regular. But the entire world shifted its position."

"Either that," Stig said, leaning against his ATV's saddle, "or Skadi is a cruel and fickle bitch."

Val didn't put much faith in Skadi—the goddess of winter—having anything to do with it. She wondered briefly whether the statement from Stig, the perpetual complainer, was a dig at her, but she thought better of it. In the last few days, Stig had decided to side with Ulrik on any disagreement, and she had noted the heavy man was no longer sitting near Morten and Oskar when given the chance at night.

Unfortunately, Morten and Oskar had become bigger complainers than Stig, challenging her decisions at every opportunity.

It will soon be time for another lesson, she thought.

But for now, the turn in the weather concerned her. She knew the ATVs could move in light snow—Halvard had told her so, and Erlend had confirmed it. Erlend had discovered the vehicles the previous year, when an old man who had been caring for them died. It was not unusual for a piece of technology or some knowledge from the Old World to be cared for and handed down generation after generation. Halvard was proof of that with his book learning and knowledge of the sciences. But Erlend admitted that nine ATVs had been the find of a lifetime.

They were in bad shape when he had found them. The old man who had been keeping them in a barn had not tended to them for over a decade. It was Erlend who had converted the engines from running on Old World fuel and oil to running on propane. With Halvard's guidance, they had worked a miracle.

As Val glanced at the hard gray sky and the snowflakes that were growing in size with every moment, she knew she might need another.

"Let us go," she said. "We should get as far as we can before the storm forces us to stop."

As they mounted up and started their engines, Ulrik raced up next to her and pulled hard on his brakes, his ATV already skidding in the light covering of snow on the ground. He spoke softly, so only she could hear him. "We are close to the border. Or perhaps we have already passed it. Are you certain you wish to travel into unknown lands with reduced visibility?"

Val recognized the question for what it meant. There had long been rumors of the horrors in Southern Sweden, and no one who had ever gone to investigate the truth of them had returned. Ulrik was not challenging her, but offering wisdom.

"I know," she said. "But we'll have to go through it sometime. The further south we get, the warmer it will become."

He merely nodded, then took off and circled back to ensure the others were all ready to depart. He was good with the logistical aspects, and not for the first time, Val thanked the gods that she had him with her. The others would be far more difficult to manage, although Trond seemed to have taken a liking to her. Not in a mature way, but more the way a puppy will choose a favorite human to be near. She could think of worse situations than the massive man having her back.

They set off into the storm, the clouds blocking the sun and making the day nearly dark. As the snowfall intensified, Val and Trond led their convoy, but they could barely make out the road ahead of them.

Although she had never learned to read, Val consulted Nils every day on the map, asking the names of places and memorizing their letters and their locations. While the others had debated whether they were still in Norway or had entered Sweden, she knew they were already in the unknown lands. Nils knew it too, but he kept quiet, unless she was asking him questions.

Soon the blizzard grew so thick she could barely see past the extent of the quad bike's headlights. "Turn off here." She turned her bike off the rutted and bumpy road, deep into some close-growth trees, working her way down a natural path. As always, they went a short distance from the road so they couldn't easily be seen, should anyone—or anything—take that easy path in the night. In this case, the snow, which had already accumulated a few inches on the ground, would soon cover their tracks.

Morten pulled his ATV up alongside hers as she drove deeper into the woods. "Is this wise?"

The same question, every night, she thought.

"Morten, I will not—"

CrackCrackCrackCrack.

The staccato crunching noise was louder than the engines of the ATVs, and she slowed to a stop, looking down into the snow, without finishing the sentence.

Morten stopped also, and jumped off his ATV, pulling his sword. "What is this?"

The others all pulled up, and seeing Morten armed, they jumped to the ready, pulling swords and axes from scabbards, sheaths and belt rings, where the weapons had been dormant for days now.

The snow in the forest was deeper than on the road. They had been heading further into the storm. But while it came to their ankles or mid shins here, it was not deep enough to cover what had been on the ground.

Jumbled across the ground, many sticking up at strange angles like the toppled buildings of Stavanger, was a sea of bones, poking through the snow. Val recognized the skulls of bears, and the leg bones of reindeer, which were both plentiful in this part of the world. She realized with a sick sinking in her gut that the rapid-fire popping noise had been when they had driven over the bones and into the—

Oh no, she thought. *It is a nest.*

Something had killed and eaten all the animals, upon whose bones they now stood. Something that had dragged the carcasses to this location in the forest, this small clearing, and consumed them.

The wind had been in their faces for much of the journey through the storm, and now, without warning, it died.

The snow was behind them, and in another minute, the clouds overhead lightened. Val glanced behind her and the wall of weather was nearly black as it receded into the distance.

"Vidar's balls," Morten said. "Look at how far it goes."

Val turned again, and the sky ahead of them had cleared to a thin hazy mist above. But the ground was well lit, and she could see that the bones jutting from the recent snow stretched on ahead of them.

For miles. It wasn't a small clearing. The land opened up to a treeless, sloping valley.

And it was completely covered in bones.

Now that the weather had cleared, Val could see that some of the discarded bones were human.

She was about to order everyone to get back on the ATVs and head back the way they had come, but it was too late.

The roar that came out of the storm behind them was deep and loud. It rumbled the ground they stood on. It was alive, and coming their way.

10

The ground rumbled from repeated impacts that shook up through Val's legs. She leapt onto her ATV and shouted over the noise. "Scatter! Get the quads away from the path. Deeper into the bones."

For once, Morten followed an order without debate. He leapt onto his green ATV and took off in a straight path through the bones to the left of the trail they had taken into the nest. Oskar was quickly behind him.

Val broke right, and Ulrik, Trond and Nils were with her. The others were already gone from sight. But Val didn't look for them. Her attention was completely enveloped with the sight of the thing rushing out of the storm toward them. The smell hit her first, like a pulsating wave of death, and she realized when the creature roared again that it was the thing's breath she was smelling.

To call it a bear was to call a puddle the sea. It was half the height of the trees—twenty feet tall at least. Its arms ended in paws that held far too many claws for them to even be effectively functional. Like a handful of loose straw all different lengths and angled in different directions. They would be useless for digging but perfect for eviscerating prey.

The creature moved on its hind legs only, which she had never seen before. Bears were known to stand, but never run on their hind legs. Unlike the deformed polar bear she had battled as a child, this creature was brown and black, and nothing like any bear should be. It had fin-like ridges protruding from under the fur on its back, almost like a whale fin. The rest of its body was covered in fur but rippled with mounds the size of human heads, like tumors pushing up under the skin.

But the monster's head was its most terrifying feature. Its snout was distended, and the jaw hinged three ways—ahead and to each side, with three sets of jaws, as if it needed to eat on three sides of its head at once. One of its black dead eyes had been clawed out—by another creature or maybe by itself, but the wound was infected with oozing yellow pus. Deep long gashes trailed from the mangled eye socket up and over its head.

As it chased after her group, Val noticed the massive creature's spine had picked up a few more protrusions. Arrows. Anders was in the trees somewhere, firing arrow after arrow into the creature's hide, but the assault didn't slow the monster's frantic sprint into the bone nest.

It roared as it ran. The thunder of its hind legs striking the ground and crushing bones as it rushed after them, combined with the buzzing engines of the retreating ATVs and the continual cracking of the bones under the wheels of the quads, was a cacophony of sound that was almost as bad as the wretched smell of decay and putrescence that preceded the monster like an advanced invading force.

"The trees," Ulrik yelled at her. She saw that he was right. He was arcing his ATV around and back toward the forest that had acted as a barrier between the road and the bone nest. The tall conifers would probably not stop the rampaging mega-bear, but they might slow it.

Trond must have already made it into the cover of the huge spruce and pine trees. Val couldn't see him anywhere. Ulrik raced ahead of her, and was nearly to the treeline. She was fifty feet behind him. Her ATV skidded left and right as she tried to navigate the recently fallen snow and haphazard bones.

Only then did she realize that the jagged snapping bones had the potential to puncture one or all of her tires. She swore aloud and hoped the gods would prevent that from happening. The pursuing mega-bear was only a hundred feet behind her as she raced in an arc back toward the trees. The slightest delay and the creature would be upon her. The only question in her mind was whether it would eat her or simply crush her in its rush to get to the others.

The creature roared again, and this time she could feel the pressure wave of its breath blasting across her back and neck like a hot wind. Then she was in the trees, the ATV's knobby tires gripping the smoother ground. The snow wasn't as deep here, since the tree cover overhead was thicker. There was no clear path through the trees, but she threw her body left and right, weaving around the two-foot thick trunks.

Then trees snapped behind her, the sound like the wrenching of the world, with groans, creaks and explosions of wooden splinters. The trees wouldn't slow the monster much.

She had lost sight of Ulrik, but kept moving straight, steering around whatever trees crossed her path. Her hope was to reach the road, where she could outrun the monster, and she figured that was where Trond and Ulrik had gone as well. But then she saw a sparkle of light on metal to her left, and when she glanced that way, she saw a parked ATV, missing its rider.

"Where the hell is—" she started, when she burst out of the thick tree cover into a small glade. A thick pine came tumbling over her head to crash in front of her in the middle of the clearing. She cranked the handlebars to the left, but the turn was too sharp, and her ride began to tumble. She sprang off it, but the velocity kept her body flying through the air and tumbling until she crashed into a thick cushion of pine needles. She thought the pine would break her fall completely, as the dark green boughs enveloped her, but then her hip and lower back slammed into a branch and a lance of pain shot through her spine up to her head.

She shouted out, and the rampaging monster bear suddenly stopped its chase. She stayed perfectly still, realizing the thing had just overshot her position, as she had plunged into the thick cocoon of needles.

But its hearing is excellent.

Val held her breath, not daring to move her body even a fraction of an inch. The horrific stench that spoke of countless dead animals for meals washed over her again. *It has turned back this way.*

Her lungs begged for air, but she refused them. She needed to move, but the movement she had in mind had nothing to do with her chest and everything to do with her arm. It was twisted behind her, and it would be useless there. She had no desire to die a horrible death at the triple jaws and multiple claws of the mutated bear. But if she was going to die that way, she would deliver the beast as much pain as she could. She slowly inched her right arm out from behind her back, pushing against the wall of green pine needles with her elbow.

Once her arm was free, she slid her hand down to her aching hip, where the metal ring that held her long ax was attached to her belt. She secured a scavenged leather holster that kept the handle of the ax from swinging when she walked.

Her eyes felt as if they were bulging in her sockets from holding her breath so long. Her lungs screamed at her with all the profanity of the gods.

She had to breathe.

Val slowly sucked in air, and the rotting aroma of the creature's breath nearly made her pass out, as her stomach wobbled and her vision narrowed.

Then two things happened at once.

The pine needle wall in front of her face burst apart, as the triple-jawed beast mashed its snout through the barrier. Its nose stopped just two inches from the rim of Val's goggles. The shiny black eye of the creature stared right at her. Long splinters of wood pierced the thing's face, suggesting that, in addition to knocking the trees in its path down, the mega-bear had also bitten through whatever branches or trunks had been near its face.

The second thing that happened was her hand reaching the holster, fingers scrabbling for the ax.

But the holster was empty.

11

The wave of stench was so thick, the air in front of her eyes shimmered like heat haze. The mutant bear lunged for her just as she rolled to her right, pulling her hand-ax from its front-mounted sheath with her other hand as she went. She struck backward with the blade, not even seeing where her arm went, and she felt the sharp blade lodge in between the teeth of the beast's side set of jaws.

She released the handle of the blade, leaving it wedged in the animal's mouth. She crawled forward through the wall of pine needles, until the barrier of green parted and she saw snow once again.

Behind her the monster roared, this time sounding irritated by the small sharp thing embedded in its face.

Irritated, but it doesn't sound hurt.

She scrabbled forward into the snow, trying to get her feet under her, but then she heard a human yell.

Val rolled onto her back in time to see mighty Trond, his huge double-headed broad ax behind his head, dropping from high up in the trees, and down into the clearing, heading for the creature's back. He swung the blade over his head with all his massive upper body strength, and brought the edge of the blade down into the mega-bear's spine as he landed atop the beast. The blade sank in deeply, and now the monster roared a high-pitched shriek of pain.

It quickly stood up onto its hind legs from where it had crouched to shove its long triple-snout through the fallen conifer. When it stood, it simultaneously dislodged Trond, throwing him backward, and lifted the entire pine tree that was still attached to its head. Now the beast had the whole tree horizontally atop its shoulders where its head should have been.

"Val," Ulrik called.

She turned her head to the left and reached up in one fluid movement, catching her long ax, which Ulrik had spotted on the ground and tossed to her. With a weapon in her hand, and the revelation that the plan was to fight the creature, she stood and gripped the end of her ax with both hands. She rushed forward and under the suddenly swinging trunk of the pine tree. The branches were not long, and the needles dipped to just above Val's head.

The bear spun in a full circle in the clearing, as it tried to dislodge the lengthy pine from its face and failed. Val rushed toward its leg and hacked twice at the back of the creature's knee, which was now at her eye level. Blood arced from the wound in spurts of crimson, along with white pus.

Infection runs through the whole beast, she thought. She wondered briefly if whatever was making it sick was going to infect them. Was it a sickness, or was it radiation? She knew enough about radiation to avoid it, when she knew it was present, even though she did not understand what it was exactly or how it worked.

She ran past and took a swing at the other leg as the creature continued to howl and spin. She missed with her second strike, but was almost once again clear of the beast when it dipped its upper body, and the attached tree came crashing down.

A thick branch cracked into Val's back, adding more pain to her already throbbing hip. She sprawled in the snow, just as Ulrik came rushing toward her and leapt up and over her, into the branches and up the trunk of the long pine.

The mutant bear growled and began thrashing with its long front paws, the multiple overlapping claws hacking and tearing at pine needles and branches.

Val rolled forward in the snow, a full somersault, then she spun around, ax in hand and ready to rush in again.

Ulrik raced along the spine of the tree to the monster's face. It was crushed tightly against the trunk, interlocking branches behind its head, holding the tree fast. Val's hand ax was still embedded vertically in one set of side jaws, the blade glinting in the seeping blood. He swung down hard with his long ax, cleaving into the beast's uninjured side jaw, the teeth and distended side snout falling away into the pine needles below.

The creature swept an arm up. The jumbled claws missed Ulrik, but the bulk of the forearm's backswing smashed into his chest and face like the trunk of a thick oak tree. Ulrik was there, and then he was gone, sailing through the air and passing backward, past the trees and right out of the edge of the forest. He crashed into the field of snow covered bones with multiple crunches and snaps.

Val hoped that none of those breaking bones were his.

She had an idea, but she needed a distraction.

Then it came, as Trond rushed back into the battle with smaller hatchets in each hand. Taking a cue from her earlier fight with Vebjørn, he slipped in under the tree and sliced both blades into the back of the animal's muscular legs, attempting to climb the beast to his still-stuck double-bladed ax in its spine.

The monster began to spin again, and Val thought Trond would be thrown, but the distraction had been long enough. Instead of getting close to the creature, she grabbed onto a low hanging branch of the spinning tree, and let it carry her away. The sticky pine sap cemented her grip on the bark. She slid her ax into its holster at her waist so she could use her other hand. Then hand over hand she climbed higher into the pine, as the massive animal spun faster. She could feel the force of the spin on her, but she moved closer to the center of the tree, which was her target anyway.

Trond shouted as he was flung away again, and she saw the man hit a tree at the edge of the clearing, before she saw the oncoming danger—she wasn't going to make it up to strike down at the head as Ulrik had done. The bear's spin had become erratic in the fight, and the end of the forty-foot long pine tree was getting closer to the wall of trees that ringed the clearing on one side.

Instead of continuing to climb, Val dropped down through the needles, her feet hitting the snow-covered ground and sliding out from under her. Her back slammed into the ground—a blast of pain shot through her frame, but she forced the pain down and gritted her teeth, rolling away just before the bear's huge leg came stamping toward her position. The bundles of claws on the hind legs were mostly cracked and broken, but she had no desire to discover whether her lithe frame could withstand the behemoth's weight.

Instead of aiming at its head, she aimed at its feet.

She pulled her long ax and swung at the thick, two-foot diameter ankle as it came around. Another spurt of thick white and red confirmed her earlier assessment—disease coursed through the monster. Then she dodged out of the way as the spinning creature turned further. She was ready to strike at the other ankle when it came around, but she heard a booming crack, as the trunk of the spinning, horizontal tree struck an upright tree at the edge of the clearing.

She had been expecting that. She had *not* been expecting that the tree would come plummeting straight down when it happened. She was crouched to attack the monster's ankles, but she didn't have enough time to dart out of the way before she was once again coated with green needles. A branch the size of her wrist came thumping down on the studded leather plate of armor on her shoulder. The impact staggered her, forcing her squat deeper, until her bottom was nearly touching the ground.

The bear didn't stand.

Val clawed her way upward through the sticky green, until she was on top of the long trunk. She was poised for action, but none was required.

The twisting tree had broken the creature's neck, its strange front set of jaws now sideways to its shoulders under the branches. One thick brown branch had splintered and driven itself into the back of the animal's neck. Her hand ax was still stuck in the teeth of the remaining side-jaws. The other side of the animal's face had been cleaved away.

The amazing thing was the beast was still alive.

12

The bear's single set of functioning jaws slathered and snapped, attempting to chew its way to freedom despite the loss of all function below its broken neck.

Val didn't know how the thing could still be alive. The hairs on its huge two-foot thick head were all standing up like thin twigs, as if the head grew out of the tree—instead of being stuck in it. The creature's huge body lay on its stomach, the long handle of Trond's double-bladed ax sticking upward out of the greenery from its back, like yet another jagged branch. Val stepped onto the creature's shoulder blade and tugged the massive weapon free. She almost dropped it when it popped out with a slurp. The weapon was incredibly heavy. But she lifted it above her head and simply let gravity take it down into the top of the mutant bear's skull.

As if electricity from a lightning bolt had been keeping the animal's hair standing on end—even on the tip of its functioning snout—as soon as the giant blade of Trond's ax sank into the creature's skull, the hairs laid flat and the head stopped thrashing.

Val fell backward, landing seated on the bear's needle covered back. She breathed heavily. She glanced around and saw Ulrik standing, leaning with his hands on his knees, heaving big gulps of air, like her. A few feet away, Trond was rubbing a lump on the top of his head, but he looked as if the adventure with the bear had hardly robbed him of breath.

Swinging her head around to the other side of the clearing, Val could see the mechanic and the historian gawking at the carnage. She had not expected the men would come to her aid, but they were close, which meant they had at least thought about it. Anders also stepped into the clearing with his bow, and an arrow nocked and trained on the bear, should it move again. There was no sign of his bird. Seeing that the bear didn't budge, he put the arrow back in his quiver and slung the bow over a shoulder. "Are you injured?" he asked.

Val barked a laugh. "Everywhere. Thank you for coming to our aid, Anders. I saw your arrows strike the beast." Then she turned to Erlend and Nils. "And thank you both, as well." She knew neither man had done a thing, but with them being unaccustomed to fighting, it meant a lot to her that they had come close to the battle. She suspected that had they seen an opening, each man would have entered the fray.

Conspicuously absent were Morten, Oskar, and Stig. *Perhaps Stig was not as won over by Ulrik's arguments as I thought.*

They each collected their fallen weapons, and within a few minutes, heard three buzzing ATV engines. Morten led the charge, riding into the clearing with determination, as if there were still a battle in which to partake. When the three of them had come to a stop, Morten looked gravely to Val. "Thank Odin you are alright. We came as quickly as we could, when we realized the beast was no longer in pursuit."

Before Val could open her mouth to reply, Trond rushed across the clearing, pulled Morten from his ATV by his neck, and carried him the distance to the nearest tree, where he slammed the Laplander's body against the peeling bark of a birch. "Where were you, scum?" The big man's voice boomed like thunder, and Val thought he looked more like a god than a man. Rage filled his face with blood and his normally pale complexion became nearly purple. "Where were you? We are companions. We are fighting for all of humanity. You will not desert us again, or I will wring your neck."

Morten clutched both hands to the big man's fingers, trying to prize them away. The Laplander's face broke out in a sheen of sweat, and his color began to match Trond's.

Oskar pulled his knife and pointed it at Trond's back. "Let him go."

Trond swung his free hand backward and smacked the smaller Laplander down into the snow, as if he were waving away a pesky black fly.

"Trond, please," Val said, walking toward the two men.

The second he heard her words, the big man let the Laplander fall into a clump at the base of the tree. As Morten slid down, he dislodged some of the paper-like bark, which fluttered down to land on his head.

Val leaned in close to Morten's face. "If it happens again, Trond will have to wait in line after me. Are we clear?"

Morten busied his hands, running them over his bruised neck. He did not reply.

Faster than the others could see, she slid her knife from its sheath and into the dirt between his legs, a hair's breadth from his groin. "Do you *understand* me?"

"Yes," the man growled, but it was soft and hoarse.

When Val stood and turned, Stig and Oskar stood by, their horrified faces nearly comical.

She stared at them. A beat of silence filled the forest, until both men understood at the same time.

"Yes," they both said.

One of the ATVs—Ulrik's—had sustained some damage, and Erlend and he set out to fix the vehicle's front left tire. The plastic fender had been snapped off, but Erlend assured them the piece was merely cosmetic. A new tire was needed, but they carried a few spares.

Within half an hour, they were ready to depart the area, and each person was eager to be away from the bone nest and the dead beast that had made it.

After leaving the forest behind, they set a slow pace on the road. The snow had stopped, and the sky was overcast, but no longer threatening. Still, the battle had sapped them of their zeal for the day's travel. Val needed to rest, but wanted to put a few miles between them and the bone nest before stopping for the day.

The battle had tested their mettle, and they had prevailed, but the entire incident raised a lot of concerns. She had known Morten—and more so Oskar—to be a backstabber, so their lack of aid in the battle had been little surprise. But she was disconcerted to see Stig flip sides again. Also, although he had been there, Anders had done little to help them. She would need to keep an eye on him.

But the group's dynamics were the least of her concerns. The battle showed her just how dangerous the world—and the creatures residing in it—could be. Halvard had warned her that it had been many decades since anyone had successfully traveled these lands. Anything could be awaiting them. Another mutated bear could be the death of them. A pack of the things would offer exactly zero chances of survival.

And then there were the ATVs. If they broke irreparably, the group would need to walk. Even if they did not, they were terrible in the snow. *Never mind a simple storm. What happens when winter comes? Will we need to sit it out in some abandoned village somewhere?* She remembered what Halvard had said the weather was like further south—in the days of the Old World, at least. If the south remained the same now, there would be no snow in the winter, except in the higher mountain passes.

If it was the same. Weather could alter drastically between single seasons, never mind over hundreds of years.

The men with her were the last hope for the whole world. They would need to learn to fight together like a unit, instead of as individuals, cowards or turncoats.

She was the right woman for this journey. She felt confident she could make it to the destination—and back. If she had to do it alone, she might be able to manage. But with the group of fighters at her side? She was less sure. Less sure she could keep them alive. Less sure she could keep them from trying to wrest control from her. *On my own, I worry only about the threats in nature. With them, I worry one of them—probably Morten—will try to slit my throat when I sleep.*

She spent the rest of the night wondering if she should leave them all behind.

13

"What in the name of Odin is that?" Morten asked.

It was night, but they had been traveling on a section of road that was mostly flat, with only the occasional ripples in it and tufts of soft sea grass growing up through the ancient asphalt. They had decided to continue well past dark when the roads were good. The need to get south and out of potential storms drove them through the night.

But now they had stopped to sleep, the thick air full of the salty, crisp smell of the sea, and the night lit up as if the sea to their right was on fire.

In the distance, a long line of golden orange light stretched out into the water, some several miles long, with two immense spikes of yellow light stretching up A-shaped towers in the middle of the horizontal, curving line. Val and the men were all looking at their first examples of electronic light since being introduced to the ATVs' headlamps.

"I had no idea it would still be here—let alone lit up," Nils said, his voice filled with awe. "What you see before you is the Øresund Bridge. They lined it with large panels in the Old World. The panels would collect the sunlight during the day and power the lights at night. It still works after all this time. Amazing."

Val noticed that there were gaps in the light, and she hoped that was a result of broken panels and not a broken bridge. If they couldn't get the ATVs across the water to the land formerly known as Denmark, their journey would become a very long walk. That or they would need to camp here for months and attempt to build a sturdy boat with which to get across the Øresund Strait, which separated the Baltic Sea and the North Sea. On the other side, the tantalizingly close ruins of Copenhagen. She would go crazy waiting months.

"How long is the bridge?" Morten asked Nils.

"Five miles," he said, uncertainty clouding his face, as if he had realized that even one missing ten-foot section would keep them from crossing. "But then it gets worse."

"Worse?" Val asked, her curiosity piqued. They had come to a halt on the road, and they were probably still a mile or two from the place where the road would become the entrance to the bridge. "How so?"

"It was a very strange design for a bridge. Meant to take vehicles like these, but also trains under the road, in a tunnel."

"'Trains.' What are they?" Stig asked Morten.

"Like large rooms on wheels, which ran on the long metal rails you sometimes see in pairs," Morten replied, and then he focused on what Nils was saying.

"Then after five miles, the bridge simply ends on a man-made island, and plunges straight down into the ground, like a passage to Hel's domain."

"It does *what?*" Ulrik said, his mouth hanging open in disbelief.

"The last three miles of the crossing is a tunnel under the water. It comes up on the other side, in Denmark," Nils said. "I have read about this bridge, and seen pictures in an old book of Halvard's. They could not make it a low bridge, because tall boats needed to pass under it. They could not make it a high bridge, because the towers on the other side would have been a problem for their flying metal birds in Copenhagen. A tunnel all the way would have cost too much time and resources."

"So they made half of it a tunnel and half of it a bridge?" Ulrik asked, traces of awe and disgust in his voice.

Nils nodded. "It was a design triumph at the time...but now?" He shrugged. "There is no way to know if the bridge to the island will be solid, and there is no way to know if the tunnel from the island will be flooded."

"Or filled with bear shit," Stig moaned.

"If it is," Val said, stepping off her ATV and signifying to the others that they would wait until dawn before challenging the bridge, "you will go first."

As pale blue light filtered into the morning sky, long before the first ray of golden sunshine that would follow, they set off on the ATVs. They came to a broad concrete expanse, where the road widened out so they all could have ridden side by side and had room to spare. Val stopped the group to assess the area ahead of them. The road was in strangely good condition here, with hardly any grasses growing from it, and Val suspected that might have been due to the sea's proximity.

Even to the right side of the road, the vegetation was small. Stunted trees and tufted grasses struggled in the sandy, rocky soil. *Not enough food for the plants in the ground, so close to the salt water,* Val thought.

The exposure concerned her. If there were hostile people or animals here, then the group had been spotted long ago. On the positive side, the smaller trees meant it would be impossible for something like the giant bear they had fought to be concealed and waiting for them. Still, she did not want to ride into a trap—or an animal lair.

In front of them, spread across the widened road, was a partially collapsed metal structure. It looked like a series of tiny linked rooms, with spaces to walk between. *Or drive,* Val thought. Then she understood the place's function, just before Nils explained it to them.

"People would collect money here, before travelers could cross the bridge."

A few of the tiny structures were little more than piles of gravel and debris, but the few still standing looked like they had been used to shelter more recent travelers. Some were missing their doors, and others their windows. One had wooden boards nailed over the gaping holes. All of them were covered in thin vegetation like the surrounding landscape. Small animals had made homes in the structures, too. She could see a few bird's nests on the collapsing roofs of the little rooms.

To her left were sets of metal rails for the trains Nils had spoken of, and beyond the rails, an identical widened oncoming road where the metal shells of automobiles had been stacked up like a thirty-foot-tall wall. She had seen the vehicles in towns across the north, but had never seen a working one. Usually there was little left to them besides the rusted out metal shells. She had seen one with its comfortable chairs and glass windows still intact. But even those were usually missing the rubber on their wheels—or the wheels themselves. Val had seen people use them as shelters, or in one case as a tailor shop.

But the mountain of ancient vehicles on the other side, and the lack of any on her side made Val suspicious.

"Let us go and see this bridge," Morten said.

"Yes," Val said. "But not in the way you think."

"What do you mean?" Nils asked her.

"I want to see the bridge, but not drive on it yet. We will take this road to the side—" She pointed, "—and we will drive around it. To the shore. I want a closer look before we try to cross."

"You suspect a trap," Ulrik said. It was not a question. It was approval.

They set off on the side road, which curved around the money-taking plaza, and onto a trail that led toward the coast. As they drove, Val's eyes scanned for danger, but she found none. She could see ahead that this smaller road would turn and run right along a sea wall of boulders that stretched in both directions along the coast. The road ran under the bridge to the left. That was where she wanted to be.

When they reached the underside of the bridge, she stopped and dismounted from her quad. The sea wall was almost twice her height, and she scrambled to the top of the pile of rocks for a better view. Above her, the bridge's rust-coated metal stretched out and curved into the sea. It rested on massive concrete supports interspersed along its length, each one taller than the last, until, at the center of the bridge, the height was two hundred feet above the water.

This close, Val could see that the structure looked deserted of animals and people. The sea was calm. The morning was warm.

Everything was perfect. Too damn perfect.

14

The group circled back around and slowly made their way onto the bridge. The road seemed to stretch forever before it reached the pylons at the structure's halfway point. There were two passageways—the one on their side and another for returning traffic. They were separated in the middle by rusted spikes. Nils suggested they had once been a guardrail.

The outer sides of the bridge had guarding fences, many of which were still standing. A few tall, rusted-metal spires climbed up out of the central divide, but their purpose was unknown, even to Nils. What he had learned about the bridge—and the entire Old World—from books, could only take him so far.

Ulrik was not concerned about the metal spires, or the fractured metal guard rails. He was more concerned about the pieces of the road that were missing, the concrete and steel under them having given way. Holes covered the bridge's surface, some larger than an ATV. He could steer around them for now, but worried there would be larger gaps, or that one would open up as he drove, dropping him down into the rail tunnel below the road, or a hundred feet further to the water. He peered into each hole as he passed. In some he had seen down to the train rails, and sometimes there was nothing under the road but the sea, far below, glittering like liquid diamonds in the sunlight. The only other detail Nils had known about this bridge was that the weather was often vicious. They had been lucky with the warm, clear sky. *But how long will that luck hold?* Ulrik wondered.

He led the way for the group with Val behind him. Trond, with his short, purple-dyed beard practically glowing in the morning sun, took up the rear. Ulrik took the path slowly. Nils had said it was five miles over the bridge, then that distance again on the man-made island and the tunnel. Val had told Ulrik to take his time.

"Safety is our main concern," she had said. But then quieter, so the others couldn't hear, she had told him, "But we need to be off this thing by nightfall, and you need to keep your eyes open. Be ready for anything."

He was. His eyes scoured the gray road, the way ahead, the other side of the bridge, the cerulean sea to either side, and the white pylons supporting the center of the bridge with cables.

It was the pylons that concerned him most.

The damn things were over six hundred feet tall. Had a lookout been perched atop one of them the previous day, they'd have easily spotted the ATVs. Plenty of time to set up an ambush.

As they got closer to the center of the bridge, the wind from the strait picked up. The day was still sunny and bright, but the air held a chill to it. The smell of the salt water filled his nostrils so completely he doubted he would have been able to smell roasting meat had it been laying in the road in front of him. He could see that the pylons, which he had thought were white in the brightness of the day, were really the sort of grayish white that old concrete gets. One of the pylons had snapped off near the top and hung from its many support cables. The rest of the cables appeared solid, but he was reluctant to move into the center of the bridge. He stopped the ATV, and waited for Nils to arrive with the others.

"Is it safe?" he asked, pointing to the dangling section of the pylon.

"Oh yes, it should be," Nils said, his confidence brimming. He had clearly read something about the cables. "They were actually just for extra support, because of the trains. Normal bridges are slightly flexible and sway in the wind. It is expected. But with the trains passing in the tunnel under our feet, the bridge needed to be more rigid. So they supported the middle with those cables."

"So it will not matter for us if they are broken?" Val asked.

"It should not. We weigh very little compared to the weights the bridge was designed to handle, and the concrete supports under the bridge are what keep it in the air."

Ulrik was not fully convinced, but he started his vehicle again and rolled forward.

Just before they reached the first double set of pylons, the gaps in the road became extensive—as if someone had tried to destroy the bridge at some point in the past. None of them knew history the way Nils did, but they all understood that many wars had occurred in the past. Ulrik believed that this damage was intentional.

The road surface was missing entirely, and only the flat metal beams underneath showed, with deeply rusted metal plates over the beams. He stopped and explained his plan to Val, and she passed the information back. They would need to keep their wheels on the plates that rested atop the beams. If a wheel rode over an unsupported portion of metal plate, Ulrik suspected the ATV would tear through the tissue-thin rust.

It took thirty minutes moving at a snail's pace to get the nine of them across the dangerous section. He was hungry when they were finally over it. He suggested they stop for food under the pylon's eerie shadow. Nearby was a door that led into the structure. Inside was a small human sized box, which Nils explained was a powered lift to get people to the top. The power was long gone, and the amount of rust on the box suggested that even stepping into it would be a death sentence.

"The elevator goes down as well," Nils pointed out.

Next to the defunct elevator was a metal ladder that stretched up into the darkness above their heads as far as they could see—even with the clever use of the headlamps on Ulrik's ATV and a carefully held hand-mirror.

"We should climb to the top," Morten suggested, eager as a small boy. "We could see the land we will be coming into, instead of going in blind."

Val took one look at the ladder and shrugged her thin shoulders, her long blonde hair dancing. "It would take too long, and leave your arms sore from the climb. I would rather get off this monstrosity." With that, she strode out of the room and back to her waiting ATV.

"What do you think, Ulrik the Fearless? Would you climb this tower to the sky?" Morten had begun asking Ulrik's opinion on routine matters, as if the sting of taking orders from Val was lessened when Ulrik agreed with her.

Looking up into the darkness, Ulrik gave it some consideration. He had never named himself 'Fearless.' It was a childhood joke from his uncle, but it had stuck with the other villagers, and eventually it had become an expectation. He had become their most fearless fighter because they needed one. But he had worries and fears like any normal man.

"Seeing far ahead would be an advantage," he began. Morten smiled and walked to the base of the ladder, already placing his hands on the rungs, as if the decision had been made. "But, should any trouble be approaching, you would be trapped up there, with no way down but to dive into the sea from the top."

Morten removed his hands from the rungs and turned around. His face was pale at the idea of that dive.

"Even I am not that fearless," Ulrik chuckled as he turned to follow Val outside.

They continued across the bridge as they had before, Ulrik in the lead, and Trond in the rear. The small flat island was visible in the distance.

His eyes shifting between the way ahead and the sea, Ulrik felt uncomfortable with the massive Pylons behind them. As he had told Morten, anyone on top of one of the massive spires would have an incredible tactical advantage. They could be watching them even now, signaling ahead.

He looked back over his shoulder to check for spies.

As soon as he craned his head around, he wished he hadn't.

Between them and the receding pylons, the sea on either side of the bridge erupted with monsters. Long, wavering tentacles reached up out of the waters and clung to the cables jutting from the concrete towers.

15

Ulrik was in full disbelief as he watched tentacles reach up and wrap the pylons from both sides. The greenish blue limbs were covered in suction cups, like those of an octopus, but he had never heard of a creature so large.

Growing up in a small fishing village, he knew about all the sea's creatures. But this was something different. The tentacles streamed up through the surface of the road, ripping up chunks of concrete, rusted steel and asphalt. They hurled debris into the air, as the snapping, waving limbs rushed through the new openings like snakes squeezing through holes in a rock wall.

He suddenly understood that the holes in the road had not been caused so much by decay as by these reaching wands of flexible fish life. Then the water on the left of the bridge boiled and a shape rose up that was so huge, he had to turn his head to see from the rounded ridges of its eyes to the back of the rounded head. It was an octopus of a kind, but its head was a hundred and fifty feet across—and it had far more than eight arms.

Then the other side of the sea frothed and a second creature of equal size rose up, scaling the bridge's central supports.

They were both the mottled yellow color of the sea floor, a sort of sulfurous shade with green-blue highlights over the eye ridges and in the deep, dark cracks that spider-webbed their massive heads.

The others were only just beginning to turn, to see what was causing the commotion in the sea. The creatures had moved so fast—like aquatic rabbits. And still, the two immense creatures, who were dwarfing the majesty of the bridge, could not account for all the waving tentacles bursting up from under the bridge.

Ulrik realized the truth in an instant. *They have young. Many of them.*

His mind sprinted through possible outcomes, but none of them were good. They had been lucky with the mutant bear. There was no way they would be able to face even one of these creatures.

"Get away! Fast as you can! Go!" Val had reached the same conclusion and was screaming at the men.

Ulrik was already past the place where the tentacles were crashing through the bridge deck, and he considered turning his quad around to help the others, but Val was racing right for him, moving as fast as the ATV would carry her.

"Go!" she screamed at him.

The others tore through the chaos of waving limbs, dodging and turning to keep their ATVs clear of the suckers and tentacles snaking through the support cables, reaching for them.

Anders ran his ATV straight at a thin tentacle snaking across the road. He threw his weight back at the last moment, pulling the front wheels up as they hit the obstacle. The quad took to the sky, as Erlend had taught them to do. Skjold circled the chaos in the sky, always tailing his master.

Nils chased after Anders, and the front left wheel of his ATV dropped into a hole in the road, spilling him onto the ground. Stig raced up beside him, and grabbed the slim man by the back of his shirt, hauling him to his feet. "On the back," he yelled. Nils straddled the twin silver propane tanks, and Stig raced off again. The others came zipping past as well.

All but Trond.

He was too far back. Between him and where Ulrik stood, there was now a forest of tentacles rising up from the road, many only reaching as high as a man, but many more reaching half as high as the pylons, while the two giant octopuses seemed to be fighting over the top of the bridge, their snaking tentacles vying for supremacy.

A thick barrier of horizontal tentacles prevented Trond from moving forward. Ulrik wanted to call to him to just leave the ATV behind. They would double up like Stig and Nils. But the man was too far away to hear him, and the water crashing down from the mighty animals was like a torrential downpour. The water brought the creature's stench, filling his nose with the smell of rot and fish. There was no way for him to get to Trond, past the tentacles, but he considered it anyway.

Run back, Ulrik thought. *Go back, big man. You cannot win this fight. These are too big.*

Then as the warring giant octopuses intertwined across the surface of the bridge, Ulrik noticed that the big creatures' movements were synchronized. As the one on the right advanced, the one on the left retreated.

Trond stood on the other side of the wall of reaching, grasping suckers, unsure of what to do. Slithering tentacles slipped behind him.

The huge creature on the left tugged its way up the pylon, bringing its huge eyes level with the roadway, as the monster on the right dipped down.

Ulrik's already sky-high level of horror climbed a notch more, as he realized why he had not seen the young creatures yet.

There weren't any.

There weren't even two giant octopuses—there was just one, its body stretched under the bridge and rising up with a head on each end, on either side of the bridge. The smaller tentacles Ulrik had mistaken for young were attached to the beast's midsection.

Trond's heavy double-bladed ax was out, and he was slicing away at the wall of yellow-blue tentacles ahead of him, as if he were rapidly chopping cord wood for the winter. Fist-sized pieces of bloody yellow flesh sprayed around him with each swing of the mighty ax, covering the man's short purple beard in gore.

The huge man's strikes were doing damage, but not enough.

A tentacle shot over the road and wrapped around Trond's thigh, tugging him into the air. At first Ulrik thought he would lose his long-handled ax, but he clutched it with both hands and swung the blade down. The ax sliced along the length of the huge appendage, but it continued to pull him out toward the cables, where it would yank him through and down into the water.

But the creature surprised Ulrik—another tentacle from the other side of the bridge shot across the open space, wrapping around Trond's face and chest.

Then the strange, giant octopus pulled in both directions, as it had been doing all along, engaged in an endless tug-of-war with itself.

But with Trond's body in the middle this time, the conclusion was obvious.

The top half of the large man's body was wrenched off his pelvis and legs. Following a series of wet pops—the man's spine separating—a cloudburst of red mist filled the air. Then the tentacle on the right, without the pressure of Trond's body holding it up, jerked back. The long yellow limb slapped into one of the support cables and flipped the upper half of Trond's still-screaming body over the wires. His legs fell to the roadway, suddenly released by the other tentacle.

Ulrik was unable to help, but felt he should bear witness. Just when he thought Trond's upper body would scream all the way to the water, another yellow and copper-tarnished blue limb shot out and snagged him, pulling him down into the depths.

Ulrik turned and raced his ATV down the last part of the bridge's expanse, no longer caring about any potholes or missing segments. If the incredible creature behind him hadn't had humans as food before—or in a long time—he didn't want to be around when it realized it wanted a second helping.

The small artificial island of Peberholm was ahead of him. The road ran right off the bridge and onto the island, which was no more than 1000 feet wide, and over two miles long. The tiny seawall of rocks surrounding the island would not keep the giant sea creature from crawling up on to land.

He just hoped the others had made it to the tunnel, and that their escape route wasn't flooded. Or a nest for the damned, double-headed octopus.

Then he realized that even if it wasn't, there was nothing to stop the beast from following them *into the tunnel.*

He twisted the throttle on the handlebars harder, taking the ATV to its maximum speed. He bent his head low into the wind.

Faster, he thought. *Must. Go. Faster.*

16

Val stood two hundred yards from the mouth of the tunnel, next to her ATV. She was waiting for Ulrik and Trond, but she had seen Trond trapped on the far side of the horrible tentacles. She held little hope that the man would make it off the bridge. But she still believed Ulrik might make it.

And then she saw him, racing off the bridge and onto the low island, heading for her. Behind him, the massive octopus creature dropped into the water under the bridge, pulling in its long yellow tendrils down into the turbulent blue. *Does it sleep there?* she wondered. And then she had a horrible thought. *What if there is an underwater cave that leads to the tunnel?* But then the tunnel would have been flooded, and it was not.

She understood Ulrik's haste. He was concerned about the same thing. But they had no choice. The end of the island was barren, save for the entrance to the tunnel. She had sent the others through, and she prayed to Odin that it was clear the whole way. There were no boats, and crossing the bridge again would be suicide.

As he grew closer, she turned and mounted her ride, the motor still idling. She prepared to launch into the tunnel, once he caught up with her.

He slowed when he reached her.

"Trond?" she asked.

"No."

She released her brake and they both raced into the darkness.

The tunnel was clear for the two and half miles of its length with only a few small puddles of condensation and drips on the road surface. Val didn't think the tunnel would last another hundred years before the invasive water found a crack and poured in, but she really didn't know.

When she came out of the tunnel mouth, still traveling on a road that paralleled the Danish shore, she was reminded of how the octopus-thing had pulled itself up the pylons of the bridge, and she wanted to be away from the coast as soon as possible.

The others had obviously had the same idea, and were far ahead, racing away from the strait. The area around the road had once been a city like Oslo or Stavanger. Concrete and steel ruins surrounded her, the crumbled remains of buildings and structures overtaken by pervasive vines and sea grasses.

Val kept the speed on, until she overtook most of the others. She was not surprised to find Morten in the lead of the headlong rush along this new road into uncharted territory. The blackened remains of an ancient fire stretched along the sides of the road. She could see the rubble of old settlements beyond that. Thick trees and the artificial mountains of old skeletal buildings now overgrown with plant life, lined the left side of the route.

There was nowhere to turn off the road. Its surface was a soft carpet of vegetation, so she was content to continue ahead. They passed under a few bridges, and then through a concrete chute that led to another tunnel, short and clear enough to see the light on the other side. So she rode on, with Morten at her side, and the others close behind.

A few miles further, Val pulled to a stop. The road ahead had been piled high with rusting and burned out vehicle husks. Their path toward Copenhagen and deeper into the rest of Denmark had been blocked. There was no easy way forward, and back led only to the sea. But there was an exit ramp, leading up and off to the right. Val slowed at the top of the ramp, and Morten matched her pace until they came to a stop.

"What are you thinking?" he asked her.

"That I do not want to go into the ruins of the city." She looked around. At the top of the ramp they could see the curved road they had been on, and beyond the wall of cars. But a few hundred yards ahead was yet another bridge and another pile of cars blocking passage. To her left was another pile of rocks and debris stretching clear across the road. The only clear path led straight into the city, unless they wanted to slow their pace by taking the vehicles off road and attempt to skirt these man-made road blocks.

The others arrived, and Nils climbed off the back of Stig's ATV, clearly having been uncomfortable on his perch atop the secondary propane tanks.

No one spoke.

Their faces looked long and dejected after the loss of Trond. Val didn't need to tell the men that they would have a brief ceremony for Trond when the time was right and they felt safe.

Ulrik pulled up next to her, silent and waiting. His fingers stroked his beard.

"Nils? Are there other ways into Denmark, if we go along this route?" She pointed in the direction available.

"Most likely a few bridges that would still be standing." Seeing the looks on his companions' faces when he mentioned bridges, he quickly clarified. "They would be short spans, like those we just passed under."

"Then we go this way," Val said.

As engines started up again, Ulrik held back, and she could tell he wanted to speak to her.

"What is it, good Ulrik?"

"You realize we are being herded, yes?" he asked her.

"Of course. But the alternative is we take these off road." She patted her handlebars as she spoke about the ATV.

"They were made for that," he pointed out.

"But it will be slow. And we do not know the reason for the herding. Perhaps the road we wanted is closed. We are on another island, only this one is bigger. On the map, it is called *Amager*. We need to get to *Sealand*, which is an even bigger island." She pointed in the direction they could not travel. "Then another island, and then we need to get to the mainland. No matter what, we will have difficulties until we reach the continent. If there are no bridges or tunnels that way..."

"I see," Ulrik said. "Yet this path is..."

"Too convenient?" she asked.

"Yes."

"So we stay alert. We must do better than we did on the bridge. And the afternoon is fading. We need to find a place to stay for the night. I want us out of the city, if possible."

They set off again, and the road was flat and straight, strange structures lining the road until they came across one so strange that they all stopped. It was a massive white tower with spinning blades. Val recognized it as a windmill, but she had never seen one like this. There was no mill or water pump connected to the huge structure.

"What is it for?" Stig asked Nils.

"Electricity. It is still spinning because the wind does not stop blowing, but...the people needed to harness the energy are long gone."

Val hoped he was right.

17

When they reached the next intersection, they were once again herded by obstacles in the road. Gigantic vehicles were parked across streets, turning intersections into one winding road. One of the large vehicles had a long white trailer behind it. They might have been able to squeeze under it, but someone had taken the time to pile rocks and perfect rectangular blocks of concrete in the space beneath it. The other vehicles were larger and stranger, and Val couldn't guess what they'd been used for.

She shared a meaningful look with Ulrik, and the group followed the road left. A forest of sickly looking, ten-foot tall trees grew on either side of the road, once again limiting their visibility. At the next intersection, nature had helped create the roadblock—more of the ten-foot trees grew right out of the middle of the pavement. The rest of the intersection had been blocked with piles of metal girders and poles like those they had seen along the way. Val recalled similar poles on the bridge, and Nils had said they had been used to provide light for the road at night.

"We are being herded," Ulrik said to Val.

She nodded, then accelerated in frustration, her ATV's tires leaving skid marks on the ground. The others raced to catch up. The road continued through the young forest. Occasionally there was a place to turn off, but each was blocked by a single thick log laid across the road. In some cases, a metal sign was planted in the middle of the turn, with a painted arrow directing them to stay on the main road.

Val rolled to a stop, and the others joined her. Over the humming of her ATV's idling engine, she confided in Ulrik. "We have no choice but to go forward. Or do you see another option?"

"It will be miles to circle back out of this maze," Ulrik replied, thinking. "And we have no guarantee that an alternate route would keep us away from whoever has done this."

Val ran a hand through her hair, and re-adjusted her goggles. "We also do not know if the roadway's creator is still waiting at the end of it."

"*I* would be," Morten interjected. "You do not involve so many people in such labors only to abandon your snare."

"Perhaps they—" Oskar began, but Val cut him off.

"If I go in, will you follow?" She spoke only to Ulrik, and it was understood that if he followed her in, the others would all follow him.

"Where does such brazen confidence come from?" Ulrik asked. "That you would ride knowingly into a snare?"

Val smiled. "I have charged headlong into far worse—without strapping men to fight by my side—and have survived well enough that I lack the scars to prove the stories true."

The man's face showed no expression for a moment, and she thought Morten would pounce on the chance for dissent, when Ulrik barked a laugh. "Very well, then. If you said to go in blindfolded, I would go. You are our leader. And we were not chosen to run home like whipped dogs at the first hint of strife."

She drove on, deep into the artificial canyons of abandoned humanity. Many of the buildings still stood, rising three or four stories on either side of the road. The building facades, with their missing windows, resembled the smiles of old men with rotted and cracked teeth.

Despite the city's clear lack of habitation, there was something about this place that made her suspect people were nearby. It took her a few minutes following the laid out path, before she understood why.

The birds.

There were none. No birds at all. None flying overhead, no obvious nests on windowsills in the blackened eyes of the ancient structures. No chirping in the trees.

There were only two reasons an area would be completely devoid of bird life: radiation or people—enough to hunt them out of existence.

They crossed a bridge and entered the island of Sealand, where the buildings on the far side were in a worse state, as was the road. The ground was split open in several places, although the thick knobby tires of the ATVs made short work of most cracks.

The real problem loomed ahead.

The road was blocked by a mountain of long metal chassis with wheels shorn of their rubber tires. The group had seen a few of these elongated behemoths on the journey through southern Sweden. Nils had described them as 'Buses'—vehicles for moving groups of people.

The blockade stretched across their path, and as far as Val could see, there were no turns at the end of this one.

Nowhere for them to go.

Her senses heightened, searching for a trap. She slowed her ATV until she got right up to the blockade. It looked unstable. Long, thin pieces of metal flapped and wobbled in the wind.

Just before a final ivy-covered brick building with human-sized letters jutting from the roof, reading: TIVOLI, the metal fence they had driven along was flattened down. An area of the ivy on the wall of the brick Tivoli building had been cleared away, and an arrow pointed back into the opening through the metal fence. It was wide enough for them to drive through, and it was the only choice, besides backtracking to the last bridge they had crossed. They would then have to find another way on to the island, and it had been a big enough hassle reaching it the first time.

"We go in. No other choice," Val said, indicating Ulrik should take the lead.

"I will cover our rear," Stig told Val.

She nodded, and appreciated the fact that Ulrik's vote of confidence in her had worked like magic on the others. She even noticed Morten and Oskar silently adjusting their weapons for quick draw. It was apparent to everyone that if something was going to happen, it would be in the trees beyond the fallen fence. They were all ready for it.

Ulrik drove through the opening, and Val was right behind him. The barrier of thick trees was shorter than they expected—just a few feet wide, and then they came into a clearing filled with the strangest things any of them had ever seen.

18

They entered a vast rectangular clearing fringed by tree stumps and jagged bits of metal sticking up out of the ground. Surrounding the stumps were lines of sentinel trees, acting like a wall, or border. But what filled the clearing felt otherworldly. The strangely shaped buildings, tall metal spires, a huge wooden boat trapped in a pond, and red rails of jumbled metal twisted and curled skyward, felt like a slap in the face. They had been expecting an ambush, not a strange wonderland of unusual shapes.

Ulrik stopped his ATV as soon as the strange visual delights appeared.

"Nils?" Val asked. "What in the name of the gods are we looking at here?"

"I have no idea. Nothing like this was in any book I ever read."

Metal loops soared into the sky, and buildings with tops like turnips dotted the clearing. Giant human skulls sat impaled on fences, and towers dangled what looked like chairs from chains. There were huge machines that resembled spiders, with mechanical limbs. One building had multiple stacked roofs, with the corners extending past the building and turning up, as if they had curled in from the rain. But the most curious things were the winding, snaking rails of metal. They climbed, dipped and looped all through the park. White support struts held the thing in the air, like the parts of some long dragon.

"I think this was some kind of place for people to come with their children. For fun." Nils shrugged his shoulders.

Val turned to look at the historian. "For fun? This place looks like the heart of Hel's domain."

She took the lead and they wound through the strange park, passing stone lions, plastic sculptures of creatures Nils identified as 'giraffes' and low walls and bench seats made of stone.

There were countless places for people to hide in wait, but they saw no one. *But they are here*, Val thought. *They are here, somewhere. All of this is free of vegetation.* Without humans keeping the structures free of creeping vines and trees, the whole park would have been covered in an ocean of green within a decade or two.

Val stopped in front of a plastic purple octopus, whose tentacles each held a small metal car with a chair.

"They worshipped that thing at the bridge?" Ulrik said in disbelief.

"I do not think so," Nils said. "This looks like a plaything for children."

"The seats are too small for a man," Ulrik agreed.

The air was suddenly pierced by a shrill, shrieking noise that could not have come from any animal or human. It was so loud several of them clapped their hands to their ears to block out the noise.

"There it is," Ulrik said, grinning at Val while pulling his ax out of the holster on his back.

The others looked around for the source of the noise, but Val stepped from her ATV and pulled her long ax and her hand ax. "They are coming."

"Who?" Morten said, drawing a sword.

Then several ululating cries echoed around the park as thin naked men with long greasy hair, their bodies and faces covered in blue paint, came rushing from every one of the doors and windows of the buildings scattered around the park. Any space, no matter how small, belched the human-shaped blue blurs. There were hundreds of them, but they were all unarmed.

Stig and Oskar looked to Val for silent advice.

"We fight," she said.

Escape was not a possibility anyway. The onrushing wave of human limbs would hit them in seconds, and they didn't know the way out of the strange park yet.

Bodies crashed into them like a suicidal wave. The Vikings arrayed themselves in front of their vehicles. Even Erlend and Nils, armed with axes, hacked at the swarming bodies that came in wave after wave, like the crashing of the sea. The Blue Men seemed not to have any agenda or fighting skills. They just rushed at the Northmen, their lemming bodies thin and emaciated.

Stig and Morten were soon weaponless, their blades having been knocked from their hands by the crush of incoming bodies. The men resorted to punching and headbutting, dropping frail bodies with a single strike. Ulrik swung his ax wide in front of them, the blade slicing or grazing three men with each mighty sweep.

Anders plugged a dozen of the frantic runners with arrows, and then started tearing into the running men with his hands. Nearby, Skjold swooped in and razed men with its talons, before taking off back into the sky. Nils and Erlend worked together, first side-by-side, and then back-to-back, each man with a sharpened blade in each hand and spinning in a dance of death, dropping foe after foe with the slightest cut.

Val soon realized the Blue Men would fall with the slightest strike or cut—they were not used to fighting, and that meant that their only advantage was numbers. As the bodies began to pile in front of the Northmen like a seawall, Val raced atop the bodies and leapt out away from the arced ATVs, and deeper into the fray.

Her arms were a blur as she cut, dodged and stabbed anything blue in her sight. Writhing bodies spilled out around her, bleeding blue.

The onrushing wave of blue humans had lessened, but they were still coming.

Val turned and ran back to the safety of her group, who were dropping the most recent arrivals. "We need to get out of here. There are too many. Soon we will be too tired to raise our arms."

She expected opposition from Morten, but he was too busy swinging his long sword and cleaving away more of the scrawny attackers.

"Stig," Ulrik called. "Go with Nils and Erlend behind us toward the trees. Try to find a way out. Then get back here and start the quads."

The men ran off as ordered, and Val closed ranks with Anders, Morten, Oskar and Ulrik, the five of them forming a wall in front of the vehicles. Without needing to be told, they each recognized the need to keep the flailing blue maniacs from the quads. The Vikings were already short a vehicle, and if they lost more in the battle, they would need to flee the horde on foot.

Val thought that might have been their opponents' plan. Wear the Northmen down with wave after wave of human onslaught, and then seize the vehicles when they were too exhausted to fight anymore.

The Blue Men around them fell in a moaning, wailing pile. Still the slightest injury caused them to drop to the ground in the ever-expanding sea of blood and blue-painted limbs.

There was a brief reprieve as Ulrik cleaved the head off the last attacker. But they could hear the strange gargling calls, as more Blue Men rushed across the park, making for their position. Stig returned from the trees behind them, leapt atop his ATV, turned and raced back into the woods, just as Nils and Erlend ran out of the trees.

"A way out?" Morten asked.

"No," Nils heaved. "There is a fence, like at the front. But it is old. Stig will try to knock it down."

Erlend ran to an ATV and jumped atop it, kickstarting the vehicle to life. Nils did the same. Then they each ran to yet another vehicle and repeated the motions.

"Ulrik, stay with me." Val said. "The rest of you go. Get the fence open."

Morten ran past Ulrik, slowing to offer the man his long sword. Ulrik accepted it without a word. They all understood the situation. If he and Val couldn't hold back the Blue Men, none of them would get out alive. He held the sword in one hand and his ax in the other. Val stepped up next to the broad-chested man, and they waited for the running, screaming swarm to reach their position.

The others took off with their vehicles, leaving Ulrik's and Val's standing and ready, already turned toward the distant fence.

"I will come back for you when the way is clear," Morten promised, his face grim.

Val was dubious, but then the next wave of Blue Men arrived. She and Ulrik aimed for the legs, dropping man after man into the heap of bodies. The pile was now to Val's chest, and she realized that if the Blues kept coming at them, she would have to retreat partially, or they would be scaling the wall and leaping onto her from above.

Ulrik holstered his ax, and swung at the full extension of his arm with Morten's blade, increasing the killing distance to nearly seven feet.

"Back up!" Val called.

They both stepped back toward their waiting ATVs. Four blue bodies scrambled and toppled over the low wall of carnage, the men slipping in the blood as they came down the other side. One of them slid down and cracked the back of his own skull on the ground. He stopped moving immediately. Another got close enough for Val to swipe at his neck with the ax, and an arc of blood sprayed laterally away from the man before his face planted into the stone in front of her feet.

"Back again," she said, and she and Ulrik took two steps again, this time until the backs of their legs reached the parked vehicles. "Ulrik. Get on your quad and go."

Three more men climbed the human blockade and slid down the other side.

"Are you sure?"

Val swung her long ax, cleaving through two more necks before she sank the smaller hand ax into the third's face. As her body completed the turn and she came back to face him, the entire front of her body was coated in blood. "Go!"

Just then, Morten came roaring out of the trees on his ATV, and he arced in front of them both, extending his arm and clotheslining two more men in the necks, before he needed his hand for the throttle again. "The way is clear," he shouted. Then he took off into the woods again.

Val wasted no time, hopping on her quad. She and Ulrik followed Morten into the trees, and the crazed Blue Men chased after them on foot. Val had to steer between thick tree trunks, and she feared the leading Blue Man would catch up with her, but the strange, thin men moved like they were drugged, smashing headlong into trees and falling down as if they had been stabbed.

On the other side of the thin belt of forest, Val found a section of gate on the ground. Morten raced over it with his ATV, then tore off down a road following the others.

Val glanced over her shoulder to see the Blues still giving chase as the ATVs outran them.

The rest of the crazy city awaited.

19

The journey continued day after day, the eight Vikings crawling across the endless landscape on their motorized steeds. They had made it out of Copenhagen without further incident, although the roads had been similarly orchestrated and blockaded until they had found their way to an open field and out of the maze.

The rest of the trip across the island of Sealand was uneventful, until Nils spotted a bent and mangled road sign for Odense—a town they skirted. He then told Val that they had somehow crossed off the island and onto the next without moving across the body of water once known as The Great Belt.

Much discussion followed, and the consensus—and Val agreed— was that the strait had either been emptied by decades of geologic upheaval caused by the great annihilation, or perhaps mankind had changed the landscape. Proceeding south, they circumvented larger towns unless they needed to forage for more propane again. Once the southern region of Denmark turned into a never-ending progression of fields with tall grasses and shallow marshland, they left the road for good. It had been too crowded with abandoned cars and road blocks. Still, they had seen no more people—blue or otherwise.

Now the landscape was filled with grasses as high as the handle-bars on the ATVs, and their progress was slow. The day was warm, and Val was tired. The frigid winter loomed, encroaching with each passing day, and she felt some pressure to continue. But she also had come to recognize when the others needed down time.

Val raised her arm at the head of the convoy, and they all slowed to a stop. "Let us take a rest here."

They stopped single file because, to the sides of them, the grasses were a few feet shorter, indicating they were on one of the many raised dikes in the area. The land below the grasses to either side of the dike was marshy peat bog. The Vikings had been stuck in shallow bogs on many occasions. They knew to stick to the high ground now.

"It is about time. I thought we would never stop," Erlend said, stretching his sore limbs. He and Nils had begun taking turns driving their shared ATV, with the other riding on a cobbled-together saddle secured over the twin propane tanks. The passenger faced backward, offering their convoy a rear lookout. Today Erlend had been manning the rear-facing seat. "If I had known I'd be riding on the back of one of these, I would have made it a lot more comfortable."

"You could not make it better now?" Nils asked, eager for the answer. He knew he would be riding in the jump seat as soon as they began again, and already his ass ached at the thought.

"Not without more tools and materials. Perhaps when we reach the next town we can put something together."

"There is probably nothing more to see today," Val announced, ending the discussion. "More miles of farming land and bogs. We should camp here for the night. Take the afternoon to rest."

The news was greeted with great applause and hooting. They had rarely taken any breaks. The last time had been after clearing Copenhagen, when they had performed a small ceremony to remember fallen Trond.

"With that excellent news, I will venture into this bog and anoint it with my urine," Morten announced with great cheer. The others laughed, Val included.

Ulrik spread a large blanket over the tall grass behind the parked vehicles, and Val sank onto it next to him, while the others unpacked. She was grateful to take a break, herself, and laid back on the blanket. She looked up at the clear blue sky turned purple by her ever-present red tinted goggles. Her mind wandered, back to her early days after the marauders had killed her parents. After the polar bear. Then through the hardships she had faced on her own as a child on the islands of Åland, and later as a young woman on the Swedish mainland, before she had traveled to Stavanger. Her life had been filled with battle and strife, so when the chance presented itself, she soaked in the quiet moments.

"What sort of name is Val?" Ulrik asked her, startling her out of her reverie. The sudden attempt at casual conversation caught her off guard. He was not normally one to chat. "Is it a usual name for the women of Åland?"

Val laughed. "No. Not a normal name for a woman. It is short for Valkyrie."

Ulrik grunted in amazement. "Fitting. How did you learn to fight?"

Val smiled. She knew Ulrik was politely trying to press for details on her past. It wasn't unheard of for a woman to be a fighter in the north. Shield-maidens joined great battles, but more often in a support role to the larger fighters like Trond. Ulrik had rarely encountered anyone like her: a full time fighter. A traveler. A mercenary. Someone willing to fight for pay or food. Those roles were nearly always filled by men.

"Mostly by watching others," she said, looking at Ulrik. "I understood that I would not always be stronger than my foes. I needed to be faster, and more agile."

She knew the answer was vague, but it would suffice for now.

Before he could respond, Morten began yelling from the nearby bog.

He was calling for help, and the others rushed into the marsh, water splashing up above the tall grasses, splattering them with mud. They pushed through the tall weeds to a clearing with shorter grasses and spongy peat under foot. "Come quickly," Morten called, the initial panic in his voice subsiding.

All around him, across the glade, were bodies frozen in time. They were completely black, their skin and clothing alike. Many of them appeared to be clawing their way out of the earth and frozen in place. Some were on the ground in various poses. Others had degenerated to little more than skeletons before turning black and rock-like.

Val nudged the toe of one of her black leather boots against the upraised hand of one of the strange bodies. It did not give. It was as hard as stone.

"What are they?" Anders asked, his bow at the ready, despite the lack of threat from the statues.

No one could answer him. The Vikings wandered the field, examining the petrified dead. Val thought at first that the bodies might have been some macabre sculptures, like the lions at the Tivoli park in Copenhagen, but these were too life-like. The veins of the arms and even the creases of the skin were visible on the surfaces of the blackened bodies. Val bent down to the one nearest to her, and saw fingerprints on the figure's thumb. *No, these are the dead. Somehow turned to stone.*

"It must be the water in the bogs," Nils hypothesized.

"Should we get out?" Oskar asked, panic rising.

Val patted him on the shoulder. "It would have taken years for them to turn to stone like this."

They spent the next few minutes looking at the various corpses. Many appeared to have been executed. Ropes hung around their necks, petrified as much as the skin below them.

One particularly gruesome body was still submerged from the torso down, his legs extending up in the air, as if he had dived into the bog, his head stuck in the mud below the water—or he had been forcibly held down.

Morten walked across the field of the dead back to Val. "Perhaps we could find a different campsite for the night?"

"For once we agree," she said. It was habit for her to think that way, but the truth was that her estimation of the man had risen several steps since the battle with the Blue Men. According to his word, he had come back for her and Ulrik, and since that day he had been less abrasive, and often quite helpful.

The group returned to the dike and continued south, well away from the morbid field of bodies, before making their camp. Their planned day of rest had been taken away. Their dreams that night were filled with the hauntings of the aquatic creature at the Øresund Strait, the manic Blue Men and the ghosts of the murdered dead from the field that day.

The next day they made their way into an abandoned village with a sign by its road proclaiming 'Handewitt.' Nils informed them, based on the other writing on the sign, that at some point during the day they had crossed into a region known as Germany.

They came across no other people—alive or dead—that day. But Val keenly felt some sort of presence watching them. Maybe hunting them.

20

Borss detested the Blue Men. Dealing with them and their freakish cult made him feel like he needed to bathe. In acid. But he had known they would have been his best option for waylaying the Northerners on their journey into the mainland. *His* mainland. That the Blues had sent him a Holy Messenger meant they had failed.

"Their feeble dog comes now," Zeilly said. She was a dark haired witch woman, capable of using herbs and roots in unusual ways. She could cure all manner of ailments, and her cooking skills were legendary. But so was her wrath. Most of Borss's men were terrified of her, and with good reason. She was always by his side, advising and counselling. And more often than not, mocking others for his private enjoyment. She stood next to his chair as the Blue Men's pathetic vassal scurried forward in his white, open chested robe, displaying his deeply tinted blue skin.

"Honorable Kaiser Borss," the blue priest began, "I bring you tidings and well wishes from the Holy Monastery of the Sea and Sky. Our Bishop bids me—"

"You fucking lost them, didn't you?" Borss asked, sounding bored. "They got past your holy tidal wave of morons. Yes?"

"I—uh. I—" The Blue Man was clearly at a loss, and he looked around Borss's throne room, as if for help.

The space was little more than the first floor of a former office building, its walls and ceiling still intact. While many structures in Bremen still stood, few of them were dry when it rained. But Borss had conquered the place—and the town. Just like he had conquered most of the continent—through coercion, guile and force. Unbearable, overwhelming force.

"Our esteemed Holy Bishop desires to..." the priest began again, attempting to restore some semblance of civility to the conversation.

"Desires to?" Borss interrupted again.

The witch woman snickered at his side.

"Holy Bishop Adelard...wishes to...convey..." the Blue Man sputtered.

Borss had heard enough.

In a lightning fast blur of shining, polished armor, he sprang from his throne and covered the ten paces between him and the indigo clergyman. His huge fist, clad in a spiked metal gauntlet that matched his chestplate, wrapped around the squirming man's throat. Borss squeezed down hard. The feeble messenger's eyes grew abnormally large in his otherwise blue face. Behind him, Zeilly purred with some-thing like sexual satisfaction at the sight of the brutal murder. A loud crunch filled the air as the cartilage in the Blue Man's neck gave way. The priest's head flopped against his shoulder, and Borss opened his hand.

The body tumbled to the floor, as Zeilly came up behind Borss whispering in his ear. "They could be south of us already. You are sure they head for the sea?"

Borss growled, a mix of irritation at being questioned, and arousal at the thought of what the witch woman would be doing to him later. "It's what the informant said. They move ever southward. But these lands are full of those loyal to me. We'll stop them. And then we'll find out what this prize is they seek, and take it for ourselves."

Borss turned to find that Zeilly had dropped her robe to the floor around her feet. Her perfect body shone in the low light seeping in from the gauzy curtained windows. She slipped forward into his arms, careful to avoid the large spikes on his armored chest-plate. He could feel her slender hands glide up to the buckles on his shoulders.

"The Blue Men were always a long shot. They might have accident-tally killed the Northerners. And there was no guarantee they wouldn't travel around the city ruins."

"True, but our forces are not yet returned from the raid to the eastern wastes. I can't chase them all over the land. We need to send other...proxies after them." Borss smiled, knowing the way he spoke only made her more aroused.

He heard a click, and the massive spiked chestplate fell away. Zeilly deftly sidestepped, and the armor clattered across the wooden floor. As soon as the plate spun away, she slipped back to his chest, and pressed her nakedness against him. He carefully put his arms around her, avoiding scratching her with his fist spikes.

He wondered if this time he'd manage to get the gauntlets off before they began.

"Who next?" she asked. "Surely not the Völkisch?"

"They are very loyal," Borss began, as her hands slid to his waistband. The Völkisch were devoted to Borss almost as much as they were to their ancient ideology of hate. Their facial tattoos were disturbing, but Borss knew there were worse groups of human beings.

Zeilly made a scoffing noise, like the sound others made when clearing their throats. "They are loyal, but inept. They place all their faith in their weapons, and their racism."

"They are powerful, and they have the greater numbers. It should be enough."

The svelte witch woman moaned as she ran her talented fingers over his scarred chest. "And this prize they seek? It will be important?"

"It is what I have heard." Borss prized her counsel, but he would never tell her everything. At least not up front. After he had what he needed from the Northerners and had collected his reward, then he would tell her. Then it wouldn't matter anymore. "We will have it, and we will be all powerful."

That was what she needed to hear.

Suddenly she was frantically tearing at his pants with her long nails, and he struggled to quickly remove the vicious spiked gauntlets.

He got one of them off before she pulled him down onto the floor. It was hours before the acrid smell of the corpse they were lying on drove them away.

21

The Northmen traveled to the east, avoiding the city of Hamburg. They had seen flickering campfires from a distance. They didn't know how many people lived in the city, but where there were people, there was also the chance for needless confrontation. Stig had lobbied for another fight, but Val had insisted their mission was more important, and even Morten had agreed with her.

South of the city, small villages were plentiful, and devoid of human life. But each was welcomed, as they scavenged propane tanks from which they could refuel.

When they reached the small village of Greven, little more than a wide spot in the road with crumbled former dwellings being reclaimed by mother nature, their first mechanical disaster struck.

Oskar's ATV coughed and sputtered to a stop, refusing to start again.

Val had them move their vehicles off the road and into a cluster of trees. Erlend and Stig went to work on taking the vehicle's motor apart and cleaning it, laying the parts and Erlend's tools on a blanket spread out on the ground.

"I did nothing to it," Oskar declared.

"The fuel line is probably clogged," Erlend muttered, spinning a wrench in his nimble fingers.

While the mechanics went to work, Anders and Nils walked off to search for game, the former setting Skjold free to soar the skies, where it could spot prey with its keen eyes. Oskar and Morten began to set up their camp, expecting the repairs might take a while.

Val and Ulrik walked west of town toward a small river they had seen earlier in the day. They would fill the water skins and bottles for everyone in the group.

"What were you going to ask me on the day Morten found the bog bodies?" Val said.

Ulrik shrugged. "I do not remember. It was a while ago."

Val walked by his side on the road, her black leather jacket slung across her shoulder with three empty water skins. "I thought you were flirting with me."

The shocked look on Ulrik's face was enough to tell her the thought had not crossed his mind. His blue eyes were wide, before he turned his face away, pretending to scan the countryside for threats.

"Were you... Were you *wanting* me to...flirt?"

The way he asked it made Val wonder if he had ever flirted with a woman before. He was a big, broad man, and in his thirties. He had most likely been with women, but she wondered if he had ever needed to chase one. The village girls probably threw themselves at him.

She just laughed softly and said, "You were just very talkative that day. Asking about my name..."

He turned his piercing gaze on her, then returned his eyes to the road ahead. They walked several more steps in silence. Even their footsteps were quiet, muffled by the carpet of grass coating what had once been a road. As the silence spun out, she wondered if she had insulted him.

"I...was curious. I have never met anyone else from the Åland islands, and certainly never a woman like you. As you know, many women are not fighters at all, and while I have shared a battlefield with some..."

"I understand. There is not much to tell. My parents were killed when I was very small. I needed to survive."

He didn't press her for any more details, and she was grateful.

The two reached the river in silence. Ulrik's mind was filled with thoughts of the strange young woman he followed. She was an enigma, for sure. A more competent fighter than most men he had known, a good leader and a decent judge of character and personality. He had watched how she had managed Morten's small rebellions with congeniality, until the man no longer seemed interested in being a persistent thorn in her side.

Ulrik had seen Val nurture Nils's confidence, by appealing to his knowledge, and how she had steered Stig toward Erlend, reducing his initial allegiance with Morten. She had shown great respect for Trond, after the man had saved her in the harbor fight in Stavanger. She had spoken good words over him during the ceremony. The woman spoke little each day, and she pushed them hard on their mission, but she always seemed to sense when the group needed rest.

He leaned down to the river to fill the clanging metal bottles he had carried.

Val dumped her skins on the grassy bank of the slowly flowing river. Moving down-stream, she said, "It is hot today. I will take a quick bath and return to help you with the water."

He watched her walk thirty feet down the bank, before dropping her jacket and pulling her black tank top off, revealing her bare chest. He turned away, giving her some privacy. Their trip had been long, and he had seen her bathe before. Nudity was not frowned on in the North, but after her question about flirting, he suddenly found himself thinking about how he looked at her.

He set about filling the bottles. When the receptacles were full, he walked over and picked up the water skins Val had dropped, thinking to save time by filling hers. He felt no resentment at needing to fill them; it was simply expedient. He did not begrudge her a swim. The day was warm, and he was thinking of swimming, too, after the work was done. Maybe if they stayed the night in the village, he would come back again in the morning for another bath, before they set off.

When the last skin was filled, he lifted them all and slung them over his shoulder, pulling his ax out and swinging it in his other hand as he walked, balancing the weight across his body.

He walked along the grassy riverbank, the blue sky overhead warm and filled with puffy clouds, but none threatening rain, and the winter was still a few months off. The bulbous clouds just added decoration to a brilliant day. Ahead of him, Val was lazily swimming in the river. He dropped the water skins in the grass.

She hadn't heard him approach, and the loud noise of the skins sloshing onto the ground startled her. She was swimming nude, but it was not her body she tried to hide when he saw her turn, surprised.

It was her eyes.

She had been swimming with her ever-present goggles lowered to dangle around her neck. But when she saw him, she snatched them up and moved the red lenses into position over her face.

"I..." he started. He was about to say that he was just thinking of swimming, as well, if she did not mind. Instead he said, "The skins are full. We should get back to the others."

He turned his back to her, indicating he was giving her privacy to get out of the river and dress. He heard her step out of the water and pull her pants and shirt on. Then she strapped her weapons on herself and reached down to collect the full water skins. She started walking back to the village without a word to him.

He grabbed the metal bottles and walked several paces behind her, thinking of nothing but her startling eyes. He had never seen anything like them.

No one had.

22

Morten the Hammer was dissatisfied with the mission's progress. He had understood that this journey, with the goal of saving humanity, was of utmost importance. He had also realized it would be difficult and long. What he had not bargained for, was that they would suffer losses before they even reached their destination, and that they would be traveling for weeks with little to do.

On some level, Morten had realized there would be slow times, but he had also been expecting battle after battle with opposing forces. He was not prepared for day after day of riding on the ass-numbing ATVs. And when they had faced threats, their foes were inhuman, like the thing at the bridge, or barely human, like the curious Blue Men.

Now the endless fields of northern Germany were dulling his eyesight, and filling him with exhaustion. He craved a simple fight with some bearded barbarians.

"This bores me, Oskar," he said. They were once again resting beneath the shade of a tree, their mid-day custom. The others sat under neighboring trees.

"You don't consider going on alone, do you?" Oskar asked him. The thin man was loyal, but sometimes thick, needing things explained to him.

"Not that, no. Although I have been thinking that maybe we should return to the North." Morten lay on his blanket, staring up at the blue sky through the fluttering of a maple tree's yellowing leaves.

"What?" Oskar was shocked. "What about this genetic material we seek?"

"It is a mission for the survival of the human race, yes. Women cannot have babies. I understand that. But do you realize that you and I have no women? We will not be fathers if we return to the North and the mission fails, but neither will we become fathers on this journey."

They lapsed into silence and Oskar seemed to be considering Morten's words.

"If we return, we have a chance at life, and finding some women. On this trip we have seen just one since leaving the North, and she is not interested in either of us." Morten stretched his arms and sat up.

"Do you think she fancies Ulrik?" Oskar asked.

"I think she fancies the mission," Morten admitted. "But I am bored of riding ever onward. Plus, there is a bigger problem."

Oskar tried to puzzle out what the issue was, as was his way. Finally he shrugged and asked Morten.

"We are running out of food," Morten told him in reply. "Anders has been unable to find game for a few nights now. His bird can't even find a field mouse. We are bored. Our fighting skills are wasted here. And soon we will all starve to death."

Three days later, Morten's complaint was being felt by all. They had scavenged through three small villages they had passed, and come up empty. Anders had been unable to find any big game, and for the second night the company had had to go without any meat.

The group had passed several lakes and streams that had been poisoned with orange and red chemicals, which left shiny smears on the surface of the water. The Vikings had drinking water, but fish would have been welcomed. If they couldn't find a new source of fresh water soon, though, their reserves would diminish.

Ulrik knew that the lack of food would fray tempers. He had expected an outburst from Morten by now, but the Laplander had been quiet the last few nights, even shrugging off the constant peppering of questions from his companion Oskar, with one-word grunted answers.

The problems came from an unexpected source.

"When will you or your bird find us some food, huntsman?" Stig grumbled, his heart not really in the complaint. Everyone knew the bird would sometimes come and go as it pleased, not returning for days. He was speaking more to himself than to Anders. Unfortunately, everyone present heard him.

Val and Nils had scouted ahead, while everyone else rested. The autumn day was bright and clear, but the threat of winter was on the chill in the breeze. The snows would bring a different world of woe.

"When will *you* stop eating twice your share of food, fat man?" Anders retorted. The others collectively held their breaths.

Oh shit, Ulrik thought. *Here we go.*

Hunger had reduced them to children. Stig shot up and rushed for Anders. The bowman screamed incoherently in reply and ran into the charge, his long braided hair bouncing behind him. Stig was powerful and broad, but also slow. Anders ducked low in front of the charging bull and plowed into the man's stubby legs. Stig was flipped up and over the hunter, flying through the air and crashing into Morten, both of their bodies crumpling into a tree.

Oskar had not seen Stig's initial charge, because his attention had been diverted by Anders's yelling, so when he saw his cousin hurt, he instantly jumped to the wrong conclusion—that Stig was attacking everyone, Morten included. Oskar rushed in to fight Stig, throwing punch after punch. Morten scrambled up and began swinging wildly, unsure of his enemy, but certain he was the target.

Then Erlend tried unwisely to pull the brawling men apart.

In seconds, Ulrik had gone from thinking his own thoughts to watching everyone trying to beat each other senseless.

Ulrik considered just waiting the men out, but he would be risking one or more of them getting seriously injured. Instead he got up and went to Erlend's ATV, opening up the seat and revealing a hidden storage compartment. Erlend had shown him some of the tools in the cramped space, and he had explained what they were for. The item that had caught Ulrik's eye then, was what he was after now. A small metal round canister with a red plastic top. The mechanic had explained what it was, but had been reluctant to show Ulrik its use. 'It might only be good for one use,' he had said.

Ulrik thought it was worth trying the strange device now. The can had rust around its edges, and the metal was cold in Ulrik's hand. He pointed the red cone on the top, as Erlend had showed him, and depressed a button on its back with his thumb.

The resulting blaring burst of sound from the air horn was stunning. Ulrik had been expecting it to be loud, because Erlend had told him that was what the thing was for, but he had not expected it to hurt his ears worse than the roar of the mutated bear they had battled in Sweden.

His hand flinched away from the can, which fell to the ground.

The brawling men stopped and looked up at Ulrik, shock on their faces. Stig pulled himself to his feet, blood streaming from a cut on his forehead, and running out of his nose. "Odin's balls, Ulrik. If you had something that loud on you, you could have used it before half my brains were dribbling out of my face."

The other four men, still on the ground, began laughing. Morten wiped his eyes of tears and blood, while cackling on the grass. Erlend surprised them all with a guffaw-like snort that had the others in additional fits of chortling.

Despite having startled himself, Ulrik was pleased with the outcome. Until he heard Val and Nils racing back down the road on their quads. For some reason, their arrival made the others erupt in yet more laughter, when they had nearly been finished.

"Stop, you cackling fools," Val shouted. "Take cover!"

Ulrik sobered instantly, realizing his folly with the horn, as he saw the swarm of black flapping creatures following Val and Nils.

They looked like bats. Their wings stretched only a little further than the bats Ulrik knew from the North. But the creatures had thick horns on their heads, like miniature cattle.

Anders stepped up to Ulrik's side, his bow raised at the flock. Twenty or more of the creatures sped down toward the oncoming ATVs. Ulrik raised his shield, waiting for the horned bats to come, while the others all picked themselves up and made for the cover of nearby trees.

Val and Nils sped past them, skidding to a stop in front of the first tree. Nils hopped off his steed and beat a retreat into the forest. Val came forward, her long ax held aloft.

"Wait," Anders said.

Then Ulrik saw it.

In a different part of the sky, something was blasting through the air, like a lightning bolt. Aimed directly for the flock of bats.

Skjold.

The bird of prey swooped in. Its talons split the wings of two bats, before it pounced on a third, twisting and beating its wings hard, carrying its victim straight upward.

The rest of the flock scattered in a chaotic, frantic jumble, some retreating the way they had come. Others raced off to the west.

The attack was broken, but the bird showed no sign of coming back down, or sharing its supper.

Ulrik understood the bird's selfish hunger.

If they didn't find food soon, things would become dire.

23

After crossing a river which had provided water, but no fish, Val called a halt to the day's travel. "We need to find some food," she said. "Anders, please see what you and Skjold can find. Even small creatures will help us."

They made a small camp not too far from the bank of the river, in a stand of trees, where they would not be seen by anyone or anything that passed. Then several of them scoured for naturally growing vegetables and wild berries, while Ulrik and Morten attempted to make a fishing net out of a blanket, stringing it across the low river. They had tied ropes to the four corners, with Morten standing and holding the thin cords on one bank and Ulrik on the other.

The group spent hours searching and coming up with little. Val went into the next village with Nils and Stig on the ATVs, and they once again found a deserted pile of rubble that had once been homes.

"Again, nothing," Nils said. Val could tell by the tone of his voice he was only commenting on their misfortune. The complaining would begin later.

Stig said nothing. He had grown more serious about their mission, and Val thought he was attempting to fill the void left by poor Trond. Although Stig was shorter, he was still a powerful man, and she was glad to have his brawn on the team. She had begun to trust him more, although not as much as she relied on Ulrik.

A small handful of berries grew on vines tangled around a pile of plastic fencing. She picked them. But the amount of fruit would not even fill her own slim stomach. The men with her required five to six times the amount of food she consumed—and Stig twice as much again.

"Anything we find will help," she said softly.

"Val, we have looked," Stig said, compassion in his eyes. "We are doing our part, but there is no food to be found. We need to move from this barren area. You have led us this far. You can lead us away from here. Perhaps it is time to consider a direction besides due south?"

It was the most the sturdy man had said to her in weeks, and the admission of his faith in her leadership was a surprise. But then she realized it had been some time since she had heard him siding with Morten on any issue.

Low fields surrounded them, but the area had not been farmed in generations, and while the soil looked good, all it grew now were wild grasses.

"My stomach groans," Nils said.

Stig knew better than to complain about how hungry he was.

"Let us go back and see what the boys have captured from the river," Val said. She was feeling as dejected as Nils and Stig. She had been eating less than she needed so the others could have enough. Her muscles ached, and when she stood up or sat down too quickly, her vision blurred and she felt lightheaded—once nearly falling over.

Val led the way back to camp, trying hard to not think about food, but failing. When they entered the camp, they found a lumpy shape wrapped in a large tan blanket. It was not the blanket the men had used for fishing, but the one they usually laid on the ground as a tarp for their camp. Val approached the misshapen lump and tugged the edge of the rough blanket away.

Beneath it was a dead buck. If it were standing, its shoulders would have reached as high as Val's. She turned to Nils and Stig with a huge grin on her face as she poked a finger in the deep arrow hole just behind the dead animal's neck.

"Anders has come through for us," she said.

Nils and Stig both whooped.

"Start to prepare it, and get it over a fire. I will go and see how Morten and Ulrik have fared with the fish. I think we will all eat well tonight."

Val walked toward the river. She was feeling happy for the first time since before they had encountered the massive bear. A good meal would turn around morale and set them back on the path. She wanted to make good distance in the coming weeks, so they would be past the southern German mountains by the time winter gripped the land.

At the river, Morten and Ulrik were walking toward her, dragging the soaking wet blanket between them. Both men were covered in mud and dripping wet.

"Any luck?" she asked, unable to hide her grin. The looks they gave her in return answered for them. "It is of no concern. Anders took a huge buck. No one will be hungry tonight."

They walked back to the camp, where Nils and Stig had just finished skinning the animal. Ulrik set up a spit, while Morten made a large fire pit.

In no time they were smelling the deep rich scent of cooking meat, and their mouths were salivating at the thought of it.

The meat was ready as Anders, Erlend and Oskar returned to the camp. They all looked surprised at the spectacular feast awaiting them.

"But..." Anders began. "Who caught this monstrous deer?"

Val squinted at the man. "We thought *you* shot it."

Anders shook his head. "I have seen nothing all day. I did not fire even one arrow today."

Val and Anders looked to each of the others in turn, but they all shook their heads.

"Who in the nine worlds left the bloody deer here, then?" Val demanded.

She felt the hackles on the back of her neck raise. Without a word, they formed a circle around the camp, hands reaching for weapons. They remained that way for a long time, waiting for an attack that never came. By the time they ate, the meat was blackened, and tasted like the dread they felt in their stomachs.

Someone was watching them, observing from afar. And apparently, whoever it was, the person was a far better hunter than Anders. They discussed the problem softly for hours, with three of them always on guard at any given time. They would need to take shifts throughout the night.

"Why would they leave the food for us?" Erlend asked. "You said it was covered, Val?"

She grunted an affirmative. The conversation and speculation had continued, but she was ready for sleep.

"So obviously, whoever left it there did so on purpose, and wanted us to eat," Oskar said. "They even covered the deer to keep the flies away."

"What I want to know is how our mysterious benefactor could find and shoot such a huge buck, when—no offense, Anders—we have not seen a single animal in days." Morten ran his fingers through his shaggy blonde hair. Without the gel or animal fat he had used to slick it, back when they were in Stavanger, it had become wild and uncontrolled. Most of them could use some grooming.

The fire crackled near the great blanket—they had cleaned the buck's blood from it—and most of them reclined on it, the smoke from the flames rising up and away from them. They had considered not using a fire at all, but Nils had observed that their spy already knew exactly where they were.

"How this person could catch a deer when we cannot, is the only part of this mystery I have solved," Ulrik said, lying down and rolling to his side, pulling his blanket over him.

"How?" Morten asked.

"Easy," Ulrik said. "Whoever he is, he does not have an ATV with a loud, buzzing motor to scare away the game."

24

A month passed, and despite being perpetually on guard, they caught no glimpse of their mysterious assistant. But when food was scarce, they found game left for them near the camp or along their path.

Val nicknamed the person 'Ull,' the god of the hunt. She had no illusions that it was an actual god helping them. She knew it was a human—and a man by the tracks he sometimes left in mud. She was sure he was alone, too. But they had been unable to find him. After a while, Val had given up on it. Ull had his reasons for hiding, and would reveal them when he was ready.

They had discussed the possibility that the food was poisoned that first night, but if it had been, none of them had gotten sick—and cooking the meat thoroughly would have killed many illnesses. So they were cautious, but they stopped being paranoid.

Ull seemed content to follow them from a distance. *Perhaps making certain we are not here to kill him or anyone else we find,* Val thought. She was aware of how they looked, this rag-tag group of avenging Northmen on their strange motorized mounts.

They were a few miles to the south and east of Frankfurt when their food shortage problem ended for good. A wooden, painted sign at the side of the road read: Waldaschaffer Forest. The Vikings drove into the gloom cast by huge, looming trees lining and arching up over the road, forming a natural tunnel. The road itself was bumpy and potholed—a result of decades of frost and thaw, and no one to maintain it. Trees grew from cracks in the ancient asphalt. Many were shorter than a foot, and easily knocked down by the ATVs. Others were five or six feet tall, and as thin as a broom handle, but strong enough to stop one of the quads or knock a rider from his saddle.

Two slow miles later, the road widened a bit, and the trees fell away to reveal a huge valley, surrounded on all sides by yet more forest. In the middle of the valley were the crescent-shaped ruins of an ancient town. Beyond the rubble, strange, brownish blobs filled the fields.

Val thought they were huge boulders until she saw them move. Then she realized they were animals. A massive herd of them, spreading out farther than she had ever seen.

"Cows," Oskar said, pleased with the find.

"No," Ulrik said, his voice grim. He pulled his ax from its holster on his ATV, and stepped off the quad.

"What are they?" Val asked him, drawing her own ax.

"Pigs. If they stay calm, we should be able to slaughter a few and reach the far side. But if they are angry and stampede?"

"We will take to the trees if need be," she said. "The forest has acted as a natural boundary, penning them in this valley."

"Yes," he said. "But look at the size of the herd. They seem to be eating well. The real question is whether the herd is tended or if they just found each other."

"Well, we need some of those animals. We cannot continue to rely on our friend, the ghost."

The valley was a mile across, with the road running straight through the middle of it. The crescent-shaped ruins that nature had mostly reclaimed, sat to the left of the road. They saw nothing to indicate that the herd was tended by humans, but people had ingenious ways of hiding.

"We go off-road, sticking close to the forest, where we will have cover," Val said.

"It is a good plan," Ulrik said.

She steered her ATV off the road and down into a wide pale green field on their right, then raced along the edge of the field, never further than a few feet from the safety of the trees. Ulrik followed her, and the others went after him one by one, wary and eyeing the distant herd of animals.

Their caravan had made it halfway along the perimeter of the valley when the smell hit them. The wretched scent of feces, mud and rotting vegetation was so all-encompassing that Val thought she could feel it not only in her nose, but crawling on her skin.

"It is like a fire giant's ass crack," Stig shouted.

The mass of distant pink and brown pigs turned almost as one creature at the sound of a raised human voice. The buzzing engines of the quad-bikes had not even raised a single porcine head. But the spoken words of a human being had the entire herd turning together, like a flock of birds.

The stampede threw up a cloud of rich brown dirt and dust as it barreled across the wide open fields. Val figured they had less than a minute. "Into the trees," she shouted, but realized no one would hear her over the grunting and shrieking of the oncoming mass of thundering animals. She turned her ATV into the trees and drove several feet into the forest before parking behind a thick oak.

The others retreated into the dense woods, as she ran back to the edge, her long ax in hand. She pointed up to the last stragglers—Morten and Oskar—intending that they take to the trees to avoid the pigs.

But Morten was spoiling for a fight, and Oskar, as ever, was beside his cousin.

Val was about to argue with them when she noticed Ulrik and Stig were both gearing up for the fight as well.

Okay, she thought. *We need the meat anyway. Let us kill some pigs.*

She crouched down, ready to swing her blade down into the sow rushing toward her. The hairy ridge of the creature's back reached four feet from the ground, and it was seven feet long. But the large beasts did not have tusks. She thanked the gods for that small favor. It was the raw velocity and weight of the animals that made them dangerous. They rushed in a frenzied stampede with no coordination or ability to turn. Val expected many would run into trees and knock themselves unconscious.

With seconds to spare, Val switched strategies, hauling the handle of her ax above her head and leaping in the air. She brought the ax head down with devastating effect, her body weight driving it into the pig's thick neck.

Then the beast rammed her falling legs, flipping her onto its back. She clung to the ax wedged into the pig and was carried away, as the creature plowed into the forest.

25

Ulrik saw Val clinging to the sow's back. Then she was gone, carried deeper into the forest. He had his own problems. Three large, tuskless boars were trampling toward his position.

He had seen how Val's strategy had fared—and knew from watching her take down Vebjørn, that her ax strike was formidable. So instead of targeting the thicker parts of the animals, he crouched low and lunged out of the trees when the boars came within striking distance. His ax hummed across the field, swiping like a farmer's scythe, and slicing into the front legs of all three animals. The severed legs skittered to the right as momentum carried the animals forward. They plowed their faces into the dirt at his feet, skidding to a halt.

He leapt onto the back of a squealing animal, targeting the next couple of attackers. He swung down, slicing deep gouges in their flanks, but the frenzied swine kept up their frantic pace, disappearing into the trees behind him. The other men would have to deal with them.

Rather than chase the pigs, he decided to conserve energy and only attack those that came for him. Balanced atop the squirming, dying animals' spines, he could easily evade the pigs that lunged at him, and cleave their snouts, or split their skulls.

The herd was two hundred strong, and they kept coming, jostling each other in the frenzied crush to reach the trees. Ulrik swung down again, the ax head cleaving off a pig's ear. He kicked at the creature, pushing it back into the flow of animals pouring around his initial three victims like the sea around a rock.

He'd been worried that the pigs had rushed the group out of hunger—the animals were notorious omnivores. But now that the herd kept flowing past him and into the trees, he guessed that something had spooked them, and they were moving to what they considered safety. Perhaps to some other valley surrounded with trees, like this one. *Probably near a river*, he thought.

In what seemed like seconds, the last of the hulking beasts skittered into the woods. Ulrik turned to watch it go, and he realized his comrades had all fled into the forest—or been carried like Val.

The boar on which he stood had stopped its thrashing, after bleeding to death from its severed limbs, all while he had stood on its back and beaten off its brethren. He felt a pang of sympathy for the creature, but he knew he would feel no such guilt later in the night, when they feasted on blackened pork.

His present foes vanquished, Ulrik headed into the forest to find the others. He spotted Nils twenty feet up a tree on his right. The thin man was in the process of climbing down, so Ulrik continued onward, following the swath of destruction the pigs had caused in their headlong escape.

Next he found Morten, who was walking his way, carrying Oskar over his shoulder like a sack of potatoes.

"Is he hurt?" Ulrik asked.

Morten shook his head. "Knocked out by a tree, the silly bugger. But he is my cousin, so I promised his mother I would always take care of him."

Ulrik continued past him, looking for the others. Morten turned and went with him, still carrying his cargo.

Next they found Stig, who was seated in a puddle of mud on the ground, looking slightly dazed.

"Are you well, Stig?" Morten called to the man.

He started to get up off the ground with a grunt. "Only my ribs and my dignity bruised."

Morten laughed.

Ulrik followed the trail of pressed and broken low lying branches, and the torn up muddied forest floor. Stig joined Morten, and they followed the path for another thirty minutes until they came to another wide clearing. The field was far smaller than the last and showed no signs it had ever been inhabited.

In the center of the clearing, surrounded by close to fifty pig bodies, arrayed in a twisting path of destruction, Val hacked at the skull of the last living beast. She stood astride the creature, her blade whipping down at its skull with lightning speed once...twice...and then a third time, until the animal's bloodcurdling shriek finally ceased.

The woman was covered from her waist down in dark red pig's blood. Above the waist, arcs of sprayed blood covered her, but none of it looked to be hers. Ulrik quickly determined she was uninjured. He smiled broadly. He had taken down three of the fleeing pigs. The others had not killed any. Val had killed dozens of them by herself.

"Still questioning her leadership?" Ulrik asked, soft enough that only Morten would hear.

"Hah. No. I am instead wondering why we even needed to be here. The woman is a storm of vengeance."

Just at that moment Val looked up at them, her teeth gritted against the out-of-control rage that had consumed her and lent her the near superhuman strength to murder the swarm of pigs in a bloody haze. Pigs' blood had splashed across her face, covering her white teeth in crimson gore. "Who is hungry?"

They spent several days in the larger clearing, sleeping in the crescent shaped ruins. They needed to rest after the long days with little food. Instead of traveling, they spent the time smoking meat from the pigs and tanning some of the hides, to replace damaged garments, and to make basic leather armor for some of the men.

They had found Erlend and Anders nearby in the forest, and Oskar's injury had been minimal. Stig's ribs turned vivid shades of purple and yellow, but he shrugged the injury off as the cost of the journey, which he said he was beginning to enjoy. Ulrik suspected the reemergence of plentiful food had much to do with the man's newfound enjoyment of their mission.

The food was welcomed by all—especially because as they left the pig fields behind and headed south once more, they traveled for two weeks toward Stuttgart, without once spotting a living thing. No game, no more pigs, not even a bird.

The land was covered in a thick gray mist. The waters they found were tainted with greasy streaks of color, and the trees, when they could be seen, looked pale and sickly.

There was no new food to be found, but in return for the kindness their shadow had left for them, Val took to leaving an amount of the smoked pork behind them on the road each night.

In the mornings, it was always gone.

Although the conditions were not optimal, Ulrik found them tolerable—with food in their packs, most things would be.

The problem came during the third week of moving across the poisoned, empty landscape, when Stig woke up coughing thick, chunky phlegm, peppered with bloody specks.

26

"He is getting worse," Erlend said. "I fear he will soon be going to Valhalla."

Ulrik spat on the ground. "It is no way for a warrior to die." He stalked off across the field, anger making his arms shake.

Stig lay on a makeshift bed they had created with a heap of branches nestled between two piles of rubble and rock, near the middle of a large open field. It had been a long time since they had come across a solid structure. The day was overcast and raining on and off, with the bitter chill behind it, souring moods and implying winter would not be long in coming.

The man lying before Val had lost several pounds, and his skin had turned a pasty yellow. The hue nearly matched the heavy strand of snot that dribbled out of his nose, and the chewy mouthfuls he frequently spat aside.

Despite the midday time, he was trapped in deep sleep. Their travel time, even with Stig strapped to the rear seat of the doubled-up ATV had been cut to just a few hours each day. The man was not well enough for more.

None of the others had developed the sickness, and they debated whether it was a result of the injury to his ribs. The broken bones had begun to mend, and there was no longer a discolored bruise on his chest. But there was no denying his weakness or the non-stop production of mucus.

The nightly discussion also touched on radiation sickness or tainted pork meat—but in both scenarios, they would all be ill. Anders was suspicious of Ull and his supposedly benevolent gifts. But Val had again pointed out to the bowman that they had all eaten the meat, and no one else had contracted the sickness—and they had not needed gifts from their follower since the pigs.

Whatever the cause, hearty, robust Stig was dying, and it would not take long. The man rolled on his side and instead of spitting out a mouth full of heavy mucus, he simply opened his mouth in his sleep and let it drool out.

Erlend turned away at the sight. They didn't have anyone skilled in medicine, but he did his best to treat the man he had befriended on the journey.

"Do what you can for him," Val said, understanding this might be the last day Erlend needed to tend to his patient.

She walked a short distance away across the field, the grass sliding past her shins. She had seen a wooden fence set twenty feet inside the edge of the forest. *In twenty more years, the seeds from the trees at the edge will have filled this clearing as well.* Ulrik had stalked off a good distance, but the others—Anders, Nils, Morten, Erlend and Oskar—were huddled in a group and talking. As she approached them, they stopped speaking, each avoiding her gaze.

"I am not stupid," she said. "It makes sense to discuss putting the man out of his misery, even if it is not a pleasant topic."

Relief washed over Nils's face, and she knew that was precisely what the men had been discussing. She knew Ulrik would have no part in such a topic. He would not even consider it. Val had already accepted that Stig was dying. She had accepted that they would be unable to stop the progression of his illness. Her thoughts had already moved on to making sure no one else contracted the strange sickness, and to surviving the encroaching winter.

Morten ran a hand through his unwashed hair, his slicked-back look returning with natural greasiness. "This place is not good, Val. We need to move from here. We are all agreed."

"What would you suggest?" she asked. She would not make it easy for them.

Oskar turned away, and Nils looked down at his feet. The answer surprised her when it came instead from Anders, the quiet hunter. "We should just kill him and move on. The pork will not last forever, and the winter snows will soon be upon us. Nils has shown me the maps. If we do not get through the mountains to the south soon, we would be better served by going to the west, through France."

"That would be well out of our way," Morten said, suddenly concerned. Val was surprised to discover that he knew the route at all. He had clearly also studied the maps, although she had never seen him display any interest in them.

"The mountains are a vast boundary to the south," Anders added. "Crossing them, even with the ATVs, will be a challenge. Doing so in the winter would most likely lead to more death."

"The mountains—they are called the Alps—extend down into France, as well," Val pointed out.

"Not all the way to the coast of the sea," Anders countered. "We could then travel into Italy along the shore."

Val had spent a long time calculating the route with Nils and Halvard back in Stavanger, before they had departed. She had first proposed the sea route herself, but Halvard had warned against it. She knew little of Europe, or the few peoples still living here, but Halvard had assured her that there were, according to his scientist friend, still plenty of pirates on that sea. 'And the south of France is to be avoided at all costs,' he had told her.

"We will give Stig until the end of this day. If he is not recovered, we will give him the option of being left behind, or having us end his life. We will not make that decision for him. He has earned that much from us and far more." Val started to walk toward Ulrik.

"And the mountains?" Morten called to her.

A loud cough interrupted them. Then, "What mountains? I am ready for them."

All eyes turned to see Stig, standing next to Erlend, and shaking off a helping hand. His beard was crusted with dried snot, but he had a light in his eyes. He looked better than he had in days.

Then his chest erupted in five bursting gouts of red, spraying his blood out into the grass. The unexpected sight was accompanied by the loudest mechanical shattering sound any of them had ever heard.

Only Nils knew what it was. "Get down!" he screamed. Then he threw himself to the grass, and the others followed his lead as Stig's suddenly perforated body toppled forward. Another burst of fire from the automatic weapon strafed the field, and then abruptly stopped.

Voices shouted in German.

"Scheisse. Es ist kaputt."

"Sei still, Narr!"

Nils translated to the men on the ground, and Val could just make out what he said from her distance.

"*Shit. It is jammed.*" "*Shut up, fool.*"

"Nils, what in the name of Heimdal's horn was that weapon?" Morten hissed, from his place in the grass.

"It shoots metal pieces very fast and very far. A machine gun."

"It ripped through Stig and we never saw the man using it," Oskar said. "How can we fight that?"

"We cannot," Nils said. "But the weapon is broken. Perhaps only temporarily. Let us hope it is the only one they have."

"So we should stay in the grass, Nils?" Val called out across the field.

But their new opponents answered for him. A group of the men came running across the open field toward where they lay in the grass. The men were bald, and they wore dark pants and boots, but their huge chests were bare, and covered in raised scars that formed patterns and decorations like tattoos.

But their heads were the most unusual thing—the men had no ears. Just open holes. The lumpy, mismatched scar tissue suggested the ears had been cut off. The men wore either black make-up that covered their bald heads—or else the entire head had been tattooed black, with just small patches of untouched skin at the throat, back of the head, and on the sides.

More threatening than the makeup, the men running through the field's shin-high grass carried a long, slim knife in each hand.

"So, no more of the machine weapons," Val said, scrambling to her feet. The others stood up behind her. "Time to avenge Stig." Then she ran toward the men with the knives, pulling her ax from its holster.

As she halved the distance between her and the black-headed men, before her comrades had even begun to chase her, two more groups of tattooed attackers entered the open field.

Instead of turning away, Val only sped up.

27

The long knives the attackers carried looked crude, but deadly. They were not quite swords—about two feet long and slim. But the metal looked weak, and poorly formed. Black and lumpy. Val thought she might be able to split one with a good strike from her ax—or even the wood of its handle.

As the first tattooed man closed in, she dipped low, under his twin knife sweeps, and then sprang up into the air. She swung down with her ax, the blade biting into the top of the man's head, even as she continued her tumble forward, flipping over his falling body and tugging her ax free in the same movement. She landed on her feet behind the man, and he crashed to the grass with blood spraying from his head.

The men on either side of him stopped, stunned. Val's left hand snapped out laterally, and her hand-ax spun through the air, slicing into one man's blackened face, as she turned to the third. He pulled up his twin blades and flipped them in his hands, so the tips pointed down. His torso was twice as wide as hers, and this close she could see the patterns on his chest. They were old symbols, but still known for their association with evil—even far to the north where she had lived her entire life.

Swastikas.

The tattoo on his head was a giant black swastika. It started the intersection of its four legs at the bridge of the man's nose. The bent legs of the design wrapped under his chin, over his bald skull to the back, and across the artificially flattened sides of his head, where the missing ears had once been.

But like everyone in the North, his eyes were a crystalline blue, for a moment revealing uncertainty and awe, and then quickly sliding back toward hatred.

The man rushed at her, one downward arcing blade slashing for her chest. Val swung her ax handle straight up, the head of the weapon tangling with the man's wrist and the hilt of his blade. The strike blocked, Val snapped a booted foot straight up, catching Long Knife man in the chin, sending his head back, and tugging her ax handle from her hand.

He recovered quickly, and came back at her, the long weapons spinning again in his hands until the blades pointed upward above his clenched thumbs. He thrust forward with both hands, but Val slipped to the right, rolling her body around the outside of the man's arm, and the side of his body. Her own knife—the blade just four inches long—already in her hand. It was her last weapon. But she brought it in close as she spun, slicing along the man's side, just above his hip. Then her free arm shot up and backward, her elbow connecting with the base of the man's skull.

She spun around the Long Knife's body, even as he started to fall from the blow to his head. With the metal hilt of her knife still in hand, she threw her weight into a punch at the side of the man's right knee. The cartilage protested with loud cracking noises, as the joint collapsed inward.

The man screamed, his knees impacting the soil. Val reversed her spin, and swept her arm out, slicing through the side of the man's neck. Arterial blood arced up and over her head, as Val lunged to the ground, rolled and came up with the knife still in one hand and her recovered ax in the other.

She took a moment to orient herself. Ulrik was in the process of ramming his shield into the face of a Long Knife, as he pulled his ax free of another, his foot planted on the man's chest, heaving the body free of the weapon. Closer still, Morten and Oskar were a whirling tornado of death, sweeping through two and three men with each strike of their long swords, the weapon cleaving through the Knives' deficient metal as easily as it split Long Knife skin.

Erlend and Nils fought side by side, their blades clashing with the knives of two attackers. Anders was nocking and firing arrows, each shot finding and slipping into a Long Knife head. As she watched, one of the arrows went into an unguarded Long Knife ear hole. The man's muscled torso snapped around in a circle and dropped. The hunting bird was nowhere to be seen. It made its own decisions whether to fight or fly, it seemed and, not for the first time, she wished Anders had better control over the creature.

Val turned her head back in the direction from which the Long Knives had come. The day's gray haze still obscured the edge of the forest. But the ten new men rushing her way were easy to spot, as was the knife that had been thrown at her, spinning straight toward her face. She tilted her shoulders right, her head moving left. The blade whipped over her shoulder, the tip of it slicing through her leather jacket and nicking her flesh.

Her attention stayed on the man who had thrown his weapon. He was in the lead, the new group of attackers spread out in a wedge formation. Val stayed in place as the last two men on either side of the wedge split off, heading for her friends. She waited until the leader got closer. As he did, he swung with his remaining knife. Val swung her hardened ax over her head, like she was chopping wood, striking and cutting through the man's knife blade like it was a head of cabbage.

Before her swing was complete, she reared her head backward and then slammed it forward, mashing her forehead into the bridge of the man's nose. The hit was so hard it rammed the bone and cartilage backward through his skull, killing him instantly.

The man fell at her feet, and Val spat on him.

The five men who had stayed with the leader slowed to look at her. Then the smallest of them screamed incoherently and charged. His four comrades rushed in from all sides.

There was no way out, and she could not leap over them as she had done with the first man. Not while stationary.

So she did the only thing she could think of. She dropped down into a crouch, swinging her knife in an arc at knee height. When the blade bit into multiple limbs, she struck again and again, shredding legs too committed to the charge to veer away before being sliced open. But it wasn't enough. A tangle of bodies crumpled down on her like an avalanche of flesh, blood and body odor. She thrashed with her knife, the long wooden handle of her ax, her elbows and her head. But fists and knees pummeled her from countless directions, and eventually, the sharpened tip of one of the long knives found its way into her flesh.

28

Ulrik lunged from behind his shield, sending the man on the other side of it to the ground where he was promptly stomped by Ulrik's boot. His right heel smashed into the man's tattooed face, shattering nose and jaw. Ulrik did not know if the man was dead, but he stopped moving, and that was enough.

Val had been surrounded when Ulrik last saw her, and then the five men had tackled her. The other Vikings were all too far back to offer assistance. But Ulrik would kill every earless bastard between him and his fallen leader. His respect for her had only grown on their long voyage, and while he was not sure if his additional loyalty to her was because he had feelings for her or because he simply respected her, he knew she meant more to him than any of the men in their group.

Stepping off the fallen Long Knife, Ulrik raced for the next two, who stood too close to each other. He led with the ax, fooling them into thinking he meant to swing it overhand. Instead, as he got close, he swung out and back with the heavy ax, and brought his shield up to smash into both men, the velocity of his sprint adding heft to the impact. Knives clattered against the wood and the metal dome of his shield. Then their bodies. Ulrik turned a full circle, dropping the shield and following his ax around. He swung low, the ax hewing through the first man's thighs, and chopping cleanly through the first leg of the second man, before stopping an inch into the inner thigh of the fourth leg, where resistance tugged the handle from Ulrik's hand.

The dismembered men screamed in horrified pain and shock, but he just lifted a foot and stamped down on the back of his shield, driving it down on their faces. The man with one leg still attached was silenced in a barrage of crunching sounds. Ulrik pulled his foot off the shield, bent low to pull it up and rammed a fist into the blackened face of the legless man. His screaming stopped when unconsciousness dropped on him like a stone fallen from a great height.

The other man's silence had not come from the shield, Ulrik saw, but from the man's long blade, which had sliced his own throat in the second impact.

Good, Ulrik thought, and he was moving again toward the pile of bodies where Val had gone down.

Four more men came at him, two from each side. Ulrik hefted his wooden shield in his left hand and pulled the ax in close with his right, letting the head drop low to the grass, where the blood-drenched blade was nearly concealed from sight. He stood still, waiting for the men to make their move.

In contrast to his stillness, the men bounced on their feet, nervous energy coursing through them, and three of the four twirled their blades in their hands, as if to show off their expertise with the weapons. The fourth man tightened and loosened his grip on his blades. They all looked identical with their naked chests and their large swastika head tattoos, and Ulrik supposed that was the point of the design, and their naked chests. The scarified designs in their flesh were the only individual variations they had. He could only wonder at the purpose for the mutilated ears.

The two on his left—the knife gripper and the other—lunged first. Ulrik swept his ax up in a lunge of his own, releasing its handle and allowing the heavy ax head to sail through the air, its long handle chasing the pointed tip. The projectile hit the knife gripper so hard that the metal collapsed his chest inward. His already dead body spun, the long handle of the weapon striking hard across the throat of the man next to him.

Two opponents down in less than two seconds.

Ulrik was not watching the impact, though. It was a diversionary tactic against the other two, and it had worked. While they watched Ulrik's ax fly, he charged, shield held high. He brought the edge of the giant wooden disc down on top of one man's head. The now dead man fell and tangled in Ulrik's legs, sending him toppling into the other man. It was enough to knock the man to the ground, but the last Long Knife was not injured by the fall. Ulrik rolled as he went down, his grip loosening on the shield, and he came back up atop the man. His arms pumped like he was running, his fists, forearms and elbows pounding his opponent.

The man tried to crawl away, but Ulrik was on top of him, beating the bald head until it no longer resembled a head.

As Ulrik rolled off the man and pulled his shield to him, he heard a battle cry: "For Midgard!"

He looked back across the field and saw Stig had somehow survived the projectiles that had ripped through his chest. Blood poured from the corner of his mouth as he grabbed two of the Long Knives and slammed their skulls together, crushing them with his powerful arms. Stig was not as large as Trond had been, and much of his weight was fat rather than muscle, but he was still larger than their newfound enemies running across this battlefield. He used that size and power to his advantage, barreling into the next two men, and knocking them down. After the impact, a two-foot-long knife was stuck in Stig's chest, four inches deep, but the man just knocked it aside with his forearm, sluicing the blade out. If he felt the sharp edge of the thing in the flesh of his arm, he gave no indication.

The large man took three more running steps at an opponent, when one of Anders's arrows buried itself in the Long Knife's eye socket. Stig barely noticed. The man was dead, so he was no longer worthy of receiving the big Viking's pent up rage. Stig continued on toward the men piled atop Val.

He only made it halfway there before the cumulative effect of his multiple injuries and his illness caused him to crash to the ground, just as Ulrik was running past him for Val.

Behind him, Morten and Oskar whirled in their devastating back-to-back ballet of death, assailants dropping all around them.

Anders was reduced to plucking his already expended arrows from the heads of his previous victims before firing them across the field to drop the newcomers. But the battle was nearly over, and only stragglers were still running onto the field.

"Das ist es!" "Sheißen!"

'That is it!' 'Shoot!'

Nils heard the shouts and knew what they meant. He had been waiting for any sign that this might be coming. He thrust his shield out, smashing it into the face of the man he had been fighting. Then he dropped his ax from his left hand and grabbed the horn on his waist, pulling it to his lips as he leaned back from the return attack. The man's long knife clanged into his shield just as the mechanical chattering thunder boomed over the field.

Nils blew his horn, the sound echoing over the clearing even louder than the machine gun. As he expelled the last of the air in his lungs, he dropped into a squat, the wooden shield over his head. The man he had been fighting was instantly perforated by the machine gun fusillade, and several rounds ruptured the top edge of Nils's shield as he held it up above his head. Then the dead Long Knife collapsed on Nils's shield, his body becoming additional protection for the Viking, as they both crunched into the ground. Nils lay under the wooden shield and the Long Knife's body.

He was pinned, but could see Anders on the ground, peering through the foot high grass. The horn blast had saved at least one of them.

Then, fainter than the first time, Nils heard the machine gunner speaking again. "Das war die letzte Kette."

'That was the last chain.'

Last chain? Nils wondered. Then he understood, blowing his horn again with two quick bursts. The last belt of ammunition for the weapon. *The morons had only ten or twenty bullets left. They should have waited until they had us all lined up.*

Nils couldn't climb free from the weight of the man on top of him, but he saw Anders take the message of the double horn blast, standing to his feet and running off to rejoin the battle.

Nils tried to squirm his body forward, gaining just half an inch with each struggling thrust of his legs and hips.

He closed his eyes with each jolt, but when he opened them, he could see a Long Knife running across the field for him, only one knife in hand.

Nils struggled faster, grunting with the effort of trying to dislodge the dead weight of a man that outweighed him by nearly double. His progress was minimal. He was stuck.

The Long Knife stopped right above him.

Nils looked up to see the man's vicious smile, as the two-foot blade began its plunge downward.

29

Nils never wanted to be a fighter. As a child, he had been small and slight, but intelligent. Despite academic pursuits not being highly sought after in this new world, after the *Utslettelse*, he had persisted in his interests, and Halvard had approached his parents, convincing them to let him train in the old ways of science.

As it had turned out, Nils had not been terribly good at science, but he had instantly been attracted to the texts in Halvard's library. The man had deemed the books 'dry histories.' *Dry to you, maybe*, Nils had thought. He had been fascinated with the Old World and all of its lost knowledge.

Now as the lumpy black iron blade plunged down at his head, Nils, for the first time in his life, wished that he had worked harder to strengthen his body. He had really wanted to see Italy.

At the last second, instinct guided him, even with his eyes shut. He yanked his head to the side. The *shckkk* sound of a knife slicing into something, came from just left of his ear. When he opened his eyes, he saw the knife had stabbed into nothing more than soil and grass.

He tilted his head up in time to see the man dropping down over him, an arrow protruding from the middle of his forehead. But the arrow and the man's face disappeared as he fell forward, his dead weight slamming down on top of the corpse already pinning Nils. The extra weight took Nils's breath when it squeezed him, and he thought he would now suffocate.

Then the pressure lifted, as the newest corpse was tossed aside, rolling into the grass in front of Nils's pinned head. Then the first body was dragged away. Strangely, his savior had not been Anders. A man was running away from him, toward the nearby battle. But Nils did not recognize the man. His legs were covered in forest camouflage pattern-ed trousers, with large stuffed pockets on the sides of the legs. He wore black leather boots, and a black T-shirt, covered with a fur vest. A two foot long wooden club dangled from his hand. The weapon had bands of black iron around the tip. Each band sported several two-inch-long, metal spikes. Most dripping blood. Below the iron bands, some of the metal spikes jutted right out of the wood. A long metal spike rose from the end of the weapon.

Nils sat up with his shield and watched the stranger sprint across the field. He had short blond hair that had been cut in patchy bits, most likely by himself. As he came across a Long Knife, he dodged and evaded the blades, his spiked club bashing into head after head.

The stranger leapt over Anders, who was tussling with a Long Knife on the ground—each man unarmed. He kept running, past Stig's fallen body, and past where Ulrik fought three men in a frantic, thrashing struggle. Nils had no doubt the men would fall before Ulrik's fury. His long blond hair, soaked from mist and sweat, Ulrik punched, kicked and clubbed the three unarmed men. His shield was as much a weapon as a defensive tool. Nils decided to learn all he could about using a shield—if they survived this bloody battlefield.

Nils staggered to his feet as Morten and Oskar stabbed the last of their opponents. They saw him looking and Oskar rushed over, while Morten limped, his leg dripping blood.

"Where is Erlend?" Oskar demanded.

"I do not know," Nils said. He pointed. "Who is that?"

The men turned to look at the stranger, who was just reaching the pile of bodies, under which was their leader.

He leaned down and pulled bodies away, flinging them with immense strength. They saw him drop his club and hold his hands out flat in front of him, then speak. A second passed, and he reached down to gently pull Val up off the ground.

Nils was shocked that she had taken his hand and allowed him to pull her to her feet. Her left arm was bleeding, but she seemed otherwise unhurt. The stranger bent to collect his club, and kept his eyes scanning the trees at the edge of the field, while Val turned her back to the man and collected her weapons from the ground.

Closer to them, Ulrik drove his fist into the face of the last living Long Knife. The opponent tumbled backward like a folding blanket, landing on the ground on the top of his head, his neck shattering with an audible set of cracks similar to the machine gun.

Nils turned back to Morten. "Do you need help to walk?"

"I will be okay."

The three of them approached Anders as he climbed to his feet. He looked a little dazed, but otherwise unhurt. Nils bent down to pick up one of the long knives, his own weapons temporarily lost. They joined Ulrik, who collected his ax, and then they all approached the stranger with caution.

Val saw them coming and shouted. "Find the weapon. This is not over if they can kill us from a distance."

Ulrik ran toward the edge of the forest, and after Morten said "Go," Oskar followed him. Anders went with him. Nils stayed with Morten, and he and the Laplander limped up to Val and the stranger.

"Who is this?" Morten asked.

Val and the stranger both turned to him. The man's short, badly cut hair was unusual when the rest of them all had longer hair. But his eyes still looked Nordic, even if his cheekbones betrayed him as different from them.

His clothes would have done that anyway.

"I am Heinrich," he said in their tongue, though it was heavily accented.

Before he could say more, Val interrupted. "He was the one who left us the food. Where is Erlend?"

The men all shrugged. They might not fully trust Heinrich, but he had proven himself to not be an enemy.

Ulrik, Oskar and Anders came jogging back from the trees. "They have gone," Ulrik called. "The weapon is broken." He explained the look of the thing, with a piece sticking awkwardly up in the air, and the links of the ammunition belt on the ground with the spent shells. He had never seen a machine gun before, but a quick look at the device in the small foxhole surrounded by sandbags had been enough for him to puzzle out how it had worked.

As they searched the field for Erlend, they first came to Stig's body, and Ulrik briefly recounted how the man had conquered his illness and his machine gun injuries to perform one last heroic, rage-fueled berserker attack. "He died well."

Morten sat in the field suddenly, grabbing his leg, before he leaned back in the grass.

"I will stay with him," Nils said. "Find Erlend."

Nils sat on the ground and pushed the body of a Long Knife aside. He had no wish to sit near the dead. When he did, though, the moved body uncovered what had been beneath it. Another, smaller body, pierced and punctured in seven different places—among them the eye socket and the throat.

"Never mind. I have found him."

30

Three of their number had died, and they were not over the mountains yet. Not halfway through with their journey. They still needed to get the genetic material and then retrace their steps back to the North. Val shivered at the thought of facing the Blue Men and the mutated octopus a second time.

Although they had lost Stig and Erlend, they had gained Ull—*Heinrich*, she reminded herself. The man had helped them cremate Stig and Erlend, and had revealed that he had been wandering alone in Germany when he had spotted them. He had been tailing them since shortly after their encounter with the Blue Men in Denmark.

"How were you able to find food, when we were not?" Anders had asked the German man.

"I was riding a bicycle," he admitted. "The noise of your engines was scaring the game away."

Val had further questioned the man to her satisfaction, and his eagerness to assist in the aftermath of the battle, as well as his timely aid during the clash, counted for much. The Vikings kept a close eye on him for the first few days, but the German was congenial and always helpful and upbeat.

Because they had not crossed many miles each day, due to the difficult terrain, Heinrich had been able to keep up with them, performing long days of pedaling on a two-wheeled bicycle with no motor. Anders, Morten and Oskar all admitted they had seen bicycles in the North, although they had never ridden on one. Val had seen one as well, but she had not joined the conversation.

When their fallen friends had been dealt with, their ashes spread on the breeze, and their spirits taken to Valhalla, Heinrich had taken Erlend's ATV, and with a few short lessons, he was competent at maneuvering the vehicle.

They had continued south, explaining to Heinrich that they had a mission on the other side of the mountains, and that they were honor-bound to finish it. With nowhere else to go, and no one else in the world, Heinrich had offered to accompany them the full way, and Val had accepted.

Now they rolled into a town with crumpled concrete walls, toppled orange tile roofs, the charred, singed remains of countless buildings and one unique architectural oddity. In fact, they would have passed the town by, for fear of yet another ambush, had it not been for that one strange feature.

While all the surrounding buildings were little more than rubble reclaimed by vegetation, one structure stood. "Ulm Church," Heinrich told them, Nils translating from German, since the man's ability with the northern tongue was limited. "It was the tallest church tower in the world once. I don't know if it still is." It climbed five hundred and thirty feet into the sky, like a charred, petrified fire giant from Muspelheim—the Land of Fire.

The darkened stone spire had been visible from the outskirts of town, and with everything else abandoned, it looked like a good place to spend the night—if it was likewise empty.

Unlike in Copenhagen, the roads were barely cleared, and in two cases they had to carefully crawl the ATVs up and over hills of uneven concrete and dirt.

Ulrik brought up the rear of their convoy, keeping his eyes on the surrounding scenery and on Heinrich. He had not said anything, but Val had understood the man did not trust the German.

The gothic towers loomed above the plaza where they parked the ATVs. It was mostly clear of the rubble, and it was obvious that since the city had fallen, the church, the only standing structure, had housed the dregs of humanity on occasion. The soaring arched doorways had been barricaded with stone and wire, but vines had long since grown over them. The coils of wire had rusted down to just a few bits still sticking up at random angles. The doors to the sides of the main entrance had been barricaded from top to bottom with rounded river stones. The tall stained glass windows were bricked up from the inside. Everything below a height of thirty feet was stained darker than the rest, a thin veneer of carbon from fires having scorched the outside of the structure.

A few of the spires on the sides of the massive structure had snapped off, and Val suspected they, like the charring, were the results of successive battles. But the main tower looked undamaged. The tower would have made a fantastic defensive position against hordes of Long Knives or Blue Men. Anything short of the double-headed octo-pus could have been repelled by just a few people barricaded inside. She wondered if they would find anyone alive inside. Or if not, how many dead would they find?

Val and the men checked the perimeter on foot, scrabbling over the detritus of city and war, until they had once again returned to Morten, who had waited with the ATVs in front. When they were sure the church was deserted, Val pointed at the door.

"Let us see if we can get it open—without destroying it." She didn't say that they might need to have a working door to defend themselves, once inside the church. It was understood. Even Heinrich nodded.

After clearing away the stones and crumbling wire, and hacking at the overgrown vines with their blades, Ulrik approached the solid slabs of scarred and dented wood that served as the doors to the old building. As he reached the door, he saw it was already open a crack. He touched his hand to it and the thing swung inward, the hinges creaking loudly.

There goes the element of surprise, he thought, but then he remembered the ATVs. He had grown used to the incessant buzzing of the seven engines, but for anyone that was hiding within, the noise would have announced the Vikings' arrival long before they had parked out front.

The interior was surprisingly bright. Light streamed in from clerestory windows set one hundred feet above the nave, near the roof. Everything lower had been boarded, bricked or covered with welded metal and concrete. Sunlight was unable to sneak through the blockades covering the windows that were once filled with stained glass, and which soared up the sides of the building.

There wasn't a single wooden church pew inside the nave. Instead, the interior had been filled with branches. The wooden limbs looked like the nest of a gigantic bird, or the fuel for an oversized bonfire that was never set to flame. The wood filled the space's center and was stacked twenty feet high.

"Interesting," Ulrik said. "We could make a campfire tonight."

Val pushed past him into the entrance hall's interior. "I think not. We could see the building for miles. A fire will be visible just as far."

"I will climb to the top," Morten said. "If there are still stairs."

After exploring the abandoned church with its strange cargo, they moved the ATVs into the building itself and barricaded the doors from the inside. They had been locked before by a thick slab of wood set into huge metal hooks. They used the wooden board, but reinforced the barrier by parking two ATVs sideways in front of the doorway. Then they wandered until they found the tower stairs. Anders and Morten went up first, and they were gone for a long time.

Val started to worry. Ulrik could see it in her face, but when the men came down, talking about how far they could see, how exciting it had been to release Skjold from the tower and that the mountains were visible in the distance, they were all excited to make the long climb.

Anders informed them that the ascent was 768 steps. At first Nils stalled at the idea, but Oskar convinced him to go. When the two men came back, Val and Ulrik began the long ascent. Heinrich would go on his own when they returned. He was trusted, but Morten and Anders reported that the final stage of the climb was tight, barely big enough for one man at a time. He said that Stig would never have fit, and the mention of the man's name dampened their spirits somewhat. Ulrik still set off to climb the steps, telling Val, "Come on. I want to see these mountains."

The top of the tower, as advertised, was a narrow concrete enclosed spiral stair with buttresses that stretched from it to the outer, lace-like, gothic structure of the tower.

The view was sensational.

The stairs opened to a small platform from which they could see the land south of the church. The snow covered Alps loomed in the distance, tall behind the nearby rolling green hills. The mountains were a barrier between their world and Niflheim, the darkest and coldest of the Norse nine realms.

"We will not make it through the mountains before the winter," Val said. Her frown revealed her dark thoughts, despite the beauty of the view.

"No. We will not," Ulrik said. Then he decided to broach the subject he had not had time to speak with her about since the river, when he had seen her swim. "Can I ask you about your eyes?"

She turned her face away from the view, and looked up at him. The platform was tight, and they stood close, so she needed to tilt her head to see his face. Her broken nose—like all of her injuries thus far—had healed completely. She reached up and pulled the tight, red-lensed goggles from her face. The rims of the black goggles had left pink indentations in her clear skin, and the lines circled her brilliant, emerald green eyes, calling all the more attention to them.

In all his life, Ulrik had only ever seen people with blue eyes. No one had ever seen another eye color. Even the Blue Men and the swastika-faced Long Knives had had blue irises.

It was one of the only things most Northmen knew of the greater history of the world. During the *Uttslettelse*—the Great Annihilation—only those of hardy Nordic stock, with bold features, blond hair and blue eyes, had survived the cataclysms. No one had seen different colored eyes since decades before Ulrik's birth.

"What is there to ask?" Val said, her face neutral. "I would appreciate it if you did not mention it to the others. It is difficult enough to maintain their trust in my leadership. Superstition would only make it harder."

"Of course," he said, giving her a curt nod. "But how is it that you are different from the rest of us?"

"I do not know. My parents were killed when I was quite young. My eyes are green for some reason. I find it is best to keep them hidden from view."

Ulrik suddenly realized the hardship green eyes would have caused a person. Any person. He felt a deep sadness in his heart for her.

"You have worn the goggles to keep your eyes hidden your whole life?" he asked.

"Not these," Val said, smiling. "I have gone through many pairs of goggles and eye covers over the years. But these have been the best."

"I am sorry. That must have been quite difficult."

"I am used to it now," she said, gently running her hand on his bare arm.

He felt a tingle race through his skin at her touch. But his attraction to her presented him with a problem. He had pledged himself to protect her and support her through their mission. If he allowed himself to have feelings for her, to want her, then she would become a weakness for him in battle. He would continually check on her in a fight—and it could cost him his life. Before he could change the subject, she did it for him.

"I thank you for your support on this trip, Ulrik. I could not have made it this far without you."

He paused a moment, considering his reply. She waited, content to let him have all the time he needed. Such was the Northern way. Silence often spoke volumes. Her sparkling green eyes filled him with confusion, but he found it hard to look away.

Eventually he broke the silence with the thing they both shared, which was more important than the both of them: the mission.

"We should go down, and rejoin the others."

She started for the stairs, and they descended in silence, to spend the night in the church, with the ghosts of the past haunting their thoughts.

31

South of the piled ruins of Ulm, they followed a thin tributary of the Danube river, never straying far from its life-giving water and the plentiful game found near it. The liquid was clear and pure, fed from the snows in the mountains that were its source and the group's destination.

With the blinding white mountains looming in the distance, juxtaposed as they were against the blue sky, it was hard for the Northmen to turn their thoughts to the difficulties that might await them. Instead they were pleased with the abundance of food—particularly Anders, who could show off his expertise and trade tips with Heinrich, redeeming himself in the eyes of the others as the better hunter and fisherman.

But the good times were not to last, and Val knew it.

Up until this point, they had been lucky to find propane along the way, which they had used to refuel the vehicles. They had found the gas in tanks attached to homes and buildings long defunct. Erlend had fitted the ATVs, which originally had tanks only large enough for one gallon of fuel, with twin eight-gallon surplus tanks on the rear. The massive silver drums added a lot of weight to the rear of the vehicles, so they had balanced the weight out by packing most of their gear on the front of the quads. He had explained that the added weight would reduce the distance they could get from a gallon of fuel, but due to the poor quality of the roads, they normally traveled at a very slow speed, thus increasing the distance they could travel on a single gallon. Ultimately, the sacrifice in distance from the weight was balanced out by the pace. They had needed to refuel only four times on their nearly 1500 mile journey.

But now the time had almost come again, and none of the standing structures they had passed in the last week had been contenders for a structurally sound propane tank. None of the others had mentioned the steadily lowering gauges Erlend had attached to the exterior of their surplus tanks, but Val had noticed that their red needles had crawled toward 'Empty,' and now all that remained was from their onboard tanks.

If they could not find more of the gas, soon they would be walking.

After passing countless crumbling farms and tiny ramshackle towns long since abandoned and reclaimed by nature, Val spotted a sprawling, low building to her right, just off the road. She raised an arm, and the others rolled up next to her on the road.

The exterior of the structure was white, though most of it was covered by trees and vines growing out of the roof and from cracks in the concrete on the side of the structure. All its windows were gone, leaving dark gaps, sometimes overhung with dangling foliage.

"Why do we stop?" Morten asked. His once neatly slicked blond hair was now simply brushed back over his head. His voice was hoarse and gravelly from not speaking or drinking for hours. Even if she didn't want to stop because of the building, they would have needed to stop anyway for food and water, and to relieve themselves.

Val spread her knee out and away from the ATV, leaning on the right footboard, so Morten could see. She knocked her knuckle on the silver fuel cap, in the center of the ATV, just in front of the black handle bars. It made a hollow *ting* noise, when she did. No words were necessary.

She had explained to them early on where Halvard had suggested they look for viable tanks of propane. Larger, industrial areas were better than small houses. And this building was the first large thing they had seen still roughly intact, since the church in Ulm.

Ulrik turned off the motor to his ATV, and dismounted. "Spread out. Pair up."

Nils went with Heinrich, who had his bow out, ready for danger or any edible animals they might encounter in or around the broad structure. Morten and Oskar teamed up, as usual, and Ulrik and Anders moved in through an open doorway. Val looked up at the low roofline of the building.

"Heinrich," she called. "Lift me." She nodded at a concrete lip too high for her to reach. The man slung his bow and laced his fingers into a step. Val stepped into his grip and sprang upward, partly from her own leap and partly from the German shoving upward with his strong arms.

She flew high enough that she could thrust her arms straight down to catch the ledge, and then lift up her right leg. Then she stood. Along the wide, path-like ledge of concrete was a string of missing windows. Above them was another lip, and she leapt up, snagging the edge with her fingers and pulling herself up to the next level, which had thigh-height windows. Then she reached the roof. She scrambled up and looked out over a sea of broken and cracked black solar panels. Trees grew from some of them. Others were covered in thick carpets of mold, funguses and lichens.

Some of the panels had large nests of sticks, but they looked long abandoned. Instead of checking them for eggs, she skirted the edge of the roof, searching for exterior propane tanks, while the men searched the interior of the building for a basement or a loading dock. The building was large enough that it had probably stored large quantities of goods or vehicles—judging by the size of some of the doors. There was a better than average chance they would find what they needed here.

Peering down to the ribbed and buckled expanse of parking lot that surrounded the building, she saw the rust-red colored roofs of several long vehicles arrayed around the structure like fighters. More of the buses, Nils had described. All were missing tires, and most were missing windows. *They might serve as a place to camp for the night,* Val thought, *if animals have not been inside.*

A loud squawking noise spun her around. Perched next to a large nest she had thought abandoned was a bird unlike any she had ever seen. It stood taller than her on yellow webbed feet, like a duck's. But instead of the smaller duck's beak, this bird's bill was longer than her arm, and had a strange bulbous throat that distended down its feathered chest. The throat looked big enough to hold Val, if she curled tight into a ball.

The bird twisted its head at her and spread its wings—four of them. One set of wings protruded out from under the other. The feathers extended to their maximum reach and twitched, like Aspen leaves dancing in the wind. Then the massive bird opened its huge maw, revealing sharp teeth lining the upper and lower edges of its spread beak, now resembling a shark more than a bird.

More so than with the lumbering mutant bear or the epic octopus, Val felt a tingle of fear zip up her spine to the back of her neck. This creature, if it turned violent, could maneuver through the air, defeating any combat strategy she could devise. The bird was clearly displeased, and telling her so with belch-like squawks.

But there was nowhere for her to go without turning her back on the creature. This side of the roof did not have terraced ledges, like the side she had climbed. It was a straight twenty foot drop to the ground. She considered getting a running start and jumping to the roof of one of the buses, but doing so might result in her plunging through the rusted metal surface. And she felt certain that if she turned her back on the bird-creature, it would attack.

Instead she took a single threatening step forward, spreading her arms wide, her long ax extended in one hand, making her 'wing' look longer than it truly was. As she moved. she shouted, "Aaaaahhhhh!"

The bird faltered for a second, probably unaccustomed to other creatures challenging its great size. Then it stepped forward as well. It dipped its head, gnashing its strange beak-teeth, and clucked, almost like a chicken.

The huge bird lunged as Val darted right, arcing around the creature in a semi-circle, as if she were trying to get to the bird's eggs. But she wasn't. She was positioning herself in front of the ledges she had climbed, her only hope of retreat.

The bird had other ideas, flapping its multiple wings. The creature banked back from its lunge, its feet left the ground and it swooped toward Val's head. Its beak split open wide like deadly arms ready to embrace her.

32

Val brought her ax handle across, smacking the bird in the side of its giant beak. The huge flexible throat wobbled from the strike. The wings faltered.

She had no wish to actually kill the creature. It was probably protecting its young. The last and only memory Val had from her childhood was of her mother, protecting her. The brave woman had sent her into the frigid sea and raced across the ice to face the men who had murdered her father. Val felt a kinship of sorts with the massive, mutated bird.

As the creature tumbled down to the roof between green-encrusted solar panels, Val decided she would retreat, leaving the creature to care for its young.

She backed toward the edge of the roof as the bird flapped up and landed on the edge of a solar panel. Once again, its wings spread as it cawed at her, a threatening posture meant to send her on her way.

Val was ten feet from the bird now, and it showed no more signs of giving chase. She thought she might be able to turn her back on it. She just wanted to take a few more steps first.

She didn't get them.

She turned just in time to see Anders standing on the edge of the roof, his bow extended, an arrow nocked and about to be loosed—directly at her face. She ducked and the arrow sailed past her, sinking into the bird's chest, ending its life with a loud squealing squawk.

Val stood again and turned to assess the damage. The bird slowly toppled left, one of its webbed feet sliding off the solar panel, and then its body collapsing over like a falling tree.

She turned back on the archer, a scowl clouding her face. "There was no need to kill it."

Anders shrugged, turned and leapt down to the first ledge. "It was a pitiful, deformed thing. It did not deserve to live. If I hadn't killed it, Skjold would have."

The people of the North had long known of creatures affected by rampant radiation in certain parts of the globe. She had encountered that attitude before. Mutated creatures were generally not eaten, and if discovered close to human populations they were killed and removed by whomever was unlucky enough to draw the shortest straw. No one had any tolerance for any kind of deformity. To be deformed meant you were weak. To be weak meant you would die in this harsh world.

She thought of her eyes and their strange green color. Would Anders, a calm and usually rational man, far more balanced than the others that had accompanied her on this journey, attempt to kill her if he saw her different eyes? Would the others? She had been stunned that Ulrik had accepted them so easily.

She spat on the roof, then leapt down the ledges and dropped to the ground unassisted, rejoining the others.

On the ground, the group had returned from their recon of the building's interior, empty handed.

"No tanks on the sides of the buildings, either," Val said. "But there are many of the long vehicles."

"Buses," Nils clarified.

"Yes," Val agreed. "We might find some of the fuel in one of those."

"They ran on a different fuel," Nils said.

"Well, look around anyway."

They found no propane that day.

The end came thirty miles further south, and just twenty miles short of the mountains. It arrived with a sputtering noise, followed by Oskar's ATV coasting to a stop at the side of the road.

"What is our plan now?" Anders asked. "We never discussed this possibility."

Val got off her ATV and looked at the gas gauges on all the vehicles. There was no way of sharing the fuel. The propane was a compressed gas, not a liquid. It was difficult enough getting it in the vehicles. As it was, without Erlend—and Stig, who had also learned how to fuel the vehicles—the next refueling would be a challenge. And that was assuming they could find more propane.

"We could simply press on without these vehicles," Heinrich suggested. "I made do for quite some time with a two-wheeler powered by my legs alone."

"For that matter, we could walk," Val said. "But there is no denying the advantage these have given us." She patted the nearly empty fuel tank on her ATV. "For now, let us try to pull Oskar behind us. We will run the tanks dry until they cannot go further or until we find more fuel."

"And if we do not find fuel?" Morten asked. He looked as if he didn't care one way or the other, and Val thought he was asking the question—acting always as devil's advocate—merely out of habit.

As the chill breeze blew her hair, she looked at Ulrik and saw that he understood without the vehicles they would not make it past the mountains before winter.

"We will deal with it when it happens. For now, let us get a rope on Oskar's ATV."

Anders, Oskar and Morten tied ropes to their ATVs. With both Anders and Morten towing Oskar as dead weight, they would split the load and lessen the increased fuel consumption on their own vehicles.

Once the rig was set, with Oskar sitting astride his quad, its transmission in neutral, the group proceeded down the road, keeping a slower pace than usual. Recognizing how vulnerable Oskar would be, Val rode on one side of the tow ropes, and Ulrik on the other, ensuring that if attack came, he would be protected.

They made it a mile, Skjold pacing them in the sky in great looping circles, before Morten's ATV died.

Another jury-rigged towing system resulted in Anders and Nils pulling Morten, with Oskar towed directly behind him.

Half a mile later Nils's ATV coughed and quit. As Anders slowed to a stop, his own quad started to make burbling noises.

"We are done," Val pronounced.

As the others pulled the quads to the side of the road, Val consulted her map.

With the ATVs off the road, Morten began unpacking his camping blankets.

Without looking up from her map, which she had practically memorized, despite not being able to read the labels on it, she spoke to him. "Do not do that, Morten. You will be moving again soon."

He looked up, not comprehending. "Is there a fuel source nearby?"

"I have no idea."

"Then what?" Ulrik asked. He looked as defeated as the others.

She stood up straight, her hands dropping to her hips. "Heinrich will come with me, and we will search ahead on foot for more fuel sources."

Morten threw his blanket down in frustration. "And what are the rest of us supposed to do? Pull these ATVs behind us, as we walk?"

Val walked toward the angered Laplander. She stopped when the rims of her goggles were fogging from his breath. "That..." she said, "...is a very good idea. I will put you in charge of arranging that while we scout ahead for propane. It is good to know I can count on you, Morten the Hammer. Thank you."

Then she turned her back on him and began walking down the road in the direction they had been traveling. Heinrich hurried to catch up with her, passing by Ulrik, whose shoulders were quivering slightly as he stifled his laughter at Morten.

Behind them, Morten seethed.

33

The Alps loomed ahead, angry white fangs stabbing into the sky. The mountain tops were coated in snow, and the clouds had pulled in around them like a shroud, promising more icy resistance in the days to come. For days, Val and Heinrich ranged ahead of the others, leaving markers when they needed to leave the road to skirt obstacles, but they found no sign of propane gas.

As they moved steadily southwest toward the imposing mountains, they noticed a building on the side of a hill. It stood out like a shining beacon. It was low enough on the mountains that it was still surrounded by greenery and not snow, and as a result, its white coloring made it stand out even more.

"A home of some kind?" Val asked.

Heinrich, despite being German, previously explained his lack of knowledge about his own country. He had not traveled far until those living with him in the northern part of the country perished. The man shrugged.

"Too large," Val grunted, answering her own question.

"A stronghold, then?"

Val considered, peering at the white structure on the hillside, glowing in the sun. It was too far away to see details, but she could tell it was huge. If they were going to find any supplies—including the propane they needed so badly—this massive structure was their best bet. But one detail stood out, and made her uneasy. The building was clear of vegetation. Someone had been caring for the place.

"We will find out," she said. "It is now our destination. We are too close to the winter now, I fear. If we find no fuel, perhaps this structure will provide suitable shelter for the winter."

Val kept her concerns to herself. If the structure was intact, they would probably need to take it by force. They had already lost Stig and Trond, two of their best fighters. And while Erlend had not been the strongest among them, his loss was keenly felt, as well. They needed a break, but the jagged white towers clawing into the sky on the horizon promised only more struggle.

She knelt down and used the pointed tip of her hand-ax to carve a crude drawing of the structure in the distance, and an arrow pointing at it. Their destination would be clear to the others. Although the structure was off their intended route, she thought the diversion would be worth it.

As the afternoon wore on and they passed by a lake, the structure in the hills resolved into the most imposing fortress either of them had ever seen. Consisting of multiple structures spread five hundred feet along a cliff top, the fortress was topped with several towers, pinnacles, statues, sculptures and ornamental turrets. While the stone walls glowed a whitish gray against the pervasive forest behind it, the rooftops and turrets were all a darker slate gray that looked like it had once been a shade of blue, before time and neglect had allowed the magnificent structure to fade under unrelenting rain and snow.

Val had seen pictures in a child's book, long ago, and the word came to her just before Heinrich spoke the word aloud, "Schloss." It was the same in German as it was in the language of the North. "It is a castle. I did not think any were left standing. It looks like the church in Ulm."

She understood that he meant it was similar in the fact that it stood, while most of the villages they had seen had been reduced to piles of cracked masonry. The castle before them was far more magnificent than the church had been. She guessed that the building was a military stronghold, designed to take a beating. The builders had done a good job. She supposed many of the upper structures—gables, dormers, tiny windows and balconies—were all more for show than for combat. While she couldn't yet see the building's base, it would need to be massive and thick to support the battlements' weight.

Nearing the castle, trees sometimes obscured their view of the building's magnificence. Along the twisting road they found destroyed and battle-scarred buildings—some showing the charred remains of fire damage. The road wound past large open stretches that were once for parking vehicles, and which were now being swallowed by green, like everywhere else in the world. When they glimpsed the castle, it was apparent that the designers had chosen their spot well—it would be virtually impossible to attack the place from any direction other than from the front.

At the end of the road, the winding path stopped at a gate, guarded on either side by two cylindrical stone towers. Arching over the gate was a huge red brick building. The gate stood ajar. Beyond it they could see the castle's courtyard. Piles of stone and wood debris rose up on either side of the doorway.

"Remains of past battles," Val suggested.

Heinrich peered at the pile to their left, going down the hillside. "The grass has grown up over it in places."

"Long past battles," Val agreed. It was unsurprising to her that people had been able to successfully fend off invaders from this fortress. The only question was, *How long ago?* She nodded her head at the interior courtyard, and Heinrich followed her in.

Past the arched entryway, which framed the main part of the castle, a thirty-foot wall stood before them. They walked around the large courtyard, looking back at the gatehouse. It was a shade of tan-orange, with a clock on top of it. There were well barricaded doors and stairwells in all directions except for one—the main stairwell stretching to the top of the wall, and leading to the next courtyard and the main building. They took the steps up to the next level, amazed at the scope and breadth of the place. The next courtyard was rectangular and pointed directly to a stairwell leading to the second story of the main building. All the lower level windows were heavily secured with wood and crossed iron grills.

Although there were tufts of grass poking up from the cobblestoned floor of the courtyard, Val noted that the vegetation was short— just an inch in length. As if it had been cut back recently.

They took five tentative steps toward the main building when a wooden door on a fifth-floor balcony opened, and a silhouette of a man could be seen.

"*Guten tag*," he called. He sounded old, or perhaps his voice had not been used for a long time. His vowels creaked.

Heinrich immediately replied in German, returning the man's greeting of *Good day.*

They exchanged a few words in German, and then the man's voice brightened slightly. He went back in and closed the door.

Val turned to Heinrich for an explanation.

"He asked if we were here to take the castle from him. I told him no and that we actually needed help. He said we should wait."

34

After a few minutes, they heard loud clunks from the other side of the second story door. It opened to reveal a small, frail, old man. He was probably in his eighties, with wispy thin hair on a liver-spotted head. He walked folded over, nearly into a right angle, and held up by a gnarled, polished wooden cane.

"*Willkommen in Neuschwanstein*," the man said in the same creaky voice Val had heard from the balcony.

Heinrich began to translate, and the old man interrupted them, speaking in the northern dialect of Val's people.

"Apologies. Welcome to the New Swan Stone Castle." He smiled a gap-toothed grin at them.

"You speak my language very well," Val said, surprised.

"It is very similar to the Norwegian my grandmother spoke," he said, dismissing the linguistic feat with a wave of his hand. "Come in, come in. It has been a very long time since I have entertained guests here in the castle." He turned and hobbled back through the door.

"You are here with your family?" Val asked, following the man through the doorway.

"No, no. All gone now, aren't they?" the man said, hobbling into a hall. The walls were adorned with paintings and tapestries, the ceiling hung with long disused chandeliers now covered in cobwebs. "Oh, this place is a beauty, isn't she?"

Val thought the man's form of speaking in questions was peculiar, and she soon realized the reason. "Are you here all by yourself, sir?"

He turned with a simple grin and nodded. "Yes, miss. Just me, Jan Werther. Last of my people. We repelled a lot of invaders when I was younger, and then they stopped coming. Well, when Frauke died—that was my sister, don't you know? Well, it was just me here. She was the last of them to go."

"I am very sorry, sir," Val said.

"Oh, aren't you a sweetie? What was your name?"

She introduced them both. "We also have some friends who will be coming this way in a day or two."

"That's fine, fine," he said, leading them deeper into the maze of halls. Val had already lost her way, spending too much time gazing at the opulence around her instead of memorizing the way out. But she felt that she could trust this old man. Heinrich likewise seemed to feel at ease.

The floors were intricate patterned woods, and then flat stone tiles laid out in patterns. The walls were a cavalcade of colors and hues, with sconces, lamps, alcoves and columns. Parts of the castle were clearly original, stemming back who knew how many hundreds of years. Other parts had obviously been renovated with modern, post-cataclysm life in mind. Once-electric lamps had been replaced with thick candles that had dripped wax for so many years that they formed thick stalactites dropping down to mounds on the floor. Under the lamps, the mounds were beginning to form their own stalagmites growing upward.

In other cases, wooden and metal structures had been set up with ladders, allowing people to reach otherwise inaccessible parts of walls or fixtures. For what purposes, Val could not guess.

"Where are my manners? You said you needed help, yes, young Heinrich? What was it you needed?" The man spoke over his shoulder as he led them deeper into the bowels of the castle.

"We were looking for propane, a fuel used in the old days," Heinrich said. If the old man heard, he gave no indication.

He led them to a small closet and opened it, revealing a room just barely large enough for the three of them to stand in. Along the wall were a twin set of ropes. Once he had ushered them in, he closed the door, sealing the three of them in the tight space.

"I've got a small garden in the back. Just enough for a lone man like me, you understand. Then there are the stores of dried goods. Yep, plenty of food here. There are also a few solar panels."

The man grabbed one of the ropes and gave it a tug, with a surprisingly strong arm. When he did, the floor of the tiny room lurched downward. Then he turned to Heinrich. "Maybe you would be so kind as to propel us, son? My arms do get tired operating the lift."

"Certainly." Heinrich stepped around Werther and began hoisting the rope, hand over hand, slowly lowering the elevator car.

"I'll let you know when we're there," Werther said. "So, where was I? Ah, yes. Lots of food. Frozen food. Jars and tins. Plenty to go around. And if you need to, this place is easy to defend. Although it's been so long since anyone has been this way. From the towers you can see forever on a clear day. I've known you were headed this way for the last week. I left the front gate open just for you. I was hoping that those fellows following you were friends of yours and not chasing after you."

Val smiled. "They are good friends. They have come to protect me on my mission."

"Good, good," Werther said, showing no interest in her mission.

As Heinrich lowered them, the open face of the elevator passed several doors, until they had descended deep underground. Heinrich let go of the rope when he could lower them no further.

Werther opened the door into a gray stone hallway, devoid of the upper floors' charm. He ambled along the hallway, heading for a metal door at its end.

"How is it you have managed on your own for so long, Mr. Werther?" Val asked him, one hand slinking down to the handle of her long ax. The change in the environment had made her suspicious, although she had noticed no change in the old man's demeanor.

"Oh, it has been lonely at times, but there's always work to do, isn't there?"

He reached for the handle on the metal door, and Val stepped ahead, reaching in front of him, grasping the handle. "Allow me," she said.

The man just bowed slightly.

She flung the door open wide, and it swung inward on oiled hinges, revealing a huge open space. The floor was flat stone. Long tubes along the ceiling glowed white like the sun on a cloudy day. In one corner of the massive room was a strange four-wheeled vehicle with large metal prongs sticking off the front like tusks. Val could tell from its design and huge knobby tires that it was meant to lift heavy loads. She spotted a flat wooden pallet, stacked high with sacks, and guessed the vehicle was meant to lift the entire pallet and all its cargo at once. Along one wall of the room were several large waist-high white metal boxes, big enough for a human being to recline in.

But Werther pointed to a different wall, where there were tall white metal cages. They were adorned with writing in German and pictures of little propane tanks, along with other diagrams and images depicting the need to keep open flames away from the racks. Inside the spaces through the cages, Val could see forty bottles of propane, each one three times the size of the ATV's extra tanks.

"Those the things you're needing then?"

35

Even with winter fast approaching, the day was warm, and Ulrik was sweating rivers down his face. He had shed his shirt and cloak, his large ax on the ATV behind him. He walked bent forward at a forty-five-degree angle, pulling the rope that towed his inoperable vehicle.

Val had put Morten in charge of the men, but each day when Ulrik moved his dead ATV onto the road and began pulling, the Laplander had been content to let him lead the procession. In fact, Morten had taken up a defensive position at the rear of the convoy, with Oskar just ahead of him, and Nils and Anders—their weakest members—in the middle. Ulrik appreciated the gesture. The Laplander wasn't trying to distance himself from Ulrik, but rather the man quietly accepted responsibility without being told.

They had started out as potential enemies, but Morten had shown his worth so far. Less could be said for Oskar. The man was, as ever, Morten's ally, but he seemed reluctant to do much of anything else, besides bemoan their fate.

"How much longer?" Oskar asked, pulling his ATV in the middle of the convoy.

It was not lost on Ulrik that Nils had the heaviest vehicle with its improvised second seat, and yet the thin historian remained silent in this company—unless anyone sought his counsel. Yet Oskar always complained.

Ulrik ignored the younger Laplander, looking ahead. "Something is coming," he said, stopping the convoy, and allowing his ATV to roll to a stop. He reached over the saddle and retrieved his large ax.

Morten stepped up next to him, peering into the distance.

Whatever was coming stood as tall as a man, yet it loped on the road like a large, black animal. A horse, or something else. Around it, in constant movement, were a swirl of short, dark, creatures filling both sides of the road, darting back and forth with frenetic energy.

"Whatever they are," Morten said, pulling his sword, "they are coming fast." He looked to Ulrik, as if for guidance, but the larger man stayed still, so he turned back to the oncoming threat and waited.

"I don't believe it," Nils said, with deep concern in his voice. As the huge black creature resolved, the smaller shapes around it were recognizable as a large pack of dogs. Many of them had beards of dripping foam at their mouths, and large boils or furless distended skin on their bodies. They darted away from and back to the dark central creature, which was taller than a man. In some cases they snapped and bit at each other. "It is an ape. It will be strong like Trond. *Stronger* than Trond."

"I will take it," Ulrik said. "The rest of you, the hounds."

And then the oncoming horde of animals closed the distance. Anders loosed several arrows, taking down dog after dog, his arrows piercing boils and spraying greenish liquid into the air. The pack consisted of thirty animals of varying size. There were breeds Ulrik had never seen, as well as many of the northern wolfhounds he knew. He had seen them in the North, surviving in forests in packs. Large animals with pointed ears, tufted fur, and long, thin legs like reindeer.

As the horde grew closer, he saw that one of the animals on the fringe of the pack, waiting for a perfect opportunity, was an actual wolf, white and gray, with black paws. Like the dogs, it was missing patches of fur, and one entire leg was hairless, with just the paw still covered in black fur, like the creature was wearing a sock. Directly on the top of its head, a massive boil had pushed upward, as if the creature's brain was trying to escape.

But the ape in the center of this strange animal grouping was terrifying. It stood slightly taller than Ulrik, and it walked on all fours, like a dog. If it were to stand on its short hind legs, it would tower over him. The creature was broad and thick, its back and hind legs a silvery white in color. The animal had a vertical scar down its face, and a look of intelligence in its eyes. Most disturbing was that it wore human clothes. Canvas trousers covered its legs, and the beast wore a blanket over its chest like a poncho, tied at the waist with a belt containing a few small pouches. It held back, as the dogs came on, like a leader sending the soldiers in first. But Ulrik was having none of that. He wanted the beast's blood.

As a hound came rushing at him, he swept his leg out, kicking the creature Morten's way. Morten promptly skewered the animal with his sword. The other dogs broke right and left, around Ulrik, heading for the others, gnashing teeth and yipping, as foam sprayed from their mouths.

He ignored them and strode toward the waiting ape. As he did, the animal's human-like golden-brown eyes never left him, and its nostrils—black as night—flared in and out, as it took deep breaths, anticipating the fight.

It is intelligent, Ulrik thought.

The creature's mouth turned down in a sneer, then it leapt in the air, heading straight for Ulrik.

Its vertical and horizontal leap was stunning, clearing five feet up and twice that in distance, bringing the massive ape straight for Ulrik's head. He lunged upward with his ax, and at the last second dove to the side. The spike at the tip of the weapon's handle, between the blades, rammed into the creature's nose. Then as Ulrik's weight pulled the ax sideways, the blade sliced across the animal's mouth and shoulder, biting deeply.

Ulrik rolled away, tumbling on the ground and twisting as he came back up, the ax at the ready for another slash.

The ape howled in pain, its mouth opening to a huge diameter, the lips peeling back. Its long yellowed teeth spread wide enough to swallow a human head whole.

Behind the ape, the dog pack snapped and bit at Nils and Oskar as the two men lunged and swiped at the canines. On the other side of the stalled convoy, Anders fired arrow after arrow into the flanks of the hungry dogs, but they kept moving, snarling and yipping, sensing a tasty meal. They might die for it, but none of the animals showed the slightest sign of backing off. Morten held three of the larger wolf-hounds at bay with long sideways sweeps from his sword.

The ape ran at Ulrik this time, lowering its shoulder, and before he could bring his ax in, the animal rammed his stomach, sending him flying backward, the ax clattering to the road.

Ulrik had wondered in his youth what flying would feel like. Now he was actually doing it. The beast had hit him so hard, his body had left the earth, though he was quickly returning to it. He did the only thing he could think of—he rolled himself into a tight ball, hoping that he would be able to roll with the fall.

When he landed in the tall grass, he was pleased to still be alive. It hurt, and it stole his breath, but as hoped, his body rolled and tumbled through the tall weeds until he was unsure of which direction was up. He could see nothing past the golden grasses, but he could hear heavy grunting coming his way. He felt the rippling footfalls of the creature barreling toward him.

And then there was another sound he could not identify. Something like a low thrumming hum.

He was down to just two knives. He grabbed both of them, blades pointed downward, and he scrambled to his hands and feet, keeping low in the tall grass, hoping the creature would not spot him right away, so he could get his bearings.

The thundering footfalls grew closer. *Coming from the left,* he thought, when he heard the animal's grunting. Instead of turning, he leapt upward and left, swinging out blindly with both blades.

As soon as he cleared the grass, he saw the situation, and realized that the ape had made an error. It wasn't running toward him—it was running beside him. Ulrik's body spun in the air like a child's thrown plaything, the tips of his knives grazing the side of the ape's head as it barreled past him. Blood arced away from the creature. It howled at the impact, but it was moving too quickly to stop.

Instead, the animal dove down into the tall grasses, rolling forward and twisting to a stop on its four limbs. The beast roared and pounded the ground in aggravation, about to lose itself in an ape-like berserker rage.

The thrumming noise grew louder, distracting the enraged ape, and pulling its gaze back the way it had come.

Something huge rushed past Ulrik, and he dove left, not knowing what it was, but recognizing that it was large and fast.

When he landed on his feet he understood.

It was some kind of massive vehicle—a much larger version of the ATVs. Val was driving the thing, and Heinrich was hanging on to its side, his cudgel in hand and already bloodied from one of the dogs. The vehicle had long metal prongs on the front of it, and as he watched, they raised slightly, moving up to chest height for the large ape.

The animal stood its ground.

Just before the vehicle rammed into it at full speed, the beast leapt at the thing.

But Ulrik didn't see the impact. Instead, something tackled him from behind, clawing at his back. He toppled over into the waving stalks of grass, losing one of his knives, but swiping with the other. It connected with something hard, but then teeth sank into his wrist.

The wolf, he thought.

He reached out with his free hand, grasping the back of the creature's bulbous head, preventing it from thrashing his arm. He thrust his head forward, smashing his forehead on the creature's snout and eyes, and rupturing the massive boil on the animal's skull with a gout of warm liquid.

The canine yelped and released its hold on him, attempting to recoil from the pain. But Ulrik would not let go. He smashed his head down again on the animal's skull, hearing a loud crack under the pus and gore, and feeling the surface of the beast's face turn to pulp. Then he hit it a third time and a fourth. When he pulled his forehead away, the animal's face was a jagged mess of bone and shiny blood.

When he staggered to his feet, he nearly dropped again, his head dizzy from the repeated battering he had given the wolf. As he looked around, he saw that the battle was over. The immense ape had been pierced through the chest by the long metal tines on the front of Val's vehicle, and the German had leapt off the side and killed another dog. He was using his foot to push it off the end of a short sword Ulrik had not seen the man use before.

Around them, there were dead and wounded dogs everywhere. The last few left breathing whimpered and squealed as Anders fired arrows into their heads and then retrieved the bolts for his quiver.

Val climbed down from her mechanical steed and walked over to Ulrik, pointing back the way her vehicle had come. She was pointing to a cart filled with cylindrical propane tanks. The cart did not have an engine or handlebars like the ATVs. He realized that Val and Heinrich had towed the thing.

They had arrived just in time. He honestly didn't think the group would have been able to take the ape. His head was still ringing, and he suspected some of that was from his trip through the air.

"We heard you needed some fuel," Val said.

"Your timing was perfect," he told her.

But instead of sharing in the joy of the moment, she looked up at the sky.

He cast his eyes up in time to see the first vanguard of snowflakes descending from the suddenly leaden sky. As he turned his head down to look at her, the flakes settled on the black leather shoulders of Val's jacket.

"You are wrong, Ulrik. I think we were far too late."

36

"I warned you the Völkisch were morons."

Zeilly pouted as she followed Borss up the snowy incline. The man pounded through the snow as if the extra weight he carried in the form of the spiked metal chestplate and gauntlets was nothing. She was not weak, but she could barely lift the chestplate. Borss was a mountain, though, and with the spikes protruding from his torso, he looked like a mountain that wanted to kill things.

She had to make her way through the drifts by following in his footsteps. In some places the snow was hip deep on her.

"Soon it won't matter," Borss boomed from ahead of her. "My informant tells me they are snowed in for the winter. In the mountains."

"Then we can pursue them. Capture them where they wait," Zeilly persisted.

Borss ignored her and continued up the slope toward a metal tower on the hilltop. She followed him to the base of the thing, the wind suddenly ripping into her through her furs, without the mountain to block the assault.

Borss, seeming not to notice the additional chill, began the ascent up the metal steps.

Zeilly followed him, counting the one hundred steps to the platform, where the messenger birds huddled in little coops. As she expected, the bird they sought—far more intelligent than the oversized mutated pigeons—waited for them on the wooden post extending from the coop.

The witch woman stood by as Borss deftly tied a tiny message capsule to the bird's leg with twine. He experienced no difficulty, even though the metal jointed fingers of the gauntlets should have made the task impossible. But Zeilly knew—from both pleasure and pain he had inflicted on her—that Borss was incredibly dexterous.

When he finished, he extended one gauntleted wrist, and the bird nimbly hopped onto his forearm. Borss brought the bird up to his face, looking it in the eye. The messenger looked like it was intent on receiving his instructions. That or it was contemplating tearing Borss's eyes out.

"Go to Kinsker," Borss told the bird. He held his arm out, and the bird launched into the sky with a powerful flapping of its wings. It stopped its ascent just a few feet above Borss's head and then dove down the length of the tower and arced out over the snowy landscape.

"Kinsker?" Zeilly asked. "That maniac? Why not use the time to pursue them across the miles. We could be there before they can cross the mountains."

Borss, ever mercurial, whirled on her. "You want to know why not?"

Then he was in motion. He grabbed her, and before Zeilly knew what was happening, she felt the icy cold tearing at her face and the wind flapping her furs. She only just processed the fact that he had thrown her off the platform and she was plunging one hundred feet down into the snowy hillside.

She started to scream, but her body crashed into the deep drift, snow ramming into her mouth. The landing hurt, but it was surprisingly soft. She began to wretch and sputter, coughing snow and lunging upward with both arms and legs.

Her head broke the surface of the snow, and she shook her head, her hair flying, as she still clawed at the snow all around her.

Eventually she stopped and opened her eyes to see she was in a waist deep drift, nearly halfway down the hillside.

She turned and looked back to see Borss slowly descending the metal steps, no apparent concern for her safety.

But she was unhurt except for her pride. Then she started wading from the deep snow back toward the path Borss had forged on their way up the hill.

Borss passed her position, striding down the path as easily as he had forged up it. "That is why. The winter will hinder our journey, just as much as it prevents them from crossing the mountains. Besides, the rest of my forces are not yet returned from the East. Kinsker's freaks will take care of them. And if they do not, it will be no great loss. I can always forge an alliance with his enemies."

Zeilly said nothing as she plunged on through the drifts toward the path. By the time she reached it, Borss was several hundred yards away.

Bastard, she thought. *He would just leave me. He would leave anyone.*

Because he was far enough away, and because she was frustrated, she called out after him. "And if they make it past Kinsker and obtain your prize?"

When the huge man made no reply, the witch woman stumbled down the path after him. She wondered whether he had realized the snow drifts were deep enough to break her fall. She honestly could not decide.

When Borss had nearly reached the edge of the industrial ruins he called 'his estate', and Zeilly was still two hundred paces behind him, he finally responded. "My forces will have returned by Spring. And the Northmen will need to return northward eventually to return to their homes. Provided my informant is not killed, we will know when they are coming, and we will lay in wait."

Finally, Zeilly thought. *Now that I know his plan, I can move on with mine.*

She had never intended to be his vassal forever. All she had needed was a way to seize some power for herself. And Borss's prize would give her just that. All she needed now was to intercept one of the messages from his informant, and hopefully determine what this elusive prize was. Then she simply needed to figure out to whom Borss intended to sell it. It was what he had excelled at. Finding what one group of people had and what another group of people needed. Then taking it through guile and force. More often the latter. But Zeilly was capable of far more guile than Borss could imagine. By Spring he would be dead, and his men, terrified as always, would be working for her.

37

The world was ice and snow. So familiar. It had been that way for most of her young life. At just twenty-four, Val was younger than all the men under her command, including the German. She had been on her own for eighteen years, scavenging, making due, fighting to survive.

All of it had taken place in ice and snow.

But now they were stranded, the drifts and ravines of snow in the mountains so deep that no man or beast could make it through the mountains until the summer. Personally, Val thought the mutant bear from Sweden would have stood a chance, but she and her men were exhausted, and despite their restlessness, the chance to heal and regain their strength was crucial and somewhat welcome.

Unfortunately, the ghosts of the last several hundred miles followed them. Werther passed away in his sleep just five weeks into their stay at the spectacular castle. The man's death, though natural and from a long life well lived, still cast a pall on the celebratory nature of the group's initial stay, as the snows and storms had swept in, blanketing the landscape in brilliant white. At first, the men had grumbled that they would be stuck for the winter. But once old Werther had introduced them to the food and wine—hundreds of bottles of different vintages, stretching back hundreds of years—the mood had shifted.

Werther had explained to them all about Schloss Neuschwanstein, the formal German name for the mammoth castle. Originally built for a king, the building had been host to visitors since 1886, and then when the annihilation times came, Werther's ancestors had cared for the palace, defending it against invasion and the passage of time, life fairly comfortable with the large array of solar panels installed high on the ramparts at the back of the castle. At the edge of the mountains, the

structure had fared strangely well in the earthquakes of the Utslettelse—
which the old man had called the *Aufhruhr*—and only minor repairs had
been needed. Werther was born in a bedroom on the fourth floor of the
castle's main building, and he had known the place as home and
sanctuary for his entire life.

Shortly before he died, he had called Val to his small study and sat
in a huge, overstuffed chair by a fireplace. The man always had a kindly
air about him, but on that evening he had been grave.

"I understand your story, dear Val. Your mission to the Floating
City beyond the mountains. If there is a chance that you can save the
remnants of the human race, you must try, of course."

Val sat silent, curious to hear what the man had to say.

"You understand that I am quite old, and I will not last though
another winter after this one—"

"Why say such things?" Val interrupted.

The old man waved his hand dismissively. "It is true, and we both
know it. Listen now. There is no one else to care for this place when
I go. I know you need to press on south of the mountains when the
weather clears and the roads are free of snow. I know. But...well,
things can change out there. I have not ventured far from this castle in
my life, but I have taken small trips. I know what waits beyond these
walls, as do you."

Val thought back on the challenges she and her men had already
faced. She stayed silent, willing the man to finish.

"This place can be yours when I am gone, Val. If things do not
go well on your mission, you can come back here to live out your
days with my blessing. Perhaps things will be different for you and
Ulrik."

She was suddenly taken aback. He was talking about children.

"Oh, no," she said, a small smile on her lips. "It is not like that
between us. We are only fellow Vikings. Warriors both."

The man grinned back at her, his eyes twinkling with secret
knowledge. "Nevertheless. If you need a refuge, you will always be
welcome here, and I will charge you with taking as good care of
her as I did, should you come."

Three days later, the kind old man had died. Unable to bury him in the frozen ground of the gardens, and with no water to send him on a Viking funeral, they had opted for storing him in one of the solar-powered freezers in the basement, until the spring thaw. The panels were slanted so steeply on the castle walls that most of the snow and ice slid right off them. But Ulrik checked and swept them daily anyway.

The bitter wind blew Val's long blonde hair over her shoulders, the red-lensed goggles hanging around her neck as she peered out a narrow window. She stood in the mini-turret attached to the castle's tallest tower. The nearby mountains were her only focus now. The snows had begun to melt in the valleys to the north, but to the south, the peaks were still encased in ice. Werther had told her it would be well after spring and into summer before the roads would be passable.

Not much longer now, she told herself.

Ulrik's injuries from the fight with the ape had been minimal. All the others were in shape, although she feared if they needed to stay cooped up much longer the men might begin to lose their fighting edge. Morten had taken to the castle's massive library, whiling away the hours and days with books. Without his conversation and comradery, Oskar had resorted to what he knew best—complaining. At least until Anders had shut him up a week after the old man's death by telling him he could learn a new skill, picking up hunting at Anders's side. It was that, or Anders would stop finding the moaning man food when they were on the road again. Nils and Ulrik worked on shoring up the castle's defenses, should anything or anyone decide it looked like a good place to winter.

Heinrich, like a puppy, had been available and at Val's side whenever she needed him. She suspected he was attracted to her, but she wasn't interested. She just wanted to get on the road again. When they were traveling, she had felt a sense of purpose beyond simple survival, which was what she had known all her life. She had feared their immobility would make the men crazy, but instead, she was the one losing her patience. Her dreams were restless. She paced the empty echoing halls of the giant building. Stagnation ate away at her.

Too much time alone led to horrible, awful questions she should have asked Halvard before departing from Stavanger. It led to thoughts of failure. What would happen to the human race if they did not make it across the mountains? And now that she had her Vikings, her berserkers, her family, what would happen to her if they all failed to make the crossing? They had fared fine without Erlend's mechanical expertise so far. They had prevailed in their battles without Trond and Stig. But would they be able to continue without Nils's steady historical guidance? Could she continue on without Ulrik's strength and support?

She didn't like to think of it. There had been wild times in her last decade, when she had been more animal than young woman. She had no desire to revisit those times. Ever.

She took one last look at the ice-encrusted crags, and then shut the window.

Soon.

She began the long descent down the stairs of the tower.

They might not be able to depart just yet, but she could get them ready. Get them packed up. The ATVs needed to be fueled. They would take whatever they could from the castle, and close it up tight. As soon as the ground was warm enough, they would bury the old man and take their leave.

She didn't think she would ever come back to the castle, despite the wishes of sweet old Werther. She had a second mission to fulfill, after the first. And of them all, she was the only one who knew what would come next.

38

"This lake is not supposed to be here," Val said, frustration creasing her brow.

Ahead of them, spread out like a glittering blanket of arctic blue, was a huge, sprawling lake. It filled the valley between the sloping hills and mountains, now green and speckled in yellow, instead of coated in white, as the Alpine wildflowers ran riot in the warm weather.

A square stone tower with not one, but two clocks on each face, jutted from the lake. The rest of the building was fully submerged under the water. There were no other indications of human habitation—or even prior existence—present in the valley.

"This is not the first time this sort of thing has happened," Nils offered. "I saw photos in one of Halvard's books of a different town here in the Alps. The entire town and all its buildings were deluged. Only a church bell tower stuck up from the water. Like this one."

"What causes it?" Ulrik asked, his ATV idling between his bare thighs. He had stripped his shirt off and wore only shorts and boots.

Nils thought for a moment. "Well, that town I saw was flooded when the river had been dammed up, many years earlier. I think a few other towns were also drowned. But it was intentional. The towns had been evacuated first."

"They had so many towns in those days that they could afford to just throw some away?" Morten asked, shocked.

"Apparently," Nils said, shrugging his shoulders.

"And this town, Nils? On the map, there is no lake here." Val pointed out at the expanse of water before them. The paved road ran right into it, disappearing in the clear blue.

"I am not sure. Maybe a collapse of one or more mountains during the *Utslettelse*? It could have blocked up the river on one end of the valley and formed a natural lake? There are not enough people left in the world to perform such a task again. Those big projects, like the construction of the bridge back in Sweden, would have involved thousands of people and taken years to accomplish."

"If we skirt the lake edge, will the road still be on the other side?" Val asked him.

"I am a scholar, not a prophet," Nils grumbled, before heading off the road and following the edge of the lake, across an Alpine field of low grass.

"He has been in a bad mood for some time now," Ulrik observed. "I will talk with him."

"No," Val said, starting her ATV and rolling forward slowly. "Leave him be. He will come around. He was not meant for this kind of life."

Then she sped off across the grass, the thick wheels of her ATV chewing muddy gouges in the field at the side of the lake.

He waited for the others to follow Val, until it was just he and Morten at the end of the convoy. Morten had yet to start his engine.

"You remember he had a cold, back at the castle," Morten said, his face creased in concern.

"It was just a cold."

But now that Ulrik thought on it, he had not seen the slim man eating much of anything in the last three days, since they left the castle.

"When the wars came, during the annihilation, many people grew ill from sickness that had been used as a weapon. Entire nations were destroyed by snot. I imagine at least one of them must have uttered that phrase you just did." Then Morten started his engine and drove across the field, following Oskar and Anders.

Ulrik waited a moment, allowing the others to gain a lead. He stared at the oddity of a bell tower rising from the depths of the lake. They had been on the road only a few days, and he was glad for it. None of them had grumbled about departing. The winter had dragged on, and they were all ready for action, but as they had finally gotten under way, there was little to be found. The roads were surprisingly good, despite the constant freeze and thaw, because the Alpine vegetation was so thin, and the soil so rocky. As a result, the road's asphalt was mostly intact, and in many places it was as smooth as a baby's face.

They still traveled slowly, wary of falling into traps, and they needed to decide where to stop for the day, when there was still light left to do it.

The only things that had concerned them until this unexpected lake, were graffiti signs they had seen spray-painted along the roads. It was impossible to tell how old the paint was, but they had seen the word several times now:

HANGERS

No one had any good guesses what it meant—least of all Nils. But it was everywhere: on the road, on low concrete and brick walls, and at a huge roadblock after a town called Imst. The sign at the front of the town was all that had been standing of the place, the rest long since burnt, either a casualty of war or natural disaster.

Ulrik scanned the valley, checking behind him, and then slowly advanced his ATV onto the field. He had seen nothing amiss besides the unexpected lake, but something still felt wrong. He stopped the ATV unexpectedly and swiveled, spotting a blur of white in the window of the bell tower. It was so fast, that if he hadn't been looking for just that very thing, he wouldn't have noticed the movement.

But he had been. And he had seen it, although he acted as if he hadn't. Realizing that the sensation of being watched was not just his imagination, he raced ahead, wondering whether the watcher was an individual they would leave far behind in the flooded valley or a capable hunter, like Heinrich, who would track them on the road.

Or worse, was it an advanced guard for an even greater threat?

Rejoining the group as they skirted the edge of the lake on low sloping hills, Ulrik sped past the others until he reached Val's position in the lead.

She looked over at him as he rode by her side.

"We were spotted."

"By who?" Val asked, but the question was answered by a horn blast that rolled out of the mountain pass ahead.

39

The thunder of several motors roared to life, echoing from the valley ahead.

A loud horn sounded again, and several large men with long beards and longer hair, came roaring down the hills on either side of a dirt road that carved through the mountains, perpendicular to the lake's broad side. They rode on vehicles similar to the ATVs, but far louder, and with just two wheels each. The two-wheelers required that the riders balance on them, and the handlebars were strangely high—higher in some cases than the rider's head—so that the vehicle's operator had to reach upward to hold the throttle. But what was terrifying about the vehicles was that they were caged and armored in bones. Human bones. An intricate framework covered the sides of the bikes, and long leg bones filed to a point extended over the front wheels of the bikes like the fenders on the ATVs.

As horrific as the bones were, the clothing on the men was worse. The leather was scabbed and scarred, but the strange leathery fabric was still identifiable as human skin, stretched and stitched into vests and coats. The still-extant human faces, their mouths stretched open in permanent screams on the chest of the riders' vests, were all the evidence needed to determine the fabric's origins.

Even though the riders' clothing and mounts would strike terror into the hearts of any passing traveler, what gave Ulrik pause was their faces. All but one of the riders had their mouths stitched shut with thick cord that could be more human leather. Some of the men had odd metal spikes extending out of their skulls, right through their scalps.

Plumes of dust rose up behind ten riders skidding down the rocky hill's slope toward the dirt path. None of the men appeared to be armed, but that was probably because they needed both hands to steer.

Val saw the men descending the hills ahead of them, but instead of stopping, she cranked her ATV's throttle, racing forward, past the bottleneck and through the pass between the hills. The others followed suit, with Anders and Nils close on her heels. Oskar and Heinrich sped away just before the first two-wheeler reached the bottom of the hill—heading straight for Morten. Instead of steering away, Morten angled his ATV to the right, close to the shoulder of the narrow dirt road. As he came along the rider, who was turning his two-wheeled steed to give chase after Oskar, Morten raised his arm from his throttle long enough to throw an elbow at the man's throat.

The rider saw the move at the last second, and released his grip from the overly high handlebar, lifting his forearm up just in time to deflect the blow from its original target. Unfortunately for him, Morten's original target had been the man's throat. The deflected elbow instead rammed into the bridge of the man's nose, knocking him back into the huge seat. In the process, his other hand came loose from the high handlebars, and the front wheel instantly jolted to the right. As soon as it did, the bike flipped, its rear end launching into the air. The leather-clad rider flew forward. The bike landed on top of the man with a rending crunch. Bones—both those from the bike and the man, cracking and piercing skin with pointed fragments.

Then Morten was past the intended blockade, as another rider came rushing in toward Ulrik from his left. Ulrik leaned hard, his ATV moving right and letting the side of his vehicle smash into the bone cage surrounding the other man's ride. The unexpected crash sent his bike off the road, careening into the rocks.

Ulrik raced ahead and glanced back to see the other riders giving chase. One rider had reached the dirt road ahead of Ulrik and was speeding away ahead of him, racing toward the rear of Morten's ATV.

Ulrik twisted the throttle, felt the burst of speed between his legs, and wondered how much fuel this chase would eat up. The ATVs had always been meant for carrying them long distances—not for battle on mountain pathways.

As he caught up with the sole rider ahead of him, he saw that the man had a word burned onto the back of his leather jacket.

Hangers.

Ulrik remembered the signs he had seen. *That explains that. They are a gang of some sort. Road bandits.*

He rushed ahead, and in the moment before he rammed the rear wheel of the Hanger ahead of him, he swerved right, riding onto the pebble strewn shoulder of an actual paved road, when the dirt pathway intersected it. He straightened out the handlebars and released the left side, still holding the throttle with his right hand. His left hand reached to the quick-draw leather holster he had created for his ax on the side of the ATV.

The Hanger glanced over at him, and realizing that Ulrik was armed, he leaned away. His bike swerved, but put the man in the perfect range for the broad-headed blade at the end of Ulrik's long ax. He swung out, letting the handle slide through his hand, until the leather wrapped pommel on the end caught in his grip. The long handle swung through the space between them, and the blade slid through the side of the man's face, cleaving off beard and shaving away the side of his head in a spray of red droplets. Then the blade continued on to its true target.

The razor edge slammed into the base of the man's wrist, cleanly severing the throttle hand from the arm, before the weight of the blade and its velocity, sent it arcing through the high-hanging metal handlebar as well.

The Hanger screamed and flailed, tugging his wheel left. The bike and the man rolled sideways over and over, leaving a long streak of machine parts, bone and human gore on the gray road.

Ulrik brought the ax back, and slid it down into the holster.

He grinned and grasped his left handle before pouring on the speed.

The road curved sharply to the right where a large, craggy rock wall rose up, fringing the roadside. Several large boulders lined the shoulder on the other side. Ulrik swerved around the boulders, slowing slightly.

As he rounded the corner, he could see that the road was suddenly straight for a few hundred feet. Val and Anders were stopped ahead, while the others continued on beyond them. Anders had his bow drawn and an arrow nocked.

Understanding the plan, Ulrik steered toward the shoulder, allowing Anders a clear line of sight. Ulrik didn't look back. Instead he pressed ahead with more speed, planning to catch up with the others. Anders released arrow after arrow, some of them whistling past, dangerously close, but still on target. Ulrik heard a few crashes behind him, as Hangers were struck by the deadly projectiles.

Val turned her ATV and raced off down the road. Anders shouldered his bow and turned his own ATV just as Ulrik closed to within twenty-five feet of him.

Over the noise of Ulrik's and Anders's ATVs, a deep, throaty mechanical growl echoed off the close mountain walls.

The surviving Hangers were still giving chase, and by the sound of the engines, there were a lot more of them coming.

40

Val had only caught a glimpse of the Hangers up close, when they had launched their initial attack, but their terrifying features—with the human leather, sewn mouths, long hair and beards and the ridiculous upraised arms on the bonecycles—had lodged in her head. Now that they fled down the curving mountain road, the angered Hangers not far behind, she realized that all the groups of humans they had encountered had been homogenous. The Blue Men, the swastika-bearing psychotic Long Knives in Germany, and now these 'Hangers'. She wondered if belonging to these groups required visual conformity. The end of civilization came with no explanations, only more questions.

And rarely the time to think on them.

"They are falling back," Morten shouted over the whine of their ATV engines. "But they are still following. And there are more of them now. A lot more."

They took the curves as quickly as they dared. They were all expert riders now, but the vehicles were not designed for tight curving mountain roads.

As long as our brakes continue to work, Val thought, recalling a time in Sweden when Erlend had needed to repair the brakes on Trond's quad.

"Press on," she told him, and she slowed to pass the message to the others at the rear of their group. When she reached Ulrik at the back, she matched his speed. "We have hours through the mountains yet. We need a plan."

"Actually..." Nils was just ahead of them, and he slowed to let them catch up, pulling on the ATV's silver brake handles. "I have a plan already."

On the front of his ATV, Nils had attached a box-like, black nylon case. When unfolded, it exposed a clear plastic window, revealing the contents within. He usually kept one of their many paper maps inside the sleeve, folded into tight squares, so he could glance at their route without removing the map—or his hands from the vibrating handlebars.

Now he took his brake hand off the bars quickly and pointed to the map under the waterproof plastic shield. "Here," he said. "We can go off the road here, and lead them up this route, into the mountains."

Val exchanged a glance with Ulrik, then asked the question both of them wanted to ask. "Why?"

"We will not be able to outrun them. At least not once the road straightens out." Despite carrying on the conversation, Nils was focusing on the twisting road, standing on his footboards, and leaning with each turn.

"Again. Why?" Val asked, mimicking his swaying hips with her own vehicle.

"Those motorcycles have much larger engines than these ATVs. They were meant for long distance road travel, and not the kind of rough terrain we can handle."

Ulrik gave a nod. "Wise thinking, Nils."

"Not only that," the small historian said. "There is a very old road through the mountains. An army road. Soldiers used it when motorized vehicles were brand new. Centuries ago. They used the trail to move supplies and weapons through the peaks." Nils was in his element speaking about history—even when he needed to shout over the roaring engines.

"Can these..." Val paused for the word Nils had used. "These motorcycles... Can they not follow us along this soldier road?"

"It would be difficult, but they would still be able to follow."

"Then how is it a better route?" Ulrik asked, his irritation slipping through, even though Val knew it was directed at the threat and not at the smaller man. "I say we make a trap, here on the road. Stand our ground."

"No, no," Nils shouted. "I am *talking* about making a trap. The place I plan to take us will be best suited to our vehicles, with one way in, and if they follow us, we can ambush them from the perfect location."

Val considered both approaches. She knew the Hangers were still in pursuit, and her men were in their territory. The motorcycle riders would know the roads. They would know the places where an ambush would work best. *But maybe they will not know the areas ill-suited for their two-wheelers.*

"Go ahead, Nils," Val said. "Tell the others your plan, and then take the lead."

Nils dipped his head in a serious nod, then sped up.

"How many follow us?" Val asked Ulrik. He looked unhappy with her decision.

"Too many for us to take them all. There were ten when they first attacked. That number has grown. Fifty is my best guess."

Val's head whipped around, but the view was obscured by the tight curving walls. She saw nothing but the plume of dust kicked up by their passage. When she looked back, Ulrik was scowling over his handlebars. His long blond beard and hair flowed behind him. His thick muscled chest had broken out in goose bumps from the chill in the mountain air.

"There are too many," he said again. "Our capable fighters have been whittled to you, me and Morton. The others will be overwhelmed by multiple opponents."

"If we make it to this army road that Nils speaks of..."

"That is a large 'if.'"

"Then we set our trap. It is either that or we make our stand here with the axes, heading to Valhalla and allowing the rest of the world to die behind us. At least this way we might have time to prepare—and pick a better battleground than this twisty road."

They fell silent, and Val felt the sting of Ulrik's disapproval. This was the first time on their journey that they were truly at odds. But she knew she was right. Their mission had to come first, even though, like Ulrik—and probably the others—she would prefer to stand and fight these Hangers. But Halvard had not sent them across the world to die in the mountains at the hands of a strange foe. He had sent them to retrieve his precious genetic material. And they were so close now, if only they could make it to the point Nils had shown them on the map.

Just a little farther, she thought.

Then the road straightened, and she twisted the accelerator, catching up to the others alongside Ulrik. Nils had taken the lead, the plan conveyed. At the end of the long stretch, as they were about to head back into another tight curve, she turned her head back. The sight that greeted her through the red lenses of her goggles was enough to make her blood run cold.

Ulrik's count had been low.

41

Kinsker had called the Hangers to a halt in the road. His lieutenants, Ruck and Faust, idled beside him, astride their hawgs, attentive to his plan.

"These flat-bikers are tough, but they don't know the area. We'll catch them before the Floating City. But I want an alternative." Kinsker's voice was rough, and he realized it had been a long time since he had needed to use it. The Hangers lived in a small town in the alps during summer, and they rode their massive Harley Davidson hawgs, with their 'Ape Hanger' style handlebars, around the mountains. There was a small oil refinery south of the mountains, which had supplied them with fuel to keep the bikes running. They rode the mountain passes, collecting whatever items the Gasmen asked for.

And they rode for the sheer joy of it.

The very few times when strangers veered into their sphere of influence, the Hangers took what they wanted. Food, fuel, water, bone and skin—and if there were women, they took them, too. Hell, Ruck had gotten a wife that way. Kinsker would have had her for himself, but he hadn't been the Keystone then, and Ruck had found her first.

"A secondary plan?" Faust asked, holding a thick thong of human leather in his hand. He'd slid it out of the intricate holes in his face like a shoelace out of a boot, just seconds before. "Smooth. What are you thinking?"

"They're heading for the Floating City. There's nothing in the wastes from the last footie hill to the First Canal." Kinsker ran a finger through his long beard, thinking.

"No chance they want to go to the Other Sea? Or the City Crumbles, Down South?" Ruck asked. He was younger than the other two men, and he always seemed to want to consider the unlikely possibilities. Instead of completely removing the lacing from his face, he had simply loosened his, and when he spoke, the leather over his mouth stretched the lacing holes.

Kinsker was sure, though. "If they wanted the Other Sea, they would have gone around the Alps—not through them."

"And the Crumbles?" Faust prodded.

"Doubt it. You've been Down South. There's nothing left to raid," Kinsker stroked his chin, wondering what exactly the invading flat-bikers wanted. He'd never seen a hawg like theirs, low and squat, with four wheels instead of two. But as soon as he had spotted them near the lake, he had known he wanted the flat bikes, and he'd been glad of the mission for the German warlord Borss. But what he wanted most was the woman. She was stunning, with flowing blonde locks, a thin trim body and an attitude Kinsker had not seen before in a woman. She even seemed to be leading the flat-bikers. The Hangers had circled around and sped ahead, lying in wait for the woman and her group, but she and her men had been tougher than expected. Much tougher.

But he knew.

He knew where they were going. He just didn't know why. "Ruck is gonna tail them."

"I am?" Ruck asked. The younger man seemed surprised at the sudden grant of responsibility. Kinsker didn't doubt it. It was a rare honor bestowed by the Keystone, one which he had never received before.

"Take forty hawgs. Follow them. Chase them tight. Hound them down. Pick them off at the edges, if you can. But don't damage their flat-bikes."

"Smooth. I can do that, Kinsker. I can do that."

Kinsker rounded on the younger man. "And do not...under any situation...do not hurt the smooth woman. Pursuit is your primary goal. Drive them on toward the Floaters."

"And what are we doing then, Kinsker?" Faust didn't sound as if he liked the plan so far. *He's probably thinking about the woman,* Kinsker thought. Faust was probably thinking what Kinsker knew—Ruck would try to take the woman if he could get her. A second wife would suit the younger man, and he would brag all the more.

"I will take the rest of the Hangers down the Lake Road at speedy-fast, and we'll cut across toward the Floaters. We'll hide and wait for these flat-bikers, intercept them before they reach the City, and then their hawgs will be ours."

Faust looked like he was about to ask about himself, when Kinsker spoke again. "Faust, ride ahead of the ambush, toward the Floating City. I have no idea why these flat-bikers braved the mountains, but if they are heading to the Floaters, then they either need something the Floaters have, or they're bringing the Floaters something they need. Verstehen?"

Faust got it and nodded. "Yeah, Keystone. I hear and perceive. Something important. Either the flat-bikers have it or the Floaters have it. Either way, we get it, and we can trade it to the Gasmen. Juice for the Hangers—maybe for years. So you want me to sneak into the Floating City and try to find what they have?"

"Almost, Faust," Kinsker said with a grin. "You verstehen only half. Ruck will have forty. I'll keep nine with me for the ambush. You'll take the rest of the Hangers with you."

Faust's blue eyes widened under the fringe of long dark blonde hair on his brow. His face said it all. He'd thought Ruck lucky to receive the responsibility Kinsker had given him to hunt down the flat-bikers. But a Keystone giving *half* of the Hangers over to a lieutenant was unheard of. Everyone knew the last time that had happened. A lieutenant named Kroll had nearly split the Hangers asunder, with internal fighting and killing. Only the strength of a man named Schlüssel—the *Key*—had been able to stop Kroll's rebellion. And he had become the first Keystone. Kinsker was the fourth Keystone, and no one since had ever given lieutenants as much responsibility as Kinsker was handing out today.

"I'm feeling smooth and sparkly with all the responsibility, Kinsker. I won't let you down." Faust paused a moment, as if a problem had only just begun creeping into his mind. "But how am I supposed to sneak fifty Hangers past the Floater guards?"

Kinsker erupted in laughter. He knew he had nothing to fear in allowing Ruck and Faust the chance to shine as field generals, leading their own teams of Hangers. Neither man had the brains to plan a revolt. "Don't worry, Faust. I don't want you to *sneak* them in."

Ruck and Faust both looked confused now.

He stopped chuckling and turned back to Faust. "I don't want you to sneak in with the Hangers, Faust. I want you to set their floating shithole ablaze. Burn it until it's nothing more than charred timbers bobbing up and down on the waves. It's time for flames."

Kinsker had his own plan for the prize the Blonde Woman was seeking. The hell with Borss and what he wanted. Kinsker would have it all.

42

Val stepped off her ATV, her black leather boots crunching on the small pebbles and grit of the dirt covered pavement. Ahead of them stood a long pinkish-white wall of concrete slightly higher than Ulrik. Morten and Oskar had stayed at the entrance to the large parking area just before the wall, so they could peer down the road and alert the others when they spotted the Hangers approaching.

Emblazoned across the wall in huge embossed letters, stretching forty feet long, was a slogan in a foreign tongue:

STRADA DELLE 52 GALLERIE

"What does it mean, Nils?" There was some kind of mural artwork next to the name, but it had long faded with age, and Val could not make it out. The site was abandoned. She was less sure of the man's plan now. This place felt like a dead end. There was an opening in the wall off to the side that was just large enough for one ATV, but there had been only the one road leading in and out.

"It is in the Old Italian language. This is our destination." The historian look pleased with himself.

"Fifty-two?" Ulrik asked. "Fifty-two what?"

"I read about this location in one of Halvard's many books," Nils assured them. "It was originally called 'The Road of the First Army.' The Italians built a long road through the mountains, and it clings to the side of the rock like a goat. The Alps seem to have been little affected by the earthquakes of the *Utslettelse*. So I thought it would be intact."

Val was less and less sure. "Tell me your plan, Nils. All of it." She turned on the smaller man with her red-lensed goggles, and zipped up her black leather jacket, preparing for the battle that would come. The Hangers had followed them up the winding path to the beginning of this Army Road, and she expected their attack at any time. They were not far behind.

"The path is narrow," Nils closed his eyes as he recalled the pages of the book he had seen, and the faded photos on those weathered pages. "The road is a trail, really, like the trails through the forest back in the North. At times so narrow that only one ATV will be able to pass. The ground is rocky and uneven. Or it was, anyway." The thin man turned to them grinning, like he had a secret that he was finally able to tell them. If he had been ill earlier, he was feeling fine now, with a renewed purpose. "And there are tunnels. Fifty-two of them."

Ulrik and Val knew what tunnels were—they had each seen a few in the North, and of course, they had raced through the broad tunnel at the end of the Øresund Bridge.

"Fifty-two?" Ulrik asked, his face a mask of pure disbelief. "Surely an exaggeration."

Nils shook his head. "I've seen pictures of some of them. Some are short, just arches through the stone. But some are quite long." He was grinning again.

The man's plan crawled through Ulrik's mind. "You mean to use your bricks from the castle. Collapse one of the long tunnels with the Hangers inside...then the far end, sealing them inside the mountain." He looked pleased with the notion.

"What are these 'bricks?'" Val asked.

Nils reached back and opened a satchel on the side of his ATV. Anders and Heinrich stepped over to see the pack's contents—a few brick-sized packages wrapped in red, semi-transparent plastic wrap. "We found these at the castle, in the large storage room where the propane was. They make things explode."

"Explode?" Val asked. She wasn't familiar with the term.

"These are very old, but you mix one of these larger red bricks with a smaller green block. The material is like unfired clay. Then you insert a detonator. The effect is like a lightning strike ripping rock to pieces."

Val leaned closer, peering at the plastic-wrapped bricks.

Nils continued, "These are a special kind of explosive from shortly before the cataclysms. They were used for construction—not for the army—but they will work for our purposes." He pulled out a small metal rod four inches long, with a black numbered dial on the end. "This is the detonator. We can set it for half an hour. We stick this in the brick, and it will take down a good part of the mountain, the way a rock will shatter when you hit it with a large hammer."

"And we will be farther down the road, out of the other end of the tunnel?" Val was starting to see the advantage of the exploding bricks.

"Yes," Nils said. "We will be well clear of the blast area."

"And how many of the bricks did you bring, Nils?" Ulrik asked.

"Seven."

"Several chances to get it right," she said. "Good. And where does this Tunnel Road lead us?"

"It goes deep into the mountains where we can either come back on an easier return road, to this very starting point, or we can go off road."

"Wait," Anders spoke up as he zipped up his leather jacket. Ulrik was the only member of their group still bare-chested. He did not appear to be bothered by the cooler air now. "What is to stop these Hangers from looping around on the easy road to the end of this tunnel trail and ambushing us there?"

A shadow crept across Nils's face. "I was hoping they would follow us into the trail. They might never have been up here."

Val considered. While it had been a long journey to reach this Tunnel Road, there was no evidence to suggest that the Hangers had no knowledge of it at all. And if they knew the place, they would know of the return road and likely follow Anders's suggestion. But if they did not know the road...

"We will go on the Tunnel Road. And we will hang back a bit, waiting for them to come. We need to see if they all follow us, or if some of them split off."

Nils started his engine and the others did the same, preparing to follow him toward the wall opening. Anders, without being told, turned back and raced across the lot to speak with Morten and Oskar, filling them in on the plan. The three of them waited behind, still watching for the first Hanger.

Val rolled up behind Nils as their ATVs crawled slowly onto a trailhead. The four-foot-wide path, covered in crushed rock, rose up sharply, winding through small trees and boulders. On the far side of the first archway was a man-made concrete tunnel. Val wondered if it was the first official tunnel. A gate blocked their path, but Nils did not slow. He rammed the edge of the rusted structure with his ATV. The barrier crumbled to dust and metal flakes.

Past the barrier on their right, crumbling, fang-like mountains, rose up. Their white and brown facades were imposing, but promised escape. Before they reached the trail's first turn, Ulrik hollered. Val twisted her head around to see that Anders, Oskar and Morten had joined them on the trail, and the men were coming fast. Morten raised his finger, pointing up the trail. The message was clear.

The Hangers had taken the bait.

43

Ruck slowed his hawg as the Hangers roared into the parking lot. He had never been this deep in the mountains. Neither had his brethren. No one knew what the place was—or what the huge letters on the pink wall meant.

But he could see the trails in the dirt, where the flat-bikers had gone, passing through the hole in the wall. "They're going dirt-riding, into the mountains."

"Should we follow them, Ruck?" Klein was next in line, in the order of command. A small man, with freakishly large hands, he had been Ruck's friend since childhood. Like Ruck, he only loosened his mouth lacing when he needed to speak. They had joined the Hangers on the same day. But since then, Ruck had realized a simple truth about Klein.

He was an idiot.

Much like what Ruck knew Kinsker thought of him. But Ruck had ambition. He had an eye for the big picture. He was just too smart to let Kinsker know that he could see his leader's true intentions. He knew that Kinsker was accelerating his long-range plan to take down the Floaters and enslave the Gasmen. Ruck also knew that Kinsker wanted the woman. Who wouldn't? Faust wanted her, too, but he didn't have a chance.

"We follow," Ruck told Klein. "Responsibility. You take the lead, Klein. Take it slow so you don't road-rash, but stay nipping at their heels. Keystone wants us to push them—not capture them."

"Smooth, Ruck," Klein was visibly puffing up his chest as he accelerated toward the hole in the wall, far more recklessly than Ruck ever would have on an unknown trail-space. The last of the flat-bikers had just swept through the hole, and Ruck had noticed that the archer brought up the rear. Ruck would have to be a complete moron to race through after them as fast as Klein just did.

He waited a beat and then followed at a much more leisurely pace, the other thirty-eight men on bikes queuing up to follow him, cranking their throttles and wasting gas, their engines filling the mountain stillness with echoing thunder.

Ruck slid his hawg through the section of the pink wall with a small roof over it. The remains of a mangled guard fence lay on the far side. The way ahead was rocky and lined with trees, but it would be easy riding. He'd just have to take it slower than the turns on the alpine roads. Beyond the jagged metal frame, he could see Klein well up the path, racing into danger with delusions of glory.

With a little luck, he'll get himself killed by their archer.

The path became steep, and the way was littered with larger rocks. Ruck realized he would have to spend more time focusing on the ground than on the possible threat ahead. He slowed his hawg, allowed five of his Hangers to catch up, and sent them on ahead with a wave of his hand. He then rejoined the flow of bikers scrabbling up the trail. If the flat-bikers left traps, he was happy to let these men find them.

Traps or not, the flat-bikers would eventually tire of running. They would stand. They looked like the type. Then Ruck would throw them Klein—if he lasted that long—and a few more Hangers, before sweeping in. He would finish off the flat-bikers, take the woman, and capture the strange four-wheeled hawgs.

He didn't give two squirts whether Kinsker wanted the travelers pushed instead of killed. Ruck would have the smooth woman, and with the Hangers's support, high on their victory and the capture of the four-wheelers, he would ride into Kinsker's small ambush and challenge the man's authority. Even if Ruck lost a few men in the mountains, he knew he would still outnumber Kinsker's group, with Faust and fifty men sent off to attack the Floaters. Plus he would have whatever prize the flat-bikers possessed. Ruck didn't know what it was—Kinsker hadn't told them—but he was clever enough to recognize that Kinsker wanted it for a reason. And the man had known the flat-bikers were coming. Someone on the other side of the mountains had tipped him off. Ruck would need to learn who that was. The last thing he would need was another challenger.

After Kinsker was dead and Ruck was the new Keystone, his group would meet up with Faust. If they had succeeded in their attack of the Floating City, Ruck would take the credit. If they were losing, he'd call them off and live to fight another day.

But first, we need to catch these flat-bikers.

The trail began to hug tight curves around the sides of mountains, and the view stretched for miles. Short green pine trees coated the low hills away to the south. Ruck snuck a momentary glance at the view's majesty, but quickly imagined himself plummeting off the side, man and bone-machine bouncing down rock strewn hills. Chased by the vision of his own road-rash gore, he turned his attention back to the ground, ensuring that the black rubber tires of his hawg stayed straight and in the middle of the four-foot-wide path.

A tunnel loomed ahead. The gray stones of the man-made archway matched the color of the mountain it cut through, the blocks machined and sloped outward in an inviting gesture.

Across the top of the tunnel were strange letters Ruck couldn't read:

MCMXVII

EX ARDVIS PERPETVVM NOMEN

There were other letters below that, but he was in the mouth of the tunnel before he had a chance to glance at them. The ground was clear, but the path turned hard to the right, and plunged into darkness. The headlamp on his hawg was broken, and he hadn't gotten a spare bulb yet. They were hard to come by, but he hadn't experienced any hardship from it yet—the Hangers nearly always rode as a group, and during the day. He had always had light to see by. But the tunnel was too narrow to ride side-by-side with another. He would have to slow and let the man behind him catch up, so he could see from his headlamp.

Ruck's lead on the next man was short. He didn't need to wait long. But sitting in the dark, he began doubting his plan. He had no idea where the tunnel went. Maybe it wasn't even a tunnel. Maybe the road just went deep into the mountain, a snake hole twisting deeper and deeper into the Earth.

Where are the flat-bikers leading us?

Just then the Hanger behind him approached, and he could see again, the black walls of the tunnel illuminated in the distance. Ruck rolled forward, moving slower than he had before, and finding more courage after his momentary doubt in the dark.

Soon he could see daylight at the end of the tunnel. He realized it was just that—a tunnel. It had only been about fifty feet long. Not some mouth leading into hell itself. As he burst out into broad daylight, his rear wheel fishtailing on the loose gravel path, he determined to catch up to Ziegel.

He could see the man in the distance, riding up the steeper trail. He would tell Ziegel to take it a bit slower. He wouldn't explain why, but if they passed through any more long tunnels, he would use the man as a light source. And if necessary, he would use Ziegel as a shield against the archer, too.

After a sharp hairpin turn, they approached another yawning tunnel. It would make the perfect place for an ambush, and he wondered if he could catch the flat-bikers in one of these tunnels.

Then Ruck's grip on his throttle loosened as he wondered if that was *their* plan.

44

The words echoed through Val's head: *Lasting renown won through tribulation.* It was the translation of the slogan on the first tunnel, or so Nils had told her. She hoped it would be a fitting epitaph for her group if this plan did not succeed.

As she blasted out of the fourth tunnel along the trail, the path became a straightaway for the next hundred feet before it angled to the right. She sped up, despite the loose rocky ground, her thick tires spitting rocks behind her. The path widened and she let Ulrik and Heinrich move ahead of her. Their ATVs made short work of the steep grade. After two more tunnels and a series of switchbacks, Val let Morten and Oskar move ahead as well.

Just outside the mouth of the sixth tunnel, she bade Anders to wait with her. Down the hillside they could see countless pines amid rocky crags, and far below was the series of switchbacks they had just driven up. Val stepped off her ATV, walked to the side of the path and picked up a large rock, just smaller than her head.

Far below, they could see a progression of the Hangers. The line of grisly men moved slowly on the loose rocky path, but there were dozens of them, and Val knew that if they were still giving chase when they returned to clear roads, the men would catch up. So she decided to rattle them a bit.

"Can you hit them from here?" she asked Anders.

The archer considered the request for a moment. "Too many trees. Probably not."

Val looked at the rock in her hand, spun around in a full circle, and pitched the missile in a high arc. It sailed out into the void. "Maybe we will get lucky. This should at least give them a fright."

Ruck happened to glance up the mountain, and the simple act saved his life. He saw a small gray shape arc down from the trail above, and beyond that he could see the smooth woman in her odd eyewear. She stood on the trail looking down with another of her flat-bikers.

Before Ruck could shout a warning through his laced mouth, the descending object crashed into a slight outcropping and bounced straight at Ziegel's unsuspecting cranium. The rock was close to the size of his head—minus the hair—and it tore the man's skull from his shoulders. A cloud of crimson detonated around the man like the seeds of a disturbed dandelion.

The velocity of the impact carried the rock, and the human head, well out into the void where they plunged downward. The momentum also tugged on the man's neck and the wrenching motion pulled his body sideways. It toppled clean off the bike, flipping through the air, before a leg caught in a tree, and the corpse came to rest at a twisted angle.

Ziegel's hawg bounced along as though it still had a rider, until it struck a rock and toppled over in the middle of the path.

Ruck was equal parts horrified and amazed. Either the woman was the luckiest shot on Earth, or she was the most skilled warrior he had ever seen. Either way, he knew what could stop her. He reached into his skin jacket, and pulled out his most prized possession.

There were not many handguns left in the world, and fewer bullets. But the top five members of the Hangers all had Glocks. They were antiques, and the men meticulously cared for them. They practiced firing the weapons once a year, especially after finding a new haul of bullets. Ruck was the best shot of the five of them. But he had only three bullets left. It had been a long time since they had come across ammunition of any kind—never mind the 9mm that the Glocks used.

Three bullets.

But he had just decided to use one on the smooth woman.

Frag her, he thought.

He already had a wife. He didn't need another.

Val spun as something sliced into her upper arm. Then a loud, echoing crack rang out across the mountains, as she twisted and slumped across her ATV. Anders was crouched by her side in heartbeat.

"Are you okay?"

Val turned and looked at her arm. The bullet had ripped through the leather jacket and sliced through her skin, but it had missed bone, and had not carved deep enough to damage muscle. Just a scratch, but it burned like a bastard. *And the same damn arm the Long Knife stabbed. It has only just healed.* "They will be coming. Move."

Anders rushed back to his ATV and they were off, buzzing up the trail to the next tunnel. Just before the ninth, the others were waiting for them, and Nils was off his quad. It was parked just inside the mouth of the tunnel. Nils was standing on it, stuffing one of his bombs into a crevice near the ceiling. He gave the detonator's timer dial a twist with a clicking noise and then slowly pushed it into the soft, claylike substance. Then he dropped down onto the saddle of his ATV and sped off into the tunnel's gloom. The others quickly followed, Heinrich glancing nervously up at the bomb as he passed under it. Val and Anders, last in line, did the same.

Ruck had quickly taken the saddle bags off his hawg and abandoned it for Ziegel's. Although the bone cage on the side was scratched and cracked from its fall, the hawg's headlamp worked, and at the moment, that mattered far more. He had left his hawg on its kick in the grass, to the side of the path. He took off up the hill. When he noticed Ziegel's hawg had more juice than his, he had smiled at his good fortune.

He didn't know he had hit the smooth woman with his shot until he saw blood splatter on the gray rocks, just outside the mouth of the sixth tunnel.

I actually hit her! Massive smooth!

And now, at the upper level of the switchback, he was thoroughly delighted to see that he'd exacted some blood for blood. But the smooth woman's corpse was nowhere in sight. And the blood spatter wasn't enough to suggest his shot had killed her.

It won't matter. The next two bullets will do the trick, he thought with a grim smile. Throwing caution to the wind, he sped up, passing the Hangers ahead of him until he was just behind Klein.

And then he took the lead.

The passage from daylight to darkness repeated until it was like a blur. The stunning greenery around them and the fresh, crisp mountain air went unnoticed as Val struggled to keep up with the others on the shifting terrain. Occasionally there would be a huge rock embedded in the middle of the trail, and she would have to swerve, her rear wheel gripping the path's edge.

Behind her, the maniac leading the Hangers, the man with the gun, closed in. He had put the weapon away, but it wouldn't be long before he could stop and shoot her in the back. He was no more than twenty feet back when thunder rumbled across the valley, and the ground beneath her ATV shook. Pebbles bounced across the path.

The bomb, she thought.

It was much too soon. Nils had said he was setting it for close to half an hour, but it had been less than five minutes.

Then as soon as the explosion's pressure wave passed, a second impact struck. The Hangers' leader had sped up next to her and smashed his bike into her ATV, driving it toward the trail's edge and certain death.

45

Val removed her right hand from the throttle and snapped it out, hooking it around the back of the Hanger's neck. He tried to pull away from the ledge and from her grasp, leaning his bike to the right. But her grip was like iron, and he towed her and her ATV with him.

She released his neck and her quad fell back behind him. Then she cranked the throttle again, ramming the front of her ATV onto the unprotected rear wheel of his bike. As her rear wheels tipped up off the trail from the impact, his rear tire squealed in protest, and the air filled with the scent of burning rubber.

The Hanger was thrown forward from the collision, and his forehead banged on the sideview mirror attached to the high handlebars. He swerved right toward the wall, and then left toward the drop off. Val took the opportunity to zip past him on the inside of the trail. She wanted to lift her left foot and give the crazy bikerider a swift kick, sending him clean off the ledge, but she needed her weight on the footboards to steer the ATV properly, and the path was too narrow. In her zeal to send her foe to his demise, she might follow him into the abyss. So she focused on retaking the lead and pouring on the speed, getting ahead of the Hanger before he fully recovered.

It didn't take him long.

As she swept into the next tunnel, a loud crack filled the air and something pinged off the tunnel wall with a burst of sparks. At first she thought Nils had set another explosive, because of the report's volume. But then she realized the Hanger had pulled his gun and fired another of the small metal projectiles—*Nils called them bullets*—at her.

Thankfully, he had missed.

The tunnel felt darker than the others she'd been through, and she realized that the light shining from her ATV was uneven, illuminating the left of the cavernous tube more than the right. *One of the lights at the front must have broken when I rammed him.* The tunnel rose up at a steep grade, the ceiling just above her head.

She leaned forward and ducked low beneath the ceiling. The motion saved her life as another bullet whizzed just over her head, ripping through the leather pack attached to the front of the ATV, just above the headlamps. The reverberating report felt like a thousand claps of thunder. Her ears rang louder than her ATV's constant buzzing and the deep growl of the Hanger's two-wheeler.

She forgot about the ringing when she saw the tunnel's end ahead, someone standing in the path. It was their pre-determined signal, and she sped up in anticipation of what she knew would come, keeping her head low, behind the front satchel.

Fifty feet from the end of the tunnel, Anders was hollering for her to stay low. She couldn't hear him, but his waving hand was clear enough. *Get down*, which was easy to obey since she was already as low as she could get. Anders let three arrows fly down the tunnel. Then he turned and hopped back onto his ATV and tore up the trail.

Val didn't see or feel the deadly bolts clear her head, but she knew they had or she would have either felt the agony of having been hit, or she would be dead. She raced out of the low tunnel and raised her body into a normal riding position. But she didn't slow or turn around to check on the Hanger.

There was no time.

She knew what would come next.

The next tunnel would be a long one, and she needed to get to it and through it as fast as possible. Anders slipped into the tunnel's mouth. She was close to the black entryway when she started to hear the whining buzz of her own motor again. As the ringing faded, she heard the throaty burble of the Hanger's engine, too.

He was still behind her.

Val cranked the ATV as fast as it would go, launching into the dark tunnel. She knew the tunnel would be straight, so she would be in no danger of crashing at such high speeds. Nil's plan had been to set the explosives at the end of the longest, straightest tunnel they could find.

She passed through a hundred and fifty feet of darkness before she could detect the faint glow of dim daylight at the end. Anders was already out the other end, beyond her field of view. She leaned down again, not because of low clearance but to reduce her air resistance and squeeze out every last bit of speed out of the sturdy vehicle.

As soon as she approached the end of the tunnel, she slammed on the brakes. The tires locked up and the ATV skidded out of the tunnel and into the open on a wide section of the path. Nils had chosen well. The ATV turned sideways and slid to a stop. She hopped off the vehicle and ran back for the mouth of the tunnel.

Anders, positioned on the slope to one side of the trail, nocked an arrow. Nils, whose two-seater ATV was further up the trail, hopped on to her quad and steered it back in the right direction before powering up the path with it and coming to a slow stop ahead of his own vehicle.

Val scooped something off the ground at the side of the tunnel entrance, then stood in the path, listening to the Hanger coming on and waiting for the light of his headlamp to turn the front of her black leather jacket orange.

Then all of a sudden the man's shape was visible in the light shining into the tunnel's mouth. He had been driving without the headlamp, and was nearly on top of her.

46

Ruck was furious, and he saw the world through a haze of red. He'd forgotten that he had fired his three shots until he tried for the fourth. He slid the Glock back into the holster inside his denim jacket and gripped the handlebar until his knuckles started shaking.

He was thirty feet from the end of the tunnel, running without his headlight. The smooth woman stood defiantly in his path. And while he couldn't shoot her, he could damn well run her down. He might take them both off the edge of a cliff, but he felt it would be worth it.

You just stay right there, Smoothie.

She stood perfectly still, the sun glinting off the sheen of her leather jacket, with its armored pads, metal studs and white fur collar.

Twenty feet.

Ruck leaned forward, bracing for the impact.

Then the woman became fluid motion, swinging her arm up and hurling something the size of a rectangular rock into the mouth of the tunnel. Then she rolled to the side, her body disappearing behind the tunnel wall.

Ruck had just a second to be startled by her sudden departure, and then the world turned to fire and noise. The tunnel erupted around him. Fist-sized chunks of rock pummeled his body and his ride. The noise shattered his eardrums, which bled down his shoulders. His head roiled from the chaos until he found himself lying on the ground, his body tangled with the hawg and pinned by immoveable piles of stone.

The headlamp from the hawg was on his stomach and lit, but the handlebars were gone. His head ached, and his arms were numb from the shoulders down. The beam of yellow light struggled to pierce the cloud of dust and smoke in the air, but it slowly increased over the next few minutes, brightening a cave no larger than how far Ruck could spread his arms—if he could have done that. But his arms were useless.

He couldn't move his legs either. He could only move his head slightly, side to side, but it filled his eyes with starbursts, so he stopped, and remained still.

A fresh mountain breeze snuck through the smoke. It was enough to clear Ruck's fogged-in mind. The woman had somehow collapsed the tunnel. The small space around him was enough to move in, if he could get his arms or legs working.

He shouted for help, but heard nothing. His ears throbbed with pain, and the world was eerily silent. There was no one to help him. The smooth woman, if she was still alive, would not lift a finger to assist him. He decided to wait a while, and then call out for his brothers.

He wasn't panicked. He knew he could get out, even though he couldn't see much more than the walls around him. He would just rest for a while. It would all be okay. Kinsker had given him the responsibility. He needed to be a calm leader.

He drifted off to sleep.

When he woke, he had no idea how much time had gone by. The hawg's headlamp had died. He could still feel it there, pressing uncomfortably on his hip bone. The cave was completely dark now. But the fresh breeze was still rolling through. He still could hear nothing, though. And his legs would not move. He tried to move his head again, and once more the shower of green and pink sparks radiated around the inside of his eyelids, but cast no light in the darkened cave.

He screamed, but still couldn't hear his own voice. He could, however, feel his throat going hoarse. An hour later, he couldn't feel his throat anymore. His mind had fled, leaving him a screaming, gibbering maniac trapped in the dark.

He screamed for two days before he died.

Val had thrown the makeshift bomb, after twisting the dial on the detonator with her thumb, nudging it just a few clicks around. The previous bomb had detonated much too soon, so she figured the detonators were not working properly. But if she had set it for too long, the Hanger would have come ripping out of the tunnel, crashing into her.

She had placed her faith in the short timer, and rolled to the side of the tunnel.

The explosion was devastating. The mountain shook, the pressure stole her breath and the mouth of the tunnel fired stones as if they were bullets. Anders dove behind a craggy knob of stone on the hillside, and covered his head with his arms as a fusillade of rubble pelted him.

Val was protected from the projectiles, but the searing heat and scorching air filled her lungs as she breathed deeply following the initial pressure wave that mashed her against the wall. The mouth of the tunnel held, but the roof collapsed, turning the passage into a wall.

When the conflagration was done, Val staggered away and checked on Anders. He had a few small cuts on his forehead, but he waved her off. She leapt down the low hill to the now debris-strewn path, taking long strides toward the two parked ATVs, where she had last seen Nils. But she didn't see him now.

As she got closer to the vehicles, she could see that her ATV had been battered by flying debris. The green plastic fenders had been cracked and shattered. The whole side of the vehicle was covered in gray dust and small pebbles.

But then she saw that the damage was more severe. A jagged, elongated stone, like a squeezed dinner plate, had punctured the side of the fuel tank, and the invisible fuel was hissing out of the rupture. She could detect the faint smell of rotten eggs. Nils's ATV was parked just beyond hers. It had been shielded from the blast by her own ride. As she walked around the vehicles, she spotted booted feet on the ground. She rushed around the fenders and saw Nils. He was rubbing a knot on the side of his head where he had been hit by a flying rock.

"Nils, will you live?" she asked him, but her voice was soft and playful. She knew he would be fine.

He groaned and stood up, dusting himself off, then checked his two-seater ATV for damage.

Val pointed to her own punctured fuel tank, as Anders came walking up the path toward them. "It looks like you and I will be riding together from now on, Nils."

He looked at the rock that had punctured her fuel tank like an arrow head, shook his head and then motioned toward the jury-rigged extra seat over his ATV's rear propane tanks, inviting her to hop on.

Val walked around the ruined ATV and gently pushed Nils out of the way. "Yes, that is where you will ride, Nils," she said, swinging a leg over the saddle of her new ATV.

47

Seagulls swooped overhead in great armadas of wings and claws. They were huge, with wingspans ranging from six to ten feet.

Val and the Vikings stood next to a twenty-foot-high curved stone column. They could see the remains of a second on the far side of the road, but it had long ago been shattered, and now only a rounded stump remained. Ahead of them, the road dropped away, crumbling bits of asphalt filling the shallow waters. In the distance, a mile across the open harbor, they could see a low island, it's surface completely covered with red-roofed buildings. A ten-foot-tall wall of steel surrounded the island, hiding the true size and scope of the city within.

The only thing Val could determine for certain, was that they were not going to be driving to the city formerly known as Venice, Italy. Part of her couldn't believe they'd made it to the first of their destinations, though only she knew about the second. The journey here had been arduous. Many had said it wasn't possible. But she was now looking at Venice with her own eyes. The question was, would they find the man named Troben inside? And would he have the "genetic material" Halvard had sent them after so many months ago?

They had parked the ATVs in the squat trees growing along the arrow-straight road, and done their best to conceal the vehicles with fallen leaves and snapped branches.

Then the group had stared at the distant island until they had heard the birds. They crouched low in the bushes, concealed from the mighty winged creatures. The birds swooped and dove at the water, rising back up with four-foot long struggling fish clamped in their oversized beaks. Mighty Skjold, dwarfed by the giants in the sky, wisely stayed on Anders's shoulder, even without its leather hood.

The hungry birds passed by, receding into the distant sky. Val stood up and walked back to the water's edge.

"Will we swim or make a boat?" Ulrik asked. "There are plenty of trees. It would not take us long."

"No," was all Val would say. She lingered at the edge of the shattered road, waiting.

The others stood quietly for a while, but their curiosity got the best of them.

"Are we expecting something?" Oskar asked. "We have come this far. Let us get to this island and retrieve what we came for."

Val said nothing.

"What you have come for..." Heinrich said. "It is inside this floating city? This 'genetic material' that will save all life?"

"Yes," Val said. "Just wait. I was told we should wait."

Ulrik stepped up beside Val, peering out to sea. Morten joined them at the water's edge, and then Nils. Anders hung back in the trees by the ATVs. He looked bored.

"Are those..." Ulrik started to say.

"Yes," Val said quietly.

In the distance, small white objects zoomed past the front wall of the city. They looked like more of the gigantic birds, buzzing the surface of the water.

The shapes zipped left and right, leaving streams of white water behind them. As they got closer, Val saw them for what they were. Boats. Small white boats which were incredibly fast.

Faster than the ATVs or even the two-wheeled bikes of the Hangers, she thought.

She stayed in place, but her hand slid down to the head of her long ax at her side. Two of the boats stayed a long way off, darting back and forth, and then making sharp turns, carving up low walls of the white-frothed green water. The third boat slowly approached the fractured road where Val stood. Behind the boat's small windshield, holding the steering wheel, was a small man with short dirty blonde hair and blue eyes. He was slim, like Nils, but the man's face was shaved clean despite being at least fifty. His skin was tanned and leathery from the sun, but his cheeks suggested his ancestors had come from the North. Beside him was a broader man, who also had Northern looks, but his skin was paler, as if he ventured outdoors only rarely. He was armed with a black metal crossbow, and the tip of the weapon was pointed at Val's chest.

The boat's pilot threw the engine into reverse, and the vehicle slowed to a stop, the water from its wake rushing up to lap at the broken edge of the road, keeping a safe distance. If the Vikings were to attack, they could turn and be gone in seconds.

The man with the crossbow spoke in an old and very formal version of the Northern dialect the Vikings all used. "What do you seek?"

"Halvard from Stavanger has sent us," Val said.

The man looked to the boat's pilot, whose face showed just as much surprise. When he looked back to Val he said, "Odin's beard, we were expecting you months ago."

"We had to winter north of the mountains," she explained.

The pilot maneuvered the boat so its side was parallel to the broken edge of the road, and just before the sidewall of the vessel reached the asphalt, the larger man lowered the crossbow and tossed rubber fenders—cylindrical tubes with ropes—over the side to prevent the boat from scraping the jagged road.

"Come aboard, quickly," the man said.

Val and Ulrik stepped aboard the white boat, then Nils and Heinrich joined them.

Morten called Anders, and a second boat came in to the shore to collect the two of them and Oskar.

Then the three boats drove away, the man with the crossbow warily checking the shoreline as they departed. "Have a seat," he said. "The ride will be bumpy."

Val and the others sat in chairs with leather coverings that looked as new as their ATV saddles had when Erlend had first shown them the quads. The crossbowman sat as well, and the pilot stood in front of his seat, gripping the steering wheel. He sped the boat up until it skipped across the water's surface.

The jouncing ride was mercifully short, and they soon approached the rusted steel wall that rose up out of the water around the city. Green algae crawled up the sides of the wall. Lumps of sea life grew under a film of dark brown slime.

Two towers climbed up from the top of the wall, and between them a large steel gate rose up, hoisted slowly by metal chains—and from the slow and jerky ascent, Val assumed there were people inside the towers tugging on the other ends of those chains.

When the bottom of the gate was high enough that the bow of the boat could clear it, the pilot inched forward.

The pilot leaned down, so the climbing gate would not need to go higher, nor would he have to wait any longer. Val and her companions ducked their heads as they passed under the dripping wet gate. She looked back and watched the second boat, with three of her men, do likewise. The third boat had turned off, back to whatever its normal task was when strangers were not showing up at the end of the missing bridge.

Inside the walls was another world.

In all their travels, the towns and cities they had seen had been mostly destroyed. This town, this floating city, was bustling and alive. And yet, the buildings all strangely rose up out of the water. Instead of roads there were canals, and tight little waterways between the tall, narrow buildings that were too tight for their boat to pass.

The buildings were all three and four stories, with orange terracotta tile roofs. Windows and water-stained brick and stone lined the waterways, as the boats crawled through the tight canals. People bustled about, hanging laundry from lines to dry, and popping in and out of windows, all of them with a nod or a salute to the boats, as if the occupants of the boats held some position of rank in the society.

The boat pulled up to a low stone dock, with two badly canted wooden poles rising up from the water. The crossbowman tossed out the rubber fenders, and then hopped out of the boat, beckoning Val to follow him, and leaving the pilot to tie the boat up at the post. The second boat carrying Morten, Oskar and Anders pulled in right behind the first, and Morten was quick to leap out and hurry up to Val.

"This feels wrong," he said softly. "A trap?"

"I do not think so," Val said, speaking normally. Then softer she said, "but be on your guard anyway."

The building was orange stucco with patches of white, and exposed brick underneath. Nothing to suggest that they were being taken to this city's leader—or its prison. On the roof of the building, Val had spotted a wire mesh cage, similar to the one Halvard had used in Stavanger to house his mutated messenger birds. The crossbowman led them into the darkened interior of the building and a set of rickety wooden stairs at the end of a damp hallway. The lowest two steps had buckled from water exposure. Val stepped over them as the crossbowman did, climbing the stairs into the dim second story hallway, and the other Vikings followed her.

The second story of the building was brighter and breezy, as the windows of the rooms were open to the outside. The doors to the hallways were propped open with thick rubber wedges to permit a cross-breeze. The slightly foul harbor smell of the canals wafted through the hall, as the man finally came to a closed door and knocked twice, before opening it.

Inside was the oldest man Val had ever seen.

"The people Halvard sent have finally arrived," the crossbowman announced, and then he turned and left, allowing Val and Ulrik to enter the room.

The elderly man was tiny, just under five feet tall. He had wispy, white hair that trailed down his shoulders. *And he has the same crystal blue eyes as every person on the planet but me,* Val thought. He walked with a black wooden cane topped with a silver knob. Despite his obvious age, he moved with swift efficiency.

The room was a small kitchen, and the man had been slicing open a large fish with a thin fillet knife. He set it down on a thick wooden cutting board that rested on a wooden table.

"Do come in, all of you, come in." The man's dialect was different from the way people spoke in the North, but Val still understood him well enough.

He hobbled over to a closed, brown door.

Val walked toward the man, and was about to pepper him with questions, when he opened the door and pointed in the room.

"What you have come all this way for." The man's speech was stilted, as if he were remembering how to use Val's language, after many years of it rattling in the recesses of his memory but not touching his tongue.

Val peered into the room, and saw a teenaged girl with long, straight blonde hair sitting on a bed. She was reading an old, weathered book. She glanced up at Val.

The girl's moss green eyes stole Val's breath.

48

Kinsker knew he needed to save this stabby mess somehow. He had stood on the side of the road with Faust and fifty-eight Hangers all waiting on him as he peered through a brass telescope. He had seen his whole plan come apart. The smooth woman and her crew were riding out of the mountains with their strange flat-bikes, and his forty Hangers—*Forty of them!*—had been nowhere to be seen. Not even one of them in pursuit of the foreigners as they drove out of his mountains.

He'd made the decision then, much to Faust's obvious displeasure. He would keep the remaining men together, and they would let the flat-bikers ride to the Floating City. Then they would seize the vehicles and attack the city itself. Together, as a group, and after the damnable blonde had what Borss was after.

They stood at the shore, the Floating City and its defiant steel walls in the distance. They had spotted the flat-bikers on boats, moving out to the walled compound, but when they arrived at the very edge of the road, ready to collect the vehicles, they were gone. All of them. The Hangers had spotted the smooth woman and her team on board the fast boats the Floaters used as attack and defense vehicles. Kinsker had seen them up close. There was no way the Floaters could have gotten a single flat bike on the tiny boats. And there had been just the three boats. They must have loaded the bikes onto some broader, flatter boats, but he didn't see them anywhere.

He crept around the edge of the big stone monument that bordered the edge of the broken road, careful to keep the bulk of his body hidden from view. The Floating City's spotters were always alert, and they would be looking for the Hangers to pursue the woman—especially once she told her story of encountering them in the mountains, and whatever fate had befallen Ruck.

Doubt crept into Kinsker's head. Had Ruck and all those men faced off against the smooth woman and lost? Had he and the others split off, perhaps back up toward Innsbruck?

No, Kinsker assured himself. *Ruck would have wanted the woman. If anything, he would have disobeyed me, and attacked them, thinking he would be a hero.*

The more he thought about it, the more certain he became. Ruck had screwed up, and the smooth woman had lost only a single flat-bike, while Ruck had cost the Hangers forty hawgs and their riders.

No, I cost us that. That is how the others will see it. We need a win. We need the bikes, the prize, the woman and the Floaters.

"What are we going to do, Kinsker?" The irritation in Faust's voice was obvious. He was angry that he'd lost his chance to shine, and he blamed Kinsker for Ruck's failure. As if Faust, in Ruck's place, wouldn't have made the same mistakes—or worse.

Kinsker ignored him. The more he thought of the boats he had seen the Floaters use, the more he realized how impossible it would be for them to get the flat bikes loaded and back to the city before he and the Hangers had arrived.

No, he thought. *They didn't take the bikes to the city. They moved them somewhere else.*

"Kinsker?" Faust prompted.

"Shut it. I know where they took the bikes. Two miles north, along the shore, is a place where men used to store huge machines, before the cataclysms. Machines that could fly through the sky like birds."

Faust's expression said he had never heard of such a place. It was deep in Floater territory, and only Kinsker knew any of that area. Faust frowned and then said, "Like down in the ruins, we saw that big metal tube with the chairs in it."

Kinsker remembered when they had scavenged in the ruins of Rome, two years previously. They had indeed checked out the city's abandoned airport by the coast. They had found little of use, but the sight of giant metal bird carcasses had been thrilling.

"Exactly. Just like that. The Floaters have a place like that north of here. Two miles." Kinsker pointed. "They took the flat bikes there. No way they could have gotten them on a boat that speedy-fast. So we ride for them now, while they're least expecting an attack. Before they have a chance to get the things to the city on one of their larger boats."

"And then?"

"Then you're gonna stay there, so you can kill anyone who comes back from the Floating City. The rest of us are going to ride out on Floater boats and set the entire city on fire."

Kinsker walked back to his hawg and kick-started it, the engine growling loud, as if in anticipation of his coming victory. The rattling generators out at the Floating City and the buzzing of their boats would drown out the noise of the hawg, so Kinsker had no worries about the sound travelling across the water.

"I don't get to join in on the attack?" Faust shouted over the engine's grumbling.

Kinsker throttled the bike, its engine drowning out Faust's words, then he turned and sped off down the road. Fifty-eight other engines sprang to life, and the Hangers slowly turned their bikes and followed their leader. Faust was left standing in the road.

Ten minutes later, Kinsker saw he had guessed correctly, as six of the Floaters—skinny bastards with short blonde hair, and hardly any clothes, just short pants, and sleeveless shirts, with no shoes—wheeled the flat bikes inside a fenced off area. He could see one of the men trying to close the chain link gate when he had heard the rumble of the Hanger's bikes approaching. Kinsker was two hundred feet from the gate when a second and then a third Floater rushed to the first man, helping him close the stuck gate. It was just a fifteen-foot-tall wall of wire with a few metal poles lending support. They swung the gate into place, and quickly fumbled with a lock to secure it.

Kinsker sped toward the gate. The floaters had just about gotten the lock fastened, when he rammed into the wire mesh at 50mph. The front bone spike on his hawg slammed into the metal chain so hard, the gate snapped back, flinging the bodies of the three Floaters in the air. The metal wall snapped open and swung and clanged against the inside wall of the fence.

Kinsker held his handlebars, and pulled the big bike out of a slight wobble, but he stayed up and raced into the confines of the fenced-in field. The ground had been covered with hard, flat concrete, and the Floaters had kept its surface free of plant life. It was some of the best riding Kinsker had ever experienced. The three Floaters ran for their lives.

But they wouldn't make it far. Kinsker leered as he revved the hawg's engine and chased after the skinny men, running them down one at a time. He thought he'd add their faces to his vest.

49

"Say hello, Agnes, darling," the old man said.

The girl, pleasant but meek, softly replied. "Hello."

The old man closed the door, leaving Val to stare dumbfounded at him outside the small room, where the girl with the green eyes happily had gone back to her book as the door had begun to swing closed.

"What in the name of Odin's sweaty crack are you and Halvard playing at?" Val shouted, anger erupting from her like liquid boiling through a waterfall created by narrow rock.

The old man patted the air, attempting to calm her. "Come and sit, Val. My name is Troben. Halvard will have told you a bit about me."

"Yes," Val spat. "But he never mentioned that your 'genetic material' was a twelve-year-old girl."

Troben eased himself into a kitchen stool and urged Val to take the one facing it. The men stood against the wall, by the hallway door. "She is sixteen," he said, smiling kindly. "Agnes is a genetic abnormality."

"What does that mean?" Val asked, finally taking a seat opposite the man.

"It means we men of science have no idea how she could be possible. Her parents are as blonde as you are. And their eyes as blue as I assume yours are under those red lenses."

Not quite, Val thought, but she made no mention of it.

"I've tested Agnes's blood in the lab. She has different genes from you and me. Exactly what might be needed to jump start the human species."

Val's hackles rose on the back of her neck. "If you think I'll let you and Halvard mate with her..."

Troben laughed. "Not even something we considered, I assure you. I am a very old man, and Halvard tells me much of how he loves his wife in Norway. Besides, one man impregnating Agnes would not be enough to save the human species—even if a baby resulted from the union. It is what her blood holds, you see. And before you consider the notion, we do not want to kill her either. But small vials of her blood, taken with a needle, will be enough for genetic scientists with the proper equipment to analyze. They can see what makes it different, and create something new, which we could then inject into every woman, allowing them to conceive again. It might mean some babies will be born with green eyes like Agnes, or the differences might even yield other changes, like hair color or their resistance to illness."

"Whose idea was it to not tell me we were riding across the world to collect a living human being?" Val asked.

"It was Halvard's. But ask yourself. If he had told you what the journey would entail, would you still have undertaken it? I am shocked you made it here at all."

They spoke for another thirty minutes, Val's anger cooling. She related the trials faced as the group had crossed the European continent. Troben told her a bit about the Hangers and the Gasmen—a group on the far side of Italy who manufactured the fuel the Floating City required. He also told them a little history of the Floating City, which he referred to by its ancient name of Venice. He told them about the roving motorcyclists and how they controlled the mountains. He was surprised the Vikings had made it past them.

"You must understand, getting Agnes back to the North—to Norway, where Halvard has the means to utilize the precious cargo of her genes—is your most important mission. You must protect Agnes at all costs. I am ninety-four years old, and in all that time, I have never come across someone like her. What she carries in her blood can fix the human race. It is our only way forward."

"What about her parents?" Val asked. "Will they not miss her?"

The old man's kindly look melted into sadness. "I am afraid they are both dead now. Venice has long been under siege. Various factions see what we have here in this walled community, and they want it for themselves. They have all tried. The Hangers, the Gasmen even—although they will still trade with us—and every group of men that arrive overland in this part of the world. But the true threat are the pirates out at sea. Their attacks come monthly. And with no new generations of Venetians, sooner or later the city will fall. Until now, our only hope was that these invaders would die out before us. Halvard was too fragile to make the journey here, but you *can* take Agnes up to him in Norway."

"And you have explained all of this to the girl?" Ulrik asked from across the kitchen.

"She is eager to help and to see what is left of the world."

Just then the man with the crossbow burst into the room, his weapon up and at the ready. Hands all around the room went to weapons as the man shouted to Troben. "The city is under attack. We need to get them and Agnes to safety."

The old man stood, surprisingly fast. "Calm yourself, Kristian. The wall will see us through, as it always has."

Kristian shook his head back and forth on his thick neck. "You don't understand. They came in disguise, on board our own boats. The gate is lodged open on one of the wrecked boats. They are already inside the city walls."

Just then they heard a frantic peal of a bell, clanging in an unending clamor.

Outside the building, people rushed to battle stations and speedboats ripped down the canals at reckless speeds.

Troben's face changed as the gravity of the situation overcame his calm. "They must not get their hands on Agnes. Quickly, Kristian, get them to the boats and out of the city." Then he turned to Val and laid a hand on the armored pad of her jacket's shoulder. "Val, you must get her safely to the North."

"We will," she said, then she opened the door to the girl's small bedroom. To her surprise, Agnes was already up and rushing about the room. She had pulled on some durable leather boots, and thrown a thick shawl around her shoulders. She was picking up a battered bag from the floor when Val entered. "Agnes, get everything you need."

The teen girl turned to face her with her bag clutched firmly in her arms. Val could see a thin rolled blanket strapped to the top of the bag. The girl had already been prepared, and her bag packed long ago. "I am ready." The girl's face showed only determination, and not the slightest hint of fear. Val liked her already.

Val reached out and grabbed the girl's arm. "Come with me. Keep up. Do not talk. There will be time for your questions later. Do you understand?"

Agnes nodded, her long blonde hair bouncing behind her in a ponytail.

Kristian led the group down a back staircase to a new canal. Troben remained behind in the small kitchen. Val spared a thought for him, wondering how he would get to safety.

They boarded two long sleek and black speedboats, each with thin red stripes running down the sides. When they were aboard, Kristian piloted Val's boat rapidly down the narrow side canal. Then they swung a sharp right into a much wider canal that looked like a major river running through the city's center. All around her, buildings burned, orange flames crawling higher as smoke billowed into the sky.

The entire city was on fire.

Then she realized the old man would not get out at all. He had no plans to even attempt it. He was dead, as was every other resident of Venice.

50

The twin speedboats shot out of the wide canal and raced toward the already-open rear gate. The flames of the burning city rolled toward the wall, and the men who had raised the gate were already boarding their own escape vessels. The green water was littered with floating, flaming refuse, and several unmanned boats cluttered the way ahead, their bows crushed from collision or their decks aflame.

Kristian piloted the sleek black boat like he knew what would be coming, swerving the boat with practiced ease. With him in the first boat were Val and Agnes, Ulrik and Heinrich. The others were close behind in the second boat. As the second boat cleared the mouth of the canal behind them, Val saw two white, stubby speed-boats giving pursuit. And she recognized the man behind the wheel of the first white boat. He had been in the first group of Hangers they had encountered.

"We are being chased," she told Kristian.

As soon as the speedboat cleared the gateway out of the city, Kristian threw the boat's throttle lever forward, and the boat jolted ahead like lighting, throwing Val backward into her cushioned seat.

The boat hugged the outer wall of the city, which made a sweeping right angle turn. The second boat was close behind them, and Val could see that Morten and Oskar had drawn their weapons, ready to battle, should the pursuing white boats catch up.

To their right were two smaller islands that looked as if they had been stripped of anything useful long ago. Jagged chunks of concrete and stone were all that remained, clustered on the surface in tall seaweeds.

Behind them, a wider channel ran between the abandoned outer islands and the rusted-steel walls of the burning city. Six more white boats rushed out of the channel.

At first, Val thought they were more Venetians fleeing their former city-turned-inferno. But the long scraggly beards and laced-up mouths of the men aboard the boats made them easy to identify. The Hangers had taken the boats before torching the city.

Val worried briefly that the Hangers would be armed with guns, like the man on the Tunnel Road. Her arm still stung from the grazing she had received. But the men in the boats had nothing in their hands. Still, there were enough boats and enough men that they could easily overpower their party.

Kristian hugged the wall with the boat, rounding the southeastern tip of the island. The buildings inside were a roaring inferno now, and the steel wall bulged from the intense heat. Val saw sea life—stars, barnacles and the like—bubbling and popping off the base of the massive steel plates, where it met the water. The heat baked off the wall in convection waves, making the distant outlying islands hazy in her sight.

To her side, Agnes clung to a thick plastic handle, her face a mask of terror, her eyes wide and unblinking, as her entire life was turned to ashes.

Behind her, Ulrik laid his large ax on the floor of the boat and took out a small hand-ax. He eyed the flanking fleet of Hanger speedboats. The boats were gaining, and the bearded men inside them were holding large rocks in their hands now.

Then Kristian cranked the wheel sharply, bringing the boat in a ninety degree turn around a corner formed by the heating steel wall. Beyond it was a narrow channel between the wall on the left and yet another low lying, nearby outer island. Agnes leaned over the sidewall of the boat and vomited a soup of chunky yellow into the water, as Heinrich staggered to keep his footing in the stern of the craft.

The second black boat did not take the turn, instead shooting straight, no doubt intending to go around the back of the outlying island. The lead Hanger boat followed Kristian, and the second white boat from the main canal followed Morten's crew. The rest of the Hangers pursued Val. *One less boat to deal with,* she thought.

The channel was too narrow for the pursuing white boats to pass them, but their leader edged his craft right up to their stern. As soon as the long black boat was past the tip of the outlying island, Kristian cranked the wheel again, jagging the boat to the right, and cutting off the pursuing white boat. At the last second, the Hanger swerved left, smashing into the heated wall around the city, where it skipped along the edge, scraping the fiberglass hull with an ear-splitting shriek, before he steered the boat back toward his prey.

The second Hanger boat had time to see Kristian make the sharp turn, and quickly took the lead, coming up behind them.

Kristian darted left, moving the sleek boat wider and out into open water, and throwing the throttle to its stop, hydroplaning the boat as it leapt like a tiger into the wide open bay. Off in the distance, Val saw the second black boat, with Morten, Oskar, Nils and Anders aboard, come shooting out from between two tall clumps of pale green and yellow sea grasses. The white Hanger boat was still chasing them down.

Wind blasted Val's face, whipping her long blonde hair back. Spray from the water spattered against her red lenses, but she could still see just fine.

Then three things happened at once.

Across the bay behind them, Morton's boat was boarded by four Hangers. Oskar, Nils and Anders were bowled over by the men crashing into them, and five bodies tangled to the deck of the black boat. Morten and his opponent collided, too, but he was larger, and ready for the impact, delivering an elbow to the man's throat and knocking him off the boat in one swift move.

While that was happening, two Hanger boats pulled along each side of Val's boat. On the left, the leader of the Hangers had passed off the wheel to another man. He pitched his arm backward and hurled a head-sized rock at Val's boat. On the right, the second white Hanger boat was inching closer, nearly in range for a boarding party.

Ulrik lunged up on the back of Val's seat and flung himself from the black boat, his body flying through the air, his small hand-ax leading as he careened straight into a group of four Hangers. The pilot tried to steer away, but his timing was a second too late. The boat peeled away as Ulrik began flailing with his ax, fists, elbows and forearms, smashing targets all around him in a tornado of frenzied activity.

Val's line of sight turned back to her own vessel just in time to see a another rock—this one massive—slam into Kristian's head, shatter his skull and wedge itself inside the man's head, like a small rock dropped in the top of an egg. A sludge of blood and brain swept up and over the back of his head, where it was scoured away by the blasting wind.

As Kristian's body slumped in the pilot's chair, Val dove for the steering wheel. She quickly realized she had no idea how to drive the boat, and she had no idea where Kristian had been taking her.

51

Val tugged the slick plastic wheel to the right, chasing after the boat Ulrik had attacked, and pulling away from the lead Hanger boat, in case the man had any other boulders to hurl.

The lead Hanger boat followed, but fell behind as Val realized the throttle was still thrown to full forward. The operation of the craft was not as difficult as she had imagined—there was a wheel to turn left and right, and the lever to her right controlled speed and acceleration. She looked for a brake and then realized there wasn't one. When the time came, she would just have to reduce the speed, or throw the boat's motor into reverse.

On Ulrik's boat, he was hurling bodies overboard, where they cartwheeled across the water and quickly sank from view, pulled under by their heavy leather clothing. Heinrich stepped up next to Val at the front of their boat. He watched Ulrik's frenzied battle fury. Val saw him looking and said, "That is why he is called 'Fearless.'"

Across the bay, Morten pulled a Hanger off Anders and flung the man, one-handed, over the gunwale of the boat and into the frothing bay. With his other hand, he yanked a second man up, slammed his forehead into the man's nose, and chucked the limp body over the side. "And that is why *he* is called 'The Hammer,'" Val added, laughing.

"I fear I will be known as Heinrich the Seasick," he said, as Val jerked the boat in a zig-zag pattern, trying to throw off her pursuers.

At that moment, Agnes pulled her head back over the side and wiped a long sticky strand of saliva from the corner of her mouth with her forearm. Her face was pale, and her green eyes were wide and the color of the water. "I think I will have that nickname before you."

Ahead of them, Val could see a large artificially flat stretch of coastline. Parked there were two more of the white speedboats. She didn't know how many more Hangers might be waiting on land, but she knew her Vikings would fight better with solid ground under foot, so she aimed the boat for the spot.

Across the bay, she could see Morten piloting his black boat—Oskar and Anders were lowering the Venetian pilot's body into the water, while Nils clung to the side of the boat, looking as seasick as Agnes. Morten gave Val a wave and altered course, so they would meet each other at the shore. Then he threw his throttle forward and the boat leapt ahead, even faster than Val's boat.

Ulrik had taken the white boat, and steered to follow Val. The rest of the pursuing white boats fell behind. In open water, they were far slower than the sleek black boats. But they drew into a pack and stayed on course, following Ulrik and Val toward the shore.

Ahead of her, Morten slammed his motor into reverse and turned as the boat came into the concrete dock. The side of his boat bumped into the solid structure, and Oskar and Anders leapt to shore. Morten followed as Nils scrambled up from out of the boat's stern. But Morten's leap had shoved the vessel away from the dock, and Nils plunged into the water. Spluttering, he slowly climbed out of the water, pulling himself up onto the dock.

Val brought her own boat against the dock in a similar move. Agnes and Heinrich climbed ashore, and then Val lunged to the dock as one of the pursuing Hanger boats came in at full speed, ramming into the longer black boat. The white boat flipped up and over it, and as Val rolled on her back away from the collision, she watched as the white boat—still filled with three Hanger men—toppled over her head and then mashed into the concrete surface beyond the docks, skidding and scraping its way across a huge lot.

At the far side of the wide open space, she could see the ATVs and a dozen two-wheeled bone-clad motorcycles. Running toward her were ten bearded men wearing the skins of their enemies, their faces sewn up tightly. But the flipped boat toppled straight for them, forcing the group to scatter. Two men were too slow, and the crumpling, scraping speedboat smashed into them, sending their bodies flying the way the boat's occupants had been flung once it hit the ground.

Morten and Oskar descended upon some of the fallen men, skewering them with swords. Nils ran to the side of the action, heading for Agnes. When he reached her, he grabbed her arm, and pulled her with him toward the distant ATVs. Anders stood behind the cover of the wrecked speedboat, firing arrows at the foes attempting to flank Morten and Oskar, as the Laplanders performed their back-to-back sword dance.

Val rolled to her hands and knees, about to stand, when a booted foot connected with her stomach hard enough to launch her vertically. The strike ripped all the air from her lungs, and every nerve ending burned as she soared upward. Before she landed, the Hanger who had kicked her, struck out again, this time with a fist, hitting her in the side of the head and sending her now falling body spinning away from him.

She crashed to the ground, and the impact launched a mouthful of spit through her bloody teeth to splatter on the ground in front of her. The man rushed for her, his dark brown leather boots clomping on the concrete. Val tried to scramble to her feet, but her arms and legs would not yet obey her commands.

All she could do was flop over on her back. As the man nearly reached her and pulled his leg back for another walloping kick to her side, Val found a slim reserve of strength and hauled her legs up over her head, rolling backward into a small reverse summersault. She sprang backward and up, but her angle was wrong, and instead of rising to her feet, she launched backward, sprawling to the ground with a groan.

The Hanger's kick missed, and continued upward, reaching so high that it threw him hard onto his back.

Val tried to move again. To take advantage of the man's blunder, but her body fought against her will, seized by pain. And the man began to stand. Her head lolled to the side, as she tried to find some last sliver of strength with which to rise and fight. Then she saw her end rushing toward her.

A speedboat caromed off the edge of the dock and launched itself into the air, just feet from the ground, like an arrow aimed at Val's supine body. She held her breath and waited for death, but she did not close her eyes. She had known this moment would find her eventually, as it did all warriors. She would be damned before she didn't face her life's end head on, just as her parents had.

52

Kinsker had allowed the other men to move ahead and into the fray, skirting the battlefield and moving for the true prize. He had made for the cover of some small bushes growing along the airport's fringes, concealing himself from view, and waiting for the perfect moment to strike.

As his quarry made for the parked flat-bikes, he spotted Faust. The man had been waiting near the shore. Kinsker had sent him a small group of men at the airport, and they had run across the field to attack the Northerners as they disembarked. But one moron—he thought it was Werner—had slammed his boat into another, flipping and crashing up onto the airport's field, throwing the men into chaos. Faust had wisely stayed separate from the others, and now he took the perfect opportunity to deliver the mother of all kicks to the smooth woman when she was on the ground.

Kinsker almost cheered, but held his tongue as the slim Northern-er and the young girl they had acquired in the Floating City ran past.

He lunged out of the foliage, swinging his arm hard into the slim man's chest. His arm clothes-lined the smaller man, knocking his feet out from under him and slamming him on his back. Kinsker kicked out with a booted foot, his heel connecting with the man's jaw. The North-erner stayed down.

The girl kept running, but he caught her in just three long strides, spinning her around to confirm his suspicion. He'd caught a glimpse of her during the chaotic boat chase, but as he spun the young girl—she probably was not yet eighteen years—he saw her face up close.

Her eyes were the most startling shade of green. The hue of sum-mer leaves on trees. Kinsker did not know what the girl's value was, but he knew he had never seen a person with green eyes, and he had never even heard of such a thing. He knew instinctively that the girl was the treasure the Northerners had come for, and for which Borss had prom-ised him a fortune.

But now that she was his, he thought he might find better uses for her than Borss's promised treasures. Then again, maybe Borss would pay more. Maybe a lot more.

He glanced back across the field and saw that the Northerners were decimating his men. The battle would soon be over, and it looked like the Hangers were going to lose.

Faust tried to kick the smooth woman's face—a shame—but she rolled away, and the fool fell flat on his back.

Then an engine roared, and Kinsker saw that the last Northerner—the big one—was driving his boat off the bay and up onto the airfield!

The boat skipped up into the air, heading right for Faust and the woman. She stayed down, watching the boat come, but Faust was just getting up as the flying speedboat slid through the sky over them. Its bow angled up and the free spinning propeller at the end of the boat's outboard motor sliced right into Faust's head. One second Faust had a head and was getting to his feet, and the next second his headless corpse was pitching over onto the woman, as the boat continued past.

The Northerner leapt off the side of the boat with the biggest damn ax Kinsker had ever seen. He swung it wide in front of him, cleaving into three Hangers, before he crashed to the ground in the midst of their lifeless limbs.

Kinsker had seen all manner of men in his day, some of whose skins now clothed his body, but he had never seen warriors like these.

The girl struggled and pulled, trying to free her arm. He broke into a run, dragging her with him. As he neared the fence, he saw the parked flat-bikes—*his* captured flat-bikes—and the hawgs all lined up near the gate he had smashed open.

One of the flat-bikes had two seats—the regular seat, and a make-shift saddle that had been fashioned across the rear fuel tanks. He pushed the girl onto the rear seat, and she struggled, thrashing her arms and legs.

Kinsker punched her in the mouth, just hard enough to end her resistance. He climbed onto the saddle of the flat-bike, and with one hand tangled in the girl's long ponytail, and the other for the throttle, he kickstarted the ATV.

It rumbled to life, much quieter than his hawg, but he liked how stable the vehicle felt. He had examined it earlier, before the attack on the Floaters. He liked that the four-wheeled vehicle had no manual gears to shift through. Just a forward, neutral and reverse setting. With a final glance back at the chaos winding down behind him, Kinsker sped out of the airfield, his woozy hostage dangling over the propane tanks behind him.

Ulrik stood and exhaled hard, then he blew snot and blood from his nose, where one of the Hangers had tagged him in the face. Five bodies lay around him, three headless. Only one of the men was still moving, but he was missing both of his hands, and Ulrik no longer considered him a threat.

The scent of blood that filled the air was stronger than the tangy odor of the bay and harbor. Around him, Morten and Oskar were cleaning their blades, and Anders was recovering arrows from the men he had shot. Heinrich was helping Val up off the ground. Ulrik saw no sign of Nils, and he turned in a full circle looking for the little man. Just as he spotted the man climbing to his feet near some distant bushes, he realized who else was missing.

"Val," he called. "The girl."

Val and Heinrich ran toward Nils and Morten and Oskar began scanning the edges of the great clearing.

"Where is she?" Val said when she and Heinrich had joined him.

Nils was moving toward the ATVs near a silver chain fence. He yelled over his shoulder. "They took her. Bastards took her."

"Shit," Val yelled, and she sprinted for the waiting quads at the fence-line.

The rest of the men rushed to keep up with her.

"One of the ATVs is missing," Nils yelled. "The two-seater."

"Go," Val shouted to Nils, since he was ahead of her and had reached the ATVs first. "Just go! We will take the two-wheelers."

Nils hopped on the first ATV he reached. He kickstarted the vehicle and blasted out of the yard, heading for the open gate.

Val reached one of the Hanger's huge bonebikes, but it was laying on its side, on the cage. She bent down to pick it up and found she couldn't budge the thing. "Ulrik," she screamed. "They are getting away."

Morten, Anders and Oskar leapt onto their ATVs and rushed out of the yard. Heinrich was about to move toward Val, but she shooed him away with a wave of her hand. He was too slight a man to help her with the huge bike, and Ulrik was already bending to lift it. Heinrich turned for the last ATV, while Val and Ulrik hefted the fallen bike up onto its wheels. He steadied it for her, while she tried to start the vehicle. She balanced the heavy bike between her feet, got the engine running, then tried to take off. The bike coughed and died.

Ulrik had moved off for one of the other Hanger bikes parked on its kickstand well away from hers, near the fence.

She looked at the bike and remembered Erlend explaining the operation of the ATVs to her that first day. He had told her how the ATVs were automatic, and there was no need to shift between gears. Checking the handlebars, she saw the clutch and then she looked down for the foot pedal to change the gears. She understood how to operate the vehicle, but she had never needed to deal with such things on the ATVs.

She tried again, and the bike stalled once more.

She made a quick prayer to Odin, and cursed the name of the bastards who had taken Agnes, then she tried the bike a third time.

It jolted forward, and then died.

And then it started to tip over.

53

Val screamed from the depths of her being, letting all her anger flow over the bike, as she smacked her fingerless-gloved hand on the handlebars and lunged with her leg, straightening the tipping vehicle.

Now using the clutch, she started the bike again. She released the clutch slowly while increasing her twist on the throttle, and the bike started slowly in first gear. The huge handlebars made the two-wheeled motorcycle strange to steer, but its heavy weight kept it on a straight path. As she made her way toward the gate, she sped up, and when the motor sounded like it was about to leap out of the bike, she tackled the clutch again, and shifted into second gear.

The bike raced out of the airfield and onto a small road that had been cleared of debris and vegetation. The road was wide and fairly straight, and far in the distance across the flat terrain, she could see a hint of the Alps, some peaks still sporting a fringe of white on top like the tufts of hair remaining over an old man's ears.

Ahead of her on the road she could see some of the Vikings on ATVs. Without a thought for Ulrik and how well he might be managing on his motorcycle, she sped up and shifted again. Her transition into third gear was not as good as her shift into second, but by her move into fourth, she felt she had the hang of it. As she moved up past a dangerous 40mph, she shifted into fifth gear.

She passed Anders, Morten, and Oskar as if their vehicles were standing still. The blast of the air in her face shook the last cobwebs from her mind after the beating she had taken at the hands of the Hanger before the boat had decapitated him. She also let her fury over the operation of the bike seep away, replacing it with a cold, calculating rage.

Ahead of her, Nils tore up the road in pursuit of the Hanger who had taken Agnes. Val shifted up to sixth gear, roaring past him at 55mph. The road was better than most they had seen to the north, and the bike handled perfectly, its tires chewing up the miles as she raced after the Hanger.

A moment later she spotted him in the distance.

The thick knobby ATV tires cast a thin plume of dust from the road, as the man took the ATV onto the shoulder. He had taken a side road—*an exit*, Nils had called them—from the main road, and it swept around to the side of the road before moving up an embankment. It then crossed a seamless bridge over the original highway, before descending to join another major road, this one moving west. Val was catching up to the man before, but his need to slow down on the curve allowed her to gain on him even more. By the time she descended the far side of the ramp and merged onto the new road, he was no more than fifty feet ahead.

She could see Agnes on the back of the ATV, holding on for dear life. The driver had his hand woven through her long hair, pulling her head around him, so he could hold her and the handlebar grip at the same time.

He sped up once his tires hit the main road, passing random rusted metal poles and trees lining the edge of the highway. He passed under a large, green, metal sign hanging down above the road at an angle. On it were the numbers 90 and 60, painted on white circles ringed by red, and a small icon of a truck.

The road was completely clear of obstructions. No derelict cars or fallen tree trunks, and Val realized this was a main route regularly used by the Hangers—and the Venetians—when they traded with the Gasmen, about whom Troben had told her. There was no way she would allow the man to take Agnes to the Gasmen as some kind of trade.

She twisted the throttle and raced forward until she was nearly on the tail of the racing ATV. Then she swerved out around it and put on a burst of speed, swishing past the Hanger.

She didn't give the man a second glance as she sped past. Instead, she kept going at her breakneck speed, rushing a hundred yards ahead. The Hanger slowed the ATV, and as she watched him in a small mirror hanging from the underside of the handlebar, he looked back, thinking to turn and retreat. But far in the distance, just coming down the exit ramp, three more ATVs had joined the chase.

There was nowhere for him to go.

Val sped ahead, and then slowed rapidly, pulling the clutch and crushing her brakes. She brought the huge bike to a stop and parked it across the road. She set the stand and hopped off, stepping between the motorcycle and the onrushing Hanger.

"Nowhere to go," she said aloud, even though the man was not close enough to hear her.

The Hanger showed no sign of slowing. Seeing no way out, he did the opposite. He sped up, steering to the shoulder of the road so he would race right past Val.

She pulled her ax from its holster on her waist, then ran at the front of the oncoming ATV, angling to intercept him. The Hanger leaned forward and sped up, swerving even harder for the shoulder. Val adjusted course, but she wouldn't be fast enough to get in front of him.

Behind the Hanger, she saw the others coming hard on their ATVs, and Ulrik was coming up fast on one of the motorcycles. He slid ahead of the ATVs, and then the men formed a wall of vehicles, side by side across the road. The Hanger wouldn't be able to turn back, no matter what.

Val knew she wanted to attack the man, but she didn't dare risk hitting Agnes with her ax, or causing them to crash. She wasn't able to come up with a different plan, so she carried on running, and as the vehicle was nearly level with her, she leapt, one arm reaching out for Agnes, and the other swinging the ax toward both riders.

Her left arm slid between the Hanger and Agnes, grabbing the girl and tugging her off the back of the ATV. The Hanger still had a handful of the girl's hair, which ripped clean out of her skull, spraying a thin arc of blood from where a chunk of flesh had stayed attached to the hair tugged out at the roots.

Still airborne, Val hugged the girl close with her left arm, while finishing the swing of her right arm and letting the ax fly. She saw the blade sink into the Hanger's back, at the shoulder blades, but she was twirling and spinning through the air, with the girl's body slamming into hers. Her vision was obscured by what was left of the girl's long hair, and then her back made contact with the pavement.

Agnes's weight crushed the air out of Val's lungs, and her chest compressed, a rib painfully snapping. Her skin tingled all over, her body's pain receptors dancing in anguish.

She threw her free arm out for balance and to stop her from rolling onto her precious cargo. Instead, they skidded on Val's back. Her head, on the bottom of the sliding human tangle, snapped and bounced back off the ground, and then her stomach lurched. She realized their skidding journey had come to a halt.

The world was a blinding blue and green, as Val took in the spinning sky. Then as Agnes slowly raised her head up, and into Val's view, looking down at her with wide eyes, Val realized what she was seeing.

Color.

Her goggles had been knocked off her face and down around her neck.

Agnes looked down at Val's face, staring into the first set of green eyes the girl would have ever seen that were not in a mirror.

VECTORS

54

Quiet.

Val thought of the word often. It was the one she had uttered to Agnes before rolling the girl off her stomach and quickly pulling her red-lensed goggles back into place over her eyes.

"Quiet," she had said.

Agnes had obeyed the command, and to Val's surprise, the girl had never asked another word about it. But the look on her face had said everything about a lifetime of being ostracized, about the girl's sense of isolation and about her shock and relief at seeing there was another person in the world like her. Val understood perfectly. Those were all the things she had felt, when she had first seen Agnes in Venice.

The Hanger had survived the ax embedded in his back, but all the fight had drained out of him, and he had simply coasted to a stop further down the road, slumped on the handlebars of his hijacked ATV.

Val approached the man and saw that Ulrik stood over him, ax at the ready. But Ulrik had thought the same way as Val had—this would be a great opportunity to find out how the Hangers had known they would be coming through the mountains after wintering in the castle. It was clear to Val that the Hangers had been lying in wait. The question was why.

"Who are you?" Val said.

The man's reply was hostile and in German.

No problem, she thought. *I have Heinrich for the German, and Ulrik's ax for the hostility.*

She called Heinrich over, and told him to pass on the message about the ax. The Hanger responded with a quieter tone.

"He says they were told we were coming through the mountains," Heinrich translated.

"Who knows of our journey? And why would they wish to stop us?"

Heinrich translated her questions, but the Hanger made no reply.

Ulrik stepped forward and dropped the pointed tip on the end of his ax head downward, where it landed on top of the Hanger's booted foot with a thud.

The man jerked in pain, but did not scream out. He did, however, start rambling in German. Heinrich had a hard time keeping up.

"A man named Borss contacted them by bird. They were told we were after the genetic material, and when we would be coming. The Hangers were promised a fortune if they would deliver you and Agnes back north of the mountains."

"Wait, Heinrich. Did this Borss know of Agnes? Did they know what we were looking for?"

Heinrich translated the questions and the Hanger mumbled his answer, still not removing his head from the handlebars of the ATV.

"No," Heinrich said. "The Hangers knew only that we were after a 'prize' of some sort."

"And this Borss? I want more information on him."

Heinrich translated, but no reply came. He looked at Val and shrugged his shoulders.

Ulrik stepped backward, swinging his ax head up and around, before allowing the blade to cleave through the Hanger's booted foot.

The man didn't move.

"This one is done playing," Ulrik said before striding away.

With Agnes safe—except for some lost hair and a small flap of torn skin, which healed a few weeks later—they had recovered the stolen ATV, and with their two new motorcycles, they continued west.

They had run out of fuel for the big motorcycles before Milan, and rigged a second seat on another of the ATVs, managing eight riders on the six remaining quads. Agnes always rode with Val, who never let the girl out of her sight again.

They gave Milan and Turin wide berths, avoiding the Gasmen's sphere of influence. With pursuit gone, and no more threats to face, the group had quickly lapsed back into their old travel routines, clearing many miles during the mornings and then scavenging for propane and hunting for food in the late afternoons.

Val's injuries—a broken rib and some burnt flesh from road rash— were the worst they had sustained, and the sharp stabbing pains in her chest had dissipated after a few weeks, until they coalesced into just a dull throb in her chest. The bullet wound on her arm had healed faster. The other Vikings had been knocked around, but no one complained about their injuries. Nils's jaw was swollen and purple, but even he said nothing about his pain.

Things were fine until they reached the French foothills of the mountains, and discussion turned to how they should proceed.

"The passage through the mountains is smaller here," Nils said.

"I do not dispute that," Ulrik countered. "I am simply saying we should return to the castle once we are on the far side of the range. It was a safe location, and we know the way. We know where to find food and water."

"Yes, but we also know the challenges awaiting us in that direction," Anders countered. "Are there still more of the Hangers in the foothills on the German side? More of the swastika-faced Long Knives? What about the Blue Men in Denmark? Is this Borss still hunting us?"

"Forget about Denmark," Morten said, poking at their campfire with a long stick from where he sat on a dry log. "I have no wish to face the sea creature under the bridge again. Whichever way we return to the north, crossing the water will be our biggest challenge."

"Morten is correct," Ulrik conceded. "But returning along our path through Germany is at least known territory for us, whereas this plan to go through France..."

They had heard rumors of hideous creatures in France from as far away as their homeland in the distant North. Seafaring Northern-ers had brought back tales of vicious pirates patrolling the waters of the North Sea, and the English Channel. There were also horror stories to scare small children, of sea creatures that had come ashore to claim the world as their own. They were alternately described as an army of monsters that moved like sharks with the legs of horses or as the bastard aborted children of the sea goddess, Ran, intent on chewing a hole in the world.

Either way, everyone was skittish about traveling through France.

Anders had suggested they make their way through France to Belgium and the Netherlands, stealing or fashioning a boat to get them to the shore of England. Then they would travel north and finally cut across to Stavanger. Ulrik favored the familiar path, and Morten had actually sided with him. Heinrich had been quiet, and Nils only contributed geographical information to the argument. Oskar seemed uninterested, as he roasted a long-legged rabbit on the fire.

Agnes slept nearby, and Val sat observing the debate. She already knew which way they would travel. Although she had collected Agnes successfully, her mission was not yet complete.

Finally, Anders turned to Val and said, "What do you think, Val? Surely the sea is the better way to return home, pirates or no." His hooded bird slept on his shoulder.

Val stood and walked to the fire. She reached into the spit and pulled the rabbit Oskar was cooking away from the flame, then used her knife to slice away a piece of meat, handing Oskar the rest. "There is more to our mission that Halvard did not share with the rest of you."

Her comment was met with stunned silence.

"As he did with his 'genetic material,' he did not give all the facts up front. If he had, it might have been quite difficult to find those of us willing to take up this task."

"What else is there?" Ulrik asked.

She sat and took a bite of the seared rabbit flesh. When she had chewed and swallowed, she told them. "It is a special machine part. I have a drawing of it. Halvard said the machine part is as important as Agnes," she smiled at them, "although he did not call her by name, of course. I am interested in having words with the man about his methods when we return, but it changes nothing. We each took on this journey for a single purpose—to save humanity. Without Agnes, and without this machine, Halvard has assured me that the human species will die out. If we had only his word for it, I would question whether to trust the man. Especially now, after his deception with Agnes."

The men grumbled their agreement.

"But the lack of births..." Ulrik said.

"Precisely," Val agreed. "We have the proof. If we ever want to see another child born into Midgard, we need to succeed."

"Yes. This is what I am saying," Ulrik went on. "Surely the safer path—"

"I am sorry, my friend," Val cut him off with a wave of her knife and the last bit of blackened rabbit she trapped against the blade with her thumb. "But the machine part is very specific, and can be found only in one place."

Knowing what was coming, Ulrik sat heavily on his log, sticking his tongue into his cheek thoughtfully, as if grasping what this new stage of the journey would entail, despite his complete lack of knowledge on the unknown terrain.

"We go through France."

Anders nodded as if she had made the only sensible choice. His fingers nimbly fletched an arrow, replenishing his depleted stock with a minimal amount of movement, so he did not disturb Skjold's slumber.

"And then, if we live long enough, perhaps we will take the sea route home."

In their quieter moments wintering in the castle, Heinrich had told her stories of the creatures that had come into Germany from France. She looked at him now and saw his face was haggard and gray in the firelight. He met her goggle-covered eyes, with a look of resignation.

Neither of them thought the group would make it through France.

55

France turned out to be fine. Until it wasn't.

Five days into their journey across relatively peaceful fields and derelict towns, cruising on mostly good roads, the worst they had seen was a two-headed wild boar that Anders had passed up, fearing that the meat might be more harmful than a night without supper.

They were off the ATVs for their mid-day break, which was growing longer as the warm spring days turned to summer humidity. They had set up a camp under a large elm tree, with their ATVs parked a hundred feet away across a field, under a line of pine trees. Blankets were spread out on the ground so they could nap in the afternoon heat under the shade of the tall elm in the field, away from the heat reflecting off the strip of blacktop. The shelter from the blazing sun dropped the temperature on their skins slightly, and the occasional cooler breeze made the weather perfect for napping.

It was too good to last.

"More of the slime trails," Nils called from further out in the field, where he had walked to relieve himself. His spirits had long since returned. Val had spent more time with him of late, talking well into the night, and learning as much as she could from him about the world.

"How many this time?" Val asked from her blanket. She was only half interested.

For the last two days they had periodically seen long thick streaks of slime across the road or in the fields near it. The stripes of greenish mucus-like substance were often a foot wide, and would stretch for fifty or more feet before abruptly ending. She and Nils had discussed what they might have been with Anders, who was their resident expert on animals, and with Heinrich, who knew the creatures in this area better than anyone else.

But the thick bands of slime had left them all shaking their heads in confusion. They were either left by the world's largest snails, or by something they could not even imagine. The only thing they were sure of was that the slime was organic.

"Many," Nils said, turning to come back. "Every few feet."

As she watched him, Val noticed something in the distance, well across the field, beyond Nils. Frequently scanning for the often absent Skjold, had left her distance eyesight keen. Dozens of dark humps in the grass, like horses or large dogs, if they were laying down on their legs. The lumps appeared to be stationary, so she took her eyes away from them, looking back to Nils as he approached.

But then movement pulled her eyes back across the field. The shapes were approaching—and fast.

She lunged to her feet and pulled her ax from its black holster. "Nils!"

He turned to look behind him when he saw her armed. The move would cost him. One of the creatures was moving on a collision course for Nils. As it got closer, she could see it clearly, but still had no idea what it was.

"Up! Wake up!" she yelled, as she ran toward Nils, and pulled her smaller hand-ax with her left hand.

Ulrik was the first to his feet, ax in hand. He ran for Val, but would be too late.

The animals were strange. Their faces were all teeth in wide open, circular mouths. Thick curved horns, like those on a ram, topped their heads. The bodies were long, as tall as a human, with flat, beaver-like tails that drooped down behind them. The creatures' skin was slick and shiny, like a fish, and slime oozed from the flat tails. The creatures hunted in a pack like wolves, and they were fast.

Really fast.

Nils was just pulling a small ax from his belt, when the first creature leapt at him, its thick horns headed for the man's chest. But the creature didn't gore him. Instead the animal's tooth-filled maw opened wider, like a snake about to swallow an egg, and the teeth clamped on to Nils's face. Nils flailed backward, the animal toppling with him, its tail twitching and flapping like a fish pulled out of water on the end of a line.

That thought triggered recognition for Val, and she knew what this animal had once been: a lamprey. She had seen the eel-like things attached to trout that men had caught in the North. Although those were usually no longer than a foot in length, and as narrow as a finger. Their leech-like mouths attached to prey and sucked on, rarely letting go until there was no more blood on which to sup.

Before the attacking animals had cleared Nils's fallen body, Val's ax blade sliced through the creature's mid-section, severing the lower legs and tail from the upper part of the body. Instead of blood, a gout of the slime spurted from the animal. Val wanted to pry the rest of the thing off Nils's face, but there was no time. Two more of the creatures had lunged upward at her on their powerful legs.

She reversed her strike with the smaller, sharper ax leading, and cleaved one animal right down the middle of its face, each thick ram's horn passing on either side of her wrist. The beast's momentum propelled it onward, adding strength to the cut. A burst of the slime shot forward, coating her arm up to her shoulder.

The second lamprey creature struck out at her other arm. The mouth closed over the elbow of her black leather jacket. Sharp teeth slid through the fabric and into her skin.

She screamed as the teeth sank in, but spun and tugged her hand-ax from the bifurcated face of the other lamprey. With a quick swing, she cleaved the creature clinging to her elbow, just behind its eyes. As the body fell away, she was horrified to see its bodiless head still sucking at her elbow. She jabbed the tip of her hand-ax under the creature's lip and pried it off, flicking the open ring of mouth and teeth through the air.

As she ran for the next attacking lamprey, Ulrik was by her side, hacking at the creatures before they left the ground. While the others joined the fray, Anders hurried to Nils's side, struggling to remove the monster from his face, but she knew the sad truth of it.

He would be too late.

The thought filled her with a sudden fury.

She screamed again, but this time in anger. She rushed ahead into the herd of the lampreys, which had been whittled down to fewer than twelve, but more were coming from every direction, drawn either by the sounds of battle or scent of blood. Her long ax bit into the face of another, as its ram horn mashed into her shin, adding the irritation of a minor pain to her already pulsing anger.

For the next half an hour she murdered every lamprey she could reach, hacking and tearing at them, until she was covered in a chunky coating of slick mucus.

56

Borss was in a good mood. Despite setbacks, despite delays, despite the incompetence of the Hangers, he finally knew where he would catch up to the Northerners. He just needed to lay in wait with his men at the perfect location.

And at the perfect time.

It had taken several days' journey, but the trip would be worth it. He looked out over the industrial site and smiled. Everything he would need for his trap was here. And the location was far more suited to his personal tastes than his own building in Bremen. *I might just make this place the capital of my new empire*, he thought.

In the distance, the sounds of sword against wood, and cudgel against skull resounded and carried on the wind. Borss smiled. They had found the area occupied, but soon it would all be his.

"What makes you smile, my lord?" Zeilly asked. She was ever at his side, like a loyal dog, and now calling him 'my lord' since her mistake on the bird tower. He had forgiven her impertinence, as he always did. Her charms were too much to resist. And she brought other, larger assets—a broad power base granted to Borss through her family. He could not dispose of her, or kill her. She was far too valuable for that.

"I like this place, witch. It suits me."

"And is this place connected to your prize, my lord?"

It was amazing to Borss that this woman could sound both snarky and congenial with each utterance. Her defiance of spirit always aroused him. But he had no time for that now. Tonight, perhaps.

"The Northerners will come here next," he told her.

"Oh?" she asked him, feigning surprise. "What of the Hangers?"

Borss laughed. He knew that news of the fall of the Floating City and Kinsker's defeat had traveled to his men's ears by bird. Then the story had spread through the camp like wildfire. His men had returned from the East, and Borss had immediately ordered them to march west with him, toward this place with its strange metal appendages soaring into the sky.

"Kinsker failed, but it matters not. My informant tells me they are on their way here. They have lost another man, but they still have the girl. That is all that matters." Borss glanced at Zeilly and saw that conniving smile on her face. She was good at getting him to talk, especially concerning things about which he should stay silent. He thought about backhanding her, but just then three of his men ran up the road to him.

"How is the conquest?" Borss bellowed. "Are you done?"

"Not yet, Lord Borss," one man answered. He had slick gray hair, and wore brown and tan clothes. There was a fresh cut near his eye, and he appeared to be limping. "There is a small band of fighters still giving us trouble. The rest of the people here were easy—even their leader. But this group of five are excellent fighters and they have us at an impasse."

Borss scowled. "We shall see."

He strode past the soldiers, Zeilly trailing behind him. The road was wide and had been cleared, because some of the buildings to either side had crumbled. But the ruins looked more like the result of skirmishes than earthquakes. Most of the place was intact. Buildings, staircases, stacks of metal boxes and the thing he prized most of all: transportation. The people living here had kept the location clean of debris, and had even put recent coats of paint on some of the industrial buildings. But the proximity to salt water had taken its toll in some structures, and he could see the tell-tale rust patches creeping up metal walls and along the towers' skeletal frames.

As Borss strode forward, the sounds of battle increased—all from a centralized area. His men were right. It *was* just the one small clash left.

As he rounded a corner, a gust of sea breeze with the associated smell of rot that often filled harbors assaulted his nose. But he thought the smell was one of freedom. Of possibility. Beyond the corner he saw an open concrete courtyard, where five men armed with swords were standing in a wedge and fending off attacks Borss's men made, thrusting ahead with their wooden clubs. The attacks looked half-hearted to Borss. If his men, who outnumbered the stalwart defenders, would just throw themselves into the fray, they would be victorious. They would also lose some numbers though, and he had told them not to risk their lives unnecessarily. *No scolding needed then,* he thought. *Just a show of power. A reminder of why they follow me.*

As soon as his men saw him approach, they backed off, allowing Borss to walk past, toward the five swordsmen.

They were not much to look at, these men. Their clothes were rags and mismatched. Their hair long and shaggy. Even the swords were different types and styles. One had a huge broadsword. Another had something closer to a machete. Two of the men had thinner blades closer to fencing foils. Those would snap easily in Borss's metal-covered hands. The fifth had a curved Asian sword.

"Lay down your weapons and join me now," Borss announced, his voice booming and echoing. "It's your only chance to live."

He had no intent of letting any of them live, but sometimes the glimmer of hope was all a man needed to drop his resistance. Other times that hope fueled the fight.

All five men started to raise their swords up, but Borss ran forward. A huge man, he nonetheless was fast. Had always been. And he wore the heavy metal chest and back plates with the spikes, as well as his heavy spiked gauntlets when he trained, so their extra weight did not slow him. At his side in a specially crafted leather holster was the huge, spiked metal ball of his flail, and seated next to that was the handle. As he ran at the men, the chain jangled, almost like a lover calling to him. His hand slipped down to the handle, then he snapped his arm out, his huge muscles tugging the deadly weapon from its resting place. The metal ball shot forward and mashed first through the top of an upraised sword—one of the feeble ones—and then through the face and skull of the man foolish enough to call that a weapon.

Blood and brain detonated from the man, showering all the combatants in gore.

Borss felt a sword clang into his back, finding its way between the metal spikes of the back plate, but stopped by the plate itself. He twisted his torso, and swung the flail back toward his attacker. He heard the satisfying clink of the spikes on his back breaking the attacker's sword, just before the metal flail impacted the unarmored man's side, drawing a high pitched shriek that faded in time with his life.

Borss raised his left hand as two more swords came for him. The first—the curved Asian blade—he simply caught in his metal coated fist. He wrenched his hand back, and the sword blade simply bent to the side under his strength.

At his front, the other man with a tiny sword rushed forward, thrusting. The pointed tip of the blade mashed against Borss's chest-plate and buckled, snapping and sending a shard of metal back to impale the sword's owner.

The man started to fall, but didn't make it far. Borss tugged the flail back in front of him, swinging hard. The deadly ball arced out on its chain, first grazing across the face of the man with the shattered blade, gouging flesh away. The spiked ball continued its course, burying itself in the Asian sword fighter's chest. Ribs cracked and blood gushed from the wound. With a cough of viscous red, the man staggered back, freeing himself from the spikes, before collapsing dead.

Borss pulled the weapon again, and the ball travelled to his side.

Bodies fell all around him, and only the man with the large broadsword was left. He had backed away from the fight, perhaps with that niggling little glimmer of hope urging him on. Now he dropped the huge blade, and it clanged on the concrete ground. The man was crying and raised his hands in the air. "You said you would let us live if we surrendered," he said.

Borss snapped his forearm forward, letting the flail rocket ahead. He released his massive grip on the wooden handle, and the weapon shot across the courtyard. The flail took the man's head clean off, before embedding itself in a rusting metal wall at the back of the open space. The chain and handle banged against the wall, and then swung down like the pendulum of an old clock, dripping blood from the handle at each extent of the pendulum's swing.

"I said it was your only chance to live. I didn't say it was a good one."

57

The soaring gray tower rose up out of the urban decay of what used to be a town called Charleroi, in Belgium. It was round and flared up near its top, hundreds of feet in the air. As the only standing structure, Val walked the weary group through the rubble and ever present creeping vegetation to the base of the wide tower.

As they stood at the base of the round, conical tower, looking up at its ribbed surface, Heinrich said, "I have seen something like this in Germany. Before I was alone. It is a cooling tower from the old world."

"Cooling what?" Val asked.

Heinrich shrugged. "They were used to generate electricity. I do not understand how it was accomplished. Only that it was."

Val nodded. They had already seen some of the still lingering methods the old world had used to create power and light. All she really cared about was whether the towering structure would provide them with shelter for the night.

They found a set of ancient concrete stairs with a rusted metal rail and ascended to a hole in the side wall of the tower. There were holes near the base of the structure, behind tangled vines and pine shrubs, but the stairs seemed more inviting.

They were weary after the long walk.

The ATVs had run out of propane three days earlier—a full two weeks after Nils's death. They had taken Nils's body with them, away from the slime-coated and stinking field of death. Two miles up the road they had found a moss-coated church and graveyard. The church's roof had fallen in, but the place had seemed a better one in which to cremate Nils than anything else they had seen in France.

When the ATVs had run out of propane, they towed them for two days, searching for fuel, but after the second day, Val had declared the vehicles useless. "They have become more burden than tool. Let us proceed on foot."

Their three days on foot had been uneventful, but they were all sore, and short of patience. The tower was just what they needed to return some wonder to their worlds.

The open doorway provided entry to the strangest structure Val had ever seen. The interior was a massive, circular open space. The tower's floor looked like a series of concrete islands—seven of them—arranged around the outside rim, connected by a starburst of concrete walkways and surrounded by dark water. At the center of it all was a moss coated hole, like a drain that had long ago been filled. She looked up and understood why. Rings of spiraling ribbed walls led up to a wide, roofless opening. They were standing inside the largest chimney she had ever seen, perhaps the largest built by mankind.

"This will not keep water off, if it rains tonight," Morten complained.

"It is one of the only structures standing," Anders pointed out.

"I like it," Oskar said, his voice full of wonder, and echoing loudly through the hollow tower.

The acoustic quality to the space was amazing, sending reverberations of sound back to them in a pleasing cascade of diminishing tones. Oskar picked up a small cracked chunk of concrete from the walkway and threw it toward the distant curved wall. The man-made rock pinged off the wall, and down through the slats surrounding the floating island to plunk in the water. The echo from the projectile rippled around the tower. Oskar smiled like a small boy, as Skjold fled up and out the top of the tower, the noise having startled the sensitive bird.

Val sat down on the concrete next to the raised funnel-like hole at the center of the chamber, trying to make sense of the faded letters painted on the walls by vandals long ago.

"It is not perfect, but I fear we will not find perfect tonight. We stay here," Val announced.

Morten slumped to the ground next to her. Oskar wandered the far end of another raised catwalk, checking out the strange building. Heinrich went back out the way they had come, to collect firewood, and Anders dumped his pack before following the German.

Ulrik stood, and Agnes stood with him. Val had noticed that the girl was gravitating toward him after the attack in France. She suspected the girl was scared of her now, having seen the berserker in her set loose. She stayed close to Ulrik at all times now, and spoke rarely.

Val turned her eyes to him. He looked angry.

Seeing the larger man's visage, Morten picked himself up and said, "I think I will go and help the others gather wood."

When he had left, Val got to her feet, scraping dust off her clothes. "What is it?" she asked him, feeling frustrated that he was again questioning her decision. She knew this odd cooling tower was not the optimal place for them to spend the night, but they had seen nothing better in the miles they had covered during the day—and certainly not in the ruined town around them.

"Why did you not tell us about this machine part Halvard needs?" Ulrik dropped his sack, and leaned his ax against a metal railing, first pushing on it to make sure rust and age had not withered the metal to dust.

Val stepped closer to him. "Keep your voice down." She pointed up at the sloped walls of the tower. "The echoes will carry your words like the wings of a bird."

Ulrik's scowl said he was not concerned whether the others heard him. Agnes took two steps behind him and set her pack down, but her eyes and ears never left the discussion.

With Oskar exploring the walls fifty feet away, and the others outside the building, Val lowered her goggles and looked into Ulrik's face. He flinched as though he'd forgotten the startling green color of her eyes.

"I did not know who I could trust, Ulrik. Halvard advised caution."

Ulrik's features softened, and he ran his fingers through his long beard. "You could have been killed—at any time since we left the North. And then no one would know about this necessary piece of metal."

She hung her head slightly, and out of the corner of her eye, she saw that Oskar was returning from his explorations. She suspected it was because the volume and echo of their voices had dropped, and he was hoping to eavesdrop a bit. She slid her goggles back onto her face, then looked back to Ulrik, hissing at him. "The thing is necessary. I do not know for what. But I tell you this—there were times at the beginning I thought of leaving you all behind. I did not know you, but I knew me."

His eyes rose in shock, his thick bushy blonde eyebrows arching high on his sunburnt forehead. Before he could speak, she leaned in toward him.

"*Now* I know you. Now, I trust you. I trusted Nils and Erlend. Heinrich will forever be grateful to us that we fed him when he was out of food—as we should be to him, when he kept us from starving. And the others have been reliable, of course..."

"Then what is the issue?" Ulrik said, his voice low, as Oskar approached.

"I do not know..." she said.

"Know what?" Oskar said, stepping onto the concrete island, and walking around the deep funneled hole, peering into it.

"We were just wondering how this place was built," Agnes said, not even looking at Oskar, as she rummaged through her pack for her blanket.

Val and Ulrik looked gratefully at the girl for her quick save, while Oskar continued across to the walkway that led out of the tower, oblivious to their facial expressions.

But as he went out, no doubt looking for his constant companion, Morten, Val became more and more certain from the man's nonchalance that he had been spying, most likely at Morten's behest.

58

Anders and Heinrich set up a fire outside the tower, at the base of the stairs. After they had cooked the rabbits Skjold had brought back that day, they would cover the fire with water and smother it long before dark. They didn't know if anyone was nearby, but they had long since learned to extinguish fires before the sun fell.

Morten and Oskar had reclined on the ground by the fire, and Anders, his work for the day done, was fletching a new arrow, his avian partner having once more taken to the sky. Heinrich had taken to the task of cooking food for the group—and they were happy to let him do it. He could turn a dry burnt rabbit into a veritable delicacy with the unusual herbs and plants he gathered on their journeys. He had several small pouches in which he kept crushed and ground powders and tiny sprigs of crushed leaves. No one understood his cooking arts, but their mouths all watered when he told them he was going to try something new.

Tonight, Val noticed Ulrik being more standoffish than usual. He had sat on a low concrete wall, after scraping it clear of a creeping red vine. It was a good position to keep an eye on everyone in the group. A shoeless Agnes sat next to him, rubbing her sore feet. The both of them were far enough removed from the others that Morten felt comfortable poking fun.

"So grandfather and his young protégé are on their own tonight," he said.

The others laughed. Val said nothing. She didn't like Morten's way of denigrating everything and everyone, but she would tolerate it some, because she knew the men needed to unwind. She had been particularly wary of the looks Morten had cast at Agnes since they had collected her in Venice. It was a strange look. Val wasn't sure what it meant. Was he looking at the young girl in lust, or with bemusement at her green eyes? Was it possibly resentment because of the loss of life that had been involved in collecting the girl? All Val knew for sure was that the man's eyes lingered too long on the teenager.

"Oh, leave them alone," Anders said, still chuckling. "She is probably just terrified of your stink, Morten."

That got Oskar and Heinrich laughing harder, and Morten was always a good sport about good-natured ribbing, so he took the barb with a smile.

"I am serious when I say her eyes frighten me, though," Morten said.

"I have never seen anything like them," Anders agreed.

Val stayed quiet and forgot to breathe for just a moment, curious where this new tangent would lead.

"I have," Morten admitted, his face lost in a long ago memory.

"Oh!" Oskar blurted. "Oh yeah! I almost forgot that."

Heinrich left the rabbit he was preparing with a thick sauce. "You have actually seen green eyes before?" he asked, incredulous.

"Oh yeah," Oskar started. "It was years ago. Morten and I..."

"Oskar!" Morten snapped at the younger man.

Oskar's mouth snapped shut with an audible clack of his yellowing teeth.

"Is it a secret?" Anders asked, suddenly interested. "I would hear of this encounter with another green-eyed person."

Morton raised his hand and said, "It was—"

But Val stood and said, "I, too, would hear of this strange encounter. Come, Morten. Tell us."

A dark look floated across Morten's face, and it did not escape Val's notice that he glared at Oskar before beginning. "You must understand that it was many years ago, when we were quite young, and very hungry."

Val tilted her head to the side, as if to say 'How is that relevant?'

Morten looked lost in thought for a moment. "Oskar and I took a job to kill a man and abduct his woman. We were told that she was the wife of another man, and that she had fled with our target to a cabin by the sea. We were given vehicles with tracks for the rear wheels. They made travel through the snow quite easy. The man hired us under the agreement that we asked no questions."

He lapsed into silence. Oskar looked suddenly rebuked, as if he had only just now remembered that he should act sorry for his part in the affair. Anders seemed unaffected, as if murder and kidnapping were common occurrences. Heinrich looked horrified, and Val loved him a little for it. But she had more important things on her mind.

"You say the man had green eyes?" she asked.

"No," Morten shook his head. "The woman. Brilliant green, just like Agnes. Anyway, we killed the man, and delivered the woman. We got food and gold. We were young and we were desperate. I always thought the man who hired us was lying about her being his wife, too. I just could not prove it. We left right after the job, heading back to the sea."

Now Val's attention was riveted on Morten, and her heart jack-hammered in her chest. "Where was this green-eyed person living?" She tried to keep the venom she felt in her blood from entering her voice. She had no idea if she was successful.

"Somewhere on the gulf of Sweden. We had crossed Lapland to the south, which was why the man had given us those motorized sleds. They were like the ATVs, but with skis on the front instead of wheels. Oskar wanted to keep them, but I just wanted away from the place. It was the darkest time of my life, and I am not proud of it."

Oskar remained silent. Heinrich turned back to the cooking, and Anders continued the conversation with Morten about the strangeness of green eyes, as if an admission of murder and abduction had not been made.

Val sat still, barely breathing. Her body hummed with adrenaline and her ears buzzed with white noise. It took her a few minutes before she could even form a coherent thought.

Her mind filled with blind rage, as it would over the murder and abduction of any innocent person, but in this case there was a personal connection. Her mind flitted back to that locked section of her subconscious, where she kept her very few treasured memories of her very brief childhood.

The seals.

The polar bear.

The cold.

The house was on fire. There was a terrifying arc of blood from the man on the frozen shore. Her father.

Black smoke boiled into the sky. Someone was telling her to follow the seals into the water. She had a cloak, that fitted to her body, like a seal's skin. She couldn't breathe. She was underwater and she couldn't breathe. Looking up out the hole in the ice. Her limbs going dead.

Who had told her to get in the water?

Then it was there. Filling the surfaces of her mind.

Blonde flowing hair.

The woman's initial nonchalance, followed by concern and then panic.

And those startling green eyes.

Her mother.

Watching the woman's blood-matted hair dangling down from the back of a strange vehicle with wheels inside treads.

Morten and Oskar had killed her father and abducted her mother.

Two conflicting thoughts kept Val immobilized for another half hour as they rampaged through her mind's eye.

The first was that she was going to have to deal with Morten and Oskar. And there would be blood.

The second was what Morten had said about the woman.

They had delivered her *alive*.

59

Twenty miles north of the cooling tower, they came to the remnants of a city named Brussels. As was their habit, they moved cautiously around the fringes of the city. This one was surprisingly intact. The buildings all stood, but they were coated in the green they saw everywhere as the plant kingdom slowly swallowed the empty world. Without new humans being born, the flora faced no competition.

Val had swallowed down her fury, examining the situation from different angles. She needed to ambush the men, preferably away from each other. She felt confident she could take both Morten and Oskar in a one-on-one fight. She wasn't sure she could take them at the same time, and she was concerned that the others—particularly Ulrik—would try to stop her.

Her biggest challenge was finding a time where the two men would be apart from each other, and away from the rest of the group. And now that she had had the time to think clearly, she realized she needed the men—or at least Morten, who was the better and stronger fighter—to get Agnes safely back to Halvard. They were just ninety miles from Rotterdam, where she would need to collect Halvard's machine part. And that close to the sea, the area would likely be populated with pirates and brigands.

They had not come across many people on their travels. Most of the last vestiges of humanity had clustered in gangs and groups. Small towns and communities, often led by those who were stronger or better suited to maintaining control. She wondered about Troben and his community of Venetians, and not for the first time mourned their loss. They were the closest thing to a proper civilization she had encountered since leaving the North. While she did not particularly crave the company of civilized people, she would rather have them than scum like the Hangers.

She fully expected to find more gangs as the group approached the water. And she would still need to travel five hundred miles to reach

Stavanger. Her vengeance would need to wait for the opportune moment. And it would need to be held at bay until she extracted the information she wanted most: the location where the men had delivered her mother, and the name of the man who had hired them.

Ulrik had become silent, keeping an eye on everyone with suspicion in his face. Her own mistrust of the others had led to him mistrusting them all. Val didn't think the man had spoken a word in three days. Perhaps sensing something wrong with him, and having had time to forget the pungent horrors of the lamprey field in France, Agnes had begun walking closer to Val.

"We need to find a place to stay for the night," Val announced. "I am tired. This city looks dead. We should be safe here."

They had been following a road with a huge metal fence still standing on their right. In many places the fence had been knocked down—or had fallen down—and it was now being covered by grasses and shrubs escaping from the forest.

Without a word, Ulrik led the group into the trees. Words were barely necessary at this point in their routine. Even Agnes knew what to look for in a suitable site. Multiple exits. Cover from the road. Shelter, in case of rain. Nearby fresh water.

As they walked through the thick tangle of trees, Val caught glimpses of sunlight reflecting off glass or metal. A building was nearby. The forest was alive with the chittering of small birds. Their presence was comforting. If there had been danger ahead in the form of strange beasts or rampaging groups of people, the birds would have found another home.

"What is this?" Ulrik said. That he had spoken aloud alarmed Val. She hurried to his side, and Agnes followed close on her heels. The others took a slower pace, but followed her out of the trees and into a clearing.

Before them stood a magnificent structure of green metal bands and thousands and thousands of panes of glass. The building was reminiscent of the castle they had seen in Germany, with long halls, curved roofs, and domed cupolas of varying sizes and shapes. Some of the panes of glass were stained by generations of bird droppings, and some of them were strange shades of pink and blue, as if the glass had been dyed.

Val had seen colored glass in the North, but it was rare. Most structures were built without glass, their inhabitants spending most of their days out of doors anyway, and tolerant of insect life. But she had never seen entire palaces constructed from glass. Inside the amazing structure was an explosion of flowers and trees, often pushing right to the roof. Off across a field to their right was a wave of black solar panels, floating like suspended leaves over the undulating grass.

As they approached the building, Val shook her head to ensure her eyes were not playing tricks on her. It was raining *inside* the building, but the sky above was clear and the sun was shining.

"The panels must power a pump to spray water inside," Heinrich guessed.

"Why would you capture trees and flowers inside a building made of glass?" Agnes asked.

No one knew the answer. Walking closer through the tall grass, they saw that several of the panes of glass were broken, and in a few places tree branches had made a burst for freedom, sending thin tendrils up through the cracks toward the sun.

"It is strange, but appears safe. We will stay here tonight, after checking for less obvious dangers." Val began a perimeter check to the left and Ulrik went right.

Agnes stayed by Val's side, peppering her with questions she could not answer.

Later that night, after they had eaten a stew with wild herbs and carrots, the summer sun was finally dropping off the edge of the world. Val waited, lying on her blanket under the stars, wondering when her opportunity would come.

They had seen a sign calling the strange glass palace the 'Royal Greenhouses of Laeken'. Upon exploring the interior of the oddly enclosed structure, they had examined the flora. In many places, with the solar powered water sprinkler systems and heaters for the winter, the trees and bushes had grown so thick inside the enclosure without anyone to tend to them, that it was impossible for a man to pass through the long corridors or even into the massive domes. With the clear sky, they had chosen to camp outside the structure in the grass.

It was a full hour after the others had fallen asleep—Heinrich snoring loudly, Anders making soft humming noises in his throat and the rest breathing heavily—that Oskar finally rose, as he did each night, to go and relieve himself. Peculiarly shy, he usually went far away behind tree cover. As soon as he left the clearing, Val was up, her four-inch knife blade unsheathed. She left her axes and leather boots by her pack.

Barefooted, she moved quickly through the grass, rushing low through the wilderness, the shushing of grass against her legs obscured by the sound of a hooting owl.

She arced around Oskar's path, reaching the trees almost at the same time as he did. Then she moved cautiously through the cover of the forest toward the sound of pattering urine on fallen leaves. She was within four feet of him—just on the other side of a large gnarled tree trunk—when she heard his piss stop. She froze in place, her knife raised, thinking the man had heard her. But then he sprayed the last few drops, and sang a few words of a song to himself, before she heard the distinctive burr of a zipper being tugged upward.

His feet shuffled through the undergrowth, and Val lunged around the tree, the knife raised. Before Oskar had fully turned in her direction, she had clapped a hand round his mouth and the two of them were propelled to the ground.

They crashed into the low plants, and Val's blade came up in front of Oskar's panicked eyes. Then it found its home snug against his throat. As soon as the metal touched his clammy flesh, he ceased struggling and stopped trying to scream. The greasy man was a fool, but he knew when his life was at risk. His eyes were wide in the silver moonlight, wondering why his leader had attacked him. The scowl on Val's face left no room for misinterpretation. She meant to do him harm.

She was about to take her hand from the man's throat and speak, when she heard a soft sound to her left.

Just outside the edge of the trees, crouched in the grass, Agnes waited, watching for whether Val would slit Oskar's throat.

60

"Agnes," Val hissed. "You want no part of this."

"What *is* this?" the girl asked. She showed no signs of fear, as she had after the lamprey field and Val's killing spree. Now she seemed interested. She also showed no sign that she was going to go away.

Val turned her attention back to Oskar, who waited wide-eyed under Val's hands. Val slid her hand away from his mouth. "Do you believe I will cut you?"

"Yes," he said quietly. "What have I done wrong?"

"I need information from you, Oskar, and I will cut pieces from you and stab you here in the dirt if you do not deliver it. Do you understand ?"

"What do you want to know?" Oskar whined. "Anything."

"The green-eyed woman. Tell me. Everything." Val's knife involuntarily pushed harder against Oskar's neck as she said it, drawing a slim line of blood.

"Okay. Okay," he said, panicked. "It is like Morten told. What do you want to know?"

"Where did you take the woman? Who was the man who hired you?"

"It was nearly twenty years ago," Oskar started, his voice beginning to rise. Val quickly pressed the blade harder against his throat while clamping her hand on his mouth. She glanced back at the field, beyond Agnes and back toward the rest of her sleeping party. It would already be difficult enough to explain this to the girl. Having to explain to the others would be awkward. Oskar stayed quiet under her palm, and she slowly removed her hand.

"How many years? Exactly."

Oskar thought for a second, and Val could tell he was counting in his head. "Eighteen."

She pressed against his throat at the volume.

In a much lower voice, he went on. "We took her at Lulea, on the gulf. Then we took her with us back to a village on the sea, called Narvik.

The man's name was Vikord. I don't know anything else. It is like Morten said. We were desperate for work and for food."

Val glanced up to see Agnes attentively watching, but still rooted in place. In one swift move, Val leapt back, pulling the blade from Oskar's neck and her hand from his mouth.

"You will say nothing to Morten about this. Nothing," she hissed, pointing the tip of the blade at him. "You will continue to fight for me and for this group, to keep this girl alive and get us safely back to Stavanger. The human race is more important than this issue."

Oskar sat up, rubbing a hand on his neck and smearing the thin line of blood there. "I do not understand why you have treated me like this. Have I not always fought for you?"

Val had to control herself from lunging at the man again. "I owe you a blood debt, Oskar the Abductor of Women. The man you killed was *my father*. The woman you took...was my mother." With that she tugged the goggles from her face, her green eyes haunting in the beam of moonlight piercing the trees.

Oskar's mouth hung open in shock, his eyes widening. She watched his face, as it seemed like he was working through his chances of drawing his blade and killing her.

"I would not do it, Laplander," came a low voice from behind Val.

She whirled to find Ulrik emerging from behind a tree. In his hands he held his long ax.

"You probably would not be able to take her, Oskar. But I would definitely cleave your intestines out and drag your corpse around by them, if you did. The end of all life would be on us then, since she is the only one who knows where to find the machine part Halvard sent us to retrieve. If Ragnarok is assured, I will gut you in a second."

The four stayed quiet for a moment.

Then Oskar slowly got to his feet, his hands far from the hilt of his sword. "I will not draw weapons on my comrades." His eyes darted toward Val, with the look of a wounded dog. "Even if they would draw on me. I am sorry for what we did to your parents, Val. It was long ago, and we were dying from hunger. If I knew anything else, I would tell you."

He turned to walk back to the greenhouse, and Ulrik laid a meaty hand on the slim man's shoulder. "Not a word to Morten. If you fight well, and if we make it back to Stavanger, I will protect you from her wrath until the end. But if you falter, anywhere from here to there..." He let the threat hang.

Oskar looked back to Val. "I will keep it from Morten, and I will continue to fight for you. I was just fifteen at the time, Val. Younger than Agnes. And I have proved myself for you many times since we left the North. Hopefully you will find some forgiveness in your heart by the time we return."

He didn't wait for an answer, but pulled free from Ulrik's grasp and stalked back to the camp.

Val started after him, to ensure that his first move would not be to rouse Morten, but Ulrik stopped her with a wave of his hand. "His heart is good, despite his bluster. We have seen that these last months on the road. He will keep his word."

"Yes," Val said. "And I think we should rectify the issue with the machine part." She glanced at Agnes, who had stood from her perch in the grass. "You both need to know what it is, and where to find it."

She showed them the rough map Halvard and Nils had drawn for her in Stavanger, and a detailed hand-drawing of the wheel-like object. Then they returned to the camp, where the others were all asleep, and where Oskar laid under his blanket, wide-eyed but silent.

The next day they moved on, and Ulrik lingered close to Oskar and Morten throughout the day, watching and listening. Oskar was more helpful than ever with finding wood for the cooking fires, and he talked less, but he showed no other sign that he intended to betray his word.

Four days later they came to the outer reaches of Rotterdam, where Halvard had told Val she would find the mysterious machine part.

Winding like a snake through the crumbled and seemingly empty city, was a river running east to west. Countless stacks of metal containers reaching a hundred feet high lined the banks. The Vikings crept through the streets, staying behind cover at all times. Anders requested permission to climb a huge metal structure like a criss-crossed ladder, with rusted metal cables dangling from its tip. They guessed the thing was used to move the colorful boxes onto the huge boats—now empty carcasses—that were still moored in the deep river.

At some time during the Uttslettelse or after, the waters had risen beyond their original point, and many industrial yards and buildings were now under a foot of clear water.

They waited at the base of the large skeletal structure as Anders climbed, accessing a tiny glassed-in room at the top. From there he would have a good view of the river, and would be able to spot any obvious dangers in the town.

It took an hour for Anders to make the climb and return to the ground with the hooded Skjold, but it was well worth the wait.

"We are not alone," he said, his bow gripped tightly in his hand.

61

There were a lot of them. Men varying in age from sixteen to sixty. They wore no common uniform like the Hangers, but the men were armed at all times, carrying stylized clubs with long narrow railroad spikes that had been fitted through the bulbous ends in an X pattern.

The men roamed around the shipping yards in packs of seven, and they went about various tasks like checking the security of locks on certain doors and shipping containers, as well as moving boxes from one place to another.

Val and her people stayed to the shadows, watching and waiting as patrols passed by. They had no way of knowing whether these men might also have been searching for them. After interrogating the Hanger leader, Val and Ulrik had reasoned that the Long Knives had also known they were coming. They were possibly also working for this man, Borss. Val personally wondered about the tidal waves of the Blue Men, as well. But they had just seemed crazed. And the maze-like funnel to their park had been created long before Val had been born. But with the knowledge that someone was hunting them, and had eyes out for Agnes, Val and Ulrik agreed that any other humans they encountered were most likely enemies. As they spied on this new group, they also saw many men carrying paint in cans, marking containers with the word 'Vectors.' Heinrich explained that the word sounded more like Dutch than German, and translated as something like 'Fighters.' He told them there were similarities between the Dutch and German languages. He had understood only some of what they had overheard the roving groups saying, but none of it revealed any useful information besides the name of the place—the Authority.

The building they needed to reach was in a disused area surrounded by a lot of mud. It was adjacent to the docks where packs of the Vectors moved boxes.

"We will keep to the shadows until after dark," Val told them. If they tried to access the building in the daylight, their tracks would be visible. Her plan was to get in at night and be long gone by morning. Then they would try to find a boat seaworthy enough to return to the North. They had all agreed it was a good plan. Anders volunteered to continue stealthily exploring the location, and look for a functioning boat. If they could have a vessel ready, they could be away and across the water to England before dawn.

"You need to be extremely careful, Anders," Val said, laying a hand on the hunter's shoulder.

"If I have not returned by nightfall, I will not be coming back at all. Go on without me." He spoke softly and for her ears only.

"We will, if necessary, but do not make it so. Return."

With that he slipped away, moving from the shelter of one building to the next.

They stayed hidden, keeping low and still whenever they heard Vectors nearby, but the men never lingered long, focusing on their business. By late afternoon, no more Vectors came near.

"Everyone show me your packs," Val said.

"Why?" Oskar asked.

"You all need to carry some of Ulrik's things. He will need to empty his pack to carry the part. It is quite large." Val made a space between her hands the size of a small shield. Then she showed them the drawing of the object. It was perfectly round, with a small square hole in the center, and the thickness of four shields stacked. There were three ridges spreading from the outer edge of the wheel to the central square hole.

"And what exactly does this thing do?" Morten asked.

"I do not know," Val admitted. "But Halvard assured me he needed it, and that it would weigh a lot."

"How much is a lot?" Ulrik asked.

"You will probably be the only one of us who can carry it," Val said. "Half as much as Agnes. Maybe more."

Agnes raised her eyebrows. "That is a lot. And that building is huge. How will we find something the size of a wheel in there?"

Val nodded, as if she had anticipated the question. "If the inside of the place is still untouched, there are numbers on the shelves. We just need to follow them."

"I do not know numbers," Ulrik admitted. "I never learned them."

"I know them," Agnes assured him. "We will find it."

Hours passed and no more Vectors came, but neither did Anders, and there had been no sign of Skjold. When darkness settled over the land, Val waited two hours for Anders. When those two hours had passed, she waited fifteen minutes longer. Eventually, Ulrik stood up and stretched, his empty pack laying limp on his back.

"It is time, Val."

"Damn it," she said, standing and shaking her head. She could only hope that Anders would meet them after they emerged from the building. She refused to believe that the man was dead—or captured. He was far too stealthy to be seen and far too good a fighter to allow himself to be caught.

She stood and readied herself. The others did the same. They had discussed the plan. Agnes was to stay by Ulrik at all times. Val would enter the building first with Ulrik and Agnes, then Morten and Oskar would come next, keeping watch within the building, as Val searched for the metal wheel. Heinrich would stay just inside the door to the building, keeping watch for Anders's return or for any of the Vectors.

There was an entrance on the far side of the building they had scouted earlier in the day, but it was too close to a building that housed some of the Vector men. So they would enter and leave from the door surrounded by the thick mud. It would leave thick footprints and show they had gone both in and out the same way, but they would all walk through the footsteps of the first person, hiding the group's number.

As they slipped out of the building they had waited in all day, the night air was chilly. Val felt the cold settle on her skin like a blanket of dew. Then she realized it was raining slightly.

She took Heinrich aside and whispered some private instructions to him, then she moved to the front of the group, and stopped at the edge of the mud.

"Agnes, behind me," she said softly, then she took even, measured strides into the mud. Her feet sank six inches into the squelching muck, and each footfall sent a plume of rank stench into the air. The mud was, she assumed, from the bottom of the river, from when it had flooded last. The rain fell a little harder, and the sound of it obscured the gentle lapping of the water in the nearby harbor.

When she reached the building's door, she twisted in her tracks—not taking her feet out of the mud—and looked back at the others. Agnes was two steps behind her, the girl's hair already wet and plastered to her forehead. Ulrik was a few steps behind her, and Morten behind him, his longsword still in its sheath, but his hand on the pommel, at the ready. Oskar followed, glancing all around. Heinrich stood beyond the mud, but was ready to follow, once the way was cleared.

Heinrich watched them step through the path, each foot carefully placed in a mucky hole that Val had created with her original steps. Soon it would be his turn.

Val pulled her knife and slid it into the rusted hasp with its orange padlock. She pried back slowly, until the lock broke with an unearthly loud metal groan, before it plopped into the mud by her ankles. Everyone froze and looked around. As rear guard, and someone who had yet to enter the muddy footprints, Heinrich quickly spun around, looking for any sign of the Vectors.

All was quiet.

When he looked back, Val had slipped into the building, and Agnes was following her. When Oskar slid through the door, Heinrich started across the muddy path. When he reached the door, he stopped and peered inside the massive space. There were metal shelves stretching up to the ceiling, thirty feet above the door, and the aisles of shelves were full of metal crates. The racks stretched over hundreds of feet down the length of the building toward the distant Vector stronghold.

Off to one side, Heinrich could see Oskar moving into the shadows, where he would keep watch. In the other direction, the much larger Morten also moved to keep guard. Straight ahead, down one of the aisles, Val, Ulrik and Agnes hurried, shining a small hand-cranked flashlight beam at the shelves, checking the numbering system.

Heinrich stepped backward toward the doorway, then carefully walked further backward, placing his booted feet in the muddy prints. He closed the door. Then he walked all the way back across the mud. When he got to the last footstep, he stopped and reached down to unlace his boots. Awkwardly, he managed to slip one foot out of a boot and reach his stocking-covered toes to the concrete.

When both of his feet had cleared the mud, he reached back for his boots, collecting them in his hands and shaking them briefly, dropping globules of mud back into Val's very first footstep.

Then, his boots in hand, Heinrich ran off into the night.

62

Val hurried through the silent warehouse. They were so very close to their second goal. Then all that remained would be to safely return to the North. But every nerve in her body sizzled, telling her something was wrong.

She wondered whether it was the recent revelation of Morten's and Oskar's prominent part in her early life. As far as she knew, Oskar had been good to his word, and Morten was oblivious to who she was. But something *was* wrong. She could feel it in her bones. She didn't like that Anders had gone to scout for a boat and had never returned. If he had been discovered, she figured he would have made a huge ruckus, and Vector men would be running around the docks on high alert. So where was he? Where was Skjold?

She and Ulrik had split up, with him moving off to check the adjacent aisle with Agnes. He used a small flashlight powered by a solar panel that had been charging in a beam of sunlight all day. When he held the button down, it shined a painfully bright light. Val's own flashlight was not as bright, and not powered by the sun, but by a small metal arm that she cranked. One revolution of the crank arm would power the light for about a minute. Instead of keeping it on all the time, and cranking the thing until her hand was sore—and having the device continually produce the whining metallic whirr it made—she turned the light on only every few feet.

She swept the beam at the metal stamped numbers and letters on the shelves. *QAB477, QAB478, QAB479.* Then she turned the light off and continued down the aisle in the dark. She was beginning to understand the number and letter system. She had learned numbers when she was young, and she knew the letters as well, even though she could not read complete words. Amazingly, most of the metal boxes were still on the shelves, coated in decades of dust. All that was left was to follow the codes and hope the box she needed was still in its designated place.

The vast warehouse loomed in the silence. Val dropped her goggles around her neck so she could see better in the ambient light, which was minimal. There were some skylights far above her head, but with the rainfall outside, little illumination penetrated the dusty gloom. She found herself holding her breath so she could hear the open space around her. If she listened hard she could hear Ulrik's footsteps in one of the other aisles, and every once in a while she could see the flicker of his light as he checked the tags on the hard metal shelves.

She couldn't hear Morten or Oskar, but they had been told to stay back near the exit of the building, hidden in the shadows. She cut over an aisle and once again checked the numbers.

RIJ522, RIJ523, RIJ524.

Almost, she thought.

She was in the correct aisle. The number Halvard had given her was RMN643. The entire aisle seemed to be the same first letter. The next two letters denoted sections of the aisle, and the numbers were for the shelves and the actual items they housed.

She sped up, still stepping lightly and straining to hear in the dark.

She stopped and cranked the metal arm on her light to check the shelf numbers. RQR246. She had overshot her target.

She turned in the dark and stopped, certain she had heard a small shuffling noise on the dusty concrete floor. Straining her ears in the dark and hearing only the thrumming of her own blood pounding through her veins, she stepped to the side of the aisle, leaning into the heavy shelving unit.

She paused, keeping perfectly still.

Two aisles away and much further back toward the door, she saw Ulrik's brilliant blue-white light flicker on and off. He was too far to have made the scuffling noise she had heard.

A rat, she thought. *This place must house many.*

But in her heart she knew it was something else. Moving on instinct, she slid sideways along the shelf, feeling the metal crate behind her back. All the boxes were roughly the same size—four feet wide by three deep and two tall. The shelves had been stacked in an orderly fashion, with a foot and a half of space between each crate and the upright metal support posts. Val felt her way in the dark to one of these empty spaces, pulling herself up in a chest high gap.

The sturdy old shelf did not move, and it made no creaking noises as she climbed into it. She paused, listening for another sound, but hearing nothing.

Then she moved again, feeling her way to the shelf's edge and pulling herself up onto the next shelf. Then another and another, until she was close to the building's ceiling. After another brief pause, she moved back up the aisle, walking on the tops of the crates and then paused, listening again.

From her new vantage point, she could see Ulrik when he flicked his light on, and she used the brief flash of brilliance to scan her own aisle twenty-five feet below her.

When she was sure she was alone, she placed her flashlight inside her leather jacket to muffle the sound of its crank arm. She cranked it three times, then withdrew the device, not yet switching it on. She leaned over onto her stomach and out past the front edge of the shelf. Then she slowly pulled her black shirt out of the front of her pants, and stretched the fabric over the light. Squirming forward on the hard metal shelf, she felt for the metal number tag with her fingers. When she had it, she placed the light close to it, and lifted her T-shirt slightly off the light. She leaned her head close. It wouldn't block all the light, but it would reduce some of it.

RMN648.

As soon as the light flicked out, she breathed in and held her breath. She heard a noise far across the warehouse, but it was most likely Oskar or Morten. She noticed Ulrik's light was no longer flicking on and off.

Has he heard something, as well?

She stayed motionless on the shelf while she calculated how many levels down she would need to climb to reach her target. Then she waited longer, hoping to hear that shuffling scrape yet again, but knowing she wouldn't.

Damn you, Anders, what happened to you? Why did you not return?

She climbed down in the dark, lowering herself shelf after shelf and pausing on each to listen for movement.

When she reached the correct shelf she waited again, counting down the seconds. Then she repeated her trick with the light, first muting the sound of the crank handle in her jacket, and then diminishing the glow of the beam with the fabric of her shirt.

RMN643.

At last, she thought.

She had seen the latches on the metal crates near the front of the long warehouse, and feeling in the dark, she let her fingers walk across the cold metal surface to them. They had buckles with a thin bit of wire on them, and the wire had been sealed with a thick glob of clay-like metal. Some of the propane cages they had found on the road had been similarly sealed. She knew that she could twist the rough textured glob, and eventually the thin wire would snap under the torsion.

The tips of her fingers grazed the glob on one buckle and she paused, once again listening for the phantom sound in the blackness. When no noise assaulted her senses, she quickly twisted the metal until the wire snapped. She felt it go under her fingers, but the break made no sound. Then her hand slid across the case to the other buckle, and she was pleasantly surprised to discover there was no wire present on it.

She took a deep breath in. Then she crouched over the case, holding the unfinished metal surface of the shelf above her head with one hand, while she unfastened the buckles and raised the lid of the case with her other hand. There wasn't enough clearance for her to raise the lid the whole way, so she propped it open with her elbow, while pulling out her flashlight again. With no free hand, she pressed the metal of the device's lever against her thigh and managed an awkward half crank.

Good enough for a look.

Flicking the light on and popping her elbow upward to raise the lid further, she peered inside the crate.

Inside was the metal part—a slick, perfectly machined wheel with ridges and a dark black square hole in the center. The part was resting in blue foam padding.

Val smiled.

She turned off the light, lowered the lid and waited in the dark for the sound once more. Certain she was alone now, she put the flashlight in an inside pocket, then climbed down the three shelves to the ground. When she reached the concrete floor, she took the flashlight out again, and she gave it a few silenced cranks.

She took a few steps back in the direction of the door and her Vikings.

"Ulrik," she hissed in a loud whisper. "It is over this way. Come. I will need your help."

She heard a footstep in the dark, but it had come from behind her.

When she whirled around, her arm snapped up and the light blazed on.

She had just enough time to recognize the man looking at her in the dark before the fist that went with it slammed into her face.

Anders.

63

The sounds came from everywhere. Morten the Hammer heard the unmistakable thrum of rushing footfalls, and he realized three things: his cousin Oskar was in danger, the Vectors had been waiting for them, and there were far too many men closing in for the Vikings to have any chance of escape.

"Oskar! Val!" he shouted into the dark. "Fight!" As he shouted, the first part of his call had been drowned out by someone screaming in the dark, but he hadn't made out the words.

He abandoned stealth, instead opting for speed and violence. His sword was up and out in the dark as he raced past the ends of countless racks of shelves.

Shadowy shapes flitted through the doorway as he approached, just barely visible in the slight ambient light from outside. The silhouettes carried the thick clubs he had seen the Vectors using earlier, long wooden things with X-shaped metal spikes the thickness of his fingers. The only advantage he had was his sword's longer reach and that the men wouldn't expect him to barrel into them.

He let out a scream in the dark as he swung his sword across the aisle, the sharp blade sluicing into flesh with its customary thunking noise. Men shrieked in the dark. A club swung in from his left. He pivoted right and the weapon slammed down into the concrete floor hard enough to crack it. The man dropped the club and staggered backward.

Morten threw his weight further right, his elbow smashing into a face, as another club went toppling into the metal shelves with a clang. Morten swung his sword back again.

This time the screams were met with a spray of blood that coated him, and he knew he had hit an artery—probably on an arm. Then a man slammed into him from behind, as if he were rushing into the fray and didn't realize Morten was right there. Morton threw his head back, slamming the top of his skull into his attacker.

Cartilage crunched.

Morten dropped to a crouch and swung a full circle, his blade chewing into legs, slicing muscle and tendon. Inhuman howls of pain and surprise filled the air.

Wasting no time, the Laplander sprang up, crashing into the tumbling bodies that crowded around him. He didn't bother finishing them off. These men were down, but there were plenty more flooding into the building, and he could hear Oskar slicing and grunting a few aisles to his side.

Further away, Morten could hear more running feet. They were heading for Ulrik, Agnes and Val, but he was too far away to help them. They would need to rely on Ulrik's brawn until he and Oskar could get to them.

If Morten could just get to Oskar. He and his cousin had fought side by side for decades. They knew each other's moves and thoughts, and even in a fight such as this, in the dark and outnumbered, they could hold their opponents at bay and triumph. They would fight back-to-back, as they had on many occasions. He just needed to get there.

"Oskar, I am coming," Morten shouted. Then he dodged left in the dark, so his voice would not betray his position. From the fact that the Vectors were disorganized, and one had even walked into him, Morten assumed they were having just as much trouble seeing in the dark as he was.

"To your left," was Oskar's calculated reply from the dark. He spoke in the Lapland accent that only the cousins would know, and he meant that Morten should stay to the left of the corridor, joining up with Oskar, where he would be waiting on the right, so they might fight in their circular dance of death-dealing. "Light in five," came the next instruction.

Morten knew his cousin was about to use a light, and he remembered the solar-powered light Oskar had, which was identical to the one Ulrik used. They had found the items in the German castle, and had used them many times at camps in the past. The instruction was not just a warning to shield Morten's vision, but also another audio clue as to Oskar's position.

Morten poured on the speed, colliding with another body and flinging it aside before spinning around, his sword raised at neck height. He felt a brief resistance as he spun, and then he was running again, chased only by the sound of a body tumbling to the floor.

"Now," Oskar shouted.

A brilliant and blinding white glow filled the corridor at the end of all the storage aisles. It stretched most of the way back to the door. The Vectors shouted out, all instantly recoiling and covering their eyes. Morten, forewarned, had already shielded his face with his hand, and still the light was almost too bright with its otherworldly blue-tinted glare.

Now Morten could see the situation around him. He was ten feet from Oskar, who was surrounded by five Vector opponents. They all wore grimy clothing, as if they had crawled through the mud. Their hair was uniformly short, and most of the muscular attackers were between twenty and thirty years of age. One of them was much older, sporting a scrub of white beard on his chin, but no mustache.

Behind him on the ground, Morten counted three more tangled bodies, one desperately clutching at his throat, and doing a terrible job of holding in the spurting arcs of crimson that pooled around him on the dusty concrete floor. Further down the corridor, the way Morten had come, more of the Vectors rushed toward them.

Morten leapt ahead, swinging his sword as far out as he could, but the Vectors saw it coming and all but the nearest of them lunged away from the strike. The nearest one moved his head just enough that only the tip of the long blade struck, severing the top of the man's ear.

The yell was strangled and high-pitched, and as the Vector spun away, Morten got a good look at the face attached to the muscular body.

It was a woman.

Her face was clean and soft, but he could see her femininity in the shape of her cheeks and lips. Her body, however, was as muscular as the others, who were all clearly men. Morten saw no indication that her tight-fitting shirt hid breasts. Her chest was muscled, but flat. She raised her heavy spiked club, the bulky muscles of her biceps and triceps rippling, but Morten was past her before her foolish swing.

It overextended her, and if he had still been there, he would have dealt her a deathblow while stomping the weapon out of her grip with his boot. But he needed to run the last five feet to his cousin.

Oskar had pulled a long knife, and darted it back and forth at one of the Vector men, while his long sword thrust at a second, skewering the man in the lung. As the blade came slipping out, a harsh gust of air burst from punctured chest before a whistling sucking noise followed it.

But then another sound took over as Morten lunged the last few feet to his kin. His sword was extended outward ahead of him as he flew over the floor, his body like an arrow seeking to pierce its target. Ahead of him, the older Vector with the chinstrap beard swung his mighty club downward, from where it had been raised over his head, at the highest extent of his thickly muscled arms. The wooden club hummed as it bore down toward the back of Oskar's head, the dull metal spike leading.

64

Val tried to dodge as the fist came for her face, but she wasn't fast enough. She turned her cheek slightly and the knuckles rocketed into the side of her jaw, snapping her head sideways. Her body flew backward, and the flashlight launched from her hand. The device clattered to the floor and spun on the flat concrete. Its fading light pirouetted around the space.

Val tumbled to the ground, her stomach scraping the floor. Her head vibrated, like a numb limb after sleeping on it wrong. Her arms took the brunt of the landing, the thick leather sleeves of her jacket sparing her skin from being torn. She slid on the dusty ground before coming to a stop, her back to Anders.

Dust poofed up in a cloud around her head, making breathing that much more difficult, as she shook her head.

Unsure of what was happening or why, she knew only that she needed to get away. She tried to scrabble forward as the light from her crank flashlight faded from white to orange, the device now pointing off to the side.

Her fingers scrambled forward, clawing at the concrete to get her away, but it was too late. She felt a pressure on her ankle as Anders grabbed her and tugged her backward. The pull was so startling that her forearms went out to the sides and her forehead smacked into the floor.

She screamed in frustration and rage, her hand slipping down to the head of her long ax, which had slid out of its holster as her body was pulled back and away from the weapon. Snatching it up, she swung backward blindly. She didn't connect with anything, but her ankle was dropped as her opponent stepped out of range.

Val let the momentum of her arm pull her body over onto her back, just as the last of the light from the crank flashlight died, plunging them both into blackness.

Val flipped over backward, staggering to her feet, her balance still off from the shot to her face. In the last sliver of light, she had seen

Anders take a step backward, allowing himself room to maneuver and space beyond the reach of her ax. The man's determined face suggested he had no plans of fleeing from the fight.

It is him, Val thought, still struggling to believe it. *Anders is our betrayer.*

All at once, his long hunting trips with no yield, and the extended absences of his bird made sense. *He has been informing someone of our movements.* Then she realized to whom. *Borss.*

In the absolute dark, Val listened, and this time she realized she had in fact heard the scuffling noises of movement before—it was Anders, stalking her in the shadows.

But why?

"Why?" she shouted, her voice echoing around the huge warehouse. She slid silently across the darkened aisle as soon as the word slipped past her lips, cognizant of her opponent marking her location by sound.

Instead of her word ricocheting off the metal crates back at her, she heard Morten's distant shout on top of it: "Fight!"

In the rest of the warehouse she could hear the sounds of battle. Scuffling feet on concrete. Grunts and groans. Metal clanging off wood. Flesh rupturing and spraying blood.

Val's free hand went to her hand-ax, unsnapping the black leather sheath slowly, with her thumb applying constant pressure, so the metal snap would not make an audible sound in the midnight pitch around her. She slid the handle down, the wickedly pointed and curved blade scraping against the fibrous-like leather.

When she heard her opponent again, Val was startled to hear the sound come from behind her, maybe five feet further up the aisle. Anders had unknowingly passed her in the dark. She lowered herself to a squat, keeping the long ax out in one arm for balance, and as an early warning system, should Anders reverse course.

The sharper hand-ax, with a blade so fine it could split an eyelash, was gripped in her left hand so tightly she was losing feeling in the knuckles. She was ready to strike with it or throw it, whichever seemed best.

Morten's voice again called out in the echoing warehouse. "Oskar, I am on the way!"

His voice was punctuated by more sounds of battle. Val wondered if Ulrik had also been ambushed. *Have they captured Agnes? Heinrich? Why? If Anders wanted to do us harm, he could have killed us at any time. It makes no sense.*

But it did. All the attacks they had faced—at least the Hangers and the Long Knives—had been no coincidence. The question was to what end. Why would someone want to stop them from rescuing humanity?

This is not the time to wonder about such things, she decided, and she clamped down on the runaway burst of thoughts like the metal gate at Venice slamming down into the surf.

Focus, she told herself. Despite the darkness, she closed her eyes, blacking out even the slightest ambient light, and intensifying her other senses.

She did it just in time.

She didn't hear Anders or smell him, but her skin felt his body rushing at her in the dark, and she had a fraction of a second to decide on a course of action.

Keeping the hand-ax in reserve, she mashed the hand holding it knuckles down, toward the concrete floor, and threw her weight up onto that arm, kicking out blindly.

The heel of her boot connected hard with Anders's stomach, his own momentum driving the air out of his lungs with a grunt. The force of her kick sent him sprawling backward.

She extended the long ax, and took a chance on swinging hard into the dark.

She hit nothing, and was rewarded with an elbow to her ribs. She had thought he was still ahead of her, but he had again passed her in the dark, striking from slightly behind her. The blow compressed her rib to the point of cracking. At least it was on the other side of her chest. Her last broken rib had only recently healed. The long ax fell from her grip, but she still had the sharper blade, and she whirled, slicing left and right.

She heard him gasp in the dark, and swear under his breath, and she knew she'd hit him. Probably not a deep cut, but any cut was better than none.

Then Morten's voice sliced through the lightlessness. "NO!"

The scream was louder than any she had heard so far during the chaotic warehouse battle, and the voice was tinged with anger, pain and despair. Without seeing the other side of the warehouse, Val knew precisely what had happened. One of the Vectors had killed Oskar— right before Morten's eyes. Although she still felt anger in her heart toward Morten and Oskar, the desperate loss of family she heard in Morten's voice as it screamed itself hoarse, broke something deep inside her. She felt unexpected agony and sympathy for the Laplander who had become her companion these last many months.

Lashing out in the gloom, Val swung the smaller ax in vicious vertical and horizontal strikes, the sweeps of her arms coming so quickly that the whooshing noise of her passing through the air became an endless loop of distortion, masking her exact location.

Orange-red flame exploded before her eyes. She recoiled from the intense glare, her eyes snapping shut and her arm raising up to cover her face as she staggered back.

When she pulled her arm down, and squinted past her squee-zed eyelids, she saw what had caused the horrible glare. Anders had thrown something to the floor. It was a stick, half the thickness of her long ax's handle, and a foot long. One end of the stick threw off red and orange sparks of flame. Nils had shown her one at Neuschwanstein. 'It is called a flare,' she recalled him saying. But the ones he had were well past their functional dates. He and Anders had tried a few, but they had not lit. She had forgotten all about them. But now it seemed Anders had kept a few, and not all of them were dead.

Val blocked her eyes from the blinding light. She heard Anders ahead of her and running feet coming from behind her in the now fully illuminated aisle.

She could only handle one threat at a time, though, and every fiber of her being cried out for Anders's blood.

When she looked up, her eyes adjusting to the light, he stood ten feet further down the narrow corridor. In his hands, he held his bow, with an arrow nocked and pointed at her face.

65

The arrow began its trajectory in such slow motion, Val thought it was still not released. It warbled slightly and twisted as it came, and she had time to think she could easily outpace it, because it looked like it was traveling through thick, sludgy syrup.

But then she tried to move, throwing her body to the left and simultaneously bringing her arm up to hack at the oncoming missile with the hand-ax.

There was just one problem.

She didn't move.

Then she realized she *was* moving. She was just moving through the same sucking muck of time the arrow was. Her arm wasn't coming up fast enough to block the projectile, and while her body was beginning to fall to her left, she wasn't going to make it.

She thought to twist away, too, but then she was out of time. Or rather, time had caught up to her.

The arrow ripped into the meat of her shoulder, slipping under the clavicle and creasing the shoulder blade. The bladed metal tip of the weapon pushed straight through the leather jacket in front and in back. Strangely, Val felt it coming out the back of her shoulder more than she felt it going in the front.

She tried to shout a profanity, but the pain ripped her voice away just as she slammed into the shelves, where she bounced, turned, struck the protruding end of the lodged arrow and screamed again.

Without thinking, she launched her hand-ax at Anders. The blade whirled through the air, but Anders dodged as fast as Val threw. His black shirt took a bloodless nick just above the elbow.

Steadying herself on her feet, Val slid her knife from its sheath, the four-inch blade her last weapon. She scowled at Anders as she slashed at the arrow's wooden shaft protruding from her shoulder. A second and an intense burst of pain later, the black crow feathers on the end of the wooden stick fell away, and half the arrow went with it.

She switched the knife to her wounded hand, and looked down at the half inch of an arrow still protruding from her shoulder like the tip of a pinky finger.

She glanced back up and saw Anders nocking another arrow. Behind her, a rushing sound built like a waterfall, progressing from soft to loud, and she recognized the angry howl as Morten, screaming like a loon, ran to Val's assistance. All around them in the shadows not lit by the flickering flare, Val heard running feet.

Her Vikings—what remained of them—would lose this fight.

She lunged under her armpit with her left hand, grasping the arrow's haft, the bladed tip slicing into the meat of one fingertip. In the same move, she tugged the thing out of her back, and brought it in front of her, under her arm. It wasn't much, but she could use it as another weapon.

She held the broken arrow shaft in her left hand and the knife in her right, prepared to run at Anders and dodge the oncoming arrows at the same time. His eyes darkened, as if he had had enough, and he foolishly rushed forward, too.

He launched an arrow, and Val felt a hand shove her injured shoulder hard. White sparks of light shot across her vision as pain engulfed her, and she was forced downward, as a fast moving bulk leapt over her. As her vision cleared, she saw Morten, howling like an infuriated animal, as he flew over her head, his long sword stretched out in front of him.

Then the arrow plunged into Morten's eye and snapped his head around so hard that she heard his neck crack.

Even though he was dead, Morten was not out of the fight yet. He hadn't been leading with his four-foot long shining steel blade. He had *thrown* it. Like a spear. Before his body began its descent toward the floor, the long blade followed its path and stayed true, plunging deep into Anders's chest, just under the man's heart, and sinking all the way until the metal cross-guard thumped into his ribs. Anders was lifted off the ground and carried backward by the weight and force of the large sword's impact. He slammed into a shelf, where the blade punched into a crate and held him in place.

Morten's body crumpled to the ground, his head at a grotesque angle, and the arrow jutting from his eye socket making it appear as if he was looking upward and urging others to follow the line of the arrow shaft, seeing what he saw in death.

I know what you found, my friend, Val thought. *Redemption.*

Val stood and lifted her gaze from her dead Viking companion. Anders was still standing, leaning against the shelf.

Footsteps pounded toward her in the gloom, beyond the light of the sparking flare and Anders. No escape. She glanced behind her and saw six Vector men, all armed with spiked clubs. Oskar and Morten were down. No sign of Ulrik or Agnes, but she had to assume they were down, as well. And Heinrich...

"You wanted to know why," Anders said over a mush of blood that dribbled from the corners of his mouth. He slurred like a drunk. "I will tell you why. Because the bounty kept growing. Enough to let me live out my days well fed, far from the squalor of my youth, and in the company of women eager to please, or given no choice. I have traveled this part of the world before. And when the Vectors learned what you were after, they made a generous offer. All I had to do was keep them informed of our group's whereabouts. I will be as rich as a King, and you will be mine...on a leash." He spat a thick wad of blood to the floor, then pulled a knife from his belt. He took a step forward, tugging the sword out of the crate behind him.

He raised the knife, took another step forward...

...and then he ceased to be, in a glorious rupture of red liquid.

A shattering boom filled the warehouse as a metal crate dropped onto the man's head, mashing its heavy cargo of metal parts onto him. The crate compressed Anders's body, crushing his head down to his feet, crunching bone and squishing muscles. There was nothing left of him other than a pasty smear that stretched seven feet in all directions. The explosion of blood and meat covered Val in a fine coating.

The men running out of the dark beyond the crate skidded to halt, as did the six behind her.

Val's eyes slid upward to the top of the big metal shelving unit, where Ulrik, his bare chest covered in several puncture wounds dripping blood, stood heaving. He had used those massive muscles to shove one of the several hundred pound crates, and let it drop on Anders.

He looked down at the spattered human remains and shouted, "Did we come here to talk or did we come here to fight, you bowl of shit?"

Even in the face of the carnage and their overwhelming loss, Val barked out a laugh at Ulrik's comment. But the laughter left her soul when more of the Vectors—some of them flat-chested women—came down the aisle into the light. They all carried the spiked clubs, and one of them dragged a passed-out Agnes along by her ponytail.

Behind Val, more of the Vectors moved in. She glanced back up to Ulrik, and saw that men were closing on him from each side of the top shelf.

The man next to Agnes had a thin series of white scars on his left cheek, as if he had repeatedly cut himself shaving. He set his club on the concrete floor, next to the spitting and hissing flare, then pulled a knife from a sheath on his back and pointed the shining silver tip at Agnes's throat.

"*Overgave*," he said.

He spoke in Dutch—or some variant of it—but the root of the word was similar enough to her own Northern dialect, where it would be *Overgivelse*. Even if it hadn't, she would have recognized the meaning based on the posture and the threat.

Surrender.

66

Dawn limped into the world one lingering step at a time. The overcast sky threatened more rain, the scent of ozone in the air suggesting the sky might follow through on its threat.

The clouded skies cast the dockyards in a gray gloom that helped conceal Heinrich, but the Vectors would be more alert after the incursion into their territory. He had held back to the shadows all night, keeping tabs on where the men—and women—took Ulrik, Agnes and Val. There was no sign of the cousins, and Heinrich believed that both men were dead.

On the plus side, there was also no sign of Anders or his bird, so Heinrich thought there was still a possibility the bowman might return.

Needing a better place to hide while still being able to view the entire Vector camp, and watch for an opportunity to steal their prisoners, Heinrich climbed a rusty ladder on the exterior of a massive, cylindrical fuel tank. It was the first in a row of five. Seventy-five feet in diameter, and over a hundred feet tall, the tank's roof provided the perfect overwatch from which he could see across a wide open field of mud, and over to the warehouse and the surrounding buildings. Beyond those lay the river. Behind him, was more industrial dockland, and another slice of the river, revealing that the spit of land they were on was actually an island of sorts.

He belly-crawled around the entire circumference of the tank, slowly popping his head up at the edges and getting the lay of the land. Then he moved back to his initial vantage point and watched for the Vectors to emerge.

Val had given him special instructions.

She had been concerned about an ambush, and he was to hide himself away, waiting for the moment to lend assistance, if something went wrong.

And something had. Horribly.

Heinrich had first retreated to the abandoned shack they had used earlier in the day, but then he had thought better of the decision and had found a different building from which he could view the front of the warehouse. For the first few minutes of his special mission, he had worried that he had been sidelined for being the least skilled of them. He even briefly wondered if his position with the group was not as solid as he had assumed, and that Val was hoping to leave him behind in Rotterdam.

But he'd only had a few more minutes to ponder the question before large groups of Vectors descended on the warehouse door and piled inside. It had happened so quickly that he hadn't had time to respond. But then he had remembered Val's instruction. *Hide. Wait for the moment.* That moment had not been the right one.

So he had remained hidden, and eventually the Vectors had come out, pushing Val and Ulrik, both bleeding and surrounded by men and women with weapons. Behind them, more Vectors tugged young Agnes by her hair. When Morten and Oskar did not come out, the story of what had happened was easy to piece together.

They had known. They had waited. They had rushed into the building from both ends and pinned the Vikings down.

When a small group of Vectors broke away and rushed into the shack where the Vikings had hidden earlier in the day, Heinrich knew they were aware of the group's numbers. They had lost track of one.

Him.

The next morning on his new perch, high up on the fuel tank and waiting for movement, he knew Val had made the right choice. He had no idea how he would rescue them, but if the opportunity came, he would take it and succeed, or die trying.

When his stomach grumbled from hunger, Heinrich guessed the sun had been up for a few hours, even diminished as it was behind the screen of loaded clouds.

The door to a low-slung building on the edge of the great field below him snapped open. Five men—or maybe there were women in there too—strode out into the center of the large field carrying shovels. They spent a few minutes digging a deep, but small-diameter hole in the mud, until they hit much drier dirt underneath it. Heinrich guessed the hole to be five feet deep. Then the group walked off the field, taking their shovels with them.

What is this? he wondered. *Too small to be a grave.*

He would not have to wait long. Vectors began walking onto the field, lingering. They were waiting for something. Heinrich counted thirty-two. He noted that none of them had breasts, although he was certain that some of them were woman. He wondered if they were all naturally flat-chested or if the women had their breasts removed for some reason. He watched for a sign of their prisoners, and as the minutes spun out, he worried that maybe the Vectors had gathered for an execution.

Then another group of five came out, pushing Val and Ulrik ahead of them with spiked clubs. Agnes was not there. Another three Vectors came into the field as well, and the largest of them carried a conical horn. His body was armored in gleaming silver plate, and covered in deadly spikes. A dark-haired woman in thick furs walked beside him.

The big man shouted into the horn, and it amplified his voice. He spoke in a Dutch accent, but Heinrich could still make out the meaning of most of the words, because they were similar to the German he spoke.

"Vectors! Brothers and sisters! Gather and observe. Record." The man was a bit bulkier than the others—broader and barrel-chested—but his clothing gave no indication of his status.

"My brothers and sisters, long have we sought our prize. The foreigners have tried to keep it from us, killing our allies and murdering our fellow Vectors!" The man's voice, even amplified as it was through the bullhorn, was drowned out as the gathered thirty-nine Vectors shouted outraged boos and hisses.

The man with the bullhorn raised it high, and the voices of the crowd settled. "But now we have them, and soon we will use the young one to gain massive riches. But first we must deal with their warriors, who murdered our friend."

Again the outraged voices of the crowd rose in volume, and several people with thicker accents than the bullhorn-man shouted out. Heinrich could not make out more than a word, but he understood the calls were indignant cries for justice.

A man standing next to Ulrik swung his spiked club at the back of the Viking's legs. The man twisted the handle at the last second, so none of the spikes impaled his prisoner, but the strike was hard enough to take Ulrik's legs out from under him, and his large frame crashed backward into the mud.

The crowd cheered and laughed.

Ulrik appeared uninjured, but stayed on his back until another two Vectors came up on him from behind and started to yank him up. Back on his feet, he lashed out with a backhand fist, pummeling one of the two in the face before three others rushed in, driving the un-spiked tips of their clubs into Ulrik's stomach. As he dropped to his knees in the squelching mud, another man came running in and kicked Ulrik in the gut, flipping his body to land once more on his back.

For a split second, Heinrich had thought the resistance would lead to the perfect opportunity to lend his assistance, and while his adrenaline had spiked, he had been prepared to rush to the fuel tank ladder. But Ulrik was down in seconds, and Val, stripped of her leather jacket and missing her goggles, stood nearby, scowling, the blood-red hawk-wing pattern on her face smeared.

Heinrich felt helpless, as he wondered again and again, *What can I do?*

Then the armored bullhorn man shouted, "These people from the North. They came into our lands, with no tribute. Without asking permission! They hacked and killed their way across the land, all the while trying to deprive you of your hard earned wealth."

The crowd's frenzied screams and hoots rose to a crescendo.

"And now, my loyal friend Anders, is dead."

The crowd went silent, and Heinrich nearly swallowed his tongue. *Anders?*

Before Heinrich could even allow the idea of Anders's betrayal to filter through his confused mind, the armored-man took a running step and kicked the side of Ulrik's head. As the boot connected, Heinrich could hear the thud all the way up on his fuel tank, and he cringed.

"And this dog-fucker killed him! Crushed him so badly that we don't even have a body to bury! What should we do with him, I ask you all?"

The crowd erupted with screams and competing shouts. Eventually, the noise coalesced into a slowly building chant that got louder and louder.

A group of Vectors left the field and came back a minute later lugging a thirty-foot long wooden pole, like the many Heinrich had seen along the edges of roads in older towns. He finally made out the words of the thickly accented chanting.

Pin him up.

Pin him up.

Pin him up.

67

Ulrik's body ached. His stomach hurt, and his ribs were either bruised or cracked. The tingling in his arms told him they were asleep, as he had been, but a dull pain radiated from his hands to his shoulders.

The side of his face felt swollen and tight. And his jaw ached. His left eye was swollen shut, and he kept his right closed to make anyone watching think he was still unconscious. He gently probed the inside of his mouth and felt all his teeth still in place, but one molar nudged a bit under the pressure from the tip of his tongue.

Raindrops pelted the right side of his body. *I'm outside,* he thought. The ticking of the rain filled his ears, and he strained to hear anything else. When he was convinced he might be alone, he slowly cracked his right eyelid.

It was either dusk or the storm clouds had darkened the sky to a dull slate gray. He hung up high over a grassy field that was turning to mud in the downpour.

He looked up and the memories flooded back.

The chanting.

The beating.

The clanging of the big metal hammers.

The thick iron spike.

His wrists were chained to either side of a foot-long pine board, and a thick black iron nail, a foot long, had been pounded through his hands, and the board, attaching them both to the dark brown wooden pole from which he was suspended.

They have crucified me.

Ulrik's hands had been laid one atop the other, and the nail—an inch wide, unfinished iron spike—had been forced through his hands between the middle and third metacarpal bones, forcing them apart and pushing the fingers apart so his hands resembled the horns of an ox.

Blood dripped down from the holes, but it had started to crust and coagulate, despite the rain. His fingers had turned white from blood loss. The only reason his weight hadn't torn his hands through the spike was because his body was being supported by the manacles around his wrists—not the holes in his hands.

He considered wiggling his fingers, and then thought better of it. It would hurt if he could do it at all, and it would do exactly nothing for him.

He looked down and saw his bare feet dangling below him. As far as he could see, he was only attached to the pole by his hands and his wrists. The distance between his wrists was just enough to keep the weight of his body from suffocating him to death, although he was already finding it hard to breathe.

He didn't have long before whatever strength he had would leech away into his toes and flood out into the rain.

The field below him was empty. With storm clouds blocking the sky, he had no idea how long he had been nailed to the pole. It couldn't have been too long, or he would have suffocated for sure. His body felt battered, but still strong. He didn't know much about crucifixion, but he imagined weakness would come soon enough.

He struggled to open his left eye, and its lid cracked just slightly, allowing a thin sliver of muted sight. It would be enough. He craned his head around left and right, ensuring that the field below him was in fact completely vacant, and that no guards were posted in the nearby buildings. He was high enough to see the warehouse where the Vikings had been defeated, and the distant river beyond it. The building where they had been detained looked deserted now.

The rain intensified. He could no longer see the river past the curtains of cascading water. He could feel the water sliding between his aching wrists and the iron manacles around them, lubricating him to no avail. The cuffs were thick, and he didn't think he would be able to get his wrists out of them, even if he could get his hands free from the nail.

He could see only one way to do it, and it was going to hurt more than he could imagine. He needed to psyche himself up for it, and filled his mind with thoughts of failure; at protecting Agnes, in allowing Val to be captured, at the betrayal of Anders, and at the

deaths of Morten and Oskar—the latter of whom he had been marched past when the Vectors took their prisoners out of the warehouse.
His fury mounted when he thought about how he had failed not just
his people, but the whole human race. Even the Vectors would die
out if he and Val did not get Agnes to Halvard and his gene science.

Then his thoughts replayed what they had done to him. How
they had beaten him like a dog, and how they had pierced his hands
and left him to die.

But he had not died.

And they were fools.

Every last one of them.

He heaved with his massive stomach muscles, pulling his thick
thighs and knees upward, and then lowered them. It was agony,
but the pain was nothing compared to what it would be, and if he
could not perform this first stage, he would not have the strength
for too many tries.

He sucked in a deep breath and swung his legs up again, pulling
hard with his arms and sending screaming tendrils of pain rushing
down his shoulders to his heart. His abdominal muscles contorted in
on themselves, and his chin mashed to his chest as his legs swept up
over his head and over the wooden plank holding him prisoner.

He thought his neck would break, but then his ankles wrapped
around the upper part of the pole, and took some of the weight off his
bent arms. If anyone saw him now, they would think he was trying to
eat his hands off or maybe hump the pole.

The truth was more terrifying. He struggled to shinny his body
backward, until the pole was between his thick calves, and then his
knees. He clamped onto the pole with his powerful thighs driving
his knees into the sides of the slick wood, feeling a rough splinter
drive into the meat of his leg.

He would not scream from the pain. Not yet. He would need that
scream soon. Very soon. If he waited too long, he would pass out again.

All at once he let go with his thighs and pulled down with his back
muscles, his legs flipping forward. They snapped down and back and as
his legs came through the halfway part of their arc, he screamed and

tugged forward with his arms, while bucking with his back. At first the scream was a focusing of his power and rage, but as the iron nail was tugged through his hands, his scream turned into one of abject pain. His left hand—on top of the right—felt a brief second of resistance, before it snapped free of the spike and the arm started to flop out into space. The right followed closely behind it, and then both arms jolted to a stop as the chains around his wrists were fully extended.

His ankles wrapped around the pole below him, and he pushed up against it, his legs slipping on the wet wood. His hands still functioned, but burned with each movement.

But Ulrik did not care.

He pulled against his left wrist and reached up with his right hand. He grabbed the blood-slicked nail. The muscles of his forearm shook and vibrated, but his hand held on to the nail, and he pulled himself up slightly. He could feel the edges of the hole in his hand stretching under the strain.

Then he raised the left wrist and banged the metacarpal bone under his thumb against the tip of the nail until the joint broke, and his wrist collapsed, sliding cleanly out of the iron manacle.

Now partially freed, he released the pole with his ankles and let his body spin from the ruined hand grasping the nail. His vision clouded with a fugue of red hatred.

When his body faced the pole, he wrapped his powerful thighs around it and pulled himself up with the manacled hand, shinnying his legs up and taking the strain as soon as he was able.

With a final burst of strength, he hooked his arm under the pine board, and threw his body backward. The nail shrieked and squealed, and then the board, the nail and the chain all ripped loose, smacking him in the face before it fell away to hang from his wrist by the chain still attached to his right arm.

Pulling back in with his abs, his chest hugged the pole. He swung his right arm, flinging the chain, board and nail around the back of the pole. He tried to catch it with his left hand and missed on the first attempt.

Lightning flashed somewhere close, sizzling the sky and his retinas, before the roar of the Thunder God filled the sky. Ulrik screamed again in rage and black hate. He swung the chain again and the board slammed into the back of his left hand as he grasped for the metal links, filling him with a white hot light. His roar was lost in an-other peal of thunder.

He started laughing as he swung the chain a third time and filled his heart with the promises of pain he would inflict on the Vectors. This time, his mangled left hand caught the chain. He pulled the thing tight, tugging it hard and leaning backward. He slid his feet to the front of the pole and pushed against it. Then all in one move he released the vice grip his knees had on the wood.

Tugging on the chain and pushing against the front of the pole, he ran downward. In what seemed just a few steps, his ankle mashed into the squelching muddy ground. His left hand released the chain and his body fell to his right, collapsing in the soft muck.

He pushed himself up in the mud, and in the distance he saw Heinrich, good Heinrich, running toward him through the rain. As good as it felt to see a friendly face, he was filled with rage.

But he was still laughing.

And they were going to pay.

Every last one of them.

68

Val was being held with Agnes in a small room with a bed and a wooden dresser. Overhead was a single bare light bulb that filled the room with feeble illumination. Silk tapestries had been hastily hung from hooks on each of the walls, with the only bare spot being a foot-wide stretch from which protruded an opened fuse box. Springing from it was a jumble of black and red wires, portions of them stripped of insulation and twisted together.

The room smelled faintly of perfume and the salty scent of tears.

Val didn't know where the flowery perfume had come from, but the tears were from Agnes, who had sat silently in the corner and sobbed after they had been forced to witness Ulrik's execution.

The Vectors had brought the two of them into this room, threw them on the mattress, and then slammed and locked the door. There was nothing else in the space, and the concrete walls held no windows. Just outside the door, was a smaller room, where Val had been stripped of all her belongings save her tank-top and pants.

She had been surprised that the Vector men had left the two of them unmolested, but the room presented a wide variety of potential outcomes, and she had no desire to see any of them. If it came down to it, she would kill Agnes—and the whole human race—with her bare hands, snapping the girl's neck, before she allowed the Dutch men (and possibly the women) to rape the girl. But she hoped it wouldn't come down to that.

Periodically over the last three hours, a Vector would unlock and open the door, checking on them. Then he would leave and lock the door again.

She knew her weapons were in the next room, stacked on a matching dresser to the empty one in this room. Every time the guard opened the door, she caught a glimpse of her folded leather jacket, and the long ax resting on top, the end of its leather-wrapped wooden handle tantalizing in its nearness.

Each time she heard the door lock begin to turn, Val poised for action, unsure whether it would be time to fight or die, but so far, their captors appeared to be interested only in keeping her and Agnes prisoner.

She had already decided she would make her move the next time the guard popped his head in the door, but before she had a chance to formulate a plan, the lock clunked.

The solid metal door opened a crack, as usual, and the Vector, a younger man of maybe twenty years, poked his head in. This time he glanced back into the outer room, and then slid inside, and closed the door behind him.

Val noticed two things immediately. The man had left his club outside in the outer room, and he had brought another, much smaller one, in his pants. Summoning up every ounce of acting talent she had, Val smiled sweetly at the man, and waved him over.

They had left her sterile gauze, which she had stuffed into the open, oozing hole in her shoulder, before using the bandages left to wrap the joint. It still hurt, though, and the rest of her body ached from the damage she had taken, but there was no way she couldn't handle this young man.

The only question in her mind was how badly should she hurt him. When his left hand came out of his back pocket with a straight razor and his right hand reached for his zipper, she realized the answer to her dilemma.

She was going to hurt him a lot.

She smiled once more in her best 'come hither' look, pulling her legs back as if she were making room for the man on the bed. She positioned them under her. The man, with a slack-jawed look of complete lust, was clueless. He lowered the straight razor, thinking he wouldn't need the weapon. Val lunged, leaping upward off the bed, the top of her head grazing the lone swinging light bulb. It moved in a pendulum arc across the small bedroom, and her knee cracked into the underside of the man's chin. His arms flew out to the sides for balance, as Val landed on one foot and kicked out again, this time driving her foot into his chest like a piston. A loud crunch from his sternum echoed around the room.

The Vector's body flew backward and his back connected with the exposed wiring from the fuse-box. He spasmed as power surged through him, dimming the overhead swinging bulb to a faint glow. Val had not heard any power generators, so she assumed the building had a reserve power supply from passive solar panels, like those she had seen on her journeys. She didn't know if the amount of electricity in such a system would be enough to kill the man, but she stepped over to the empty dresser, and tugged one of the wooden drawers free. She swung the empty drawer, shattering it against the man's head. His body flew to the floor, where it twitched briefly. A thin curl of smoke rose off his back.

More smoke sizzled up off the fuse box, but the nearly dormant swinging lightbulb returned to its regular but low level of light. Val dropped the broken slats of the dresser drawer on top of the man's head, and beckoned to Agnes, who had stopped crying. Instead her face wore an expression of awe.

"You have not seen anything yet," she told the girl.

Agnes leapt up and Val tugged the door open.

The outer room was empty, as she suspected it would be. Val reached through the doorway and snagged her ax. It never left her hands as she quickly donned her jacket, and slipped her boots on.

Agnes slid her own shoes on, but none of their other camping equipment or bedrolls were in the room. There was nothing else for Agnes to collect.

Val strapped on her holsters, the knife and hand-ax. Even her goggles were on the dresser's wooden surface, and she slid them on her forehead. Her shoulder wound had been aggravated during the scuffle, and had started bleeding again. She could feel the blood running down to her elbow.

She quickly pressed her fingertips to the wound, covering the digits in blood. She raised her fingers and planted them on her opposing cheeks, painting her face with the distinctive feather pattern that looked like dried blood.

Only this time, the blood was real.

She slid the goggles over her eyes, then pulled her sharp hand-ax.

"Do we have a plan?" Agnes asked.

Val nodded down at her waist. "Take my knife."

The girl did as she was told, and held the knife up at the ready, a determined look on her face.

"The plan...is that we will kill every goat-fucking bastard between us and the sea."

With that she flung open the outer door.

On the other side was a long rectangular room with a row of wooden tables covered with dishes and serving platters of food. Metal stein cups were everywhere. At the far end of the room was another door, to the outside.

And seated along the benches were twenty men and women in the midst of eating their meal, not one of them armed for battle. Not one spiked club to be found in the room. At the far end of the table was the raven-haired woman Val had seen with the Vectors' leader, the man she assumed to be Borss. Val's eyes locked with the woman's. Then the woman dropped her plate and darted out the door at the room's far end. Val was determined to get to her.

"We will start with these," Val said through gritted teeth.

She lunged forward and up onto the table.

Then the carnage began.

69

Val sliced into three bodies before anyone at the table had a chance to move. Her ax sliced through the room in vertical chops, spraying arcs of blood up to the ceiling with each tug from a cleaved skull.

At the other end of the room, Vectors screamed and shoved their way through the door and out. Behind her, Agnes was using the knife's pointed tip, jabbing two quick thrusts into the chest of any Vector still moving after Val had passed them.

Four more men and women fell at Val's hands before the room had cleared of the living. She knew they would go straight for their weapons and then return—most likely in greater numbers.

"Let's go," she said, and Agnes followed her across the tabletops to the end of the long room.

Val sped up and leapt head first through the doorway, swinging her hand-ax to the side of the frame as she came through. The blade sank into the upper arm of a Vector who had been waiting with a raised club. The sharp tempered steel sliced most of the way through the arm—and all the way through the bone—before Val's tumbling body was gone from the doorframe and rolling on the ground beyond it in a somersault. She came to her feet and whirled in a complete circle, taking in the screaming Vector, whose arm hung and flopped from a hinge of still-attached skin.

She stepped back and dispatched the nearly amputated foe.

The immediate area was clear, and as Agnes rushed out of the long dining room into the rain, Val saw there was no sign of the raven-haired woman. Agnes hurried up to Val, her eyes darting all around. Rain poured from the heavens, but the sky had lightened to an off white.

"Back to the warehouse," Val said.

"What?" Agnes was shocked that Val would want to go back into that place, after what had happened just hours ago.

"We still need the machine part," she said, and then took off running. They crossed a road, and a line of dull trees that grew up alongside it. On the other side was a large open space—once a parking lot or a loading lot, but now coated in a fine moss. Rotting shipping containers were stacked in piles, like miniature skyscrapers of the old world.

To their right was the white warehouse with the steel wheel they needed. Running from the river to their left were close to forty Vectors, now armed for battle.

"Hurry," Val shouted, and she sprinted for the warehouse door.

She hadn't understood the shouting of the Vectors when they had beaten Ulrik, but she understood that their leader was the man named Borss, and Anders had been working for him. The only advantage she had now was that she had never told Anders the number of the crate. The Vectors would not know which item she had been after. Heading back inside now was a calculated gamble, but there was no choice.

Val burst through the door, and Agnes, on her heels, tried to close it behind them.

"Leave it," Val said, racing to the start of the R aisle. She was greeted by a grisly sight that took her breath away. She skidded to a stop, and Agnes crashed into her from behind. Then seeing what had brought Val up short, Agnes shouted out.

"Ulrik!"

The man looked like an animal that had been set loose from Helheim, the land of the dead. He was covered in blood from his crusted beard to his bare feet. His hands were wrapped in thick wads of cloth, but he still managed to hold his heavy ax, the shaft of it stretched across his body as he lumbered forward. The head of the ax was coated in so much blood it was dripping onto the concrete floor. He wore no shirt, but there were thick brown leather straps over his shoulders, the pack on his back weighted down by something heavy. Behind him, and sporting twin long knives like the black-faced swastika-adorned crazies from Germany, Heinrich was also covered in the gore of his victims.

Ulrik saw Val and Agnes, but the look of murder did not leave his eyes. "I have it. We should go. There will be more."

Val pointed. "They come already. Back to the center of the aisle."

Heinrich turned and started jogging back down the aisle. The warehouse was dim, but there was enough light from the skylights that they would see well enough to fight.

Ulrik held out his arm like a barrier gate, preventing Val from passing him. "You should take this thing and get her out of here, while we hold them off."

"No," Val said.

"You should—"

"No." She said it louder, and she saw his eyes narrow. "We will live. All of us. *That* is the mission now."

Ulrik lowered his arm, and as she moved past him, he said softly, "Yes, my Valkyrie."

Agnes grinned at him as she went by, and then he turned and began a limping, hopping, lope of a run, back toward the center of the aisle.

A second later they heard a cry rise up as Vectors funneled into the building, again from both ends. The men and women came, yelling and hooting, swinging their spike-laden clubs, heedless of danger, rushing into the aisle. They came looking for revenge, or for battle or for blood.

But the four remaining fighters had a higher purpose. They would save the world, or they would die. But if they died, they were going to send as many Vectors as they could to hell before their end came. They took up positions a few feet apart, Heinrich next to Val with his long knives. Behind them Ulrik stood in the middle of the aisle, and Agnes stood just behind him, her knife ready to jab at anyone that made it past the fighters.

There was no pause, no posturing. The Vectors just ran in to their deaths.

Val swung her hand-ax low and at her side, cleaving into the first man's upper thigh as if she were a butcher cutting meat. With the handle of the long ax, she blocked his club's blow overhead, then reversed the swing. She slammed the head of the ax out, slicing into the ear of another man who would have run between her and Heinrich. For his part, the German had stabbed one long knife through the throat of the third man in the vanguard, and jabbed left into the other ear of the man in the middle.

The first three bodies collapsed in a bloody heap at their feet, as the second wave came in, still screaming and swinging their clubs. Val stepped forward, and placed a foot on one of the bodies below her, climbing slightly higher. She refused to give the Vectors the high ground that the mound of bodies would soon form. She would soon be standing atop a mountain of dead—if the manic Dutchmen were foolish enough to keep coming. She only had to keep an eye on the shelving to ensure she was not flanked.

But then, like most battle plans, it fell apart shortly after the first bodies fell.

A Vector woman dropped off the top shelf high above them. Her feet pounded into Heinrich's chest, taking them both down behind Val.

Ahead of her, three men dove forward at the same time, all leading with their rounded club tips, as if the weapons were spears.

The defensive line had been breached.

70

The crazy woman landing on top of him wouldn't have been so bad if it wasn't for the damned spikes on her club. Heinrich had been surprised by the falling missile of a woman, but he had thrown himself backward, taking the hit and relying on his teammate for exactly what she provided.

As soon as he hit the ground, Agnes turned and jabbed her knife into the Vector woman's back twice, sinking the blade to the hilt each time. With both lungs punctured—and probably her heart sliced as well—the Vector woman was out of the fight. Heinrich shoved the body hard, and by that point, as the weight of her rolled off of him, Agnes had already turned to finish off Ulrik's new victims.

Val was about to face off against three foes at once because Heinrich had been forced from his post. He wanted to get back into the fight, but there was a problem. He looked down at where the Vector woman's club had hit his hip. The long metal spike sticking out of it had plunged all the way into his inner thigh, just barely missing his goods.

Even though the long iron nail was still sunk deep into his leg, the wound was squirting an arc of blood a foot high, squeezing out of the space between his impaled flesh and the dark metal. If he pulled it out, the blood would probably shoot to the ceiling. He was done, and he knew it. But he could still help Val in one way.

Ahead of him, the three oncoming Vectors leapt for Val. He watched in awe as she jumped up and over their extended clubs, which were pointed forward like battering rams.

She landed deftly on the shoulder blades of the middle man, and shoved, thrusting him downward with the power of her legs and bringing her arms low enough to put her axes into the men on either side. The two men screamed as they were driven to the floor, just over the first hump of bodies Val and Heinrich had created. The man in the middle crashed into Heinrich's legs, dislodging the club and its spike. Heinrich punched the man in the side of the head, his fist traveling through the spray of his own blood. Then he picked up one of his long knives and as the man tried to claw his way up Heinrich's body, he thrust the blade into the Vector's eye.

Heinrich grabbed the club that had ended his life, even though he still drew breath, and used it as a crutch to clamber to his feet. The puncture in his groin sent shivers of pain through his body, as his head and chest began to sweat.

Heinrich balanced on his good leg, and pulled his backpack off, reaching inside for what he needed. It took him only seconds. Behind him, Ulrik and Agnes had advanced into the men and women on the other side of the aisle, the big man clearing two and three bodies at a time with his mighty ax, and Agnes delivering the killing stroke to anyone still breathing.

"Go," Heinrich said, thrusting his stolen club, the nail on the end piercing the skull of the Vector who had attacked Val from the side. She lunged threateningly at the Vectors, who leaned back as a group, fear now coloring their attacks. Heinrich looked up into the shelving and saw more of the Vectors rushing along the tops of the crates. Soon they would make suicidal leaps into the battle, as the woman had done. The Vikings would be overwhelmed if they stayed here and fought.

Heinrich stepped forward on his injured leg, a buzz of angry burning torment shooting up the limb to his brain. He shoved his hand in front of Val, still gripping the item he had pulled from his pack and pulled her back a step. "Go!" he shouted at her.

She looked down into his grip, then saw the waterfall of blood pouring down his leg and the squirts that shot out of him. She took one last swing with her ax, from one side of the aisle to the other, and Heinrich smiled as the four men clustered there swayed back in terror. Behind them were probably another thirty men and women, all waiting for their chances to get up to the front of the line.

Val turned, leaned over and kissed him on the cheek, and then she ran to join Agnes and Ulrik.

In a quick glance back, Heinrich saw that the mountain of a man had cleared another twenty feet toward the door. Heinrich turned back and found the four Vector men cautiously approaching him over the hazardous tumble of blood-slicked limbs.

Heinrich raised his club in one hand. The item in the other would have to wait for the precise moment.

Val rushed to Ulrik's side, and he adjusted accordingly, reducing his ax sweeps to just the left half of the aisle. She took up the right, hacking forward with her long ax. She handed the hand-ax backward, and Agnes took it, still clutching the blood-drenched knife in her other hand.

"We need to be quick, Ulrik. Remember the tunnels." Val shouted, then hacked her way forward as she ran.

He understood, welcomed the heightened senses and rushing blood that came with a berserker rage, and surged forward, swinging the ax faster, and then knocking the next man back with the tip of the ax head.

Then he roared a scream of anger, murder and raw malevolence, that stopped the onrushing men and women. Those in the back turned tail and fled, while the last five still in their path were trampled under Ulrik as he blasted forward like a snorting bull.

He took the lead, chasing after the fleeing Vectors while still hollering at the top of his lungs. Val was right behind him, swinging at the men he had simply pushed aside, and jabbing the handle of her long ax into the face of a woman, shattering her nose and the bones of her face with a sickening series of crunches.

Then suddenly there were no more bodies to strike, and Val ran after Ulrik, her arms suddenly heavy with the slippery ax. She cast a sideways glance and saw Agnes at her side. The girl had been cast into a baptism of fire, and her face and clothes were covered in blood. Further back was a pile of bodies—what Val assumed was a dog-pile on top of poor Heinrich. He had made the ultimate sacrifice for them.

"Are you hit?"

Agnes shook her head, and put on a burst of speed, running side by side with Val. The determination on the young girl's face suggested she could fight longer if needed.

Then they were out into the rain, and the last few Vectors fled to the left, rounding some empty containers, Ulrik giving chase, lost in the rage.

"Ulrik," Val called. "Come back!"

The man skidded to a halt and turned. The pouring rain was clearing the blood from his face, but his beard was still crusted with gore.

Val pointed as she ran.

On this end of the long warehouse, the river was close. Parked straight ahead of her was a long, gray metal boat. But in front of that, was a white twenty-five-foot sailboat, its sails furled and its body clean, as if the Vectors had been caring for the vessel. Without slowing, Val ran for it with Agnes at her side, huffing and puffing. The girl might have had more fight in her, but she couldn't run forever. Ulrik reversed direction and angled to meet them at the boat.

Then he skidded to a stop, as a huge man walked from around a building, along the shore, blocking their path to the boat.

His chest glistened in the falling rain, the giant metal spikes welded onto an armored chestplate making the man seem larger than he was.

Borss.

From the huge man's gauntlet-covered hand, a giant spiked metal ball on a chain dropped to the ground. It thunked into the mud, and then Borss tugged on a two-foot-long stick at the other end of the chain, and the spiked ball came soaring up.

Val blinked in awe as the man whirled the ball at the end of its chain so fast that it blurred around him, and the chain began to look like a solid shield.

"I will deal with this," Ulrik said. Then he took a step forward and staggered, dropping to one knee and grunting in pain. His wounds had finally taken their toll. He tried to rise once more, but pain robbed his consciousness and plunged him face first into the mud.

Val would need to dispatch Borss on her own.

Not a problem, she thought. *He is too large, and his armor too heavy, for him to move very fast.*

But then Borss ran at her, moving like lightning, as the devastating spiked ball whirled for her head.

71

The man's speed was astonishing. Val dove to the side at the last second, but one of the metal spikes on the speeding ball snagged in her hair and tore a hunk of it from her scalp before she hit the wet ground. She slid several feet on the front of her leather jacket, before she rolled to a stop, swinging her ax upward.

Her timing was perfect, as the massive armored man reversed his swing, bringing the spinning death ball down toward her head. The metal ball cracked into the head of her ax, saving her face and life. The vibration sent a twang through both of her arms.

As Borss tugged on the chain, yanking his spiked flail back over his shoulder, Val rolled backward on the wet ground, distancing herself from the deadly weapon. She came out of the roll swinging her fully extended ax.

The lateral sweep would have sliced right through the giant man's calf if he had not seen the attack coming. Instead he nimbly leaped straight up, and the swipe missed. But it bought her a little more space and time to plan her next attack.

The big man wound up for another flail strike, swinging the chain with brutal efficiency. She was stunned by his speed, but now that she had the measure of him, she needed only to come up with a way to get inside his defenses. The enormous spiked chest and back plates would keep most of the man's vital organs safe from anything she could dish out with her ax.

Borss swung his flail, and Val was once again caught off guard by his strategy. He released the weapon, and the heavy metal ball sizzled toward her head, trailing its chain and handle. Val was just about to stand, and her only defense was to once more throw herself backward onto the ground. The aerial weapon missed her, sailing over her face and warming the air over her skin with its passing.

She was still falling as she heard the giant's pounding footsteps, as he raced for her position. She got her ax handle across her chest just in time to deflect a powerful punch from his metal coated fist. But the incoming hammer of a limb was still deadly, and the re-adjusted punch blasted into her shoulder, sending her flying to the side.

Her shoulder exploded with pain as she slammed into the ground yet again. But to Val's relief, instead of pressing his attack, Borss continued running right past her, to retrieve his thrown flail.

There's his weakness, she thought. He relied on the weapon and its reach too much. He had shown that he could inflict damage with just his body, but his sheer size would limit his range in close quarters combat. *Remember the Polar bear.*

As Borss reached down to collect his weapon from the ground, Val used the short reprieve to scramble to her feet. The giant stood in place, whirling the flail. He was clearly used to using his size to intimidate others in a fight. But he was no larger than the oversized oaf she had dispatched back in Stavanger. *This one will fall, too.*

She just needed to goad him.

She stood straight and placed her ax handle between her legs, running one hand back and forth along the shaft of it, mocking his display with the flail.

It worked.

Borss rushed at her, the spinning flail off to his side.

Val held her ground, and her pose. She didn't want to give anything away. Her shoulder ached, and she wasn't sure whether she could withstand a direct hit from Borss's fists. Keeping him reliant on the flail was the only way she would survive. But a single strike from the huge weapon would probably turn her into paste. Timing was everything. Just like the bear.

She waited almost a hair too long.

Borss was huffing as he raced toward her, his immense, tree-trunk-like biceps straining as he swung the vicious weapon with what had to be all of his strength.

Val dropped to a squat and lunged sideways, sweeping her ax for Borss's ankle as she flew under his strike. The spiked ball came down and clipped the sole of her boot, but she scored a hit, the fine edge of her ax, chewing through the unprotected skin of the man's leg.

Borss screamed and dropped to his knee, taking pressure off the wound, but Val had dropped her ax and rolled with her fall, coming up on Borss's side, on her feet in a crouch.

Val scrambled up the side of Borss's arm as he tried to stand and recoil from her at the same time. She went up and over his huge spiked gauntlet, and up the beefy biceps. Then she reached out and grabbed the side of the man's unprotected face, the tip of her middle finger digging into and popping his eyeball with an audible smacking noise.

Borss shrieked. But Val wasn't done. Using her hand like a hinge, she swung behind the man, stepping on the tops of the backplate's spikes. Her other hand snaked out, and she grabbed around the other side of his head, her other middle finger finding the softness of his remaining eye.

Understanding through his pain what was about to happen, Borss tried to raise his right hand to his eye, but his big metal glove was still tightly wrapped around the haft of the flail's handle. The tip of it cleared Val's wrist and smashed into his own temple.

Val yanked with both hands, the tip of each middle finger digging into an eye socket, and she climbed higher until she could thrust the sole of one boot against the back of Borss's neck. Pulling with her hands, and thrusting out with her foot, Val threw her weight backward.

A giant crack reverberated out of Borss's neck, and the noise was so loud, Val almost mistook it for a shot from a gun like the Hanger man had used in the Italian mountains.

Borss's head flopped sideways, and his huge frame began to sink toward the ground. Val jumped backward, but she didn't stick the landing, her ankle turning under her.

She hit the ground once more, this time cracking her skull. She saw a burst of stars, but then immediately, two sets of hands were helping her up.

Agnes was on one side of her, and Ulrik, looking pale but awake, was tugging her upward. "I have her," he said.

Val could hear the exhaustion in the big man, and she knew it might not be long before he passed out again, but for now, he helped her manage her own weight.

She shook her head to clear it, and her vision returned to a sharper focus. "I am fine. Go. Heinrich can only buy us a small amount of time."

Agnes, familiar with boats from her life in Venice, raced straight for the bow line, and quickly cut it with Val's hand-ax. Then she shoved the bow of the boat away from the dock.

Val angled toward the stern, but Ulrik got there first, swinging his heavy ax, and slicing through the finger-thick white rope that held the boat to shore. Val leapt onto the boat and Agnes climbed aboard after her. Ulrik threw his ax into the stern of the craft and shoved the hind quarter of the boat before leaping after it.

The boat was large, and it inched away from the shore. Val had picked up the big man's ax, and now she leaned it over the side, using the head to push the stern further away from the dock.

Agnes climbed a short ladder to a second story bridge, and grabbed the wheel of the vessel from inside its glassed-in booth. She cranked the wheel hard and the bow began to turn out into the current of the river.

Still the progress was too slow.

Val saw the first Vectors running out of the open door at the end of the warehouse, two hundred feet away. They had made it past, which meant that Heinrich was dead.

Then a shockwave slammed into them, knocking them all down, before rolling into Val. She threw herself down, as the warehouse erupted in a fireball, and the thunder god's fury raged across the docks.

The entire warehouse was engulfed. A billowing tower of dark smoke and flame shot up into the raining sky, before the moisture pressed back on it, forcing it down.

Heinrich had only shown her the one block of plastic explosive clutched in his grip, but he must have had more in his bag, and the warehouse was probably stockpiled with explosive materials. The bang was too large. Much larger than the one she had witnessed in the mountains.

As the fire roared, Val looked for surviving Vectors, but all she saw was smoke, and then the current of the river pulled their stolen boat past a permanently moored slate gray ship, obscuring her view of the maelstrom. The ship was easily a hundred feet longer then their stolen sailboat, but without sails or fuel, the behemoth was just another relic of the old world, and it would rot in place forever.

Ulrik unfurled the yacht's canvas sails, and hoisted them up the mast. Agnes had already stopped looking at the tumultuous fire, and was focused on safely navigating them to the sea.

Val pulled the goggles from her face, dropping them to the fiberglass deck. She hung her head and breathed in deeply.

We are alive.

And she meant not only the three of them, but the whole of the human species.

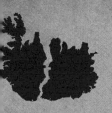

EPILOGUE

Epilogue

Winter had come early to Stavanger, but the sea had still not frozen. It would happen soon though. The boat swayed and creaked under the weight of the frost and ice that had formed on its lines and mast. People had gathered around the shore and its long wooden plank piers to watch the mysterious sailboat come in.

The townspeople had fought off raiders from further north along the coast earlier in the year, but the pirates attacked with multiple wooden longboats. Nothing like this white shining vessel.

As the boat came closer to shore, people cringed back from the man standing on the bow. He was a brute, probably two hundred and twenty pounds of muscle, with a frost encrusted beard that fell halfway down his broad chest. He wore a thick bandage over one half of his head, concealing his eye, and his hands were covered in thick gloves.

He wore black leather over his broad chest and legs, causing him at once to resemble both a pirate and a nightmare version of Odin himself. But the man's hands stayed at his hips, and he showed no sign of emotion on his face. He did not look angry, even though his appearance was enough to send some of the villagers running.

The sails lowered and the woman who had taken them down, also dressed in black leather, stepped up by the man's side as the boat slid against the pier. Her long blonde hair had been braided, and her face was covered with red makeup like the wings of a bird. Red-lensed goggles covered her eyes.

She leapt off the boat onto the creaky pier, and marched toward the pebbled beach. The man followed her, and a moment later a younger woman—maybe sixteen, jumped onto the pier and walked after the big man. She was wrapped in layers of fabrics, and carried a sword strapped across her back.

People stepped back or shied away as the woman in the lead of the strange parade approached.

Val gave them no notice as she walked past.

She went straight to the Jarl's longhall and found Halvard seated on the piggish man's chair. He stood at once, dropping a book from his hand, shock and delight vying for supremacy on his face. Val understood that in her absence, the Jarl had died and Halvard had taken over.

"Val," he said, his voice shaky. "You made it back. I never heard back from Troben; I never knew if you made it."

"We will have time to tell you about it later, but first, I want you to meet your 'genetic material.'"

Agnes stepped up next to Val, the candlelight from Halvard's reading candlestick flickering over her pretty face.

Val strode forward toward the old man, and he recoiled at the threat she exuded.

"I... I..."

She grabbed the front of his shirt and pulled him close. Hiking one thumb over her shoulder at Ulrik, who had pulled the heavy metal disc from his pack and held it up, she shouted in Halvard's face. "I want to know, just what the hell that thing is, and why so many had to die for it."

The man swallowed with an audible clicking noise, and said "I will show you."

The four of them rode on horseback, for most of an hour, north of Stavanger's coast. It was in a direction Val had never traveled. They rode in silence, with Ulrik once again bringing the metal disc in his pack, and Agnes between the two of them on her somewhat smaller pony.

The natural coastline gave way to an industrial one, with shattered buildings and ruptured concrete docks, though many were either in good shape or had been repaired.

A white metal building loomed ahead of them, similar to the warehouse in Rotterdam, but immense. The building was half a mile long, four hundred feet wide, and over three hundred feet tall. The gargantuan white rectangular structure dwarfed everything she had seen on her epic journey to the south.

Halvard was talking. "It was essential that we get her blood—her living blood—to a genetic research facility, so we can isolate the genes that make her—"

"What in the name of Odin's tick-infested sack is that thing?" Val said, pointing.

In the distance, two men armed with longswords guarded a massive white wall descending into the water. They stood several hundred feet apart, one on each side. Halvard let loose a shrill whistle and swirled his hand in the air. As he did so, the men leapt to attention and then reached for handles on large wheels. They started cranking the wheels quickly, and a dark vertical slit appeared up the center of the gargantuan wall. Two enormous doors separated.

"I would perform the work myself, here, you understand, but I do not have the technical knowledge. Just as I kept in contact with Troben using the carrier pigeons, there is another scientist who is far better versed in genetics than I am. He is Agnes's next destination, and if you would be so brave, yours as well."

Halvard dismounted from his steed and began walking toward the ever widening doors. The others followed as something vast and blue came into view inside the gigantic building.

Val walked closer, listening to the old man prattle on, as the doors widened and she took in an amazing sight. "For a journey such as the one I am proposing now, we needed something large. Something that could withstand whatever was thrown at it. The piece you brought back from Rotterdam was the only thing we could not repair or machine for ourselves. The tolerances were too exacting. We have been working on this for many, many years. We fixed the parts and cleaned her up, we got an oil refinery working again, and made the diesel fuel for her. But the part you retrieved was just too finely engineered. And it is crucial for the engine."

Finally, they reached the edge of the inlet and stared up at the colossus before them.

It was the bow of a boat.

The hull was sky blue from a tapered point to where just a hint of red paint was visible under the gently lapping dark green liquid. Its broad deck flared out so wide it looked like the boat should topple over.

"The Maersk Triple E class. Formerly the *Marikja*, the last vessel like it the company ever made before the great cataclysm. They only ever produced twenty-five of the ships, and they were the largest ever built. This one was waiting here for a part, which was on its way from the Netherlands, when the entire world fell apart. In case you ever returned, we renamed her."

Painted on the front of the vessel were downward angled wings in dark red, exactly like those Val painted on her face. On the side of the massive boat, which looked to fill the entire majestic hangar, was the name *Sleipnir*. The name of Odin's eight-legged horse, the best of all vehicles.

Val turned to see the wonder on Ulrik's face, and pure joy on Agnes's face. She looked back at Halvard, whose tired eyes were seeking some kind of forgiveness from her, beseeching her to understand that it was all for a good cause. She understood.

"Where is it we need to go?" she asked the old man.

"Across the great ocean," he said. "To follow in the path of your ancestors. Beyond Iceland and Greenland. To the shores of what was once known as the New World. To Vinland. To America."

Val walked away from the man, further toward the immense boat, the ship so impossibly huge she could barely take it all in at once.

She turned to him, showing a wicked smile. "We are going to need some more men. A lot more men."

Epilogue II

Zeilly had only just escaped with her life. The crazed Northerners had made short work of the Vectors, and the warrior woman had even bested Borss. Zeilly had seen the fight and had watched with glee as the blonde haired woman had ended that slug's life.

But now she wished she had just taken the opportunity to flee as soon as she had left the dining hall. Instead of slipping away when she could have, she had remained too long. Long enough to see the warehouse engulfed in a tremendous ball of flame. And far too close to escape the flames' wrath. The whole left side of her chest, arm and face had been scorched in the blast. Her skin was now rippled and crusted, hard as tree bark. One eye had been spared, but her left ear was gone. She was hideous now, and covered her entire body in layers of dark cloth. A true witch woman now, for sure.

The agony had been unimaginable at first, but after the skin on her left side finished dying, she'd felt no more pain. She had covered herself in herbs and mud, soothing the drying crisp feeling as her supple body turned to stone on her. Then all that had been left was the incredibly long walk.

Weeks to get away from the Vector camp at the docks in Rotterdam. Long days of walking and fishing along the shore as she made her way north. Days when she could find no fish and had to move inland, looking for other forms of sustenance. And always the walking.

She had encountered only one group of people along the way, but as soon as she had removed her hood and revealed her half-scarred face, those villagers had run from her. Whether it was only her hideous visage or a fear of radiation sickness that made the people flee, she did not know. It didn't matter.

Only one thing did matter, and she was nearly there. Borss had been a brute and a fool, but he had excelled at manipulation, and Zeilly had eagerly learned at his feet. Over time she had worked the details

out of him about the Northerners and their quest to the Floating City—
now the Sunken City—to retrieve the young girl. Zeilly had learned that
the girl's genetic makeup was different from everyone else. That somehow, her blood held the key to the survival of the human race. But
more than that, there was someone across the ocean who would pay
enough money, men, and resources for the girl to set Borss up as an
emperor. Borss had boasted of it often.

Or to set Zeilly up as an Empress.

Zeilly would have her revenge on the damnable blonde Viking
woman. She would snatch the young girl. She would claim Borss's
reward. She would live out the rest of her days with servants tending
her brittle skin, lying in pillows of satin.

All she needed to do was to go home.

An hour later, Zeilly crested the rise of a sand dune and saw the
port city ahead of her. Boats. Hundreds of them. Soldiers—all she could
need. Food. Warmth. Resources. Not hers, but she knew she could
utilize them, the way she had used Borss and his men. These soldiers
were pirates. They made their living on the seas, raiding and stealing,
crushing any and all opposition. It was a good life if you loved the
water.

Zeilly did not.

It was why she had left here.

That and an abusive father. But that man was dead now, and
another man ruled these pirates and their aquatic forces.

But soon these forces would be hers.

It didn't take long before a small group of men on horseback
rode out along the beach to greet her. The port had many towers,
and surely she had been spotted along the water before she even
saw the city. Her black cloak would have stood out on the grainy
yellow beach like a thick spider in a bowl of soup.

The men approached her at speed, slowing their steeds only
as they came within ten feet of her. Zeilly stood her ground.

"Who are you?" one of the mounted riders shouted.

Zeilly removed her hood and savored the revulsion she saw
on their faces.

"Take me to Baron Schroeder. Immediately. He will be glad to see me, and he will have you flayed to death if he learns you delayed our meeting for even a moment."

The men seemed taken aback, but one man's face changed from astonishment to recognition.

"Quickly!" he said to one of the others. "Get her on your horse. I know who she is."

The other man did as he was told, and the five of them brought her into the city, with the first man who had spoken—clearly in charge—urging them faster and faster. When they reached the largest boat in the harbor, the men slowed and dismounted, the first man helping her down from the back of the large black stallion.

Once on the ground, the man stepped aside.

Striding down a gangplank from the boat to the dock was a tall man with dark blonde hair. The same color as Zeilly's before she had used dyes to darken it to pitch. The man wore a cape that flowed out behind him as he walked. A trim beard on his chin and a grimace on his mouth offset the sea-blue eyes.

As soon as he reached the dock, he shot a glance at the man in charge of the five soldiers, his eyes demanding an explanation.

Zeilly saved him the trouble. She threw her hood back and looked up at the Baron, her one sea-blue eye matching his.

"Hello, brother."

ACKNOWLEDGMENTS

Any time you set out to write a novel, a number of people end up helping in a wide assortment of ways. Thanks for this one are due to Britney Holtan, a wonderful model in Portland, Maine who, when we saw a photo of her, we knew at first glance we had found our Val. We spent a day in a photographer's studio with Britney, and she was a great sport, letting us dress her up in crazy costumes, making all kind of faces, and generally making silly action poses for us. In the end we got some 900 photos of her and the weapons, and ultimately we were able to get the shots used to make the cover for *Viking Tomorrow* and for two more potential sequels if this book sells well. Thank you, Britney!

Kevin Ouellette was the fantastic photographer (Amazing DJ Music / Sound and Photography) who spent the day shooting Britney in all the crazy poses for us. If it wasn't for his existing photos of Britney, we might never have found the perfect Val for the book cover. In addition to coaxing just the right looks out of her, Kevin made us all feel welcome, and kept the spirit light for everyone all day—including for poor Britney after he doused her with chilly water for just the right look. Thank you, Kevin.

Thanks are also due to Kelly Allenby, Lyn Askew, Pixie Brearley, Roger Brodeur, Julie Cummings Carter, Elizabeth Cooper, Dustin Dreyling, Jamey Lynn Goodyear, Dee Haddrill, Sharon Ruffy, Jeff Sexton, and Kelly Tyler for advanced reading feedback and typo-spotting par excellence.

Finally, thanks are due to Hilaree Robinson, Aquila Robinson, Norah Robinson, Michelle Scully, and Moira Gilmour—the amazing and fierce women in our lives!

—Jeremy and Kane

ABOUT THE AUTHORS

Jeremy Robinson is the international bestselling author of sixty novels and novellas, including *Infinite, The Distance,* Unity, *Apocalypse Machine,* and *SecondWorld,* as well as the Jack Sigler thriller series and *Project Nemesis,* the highest selling, original (non-licensed) kaiju novel of all time. He's known for mixing elements of science, history and mythology, which has earned him the #1 spot in Science Fiction and Action-Adventure, and secured him as the top creature feature author.

Many of Jeremy's novels have been adapted into comic books, optioned for film and TV, and translated into thirteen languages. He lives in New Hampshire with his wife and three children.

Visit him online at www.bewareofmonsters.com.

Kane Gilmour is the international bestselling author of *The Crypt of Dracula.* He has co-authored several titles with Jeremy Robinson and also writes his own thriller novels. In addition to his work in novels, Kane has had short stories appear in several anthologies and magazines, and he worked on artist Scott P. Vaughn's sci-fi noir webcomic, *Warbirds of Mars* as well as on Jeremy Robinson's comic book adaptation of the novel *Island 731.* He lives with his significant other, his kids, her kids, and three dogs in Vermont. He's thinking of buying a farm to house them all.

Visit him online at: www.kanegilmour.com.

SIGN UP FOR THE NEWSLETTER AT
WWW.BEWAREOFMONSTERS.COM

Made in the USA
San Bernardino, CA
29 April 2018